Infinity on Fire

The Dimensional Alliance 2nd edition, Volume 2

Bonnie K.T. Dillabough

Published by The Infinite Publishing Alliance, 2021.

Also by Bonnie K.T. Dillabough

The Dimensional Alliance 2nd edition
The House on Infinity Loop
Infinity on Fire
Mirrors of Infinity

Watch for more at https://dimensionalallianceheadquarters.com.

Table of Contents

Infinity on Fire

Book 2 of the Dimensional Alliance series

By: Bonnie K.T. Dillabough
Cover Art: Richard McKenzie

About this book:

Jenny has the weight of the multiverse on her shoulders and the fate of everyone she cares about in her hands.

Ever since her aunt, who she barely knew, left the strange little house on Infinity Loop to Jenny in her will, along with the cat, Tidbit, and a tiny key on a gold chain, everything had changed for her. Never would she have expected that an impossible door in her new house would lead her to adventures beyond her own universe with beings that seemed to come right out of the myths and legends of Earth and beyond

Now she must organize the forces of the Dimensional Alliance to fight against a persistent and formidable enemy who would enslave the population of every inhabited planet in the multiverse, if they have their way, plunging the multiverse into never-ending warfare and strife.

Acknowledgements:

Great thanks to so many who have made this book series possible. I especially want to thank my grandmother, Juanita Sherman Tussey, who encouraged my writing from the very beginning. Regardless of the holiday, one of my gifts was always a book. She read every story and every poem I ever wrote and praised me to her friends as a "born writer". Thank you, Mimi, (for this is what we called her instead of grandma) for your enthusiastic support of me from the very beginning.

Acknowledgements of help in this book wouldn't be complete without my amazing cover artist, Richard McKenzie, who really knows how to bring my visions to life. Thank you, Richard and Dee McKenzie, his very supportive wife and a fan of the books.

And I couldn't have done this without my beta reader's group, including, Carolyn Hardy Greiner, Delia D. Michael, Jennifer Dillabough, Barbara Angst Gilbert, Jeremiah Maluse, George Samuel Dillabough, Luz Rives, Cindi Jones Erickson, Lynnette Dillabough, Maria Gurriere, Angela Bryner, and Cathryn Leow.

And most importantly, George C. Dillabough (Chief Bodyguard, hubby, sweetheart, cook and care-giver). Without whose love and support I wouldn't even be alive to write these books. Thank you, Papa Bear, for being who you are, my true love and eternal companion.

Prologue:

Miriha looked out over her garden as she strolled to the still pool that lay at its center. Near the edge of its pristine crystal water was a small stone bench. There were no fish in the pond and here, in this place, there was never a breeze, so the surface of the little pool was permanently undisturbed.

A random thought occurred to her. Tidbit would not have approved. No fish and no butterflies either. She smiled. It suited her needs. She came here often now. There was so much going on in the far reaches of her former responsibility as the Gatekeeper.

Young Jenny had taken that responsibility from her own hand. But some responsibilities didn't die easily.

She remembered the day clearly, though without regret. Her death had been a necessary step in her journey and as it had turned out there was so much more to dear Jenny than any of them had perceived.

Although Miriha had her own gifts, most did not know of them or had even suspected. From the moment Lizzie had told her of her great-niece, Miriha had begun to have an inkling that there was something special about her. Miriha had encouraged Lizzie to consider Jenny as a potential eventual candidate to inherit the guardianship of the Los Angeles gate when Lizzie was ready to pass it on.

Most of the time gate guardianships passed after the death of the guardian, but in this case, Miriha knew Lizzie to be unusually fit for her age. She had not at that time yet noticed the difference in Lizzie's aura. That would come later.

So Miriha encouraged Lizzie to keep watch over this special youngling when she could. She knew Lizzie had more than one surveillance device installed in Jenny's parent's home under the guise of some kind of home improvement or other. She even had funded new computers in Jenny's schools and eventually her dorm room. The dorm managers were delighted to receive the grant that allowed them to supply each new student of the school with a laptop to do their schoolwork on, complete with all the latest software.

Jenny would have had no way of knowing, however that anything was any different than she expected and, as Lizzie stayed very busy with her responsibilities as a Guardian of the Los Angeles gate and her liaison work for the Alliance with Tarafau as her Guide, there was no reason for Jenny to have any idea that her life wasn't as normal as it appeared.

As things had fallen out, Lizzie had turned up with that deadly blood disease and had passed, but not before she had made careful arrangements for everything Jenny would need so she could take over as the Guardian in the little house on Infinity Loop.

Jenny's training as a Gate Guardian would have been a grand adventure with plenty of time to grow if not for the attack on Miriha's village which took the people of her village and all of the surrounding villages into slavery and whose depredations caused Miriha's death. Miriha had a strong feeling that Jenny's timing to arrive moments before her death in time to receive the Gatekeeper's key from her hand was no accident. Indeed, Miriha was of the firm belief that there truly were no accidents.

So, Jenny had received the key, but not before Miriha had been given a glimpse into Jenny's mind and heart. What she found there astounded her and sent her to her rest with the satisfaction that she had made an excellent choice in passing the key on to Jenny instead of allowing it to dissolve into nothingness with her death.

Now, in this interim dimension she found herself once again a guardian of a different sort. She had been tasked with the responsibility of giving Jenny an occasional gentle nudge and that required that she knew exactly what was happening with Jenny.

Through this pool she had been able to protect Jenny's dreams and to prod Jenny to confront Sam, otherwise known as Engoza, the self-styled "queen of the Groga". There she learned of the Insenium's plan to dominate, terrorize and enslave the multiverse and endured the torture of her faithful Tidbit.

Already the young woman had endured so very much, and her future yet contained more trials than any young woman her age would want to bear. But she was who she was. Her part was vital and yet to be played out. So Miriha turned to her pool to gaze once more into the life of Jenny Japhet, Gatekeeper of the Dimensional Alliance.

Chapter 1: Tale of the Cat

Tidbit said good-bye to the butterflies in the garden. He knew it would probably be a long time before he saw them again. So soothing to watch them flitting from blossom to blossom, but autumn was coming, and they would soon migrate to climes even farther south.

The aromas that wafted across the garden in a gentle breeze were a mixture of sweet and bitter and spicy. The herbs Lizzie had loved so much gave off the strong scents that told him they were at the height of their potency. The majority of them were perennials, going through season after season with no need to replant, and the matured plants were ever so much more aromatic than when they were newly planted in their first spring. Lizzie had planted them lovingly the very first year when she became the Los Angeles Gate Guardian. So many memories lived here.

He sauntered over to the koi pond and dabbled one clawed foot in the water to watch the koi evade him with little urgency. They knew Tidbit and were aware that he did not consider them a food source. His orb-like amber eyes watched the lazy, almost hypnotic undulations of the fish with no desire except to watch them weave their patterns in the water. Another delight that was denied him in his home dimension.

He could hear Jenny puttering in the little kitchen just inside the open French doors talking to Lizziebot. In not long, the weather would cool to the point that those doors would be closed for a season, but for now the air was warm and the sun showed off the black-on-black stripes of his fur to great advantage, and he knew it.

His natural form wasn't at all cat-like, of course. But while in this form, he found his thoughts were definitely affected by the natural attitudes and instincts of the animal shape he took while on Earth. After years of using this disguise, his wife often told him he was sometimes more cat than man.

He wandered through the open doors, through the dining room and into the bright living room that looked out on the front garden. He leaped up onto his favorite thinking place, the window seat, and curled up, apparently to take a nap. But his nap-like posture was a ruse, perfected over the years. No one noticed a sleeping cat or would be wary of one. Thus, he could observe, through slitted eyes, the comings and goings of the humans of this place. Only few realized that Tidbit was anything more than a beautiful, big, black tabby cat and that was exactly as it should be.

Jenny came into the living room and seated herself in her cushy armchair, drawing her legs up and tucking them up under her. "Good morning, old cat. Did you have a good night?"

Tidbit sent from his mind to hers, "*Yes. All is well on the home front, your neighbors are well, and Bob is on his way over.*"

He no sooner sent this than a knock came at the door. Bob, the neighbor across the street, had a key to Jenny's place, but he never used it when he knew Jenny was home. He was kind and very polite, for a human.

Jenny got up and let him in. "Hey, you two, ready to go?" Bob was of medium height and middle aged, salt and pepper hair and a short mustache. His seemingly infinite supply of energy was evident in his big grin, as he bounced slightly on the balls of his feet. He clapped his hands with a "smack!" and said, "Tinkering to do and lots of dastardly alien tech to learn about."

Jenny laughed. Her blue eyes twinkled. It was obvious that Bob held the same charm for Jenny as he had for Lizzie. Tidbit remembered he and Lizzie spending hours laughing about seemingly inconsequential goings on in the neighborhood over peanut butter and jelly sandwiches and cold root beer out on the patio.

"I've got my gear together, including Lizziebot, and the girls will be out shortly. They're in the gateway office." Jenny was referring to her Alliance Guards, three very different women whose sole duty was to protect Jenny from harm. As the Gatekeeper, Jenny was responsible for the entire network of dimensional portals known as gateways. No one, looking at Jenny or talking with her, would suspect she held such an enormous responsibility at her age, and she certainly hadn't coveted the job.

It was often that way, with Guardians, those who guarded the dozen known gates on Earth from incursion, but Jenny had ended up with her current additional post unexpectedly. Tidbit admired her courage in persisting to take responsibility for something that would ordinarily be considered beyond someone of her age and experience. On her right forearm was the detailed outline of a butterfly, but this was no tattoo. The butterfly had been sliced into her skin as torture for information by her former best friend, Sam, otherwise known as Engoza.

Tidbit stood and stretched. It was one of the things he loved about being a cat. No being could stretch in such a satisfactory way, starting from his front paws, digging his claws in for support and then languidly extending every single muscle in his body clear to the tip of his tail.

He hopped down and followed Jenny as she went through and secured doors and closed curtains in the living and dining rooms. She didn't need to grab a backpack or luggage, as all of that was contained in her MDP (Miniature Dimensional Portal), a plastic-like wristband that contained an entire warehouse of space for items and equipment, courtesy of the Dimensional Alliance Council. All Alliance personnel were so equipped. Since there was no weight to them and they could contain nearly unlimited quantities of items, this was a very convenient piece of alien tech, to be sure.

Bob kept up a running commentary on the state of the neighborhood as Jenny secured the house. Miss Longtree was off again on a lecture tour and an appearance on a national radio talk show. Elias Mensch, the neighborhood curmudgeon and his great Dane, Cinder, were about the same, although Mr. Mensch seemed to be walking awkwardly lately, more than likely due to extreme old age. The kids down the block were doing a canned food drive for the food bank again and the city was thinking about putting a stop sign at the juncture of the center of the figure-eight road they lived on.

Bob had decided to transfer Ignatius, his macaw, to Sanglarka on the next trip in, since it was obvious, he wouldn't be spending a lot of time at home. And he had added two more AI robots to Fidget's family, in addition to Lizziebot. He was working on some appropriate names for them.

Jenny listened with only an occasional, "oh" or "really?" as Bob rambled on. She seemed a little pre-occupied, which wasn't really surprising, considering the events of the past few weeks. Not only had she been kidnapped a second and third time since starting her venture as the Gatekeeper, but she had seen Tidbit tortured and killed, not realizing he wasn't actually in his cat body at the time. And now she was heading out to lead the Alliance in stage two of the plan to eliminate violent, tyrannical, evil entities from dominating the entire multiverse. She definitely had enough to be going on with.

Lyra, Nona and Mynn opened the door to the gateway office. This door wasn't generally visible unless you had a key or an Agent pass, but it opened inward to reveal a tidy, somewhat quaint looking office with bookshelves, odd sculptures, an old walnut desk with an antique wooden office chair and a white wicker cat bed with a big fluffy red cushion. On the opposite wall was another door which led to the infinitely long hallway of uncountable doors, known as the gateroom. These doors led to dimensions that represented billions of additional universes which were a part of the Dimensional Alliance. Since she had received the Gatekeeper's key, a master gate had appeared in that hallway that could take her instantly to any dimension in the network. She had yet to access that gate, as she had yet to require it, but it also meant she could receive visitors from anywhere in the Dimensional Alliance.

They closed the door to the house behind them. Tidbit knew that anyone wandering into that hallway now would only see a blank stretch of wall if they didn't have a key or a pass. They stepped into the gateroom and opened the door that led to the Swedish gate in Sanglarka.

As they stepped through, he felt the warm tingle of his transformation and resisted the urge to stretch again. Now, as Tarafau, he stood over six and a half feet tall, his skin almost as blue black as Tidbit's fur, bulging muscles like an athlete under his colorful robe. His eyes were the same glowing amber as his cat form, and his earlobes ended at a point that Jenny had once told him would be great for an earring. He rubbed a hand over his shiny bald head, wishing he had thought to wear a hat. Here in the mountain valley of Sanglarka in Sweden, unlike sunny California, the air was already taking on a chill.

Lova and Arvid were waiting at the gate, as they often did when they knew Jenny or other visitors were coming. Lova held out both hands to Jenny and then embraced her warmly. "*Let's get you all inside,*" Lova sent in mindspeech. "*We've got hot mulled cider and a plate of Arvid's special cookies waiting in the dining room.*"

The lodge was, as always, warm and inviting. In the dining room, several others were already gathered at the long trestle table. "*I think we're still waiting for Burt, Gariel and a few of your compatriots, Tarafau. The rest are here and ready for our initial briefing. I expect the others any time now,*" Lova said as they seated themselves.

Arvid brought them a tray with steaming mugs, napkins and a plate of spicy sugar cookies that were his specialty. His white hair stuck out all over his head. Tarafau loved this little man like a brother. As small as he was, only coming up to slightly above Tarafau's waist, he was one of the toughest people he knew in hand to hand and other martial arts, including fighting with the quarterstaff. Over many years, Tarafau had yet to beat him.

Arvid was not an Earthling, although he much resembled one of the gnomes of legend in his facial features and his body was similar to the "little people" of Earth. He was the uncle of Ingot, Chief Councilor of the Dimensional Alliance, but he had been assigned as the Guide to Lova when she had inherited responsibility of the Swedish gate. He was also the head trainer of new Guardians and the Gatekeeper.

You would never know from his attitude that he was higher in rank than any of them. He took as much delight in cooking for the team of Gate Guardians and other guests in Sanglarka as he did in handing out bruises in the workout room or acting as a liaison between the Earth Guardians and the Alliance.

"*How are you, old cat?*" Arvid sent to Tarafau. "*Recuperated and ready for some action?*"

"*You know me, dwarf,*" retorted Tarafau. "*I'm always ready.*"

Arvid chortled as he checked around the table to be sure everyone's mugs were full, and no one was running out of cookies. "*Jenny is looking a little pale. I'll be sure to get her into the workout room and work on her breathing with Lova and the girls.*"

The three bodyguards who were assigned to Jenny were often referred to as "the girls" and they didn't mind. You would never have guessed that any and all of them were as deadly as any of the Dimensional Alliance Troopers or any of the foes they had yet come across. Nor would you suspect that each of them was twice the age of the one they were assigned to protect.

Lova came back into the dining room, Burt, Gariel and Tarafau's three cousins in tow. They all found places at the table as Arvid distributed mugs and cookies. Once Arvid was in his place, Lova stood, smiling warmly at the assembled team members. All of the Earth Guardians were there and all of the mental conversations that Tarafau knew had been going on around him came to a halt as all gave their respectful attention to the tall woman with short cropped hair so blonde it was nearly transparent, dressed in archaic tracker's clothing of greens, tans and browns.

"*Welcome one and all to our conference of the Dimensional Alliance on Earth. First of all, I want to say how grateful I am to see every face here. We came so close to losing more than one of you in the past few months.*"

We have much to discuss. Yes, we were victorious in stage one of our assault on the forces of the Groga and the Fleistians. I would like to assume that Earth is now free of future Groga incursions, but somehow, I think this may have only been a holding action. Although we believe we have discovered how they were raiding dimensions within the Alliance, the threat of further incursions remains. And we still don't know the location of the Groga and Insenium dimensions.

In the final analysis, as Guardians, we are committed to not only guard our own dimension, but the Alliance as well. The Earth is still not safe until the Alliance is secured. We will find ourselves working closely with dimensions from all over the network until this threat is conquered.

This is why we're here. This is what we are up against. And although we have the might of the Alliance with us, what lies before us, all of us, is something so vast and sinister that there are no words that can adequately describe the consequences of failure."

Most heads around the table nodded bleakly as she continued. "*There is new information, thanks to the stalwart efforts of our Earth Guardians, the Gatekeeper, the Alliance and Tarafau's people. Based on that information we must form a solid plan to achieve the mission we have previously discussed. The Alliance has requested our continued support in eradicating the threat of domination, torture and destruction intended by a currently unknown foe.*

We will obviously not achieve that this evening, but we will once again set ourselves up in teams to work on the components of a plan that will be useful. Starting first thing in the morning, we will be separating into our groups. The last time we met we debriefed on the status of our past mission, but with the new information we now have acquired, we can move forward. Jenny, do you have anything to add?"

Along with the rest, Tarafau turned to look at Jenny, who stood. Jenny still surprised him, even after seeing her deal with multiple attacks, kidnapping and torture. She looked so incredibly young. And yet, Lizzie had been about that age when she became a Gate Guardian over 60 years ago. However, Jenny also had the burden of Gatekeeper added to that. One of the Gatekeeper's many responsibilities was to oversee all operations connected to the entire Gate Network. All of that on her slender shoulders and she stood up to it regardless of her fears and feelings of inadequacy for the task.

As Jenny stood, she was silent for a moment, looking into each face and gathering her thoughts. *"Thank you again for your solidarity and support. I look forward to working with all of you again and continuing my training in my posts of Guardian and Gatekeeper. I am designating Tarafau as the leader and coordinator of this mission, with Lova and Gariel as his counselors. Tomorrow we will assign team leaders and release you to your various stations. We have some additional support with us today as well. Tarafau, will you introduce us to your friends?"*

"Please welcome my cousins, Sardina, Elgyra and Desminda. They are here as specialists in interdimensional science, cultural sociology and the science of war. They will be consulting with the various teams as we move forward and will participate in all further councils among us." Tarafau said, gesturing to the three of them.

Each of them had the same ethnic appearance as Tarafau, but considering that, they were all as different as could be in temperament, abilities and appearance. Sardina was the shortest of the three; his deep-set eyes were the color of the darkest chocolate, nearly black. He wore his hair in the braided knot of a traditional Daringi scholar, and he seemed to be constantly studying everything and everyone around him. His thin eyebrows were expressive as thoughts flitted almost visibly through his mind.

Elgyra was nearly as tall as Tarafau, but he was thin and wiry as opposed to muscular and squarely built. His hair was coppery, straight and unbound, hanging nearly to his waist. His eyes were amber, as Tarafau's, but with glints of green. Constantly cheerful and optimistic, his broad white smile took in the entire assembly with confident warmth that was very inviting.

Desminda, was also tall, but muscular and solidly built. Her eyes were a startling green in her dark face and her hair was a deep golden brown, curly and cropped short to her head. She always managed to look placid and was, for the most part a kind and gentle person, but woe to the enemy or trainee who took that for meekness or weakness. She was as deadly as any warrior Tarafau had ever met, excepting Arvid, and she had a mind for tactics that even exceeded Gariel's.

The last time Tarafau had been home, he had recruited these three to add their significant talents to the Dimensional Alliance's mission to eliminate the menace of domination, torture and slavery that threatened the entire multiverse.

The enemy was a combination of three forces.

The Groga were a race of soldiers bred especially for that purpose by the Fleistians. The whereabouts of their home planet and dimension were currently unknown, as they had relocated after the last war with the Dimensional Alliance. Their only purpose was to fight for their masters, the Fleistians.

The Fleistians were one of two races living on the planet of Ludor in a dimension that was only accessible through a portal that was not in the Alliance. Their goal had been to capture and dominate the multiverse to sap it of its resources, using the Groga to raid dimensions to steal technology and other valuable things, including slaves. Their plans had taken a step forward, however when a much more advanced race had forcibly taken the reins.

Now the Fleistians served the Insenium, a mysterious species from an unknown dimension who would use the Fleistians and the Groga to achieve their mission of complete domination of every species in the multiverse, taking away every freedom to choose their own paths, down to even the clothes they would wear, the occupations they would pursue and the level of education and resources that would be made available to them.

It was obvious that this could only be accomplished by eons of war and destruction. Therefore, the Dimensional Alliance was committed to remove this threat once and for all, if possible.

Tarafau had seen war on a considerably smaller scale. Even that was devastating to a point beyond the ability of most of the dimensions in the multiverse to contemplate. Even the huge world wars of the planet Earth were diminutive compared to the destruction and loss of lives in the last war with the Groga, long before this new alliance of evil had been struck.

He watched the group as Jenny stood again. "*Thank you, and welcome, Sardina, Elgyra and Desminda to our council. Now let's all get settled. As usual, Arvid has prepared a great meal for us. Let's meet back here in 2 hours for supper together. Then the rest of the evening is yours. We will begin early tomorrow morning with our workout and breakfast. After breakfast we will get organized into teams with individual assignments. Thank you again for being here and offering your strength, talents and support.*"

They all stood then, breaking into conversation groups and many of them headed up the stairs to the various rooms and suites provided for them.

Lova was chatting amiably with Tarafau's cousins. Jenny and "the girls" were laughing and pointing at Burt, who actually stuck his tongue out at them! The various Guardians were either catching up or heading for their rooms to freshen up. Tarafau marveled at how close they had become since Jenny had joined the team and took up the reigns of leadership, however reluctantly. There was a new camaraderie brought on by a shared crisis and the need to work together closely over the past few months. But it was more than that. There was something about Jenny that seemed to encourage cooperation and mutual respect among her teammates.

Bob slapped Burt on the back and the two of them chuckled at some shared joke. Tarafau strolled over to Arvid. "*This is some gathering. Do you remember ever seeing any meeting of the Guardians so convivial before?*"

Arvid shook his head. "*Even Miriha never pulled them together like this. I feel like this portends something significant. It's like a spark has been struck into well-prepared tinder. These individuals were ready to rise to a higher level and when the opportunity presented itself, they all stepped up to the task with enthusiasm.*"

Both Tarafau and Arvid had been close to Lizzie, Jenny's aunt and the former Guardian of the Los Angeles gateway. Tarafau had been Lizzie's Guide for over 60 years and she had been like a daughter to him. Now Jenny, after inheriting the post from Lizzie, had also taken a portion of his heart. It saddened him that the lifespan of a human was so very short.

Burt beckoned him over where he and Bob stood with heads together, looking at something on a tablet.

"Hey, Tarafau, Bob was just showing me the specs on his two new bots. He had some questions about how he could enhance them to be more flexible in other dimensions, without using any D.A.T. in them."

"D.A.T.?"

"Bob's shortcut for 'dastardly alien tech,'" Burt said, rolling his eyes.

Tarafau shook his head. "O.K., would you like to meet my cousin, Elgyra? He is definitely the one to talk to you about it and you should include Sardina and Desminda in that discussion. 'Sardina? Desminda?'" he sent to his cousins who were having an animated conversation with Adelle and Dhakira. They nodded and the whole group, including Elgyra, strolled over.

Tarafau explained Bob's request and, before he knew it, they were off and running, each giving enthusiastic input to Bob and Burt. He shook his head with amusement. The creative brain power in that one group would be enough to solve just about anything given time, resources, and facilities to do so. He would leave them to it.

Jenny was talking with Lyra, Nona and Mynn as he strode up to the group. *"How about a workout?"* he asked. *"Shall we grab Arvid and use up some energy before supper?"*

Jenny smiled. *"Sounds good to me,"* she said and turning to the girls, *"How about it?"* They nodded and grinned enthusiastically.

"I'll meet you in the workout room in 5 minutes," Tarafau said and turned to the most likely place to find Arvid, the kitchen.

Sure enough, Arvid was in the kitchen energetically chopping carrots and putting them into a large simmering pot. *"Are you up to a workout, dwarf?"* he asked Arvid.

"Ready? Do you remember who you're talking to, old cat?" He turned the flame down under the pot. *"It has to simmer for about an hour anyway. I'll have Lova come in and give it an occasional stir."* He clapped his large square hands together with a solid, "Whack!" and climbed down from the stool he used in the kitchen. Arvid was short, shorter than pretty much any of Tarafau's friends, with the exception of Arvid's nephew, Ingot, who served as Chief Councilor of the Dimensional Alliance. But you only ever underestimated him once.

They walked through the dining room into the lobby which was currently hosting a few different casual discussion groups, although, at second glance he realized it wasn't as casual as it appeared. Each of the groups looked as if they were poised to start a race. Faces, as they pursued mind-speech conversations, were animated and the mood was intense. Tarafau thought that they would all have preferred to get right to work, even before supper. So, in lieu of that, they were getting a jump on it by discussing their different specialties and potential team assignments.

As they entered the empty workout room, Arvid turned to Tarafau. *"How is Jenny, really? I know she is as strong as any young person I have ever met, but the last few months haven't exactly been easy on her."*

"I think she is doing a lot better than any of us expected," Tarafau replied, *"but I also think she isn't letting on very much. I think she worries she will be a burden on the rest of us. I'm very proud of her. She is maturing much faster than most young people would at her age. Of course, in our dimensions, as long lived as your people and mine are, we don't even consider them adults until 60 or more years. They have to live fast, these Earthlings."*

About that time, Jenny and her Guards came in laughing about some private joke. They had bonded quickly in the short time her Guards had been assigned by the Alliance. "OK, let's get going!" Jenny said aloud with enthusiasm.

They all sat themselves on the huge mat that covered half of the workout room to begin their breathing and relaxation exercises. It seemed such a simple thing, but Tarafau knew that Jenny had found it to be more difficult than it appeared, and she understood the value of this now.

On two occasions, she had used these exercises to distance herself from pain and torture in extremely dangerous conditions. Lova had continued to work with her to expand her abilities which, according to Lova, were prodigious. Lova told Tarafau that they hadn't begun to reach Jenny's limitations in this regard.

As he focused on his breathing, he saw in his mind's eye, like a movie playing at fast forward, everything that had happened in the past few months. So many hurdles and so many obstacles; the price had been high, and they would soon pay much more. Of that much he was certain. His wife encouraged him and stood behind him staunchly, because she also believed in the cause he upheld, but he knew she worried every time he left home to return to his post. Guiding Jenny was high priority, if the Alliance was ever to remove this overwhelming threat.

As they all rose and warmed up with the quarterstaff forms in unison, Tarafau glanced at Jenny beside him. She was fast becoming more than a novice in her martial arts training. He couldn't help but being as proud of her as he was of his own daughters, only one of whom still lived at home. He was looking forward to the next part of her training, in which he would be introducing Jenny to his culture. They would depart as soon as they completed setting up the teams and turning their part of the mission over to them.

Jenny would seldom find herself relaxing in her little house on Infinity Loop anytime soon, Tarafau admitted to himself with a sigh. Besides training, there was an interdimensional war to win and then her final training as a Gatekeeper, upon which she would be an ambassador to all dimensions, meaning she would be traveling just as much with many more responsibilities. For now, they just had to focus on protecting the dimensions from this vile dictatorial regime that was intent on ruling the multiverse.

As they split up into dueling pairs, Tarafau smiled. Jenny seemed to have an instinct for it, once she had gotten established in the basics. She and her Guards flowed through their quarterstaff and hand-to-hand matches as if they were rehearsed. Jenny was very clear that her life would potentially be on the line if she didn't progress as fast as possible.

Arvid tapped him, not so lightly, on his elbow. "Earth to Tarafau!" he shouted. "This is not creative writing!!"

Tarafau refocused and nearly succeeded in getting a tag in. He had never managed to get past Arvid's guard in a quarterstaff bout except an occasional tap. Nor had he ever managed to throw Arvid, even though he was two feet taller than him. The little man came from a race who were known for their considerable agility and speed. And their added advantage was the fact that they were almost always the smallest person in the room. People tended to relax their guard with them until they quickly realized they were outclassed and how ferocious these tiny people were in a fight. For instance, Arvid could jump high enough to kick Tarafau in the head.

Arvid finally called a halt and every person was sweating and panting with big smiles on their faces. There was something very satisfying about this kind of workout with this group. There was not a one who did not put their utmost into it.

By the time the supper gong had rung, all were cleaned up and ready for a good meal and Arvid did not disappoint. The stew Arvid had made was accompanied by toasted croissants and a salad that was almost too pretty to eat. For dessert, a cheesecake topped with lingonberry preserves made Tarafau drool. He had learned over the years to eat many strange things, but he thought Arvid could even make cat food taste good.

Chapter 2: On Your Mark...

The next morning after workouts and breakfast, the Earth division of The Dimensional Alliance Council was called to convene by Lova. In her usual warm tones, she welcomed each member and, turning to Tarafau, said, "*Tarafau, you have been selected to lead us. We want you to know that each of us is ready to do your bidding and we have committed to do whatever it takes to complete our mission to rid the multiverse of the oppression and terrorism of the Groga and those who control them.*"

She sat and Tarafau stood. The members of this team knew that Tarafau was a man of few words and every face looked toward him with respect and anticipation. He would not disappoint them.

"*Every one of you knows why we're here, so I will give no rousing speeches. I will simply lay out our needs, assign your teams and you can get right to it. We can't afford to hesitate for a single moment. Let us use the time we have as efficiently as possible.*

Now that we know the names of our enemies and their purposes, thanks to Jenny's courageous actions in the fortress of the Fleistians, we have more than what we had before, but less than we need to stop them once and for all. We will have three main teams. The Science and Technology team, the Logistics and Implementation team and the War Strategy and Tactics team. Each team will have differing individual assignments, but at the end of each day we will do a combined meeting for you to report the progress of the day and see where the other teams can help one another. Team members may find themselves working on some projects on their own or with the help of other Alliance members.

The Science and Technology team will be meeting at Adelle's laboratory and observatory in Switzerland. The Logistics and Implementation team will meet at Juan's hacienda in Puerto Rico and the War Strategy and Tactics team will meet here. Team leaders have been assigned as follows: Science and Technology, Adelle. Logistics and Implementation team, Juan. The War Strategy and Tactics Team will be headed by Gariel. Each team will have the advantage of the specialists I brought with me and the resources of the entire Dimensional Alliance.

Your assignments have been sent to your cellphones. If you have any questions about them, ask Lova.

The Dimensional Alliance Headquarters will be sending updates to you regarding their research and at the end of two weeks we will meet at Alliance headquarters to report on our findings and recommendations. The Council will discuss this with us and then we will be given our final assignments. Jenny and I will not be back until just before the meeting with the Alliance Council, as we are taking a training, reconnaissance, and recruiting trip to my home dimension."

Tarafau grinned at the amazed and excited look on Jenny's face. He had deliberately not told her about this trip, and it was worth the wait to see her reaction. The rest of the group nodded and grinned.

"I know you are all anxious to get started. Lova has your team assignments and Arvid has 'volunteered' to run errands as needed and to consult with any of you regarding Alliance resources. And of course, he will be making sure that none of you go hungry." And all chuckled appreciatively as Arvid stood and bowed comically. *"Jenny and I will be receiving your end of day reports while we're gone. We'll be taking Lizziebot and we have MDP'd some D.A.T. to use in an emergency. If there are no questions, I will leave you to your tasks."*

There was an immediate sound of chairs scraping back as each gathered in their groups. Lova stood. *"Before we all get seriously involved in our tasks, let us send Tarafau and Jenny on their journey. Those of us who have been invited in the past know what awaits her there,"* she sent to the group.

Jenny and Tarafau were immediately surrounded by an enthusiastic swarm of happy faces. Hugs and well wishes ensued and slaps on the back and handshakes for Tarafau from the men. Tarafau sensed from Jenny that, although she enjoyed and appreciated this expression of the love and support of her comrades, she was anxious to move forward.

"You have a lot to do, one and all. We will leave you to it. I look forward to your progress reports," Tarafau finally said. He noticed Jenny's surprise when Lova did not escort them to the gate but hurried off to the situation room with Burt and Bob trailing behind her. *"Where we're going, there are no gates,"* he reminded her. He reached out and laid his hand gently on her shoulder. At once the room before them melted and they were in a meadow.

He watched her face. The absolute awe and surprise reflected by wide eyes and a glorious smile reminded him so much of Lizzie that he wanted to scoop her up in his arms. These Earthlings were fragile creatures, but their ability to appreciate beauty and radiate positive emotion never ceased to amaze him. His own people were warm and peaceful people, but the energy generated by his Earth friends was a powerful force that he was sure they didn't yet understand. To be sure they did have a dark side. Nearly every being did to one degree or another, but when they were good, they were amazing to him.

He had chosen to arrive in a large park a short walk from his home. Surrounding the grassy meadow were large war machines of various kinds, overgrown with flower vines. At a break in the encircling monuments to peace was a large stone statue of a woman, arms outstretched. At the base of the statue was written, in the language of his planet, "Peace is in your hands."

"Wow!" Jenny verbalized and then sent, *"Tarafau, what is this place?"*

"This is The Repentance," he explained. *"Long ago, only remembered in the writings of my people, we were a planet at war; constant conflict among species and nations. All of our traditions and values were attached to one thing: victory, power and gain at any cost. There were always those who desired peace, but their voices were silenced or ignored. Our planet came to the brink of utter destruction, but there was a woman of the Daringi who began to gather followers in masses from every species.*

She knew there was only one force that could stop the carnage. She and her followers had a simple plan. They went about serving in kindly ways, giving comfort to those who mourned and serving those whose lives had been devastated by the many wars. They never raised a voice or a hand in anger; never gave offense or took offense and they gave shelter to those fleeing the destruction and terror of war. They believed in this so much that they would allow their lives to be taken rather than to lift a hand in anger or take a life.

There was a turning point, when they became such a force for good that heads of government and leaders of commerce began to turn to their band of followers for counsel and assistance. Some of the fiercest of these became converted to the cause of peace.

Finally, when the majority of the intelligent beings on our planet had been convinced of the correctness of her reasoning, they issued an ultimatum to those who persisted in violence and conflict. If they wished to continue in that path, we would not deny them the right to make that choice. We simply would banish them to an empty viable planet in a completely different dimension. Since then, we have lived in harmony. When there is a dispute, we resolve it through the elders who have been appointed to hear a complaint between two differing parties and make a fair decision on the outcome. Every being on our planet has agreed to abide by that decision.

This statue and this park represent the woman who gave us peace and the reforms to allow us to continue."

"But what happens if someone becomes violent or doesn't agree?" Jenny asked.

"They are given the option to join those in the other dimension. It seldom happens."

"But can't they just transport back? Or maybe transport into other dimensions to raid and wreak havoc like the Groga?"

"Our scientists discovered long before this the gene that produces the ability to travel dimensions. Each one who is deported has that gene removed. Over the last few hundred years, as new deportees have been transported there, it is clear they are diminishing in both numbers and intelligence. A century ago, they were little more than mindless savages."

He watched Jenny's face as she took all of this in and gazed about her in wonder. *"And how long ago was this?"* she asked.

"About twenty-five centuries. But come; let me introduce you to my family and my world."

As they emerged from the park onto the broad avenue that led through homes surrounded by flowers and trees that were so different than Earth, he felt the sense of pervasive peace that always filled his soul while he was in his home city.

Jenny looked around, wide-eyed, and Tarafau kept silent, waiting for the questions he knew would come. It was good to bring visitors with him to his home. As they viewed the world in which he lived he once again could see the beauty around him with new eyes.

"I'm not sure what I expected," Jenny sent, *"But this is amazing."*

Unlike Earth neighborhoods, there was no cookie-cutter symmetry to the homes of his people. Domes sat beside tree homes and large thatched and woven houses. There were multi-storied wooden homes, and some built into hills of Earth and covered with flowers and greenery with only the windows and doors to indicate it wasn't a little hillock in the middle of the neighborhood. Some of them seemed sculpted of clay and others were built with cobbles of stone set into cement. And colors ranged from white and black to warm forest tones and gem colors in every hue.

But the variety didn't stop there. The beings walking to and fro on the smooth, paved street; were as different as those who had greeted Jenny at the Dimensional Alliance Headquarters. There were many humanoids, some covered in fur, but most in human-like skin. But there were also avians, reptile and insectoid creatures as well. The varying sizes, shapes and colors of the beings on the street would be quite overwhelming to someone who had never visited here.

However unlike at headquarters, these were all of one dimension and one planet. Although the Daringi had developed space travel many hundreds of years ago, up to this time they had not discovered a single inhabited planet in their galaxy and had not pursued intergalactic travel. However, visiting other planets, even though uninhabited, did give them access to many resources present on other planets, to the point that wealth, as many cultures saw it, was irrelevant.

Tarafau explained to Jenny that there was no one on their planet who was without the basic needs of shelter, clothing, food or worthwhile occupation and that education and health care was a universal opportunity. Their society was based on the principle of free choice. People could rise or fall to the level where they felt most comfortable without anyone telling them they should be different.

His was a culture that thrived on and encouraged diversification. Lizzie had once told him that her philosophy was, "Your right to swing your fist ends where my nose begins." This was certainly the case with his people. As long as you did no harm to another being, you could pursue whatever interested you without fear of reprisal or judgement.

Of course, people with similar philosophies formed communities and spent more time with one another, but that was a natural thing.

"But you have warriors, such as yourself. How does that work?" Jenny asked, perplexed.

"We do keep an active defensive force. We wish to be prepared for any eventuality. Mostly, the force is employed in helping communities experiencing disasters and supplementing government efforts for improvements. All of the warriors are unpaid volunteers and have other occupations they follow. They haven't had to fight but one war in over 2,500 years and that was in defense of the Alliance."

Jenny considered this. *"So, no wars...What about crime?"*

"It is rare to have someone steal anything and murder or torture is foreign to us. From time to time there are disagreements and some of the younglings make mistakes when they are young. We have no prisons, but those who have difficulties with the rules are given an opportunity to repair any damage they have done. Peacemaking is an art that is both taught and rewarded by our culture. As our young are educated, part of that education includes learning our history and understanding the consequences of violence, greed and judgementalism."

Jenny's face grew wistful. *"I wish there was a way to get to that point in my world, but I don't see it happening."*

"You are closer than you may believe. There is a movement growing on both sides of this question on Earth. Over time, it is hopeful that the peacemakers will prevail. It takes one person, to be willing to practice the art of peace to spread it to another and then there are two. Over time that can double again and again, as happened on our planet. I hope, with all my heart; that your planet accomplishes this change without going through what ours did.

Ah! We're here!"

He stopped in front of his home. Only a part of it peeked above the ground, so that it looked like a tiny domed cottage. The flowers around the edges were highlighted by the deep, dark Earth from which they sprung. Tall shade trees lined the edges of his property and a large grove extended behind that. Property had a different meaning for the Daringi than it did on Earth, but Jenny would probably think of his home as his property. The blue-green lawn gave the yard that extended between the trees a soft appearance. The dome was a muted shade of yellow. The windows were round and the door at the end of the walkway was as orange as an Earth pumpkin.

He could see Jenny taking it all in. She looked up at him in wonder. *"Welcome to my home,"* He said, opening the door and gesturing her in, ahead of him. The door opened into a tiled entry hall. On either side of the doorway was a stairway that followed downward along the inward curve of the walls of the dome. Straight ahead was their "company room", furnished with beautifully carved chairs and divans that were upholstered in muted jewel tones. There were no pictures on the walls, but none were needed as the windows were framed in prismed glass that threw rainbows over everything.

His youngest daughter, Elizabeth, jumped up from the chair where she had been reading. *"Papa cat!"* she enthused, throwing her arms around his neck. And pulling back from that warm hug that always charged him with light and energy she sent, *"And this must be Jenny. Welcome!"*

She threw her arms around Jenny, who submitted with delight sparkling from her eyes. *"Thank you, Elizabeth. I'm so glad to be here."*

"Come meet the rest of us," she said, taking Jenny by the hand.

She led Jenny down the stairs to the right to Jenny's bemused delight and Tarafau felt a surge of pride in his beautiful daughter. Typically, perhaps due to their longevity, his people had small families, two or three children. Their physical fertility cycles were few and far between. So, each family cherished their children all the more. His two sons and two daughters were his treasures, superseded only by his beautiful wife.

As they descended the stairs, the true extent of his home became apparent. The huge circular great room at the bottom of the stairs included a generous kitchen, a small prism-lighted herb and salad garden and an inviting circle of large chairs and chaises. The tile floor was covered with decorative woven rugs and there were large colorful pillows, large enough to sit on, haphazardly stacked in one area that might have been a corner in a square room.

"Ee ofela!" Elizabeth called out to the three lounging in the great room. *"They're here!"* she sent simultaneously to Jenny, as was polite. The three stood and his wife Amenia hurried over to greet them, first extending her hands to Jenny. *"Welcome, Jenny! We have been so anxious to meet you. Tarafau can't seem to tell us often enough what an amazing person you are."*

Jenny ducked her head, somewhat embarrassed. *"Thank you, you are too kind. I am so happy to be here and to finally meet Tarafau's family."*

"You have already met Elizabeth," said Amenia with the smile that always lit up Tarafau's world and had for hundreds of years. *"Allow me to introduce Felan and Melek our two sons.*

His boys looked so much like him that Amenia's mother had always said that no court would ever allow Tarafau to deny them. They, however had long straight black hair and were still youthful in appearance, only 121 and 230 years old, by the reckoning of his planet. Elizabeth was the baby, only 42 years old and nearly a mirror image of her mother. Long wavy brown hair burnished with gold and large green eyes that already had the youth in her school eyeing her with longing. Of course, he couldn't blame them, therefore he had his eye on a few of those boys. The fact that she had two burly older brothers who had more than one medal for martial arts, would keep them in check, if need be, he mused.

"I have a meal nearly finished for us," Amenia sent. *"Elizabeth will show you to the guest room, so you can freshen up. I know you have your things currently stowed in your MDP, but there is room to hang things and drawers for any clothing or whatever you would like to have handy. Please let me know if you need anything. Our home is your home."*

Jenny smiled at Elizabeth and then around at the family. *"Thank you, Amenia. I appreciate your hospitality. I am so glad to finally meet all of you. This was an unexpected treat, as I had no idea we would be coming here today."*

Elizabeth led her out of the room. Finally, Amenia slipped under his arm, pulling his hand around her waist and smiling up at him with her huge green eyes. The boys resumed the game of Lattice they had been playing, ostensibly to give them privacy for conversation.

"So," she said, looking up into his eyes with a twinkle of amusement in hers. "Is she as much as you had hoped? I know you didn't think anyone could ever hope to replace Lizzie."

"And no one can, ever," he replied seriously, "but she has great potential and I have come to think of her as a younger daughter. Lizzie was right to put her trust in her. I have never seen her be deliberately unkind, except in battle. She has held up beautifully under some great trials already. I know she wants to do her best and I also know she will do it in a way that will make us all proud. She will grow into her office with grace, I think."

"Well, we shall see, of course. My first impression is that she has some strength in her and that she has the humility to become great, depending on her choices. I look forward to facing her in a quarterstaff match. I hear she is coming along very well in that discipline."

He rolled his eyes. "She has no idea what she's getting into and I'm not going to tell her. If anyone can hone her to a razor's edge, it is you, my treasure. She has a lot to learn and she needs to learn quickly. Lova and Arvid have agreed that you are definitely the one most likely to give her the best results, as they can see she has much more potential than they originally thought. I thought it would be good if you and Elizabeth could pair up with her for awhile. She especially needs the mind disciplines. According to Lova, she has potential in that area she hasn't even touched yet. She is already more advanced in these disciplines than Lizzie ever became."

"Where do you think I should start with her?"

Tarafau considered. "I think you should put her through her paces then decide. I know you don't have a lot of time with her, which means you may have to push her more than you normally would. Arvid and Lova have a good handle on things for the moment, I think. I understand The Council will also be sending specialists in addition to Gariel to help them out once the teams have had a chance to go through the newest intelligence. They're well organized and I don't think we've come close to their potential either, when they work in teams like this."

"How much have you told her about the Daringi?" she asked tilting her head suspiciously. "Almost nothing, I'm betting. You never say much more to anyone about anything unless you have to."

"I have told her nothing, as you suspect. You are so much better at that than I. Besides, I wanted to let her experience it without any of my prejudices."

"As you say, old cat. Has she seen any of your other forms?"

He grinned at her and she grinned back, warming him. "Not yet. There has been no need and I am limited legally to what I can do on Earth. You know that."

He drew apart from her, holding both hands and backing up to really look at her. "I just want to drink in the sight of you," he confessed. The top of her head came up to his cheek. He liked the length of her. Her wavy brown and gold hair was bound up in a colorful scarf and her large green eyes were just beginning to have the smallest little crinkles in the slight tilt at the corners. Her full lips were parted in that smile she reserved only for him. The delicate fangs were slightly whiter than her other teeth which was very attractive to him. There was no excess flesh on her, neither was she skinny. Her curves were built on muscle and woe to the being who underestimated her strength.

And yet she was one of the gentlest beings he had ever met in all his hundreds of years. He twirled her back under his arm and squeezed her waist. She giggled like a girl.

"And now I must finish our supper, lest we starve. And those hulking boys of yours would be very put out, if, after leaving their wives and children to meet Jenny, I did not feed them."

Chapter 3: Family Style

Tarafau watched his family interacting with Jenny with great pleasure. Lizzie had often come with him to his home and they had grown to love her as a favorite aunt. They had mourned with him at her death. While his people tended to live hundreds of years, not all beings were blessed with such a long temporal presence.

"I wish I could speak your language," Jenny sent, looking wistfully into their faces. *"Don't get me wrong, I am grateful for mindspeech, but I know you are used to speaking vocally to one another and I would like to hear the sound of your voices."*

"We can speak aloud and mindspeak at the same time," suggested Elizabeth. *"Like this."*

Tarafau and his family were amused at the delight and astonishment on Jenny's face as they began to speak normally, while sending the translations to her. Tarafau knew that to Jenny the sounds of their language sounded a lot like songbirds. In their language, not only words had meaning, but also the intonation and pitch of their speech. To an outsider, it almost sounded as if they were singing.

So, they had enjoyed their regular supper conversation, including Jenny and explaining things that puzzled her. They laughed a lot and he enjoyed catching up with his children and knowing that for at least a few days he could stay with them, something that had happened so rarely over the last few years.

In early days with Lizzie, they had visited his home on a regular basis, but the last few years with her they had been given assignments that kept him away for long periods. And then there was her illness. Now there was this war to deal with and he wasn't sure how often he would be able to make the time to be here.

So, he resolved to enjoy every minute of his time with his family and the fact that Jenny was so obviously enjoying it as well was added spice to the soup, as Amenia was fond of saying.

"We don't want it to be all work for you while you're here, so I thought we could take you to visit some different places here and meet some of the species who share our world. Would you like that?" Amenia asked Jenny. *"We could go, just us girls, so Tarafau can spend some time with his friends and catch up with some family business."*

Jenny nodded, beaming. *"I would love that! It's been awhile since I could relax at all and I do so want to learn more about your planet and culture. I haven't had any kind of vacation in what seems like years, what with college and working and then all of this."* Jenny subconsciously touched the little key on the gold chain around her neck.

"Tarafau has told me of your needs, so we will proceed like this: Morning mental and physical workout, then we will go out and explore; mental work-out before supper and then a last workout before bed. Does that sound like it will work for you? We only have about a week, Daringi-time, together, unless something changes."

"That will be perfect! I know we are on a short schedule, but I promise, once we have completed our mission and we have secured the Gate Network, I will be happy to accompany Tarafau on a regular basis so he can spend more time with his family," Jenny replied, her face glowing with excitement.

Tarafau pushed back from the table and smiled around at his family, then at Jenny. *"We have prepared something special for this evening. It is a tra-ditional welcome. Please follow us out to the grove."*

He led his family, with Jenny, out to the grove behind his house. It was a mixture of several different kinds of trees, some bearing fruits and nuts native to his planet and some just for shade and their natural beauty. They encircled the grounds behind his home and in the center of a large open area was a firepit surrounded by benches. They all seated themselves. His sons had prepared the wood for the fire so that a touch from a firestick, similar, but not the same as the matches used in Jenny's world, would ignite the fire instantly.

The fire flared up with a satisfying crackle. The sun was just beginning to sink to the horizon and soon it would be dark with the exception of the orbiting rings above. He knew that more than one of the planets Jenny was familiar with had rings orbiting them. But, no Earthling, other than Lizzie had ever seen them from this angle and they were spectacular. The brilliant jewel-like colors reflected from those rings were like a permanent rainbow. There was no need of additional lighting and the several small moons included in the rings were like glistening diamonds of light.

Jenny gaped openly at the beauty before her. She sat on a bench next to the fire between Elizabeth and Amenia looking somewhat dazed. There was something about viewing your home through another's eyes that renewed your own awe like nothing else could. Tarafau stood gazing thoughtfully around the circle and his heart swelled with warm pride in each of them.

"This is our home. From this time forth, it is also the home of Jenny Japhet. In our home there is peace and comfort and unity. This family is one."

The others repeated in unison, *"This family is one."*

Each of them stood in turn. Elizabeth turned to Jenny, holding out her right hand. In it was a small ring with a green gem embedded in the band. *"This is welcome to you, our new sister. Wear it and think of us, as we will think of you when you are far away."*

Jenny took the ring hesitantly with tears in her eyes. *"Thank you,"* she said quietly as she slid it onto the ring finger on her right hand.

Felan stood before Jenny and extended his right hand to reveal a finely crafted compass of ancient workmanship. *"You are never lost when you are family,"* he said, placing it in Jenny's palm and covering it with his own. *"Always return to us."* Jenny sat, as if dumbfounded and looked up at him in wonder.

When Melek stood before her, Tarafau could see that Jenny was over-whelmed and knew it was important for her to be so. This ceremony was very old before Tarafau was even born. It was intended to create a bond that would strengthen family bonds beyond even the most intense friendship. It was an adoption and would be legalized the following day before a magistrate.

"You are our sister," Melek said to her and handed her a tiny marble-like light that glowed in response to the warmth of the hand holding it. *"Never stay in darkness when we can be your light, your warmth and your support. We pledge our lives and our honor to you. Welcome to our family."*

Amenia stood and holding out both hands drew Jenny to her feet. *"I am, and I will be your mother regardless of what may come. I do not replace your natural mother, nor would I want to, but when you are here, I will be here for you as I am with all of my children. Welcome, Jenny, to our family."* And she hugged Jenny fiercely.

At last, Tarafau stood again. *"Since we first met, when you thought I was only a cat, I had hoped we would someday come to this. I was still in mourning from the death of Lizzie, but there was something about you... Now, having known you and suffered with you, there is nothing I can think of that would give me more happiness than to have you as part of my family. Do you accept this, daughter, Jenny?"*

He could see that from the light in her eyes and the flush of her cheeks that she had been touched to her heart. *"I accept gladly,"* she said and his family, her new family, surrounded her in a group hug.

Afterwards, in years yet to come, he would always find tears threatening when he thought of this moment. Now she was more than just The Gate-keeper and a Guardian. She would always be part of him.

"I seem to be collecting parents and siblings," Jenny said when they all seated themselves again. *"Bob also said he considers me like a daughter. It feels good to be so loved. I know there are hard times ahead, but this will make it easier. Thank you so very much for your kindness."*

The smiles went around and then, to Jenny's obvious surprise, they began to sing. It was a prayer that had been a part of their routine since he first wed Amenia. Tarafau translated it to Jenny as they sang.

"Of all that is goodly and all that is bright,

Of all that is beauty, of all that is light,
Of all that is holy, of all that is heart,
We treasure the family of which we're a part.
To all that brings joy and to all that brings sorrow
We pledge our true unity morrow to morrow.
With pure love that needs neither vision nor voice,
We pledge hearts and hands, by our infinite choice."

Tarafau concluded: *"May The Creator of All Things, hear our voices and record our choice, one and all."*

His family chorused: *"Let it be so."*

From there on, there were stories and laughter and the light chiding and teasing among siblings as was appropriate for a family gathered together. Jenny joined in with good humor, her eyes twinkling in the light of the rings and the reflection of the firelight. By the time they were finished, it was well beyond any of their usual bedtimes.

His sons bid farewell to hurry home to their families, with the promise to Jenny that she would have an opportunity to meet them in the coming days. Jenny and Elizabeth went down to their rooms, chattering like old school friends and finally Tarafau was alone with his sweet Amenia.

Chapter 4: The Daringi

Next morning Jenny, Tarafau, Amenia and Elizabeth all went into their private workout room. It somehow seemed smaller than usual. The one at Sanglarka was large enough to accommodate a dozen or more people working out at once. This had been designed for half of that. Nevertheless, it was more than adequate for the four of them.

Jenny immediately dropped to the mat next to Elizabeth and assumed the meditation position. Tarafau and Amenia faced them on the mat.

"Before we begin, Jenny, I need to tell you what your course of study will be while you are here. Lova tells me you are adept at all of the basics and you have advanced quite far in preventing intrusions into your mind and controlling bodily functions. We are about to embark on a completely new discipline because you have already shown aptitude. Lova seems to think you have some undiscovered gifts and it will be my pleasure to see how far we can take you in the short time you will be with us. Amenia paused, looking at Tarafau with an arched eyebrow. "Tarafau seems to think that of the two of us, I am most suited to this. We shall see."

He rolled his eyes, as he knew she expected him to do, and Jenny and Elizabeth both giggled and sent one another knowing looks. It must be a thing with all species of females, he decided. Certainly, every female, including the draconian, Liliath, had all had this same thing that went beyond mindspeech where males were concerned.

"We will start with the normal breathing patterns and then, instead of resisting my mind pressure, I want you to allow me in. I promise not to peek (with a mental grin) *into anyplace private. I need to determine if the building blocks are there, before we begin."*

Tarafau watched as the three went into the meditative breathing patterns. The three faces at rest were serene and all three of them beautiful beyond any words he knew how to express. Then it was as if the already still air became calmer yet. Light began to build up in the room. Not harsh light, but like the sun filtered through spring leaves. Amenia's face took on an inquisitive look and Jenny's took on a look of amazement.

Her cheeks took on a rosy glow, not of embarrassment but of energy. He could almost see it pulsing through her body. Her breathing slowed even farther until he could barely see her abdomen rising and falling.

Suddenly all three pairs of eyes popped open, staring at one another and appearing almost startled to see Tarafau sitting there.

"Lova was correct. You have untapped potential. You may be able to use your mind in ways most beings think of as mythical. You have a strong connection to the part of your mind that was intended to do so much more than most beings ever use it for. I have heard that Earth scientists believe it isn't possible to use much more than ten percent of the human mind.

However, we have learned better. That sealed part of your mind serves more purposes than they suspect. We will now begin to train a part of that ninety percent to allow you to do so much more than you may have imagined was possible.

For this morning, let us simply go through the exercises you have been taught. Then, I think breakfast is in order. We have a lot to do and see today and your time here is short."

Jenny nodded and Tarafau joined them in their usual morning mental exercises. Afterward they all went through their quarterstaff exercises and sparred two on two, Jenny and Amenia facing Tarafau and Elizabeth. Tarafau was so proud of these three women. He reveled in their grace and competence and while he was contemplating this, Amenia tapped him lightly on the behind with her staff. Grimacing, he refocused on the task at hand.

Once they had completed their workout, showered and dressed, Tarafau led them all out of the house down the broad street that led to the heart of their city. It was a perfect day, only a suggestion of clouds in the blue-green sky. Overhead, large graceful Apella soared, their haunting cries floating down to them. He explained to Jenny when she pointed to them, her eyes wide that these beautiful dark green birds were often used as messengers and the bird was probably delivering something to someone in the city proper.

He watched her with fondness, as she chatted amiably in mindspeech with Elizabeth. Evidently Elizabeth was teaching her to speak Daringi to the amusement of both of them as Jenny tried matching the melodious sounds coming from Elizabeth's mouth.

They came to the top of the rise before entering the city and paused, the valley stretched before them, bathed in the late morning sunlight. Not far away rose the majestic pyramidal shape of The Apex. Jenny gasped. *"What is that?"* she asked, awestruck by the size and unusual appearance of the massive building.

The Apex would be very unusual to Jenny's eyes. Unlike the ancient pyramid structures on Earth, there were no sharp lines in this building. Each of the corners and the edges that extended to the peak of the building were gently curved. From the outside of the building you could see many levels and instead of a solid wall as in the Earthly designs, there was a balcony-type area that extended all the way around each level. Each of those balconies was covered in greenery. It was much like the terraced farms he had seen on a trip he and Lizzie had made to Machu Pichu, except this was not the side of a mountain, but the side of a building. At the top level of the building was a viewing platform where one could view the area for miles around and above that, like a massive transparent jewel, was the solar collector. It capped the structure in light, sparkling like a beacon during both day and night.

"*It is The Apex. It is a center of production as well as a dwelling for crafters from all over the planet. It also contains a library, a marketplace and places of entertainment. I believe it is about 10 times larger than the largest mall on your planet. The outsides of the building produce food and all the outer walls and surfaces of the building produce power for the city. It will be your first excursion into Daringi life and culture. It will take most of the day to show you even the smallest part. Tomorrow you will get to explore with Elizabeth and Amenia, but I wanted to share this with you on your first day with us.*"

"*I noticed we are walking, and I see very few vehicles. Why is that? Don't you have trouble when you do your shopping, getting your groceries home?*"

Tarafau laughed. "*I will reveal that secret to you soon. But we walk because it is pleasant, and our destination is not far. Is it not enjoyable to walk together?*"

Jenny grinned. "*Yes, I am enjoying walking with you, and walking is good for you, especially when the air is so clean. It doesn't seem like city air to me.*"

"*We once had air here much like Los Angeles, although, you have gotten some better over the years. But a few hundred years ago, we made some changes. We created systems that reduced pollution to nearly nothing and adopted a community attitude of conservation and health. Now, most people walk as you will notice.*"

Jenny nodded as they proceeded down the slope into the city. As he had told her, they now began to see many people heading into the city, laughing and talking and some even singing as they went. The colorful clothing and bright smiles of the people around them was invigorating. People he knew waved and called out to them. Several times they stopped and introduced Jenny to their various friends. Tarafau could see Jenny was both delighted and somewhat confused at the difference in the culture, but he knew her well enough to know she would adapt quickly and soon fit in well.

They walked past the park where many people were either standing in groups talking or working out in groups in the martial arts forms practiced by their people. Jenny had asked him at one point, the night before, if it wasn't a bit of a contradiction to have such an emphasis on martial arts in his culture and yet be dedicated to peace.

"Not at all," he had replied, smiling. *"We honor peace and practice it as a culture, but we are not so naïve as to believe that others feel the same. Our planet has been at peace for a very long time, but one of the things we have learned is that peace-loving cultures have a responsibility to spread the cause of peace as far as is possible, but also to take whatever measures we need to protect our freedom and our culture. Just because things are well here, doesn't mean they are well in other places.*

Can we afford to bask in our blessed state without being willing to defend those who are not as blessed as we? This is why we joined the Alliance. We lend our strength and influence wherever it is needed, as we desire all peoples to choose and to have the opportunity to live as we do. We never force our ideals on others, but we will defend others' desire to have that choice."

As they moved through the city streets on broad avenues, he pointed out various buildings and their purposes. There were shops of many kinds, as in any large city. Some of the buildings were housing units for young people just starting their lives or single adults. Others were office buildings with several different types of beings going in and out. Unlike many planets he had visited, there really was no dominant species on his planet. Daringi scientists still had come to no conclusions about how this had happened, but it was a distinguishing characteristic of the planet Ungoli.

Jenny's head swiveled from side to side as if watching a tennis match, not quite sure where to look. Finally, they stopped in front of one of four entrances to the Apex. There was an entrance on each face of the building, each one tall enough to pass a dragon through with headspace to spare and wide enough side to side to allow a marching band to pass through easily.

Beyond the entrance was a vast concourse already teeming with the various beings of Ungoli. Along the edges of the huge square were many shops and stalls with colorful signs. In the inner court was a concentric square of shops and in the square inside of that were other squares each with gathering places sprinkled randomly down wide aisles with seating and tables and an occasional platform or stage. Many of these platforms held performers of various types from musicians to dancers, jugglers and acrobats already performing to lounging audiences.

As they strolled around the edge, Tarafau explained some of the more esoteric offerings.

"This," he said, as they approached what appeared to be large fish tanks with green lobster-like creatures a dozen feet long, *"is one of my favorite shops. The creature inside this tank is very unusual. It is not a fish nor is it strictly aquatic. We call them bud-crawlers. Sometimes they live in forests and sometimes in lakes. They are very tasty, but the nice thing about them is that we don't have to kill them to eat them. Under their bodies are many long tube-like tendrils and at the end of each of them grows a type of fruit we call "buds". They taste like a cross between lobster and scallops and the texture is very nice. Every few days they can harvest the "fruit". Today doesn't seem to be a harvest day for this one. Let's move down the row and see if we can find one that is ready to harvest."*

"But, if they are not harvested, what happens to the buds in the wild?" Jenny asked in concern. It was typical of her to think about things like this. He had noticed in her little house on Infinity Loop that she had taken great care to recycle and conserve energy, telling him that everyone had to do their part. She had carefully cut up the plastic bands that held groups of cans together before throwing them away, because she didn't want some fish or bird to get caught in them and be injured or killed.

"This is much like the eggs of your Earthly chickens. When allowed to grow to the point that they develop a carapace, they separate from the parent and become bud-crawlers themselves. At this stage they are no more sentient than an egg is. The bud-crawlers you see here are domesticated as your chickens are at home, the difference being that we never eat an adult bud-crawler."

They passed three of the bud-crawlers until they came to the largest yet. It must have been 14 feet long and 3 feet wide. It had large claws and a scaled carapace and undulating in the water from under its body were hundreds of tube-like protrusions, each with a fruit the size of Tarafau's fist. A tall slender being, very pale, topped with hair that looked a little like monofilament line was harvesting the buds. She made the job look easy, her 4 arms ending with hands with long deft spindly fingers. She reached in the tank and grasped the buds firmly. As she did so, the tube stiffened, and she gently twisted the bud which was then released from the tube. The tube retracted back under the belly of the bud-crawler.

"They are best when harvested fresh," he grinned. *"I think we'll eat outside tonight."* He asked for a dozen buds and she packaged them up. He showed her his hand and she scanned a tiny tattoo on the web between his thumb and finger that Jenny hadn't noticed before. She then packaged them up in an airtight glass container and marked the container with something like a grease pencil.

"She will deliver these to us with whatever else we order from the shops today. They will put it into our box by the door. There! The secret is out. People seldom tote their purchases home, especially if they have a lot of shopping to do. It is a service that is part of the accommodations we made when we eliminated most vehicular traffic from our streets. There are tubes that run under the city. The wheeled delivery drones that run through the tubes are programmed to deliver our purchases. You never see them, because the delivery is elevated up into the box from below."

They moved on, admiring the wares of fruit and vegetable vendors. The smell of the fruit was glorious. There were potted plants for sale as well. Tarafau had always felt more than a little confused as to why Earthlings sold cut (murdered) flowers that would wilt and die over a few days. It seemed like such a waste. Flowers were meant to live their full span, allowing all to glory in their color and scent until those flowers died a natural death without harming the plant they bloomed on.

They came to a wide staircase leading up to the next level. *"All levels have stairs leading up, but there are also elevators. It is high enough that most people don't take the stairs all the way to the top, but I thought you would like the view from the balcony at the top of this particular flight of stairs."*

They got to the top of the stairs and stepped out onto a viewing platform populated with tables and chairs. Many beings sat there speaking with one another, some with exotic looking drinks in front of them. As Jenny stepped to the railing her eyes were wide with wonder. *"All I can say is, WOW!"*

The view that spread before them was like looking down at a simple maze constructed of nesting squares. Each square had intermittent entrances that led to the next layer of squares. Each square was comprised of a layer of shops facing in front and behind with a broad concourse between them. What had seemed to be the center, when you came in from the outside doors was actually just the first layer of squares. In addition to the shops were occasional eating areas. And all along these walkways were trees in planters and many blooming plants. The effect was of an outdoor market, as the glow from the ambient light from the solar plant at the top was much like being in a sunlit forest or grove.

The difference was that this area was larger than sports arenas he had seen on Earth. Bob had occasionally come over on some holidays to watch "the game" with Lizzie, and Tarafau had soon learned that arenas existed in nearly every major city. He was bemused at the idea of that much space in a city dedicated purely to the playing and watching of games.

Looking up you could see the various levels and see clear up to the top story a dizzying 130 floors above. The golden light that emanated from the massive solar plant at the top pervaded the entire building.

"All power needed for this building and enough to power the entire city is generated by three sources of energy: the sun, thermal energy from below the ground and the body heat of the beings within the entire building, and methane waste produced by garbage and hygiene stations throughout. It is part of a network of power producing efforts through passive means all over the country, as well as power conservation by all of the beings in our communities by general agreement. This building also serves as a water treatment facility, contained in the underground area of the pyramid. The underground foundation extends far below the surface and is almost a city in and of itself."

"Your culture seems so rural at first glance. You are obviously far in advance of us on Earth. You must find us quite primitive compared to what you're used to," Jenny sent, sighing. The contemplative set to her eyes told him she was taking all of this in, but he realized from the sigh that she was also feeling somewhat saddened by what she saw as the failings of her culture.

"Your Earth has made great progress in many areas. Think of it as an adolescent planet. The adolescence of most living things is a time of exploration and discovery. Earthlings are still discovering who they will ultimately become. There are many good and exciting things going forward on your planet that, if they are allowed to grow and blossom, will bear beautiful fruit. Do not despair. It is people like yourself, Burt, Bob and the rest of your team members who will win the day when all is said and done. I have observed that the beings of Earth have great potential and I believe that good will win in the end."

Jenny smiled at this. He loved her smile. He knew that as much as she had already been through in her calling, that there were more difficult days ahead, and he respected her calm determination and unwavering commitment. The Insenium were relentless in their pursuit of dimensional dominance, therefore this short respite was essential to ground her while her team prepared to eliminate the Insenium threat.

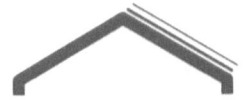

Chapter 5: Possibilities

Jenny stared around her in amazement. Beings of different shapes and sizes surrounded her and as she looked below at the crowds going about their business, greeting and interacting with happy faces, she realized there was something very different about the people she could see around her.

Unlike her recent experiences at home in a mall or a large department store, these people were looking into one another's eyes, greeting and holding conversations with evident interest. There wasn't a single device in evidence that even resembled a cell phone. From time to time she noticed groups of diverse kinds, having what appeared to be mindspeech conversations. They were honestly engaged with one another. For a moment she wondered if she would ever see that kind of interaction on her planet again.

She looked up at Tarafau. *"Thank you for this. Your city is awe-inspiring, and these people make me wonder if Earth will ever grow up."*

He looked at her and the warmth in his eyes tugged at her heart. *"You are going through a wondrous time on your Earth. The rate of discovery is escalating, and many are searching for answers to your difficulties. There may yet be some difficult times ahead, but I know enough of you to have great hope and you should also. Our people took thousands of years to reach this point and, although it may look perfect to you, there are still things we are trying to resolve."*

Amenia and Elizabeth nodded in agreement. *"And this is not a time for such woeful thoughts, dear one. Let us show you some of the crafting levels and then we should all have some lunch."*

She took Jenny's hand and Elizabeth took the other and together they entered an elevator much like those at Alliance Headquarters, large enough to hold a truck with room to spare. Based on the variations of size and body type she had already seen; she could see the needfulness of it. They ascended smoothly and got out several floors above the main floor.

Around the balcony walkway were glassed in areas, each dedicated to a different product or service, but although there were display rooms at each, these weren't just more stores. These were workshops of various kinds, from weaving and pottery to tools and cabinetry. They entered several of the glass doors along the walkway, admiring the craftsmanship of the Daringi and other beings as they went about their work. Amenia introduced her to several of the crafts folk and they passed a pleasant morning. After fully exploring this floor, Jenny could see that the people here seemed enthusiastic about whatever task they were involved in.

"These must be expensive," she sent to no one in particular, fingering a flowing scarf of fabric that was similar to silk, nearly glowing with warm colors and an elegant design. *"The craftsmanship is exquisite."*

Amenia looked at Tarafau. *"Expensive?"* she queried him. *"I don't think I understand"*

"It's an Earth concept, Amenia. Their trade system is different than ours." He turned to Jenny. *"Long ago we traded with a fiat currency system, similar to yours. Now we trade hours."*

"Hours?"

"Everyone in our community works at something that contributes to the community, sometimes more than one thing. As they work, they track their hours. These hours are put into an accounting system. A thing you might wish to buy is valued by the number of hours it took to create it. It also breaks down into minutes. There are 37 hours in a day, 8 days in a week and 7 weeks in a month. Our yearly calendar is 10 months long. There are plenty of hours available to contribute to your community to assure you have everything you need."

"But what if someone is injured or ill or very old and can't work?"

"*We honor the accomplishments of every citizen, however long and at whatever level. For instance, a mother who cares for her young children is contributing, so every hour she puts in is credited to her. An elderly person has contributed throughout their life and are given credits for that, which will assure they have all their needs met. A person who is ill or cannot contribute for a valid reason is gladly aided by the community to see their needs are met.*"

"*That's amazing,*" Jenny exclaimed. "*So, there is no currency at all? What about people, like myself, who come to visit from outside your system?*"

"*Guest-right is yours. As your hosts, it is our honor to see to your needs and we are given some dispensations to accommodate that.*"

"*What about traders from other dimensions?*"

"*That is usually more of a barter situation; we trade with them with services or goods, receiving from them whatever they have to offer. Although, admittedly that is rare, considering we do not have a gate on Ungoli. The only visitors we have are those who have been brought here by one of our citizens.*"

Jenny shook her head, trying to get her head around what Tarafau had told her.

"*It sounds like a perfect society.*"

"*Not really. We have much to learn and far to go to create something resembling perfection, but we have far less strife and difficulty than many of the cultures I have had the opportunity to observe. We are constantly striving to raise the quality of life for our communities. And we have many intelligent life forms that live here with very different needs, that must be also taken into consideration.*"

Jenny nodded. As they moved through the different crafting halls and small factories, she marveled at the diversity of different crafting methods she had never seen before. And the complex was huge! She realized that it was the equivalent of an entire large city. They couldn't possibly visit everything in a single day. She longed to stay several months, but even now she felt somewhat guilty for not being in the middle of all of the planning going on in Sanglarka. She knew this was part of her missing training, but she also realized that time was growing short if they were going to thwart the plans of the Fleistians and the Insenium.

Nevertheless, she was enjoying spending time with Tarafau, Amenia and Elizabeth. It was in the order of a deep breath before the plunge.

They ate lunch in a little café serving a number of delicacies, including some tasty buds, sautéed in something similar to fresh churned butter, with a zesty green vegetable on the side. There was a colorful salad with a tart and tangy dressing and some kind of tea with a minty/flowery flavor. Jenny found herself grateful her parents had always stressed the importance of sampling unusual new foods. Although this was different than anything she had ever eaten, it was tasty, and she wondered if Lizzie had missed Daringi food while back on Earth?

After lunch Tarafau led them to another elevator. This went up for quite awhile. *"We're taking you to my favorite place,"* Elizabeth told her excitedly. *"I can hardly wait to share it with you."* And she reached to grasp Jenny's hand.

The elevator opened out into an atrium with tall trees and flowers and a tinkling fountain. The water ascended from what looked like rocks that had been painted with assorted scenes of Daringi life and scenery from the planet they lived on. They walked around it and out onto a balcony the width of a city street. Along the sides were planters with exotic plants and even small trees. Every ten feet or so, on the outside edge of the promenade were little alcoves where people could stand and look out so far that it felt like you could see the curve of the horizon beyond.

Ever above them they could see various moons and small asteroids contained in the multicolor rings that orbited the planet. In the daylight they were even more colorful from up here than at night.

Behind them loomed the giant shining pinnacle dome of the solar plant. It reflected an iridescent light that intensified the colors around them. Jenny had to make a conscious effort to close her gaping mouth.

"This is beyond any words, Elizabeth. I can see why this is your favorite place."

Elizabeth beamed. She threw one arm around Jenny's shoulders. *"I always wanted a sister to share with, Jenny. I am so glad you are now a part of our family."*

They strolled around the outer side of the promenade and stopped occasionally at an alcove to look out. Looking down, Jenny could see how each terrace shaded the inner area of the terrace below it and left a large unshaded swath available for gardens. She could see people tending the plants, reminding her of her mom working in their family garden at home. Often a few of them would be working side by side, chatting and nodding as they went about their work.

"Anyone can have gardening space here, if they would like, but most of those you see working on the terraces actually live in apartments in the inner complex. Oftentimes their apartment looks out on their part of the gardening space," Amenia pointed out. *"Most of the produce you see in the shops below is grown in the gardens you see here. This complex produces power, food and goods for the use of all citizens on Ungoli. Of course, it isn't the only source of these things, but our world prospers by use of technologies like this."*

Jenny could see how many of the issues on her world could be resolved by copying the resourcefulness and diligence of the Ungolians. Looking out on the peaceful environs of the city below her, she noticed that although there were some vehicles on the street, most of the traffic was foot traffic as well as some rickshaw-like vehicles pulled by a contraption similar to a bicycle but propelled by the hands rather than the feet. Instead of pedals that went in a circular motion, the hands were placed on pads and they were pushed in and out, which drove the wheels below.

There was also a large outdoor market square not far from The Apex. It included a large stage with tiered seats, like a sports stadium. *"Do you hold concerts there?"* Jenny asked Elizabeth, pointing to the amphitheater.

"Yes...and theater events. We also gather there for lectures and readings from famous scholars and authors. Once a week we have a sharing time where anyone can stand on the stage and share a poem or song or any other talent. Father has been known to do his bird imitations there from time to time," she giggled glancing up at Tarafau with a wicked light twinkling in her eyes.

Tarafau rolled his eyes and Amenia laughed and nodded. *"He is actually quite famous for it,"* she said, her hand on one hip, *"but he has to be prodded to participate."*

Jenny really enjoyed the chatter and relaxed feeling of just hanging out with family and friends. She had a lot to think about and could see why this might be an important part of her training. There was so little time for personal indulgence, but she knew this time with Tarafau's family, now *her* family, was giving her a perspective she hadn't considered in the looming conflict to come. This wasn't about trillions of people in the multiverse. It really came down to individual communities like this one.

She could never possibly get her head around trillions of lives. But she could envision a community like this one, a family like this one, and how they would be affected by the incursions of the Insenium and their minions. It wasn't just about Earth. It wasn't just about the Alliance. The freedom and lives of all beings was at stake here and each civilization really boiled down to individuals and families and communities like this one.

"We should go up into the solar plant, so you can see it in action," Tarafau said, seeing Jenny's somber expression. *"I think you will find it interesting."*

They walked back through the atrium to the elevator and headed up for a longer time than Jenny expected. They stepped out onto a large platform, about half the size of a tennis court surrounded by heavy glass windows. The room glowed with sunlight. Looking down into the solar plant, Jenny noticed that hundreds of large magnifying glasses about 20 feet across were focused into spherical containers which had large pipes running downward from the bottom and similar pipes descending from the ceiling into the containers.

"We are able to multiply the energy of the sun by focusing the rays into a viscous solution that then transfers a thousand times the energy for each unit into the power grid for our area. This power plant is completely pollution free, putting out no harmful radiation or gases, just pure energy to meet all of our technological needs. It is very hot in the room you see before you. Only this special reflective glass in this temperature controlled room allows us to see the inner workings without danger," explained Tarafau. *"And now let us go home. There is no way we can show you every wonder of our city in a day. We need to prepare first-supper and get in some more training before we sleep."*

Amenia had explained the night before that, because of the 37-hour day, they generally ate 4 meals a day; breakfast, lunch, first-supper and second-supper (the lightest meal of the day, more like a large snack than a meal).

Tonight, it was the "boys" turn to make supper. Evidently household tasks were shared by all family members, not just the mother or other females in the home. Elizabeth's brothers had returned, having obtained permission from their wives for one more evening with Jenny. So, the men rattled around in the kitchen, making the house smell amazing. It was roasted buds and vegetables for supper, since the buds Tarafau had ordered at the Apex had been waiting for them when they returned in the refrigerated part of their delivery box.

Amenia suggested that Jenny take some time outside in the grove while she and Elizabeth caught up on some things they had laid aside for their trip into town.

Jenny walked out to the grove, greeted by the crooning of the Linklings. After wandering for a time under the trees, enjoying the peace of the place, Jenny finally sat down on one of the seats surrounding the fire pit, leaning back on the comfortable slanted back and closing her eyes. The filtered sunlight played on her eyelids and soon she found herself drifting off. The 37-hour day took a little getting used to and she had already had a full day on her inner clock.

She dreamed she was cuddling with a stuffed toy of her childhood and was startled awake, when she realized it wasn't a dream. There, in her lap, crooning softly was a Linkling, her huge eyes looking up at her. Her fur was extremely soft, and her breath had a gentle smell of something like eucalyptus. Her pale green fur contrasted sharply with the long dark green moustaches that hung down to the base of her neck and her startling blue eyes were surrounded by a ring of white fur below dark green fuzzy eyebrows. Linklings reminded Jenny of the Emperor Tamarin monkeys of Earth. Jenny wasn't sure how she knew the little creature was female, but she did.

Softly she sent to the little creature, *"Who are you, little one?"*

"This one is Chidwi. Friend to Jenny. Linked to Jenny. Forever to Jenny." Her soft mind voice was serious, but not somber. Jenny could feel a kind of excitement emanating from the little creature.

"Linked? I don't understand."

"We link to one, friend to one, forever. Like the Lizzie personage. I am your Linkling and I will serve." She placed her tiny hand gently on Jenny's wondering face.

"Thank you, Chidwi. I am glad to have a new friend. Right now, friends are very important. I love your song and you are very beautiful."

"As are you, Jenny. You have a beautiful mind. You think big things, like Lizzie."

"You can read my mind?"

"Your mind is open to me. All minds are open to Linklings. Some are dark, some are light. Your mind is light, but is often attacked by darkness, not of your doing."

Jenny tried to take this in, a fully telepathic species with no boundaries. What could the implications of that be?

Suddenly, the Linkling disappeared. She could still feel the slight weight of the creature on her lap, but she could no longer see her.

"Chidwi? Where'd you go?"

"Chidwi is here. I turned off my reflection."

"Turned it off? What does that mean?"

"When light reflects from solidness, eyes can see. When you turn off your reflection, eyes cannot hold the image. It is special thing of Linklings. If you wish to see me or for others to see me, tell me, 'Chidwi, on.' Then you and others will see me. If you wish not to see me or others not to see me, tell me, 'Chidwi, off.'"

"Chidwi, on," Jenny told her new friend and Chidwi faded into view, her little nose wrinkling up in what Jenny could tell was a smile.

"Chidwi stay with Jenny forever?"

"Yes, please," Jenny replied with her heart in her throat. *"May I ask you a question?"*

"Chidwi will answer as she can."

"What happened to Lizzie's Linkling? Lizzie died."

The reply was tinged with sadness. *"Lizzie was a friend to my friend, Ynni. She was much beloved by my clan. Ynni feels her still. Linked forever."*

"Linked forever," Jenny repeated, dazed. *"Even though she is dead?"*

"That word does not mean the same to us. A better word is 'separated'. She no longer dwells in her last form. She awaits her final form in the dimension of light."

Jenny blinked away tears and then remembered something Miriha had said in one of her dreams. Something about...more dimensions than she could imagine? Did this dimensional war affect them in those dimensions where a person's spirit might reside? The implications made her head spin. What could her team possibly come up with that would combat a threat that might even affect the spirit dimension?

Chapter 6: Get Set...

Bob watched Tarafau place his hand on Jenny's shoulder and fade into nothingness. He subconsciously reached a hand toward the space where they had been moments before, and he sighed. He had known she would have to leave to work on her training while they worked the problem before them, but he knew he would miss her terribly.

He noticed Burt's brows were furrowed and realized the young man was also staring at the empty spot just feet before him. "Well, buddy, let's get to work. She has her part to play and we have ours. The quicker we get to it, the safer she will be." He laid his hand on Burt's shoulder. "Tarafau won't let anything happen to her, kiddo."

Burt smiled and clapped his hands together with a loud "POP!", as Arvid often did when changing focus, and nodded. "So, let's get this show on the road!" He mindcast to the milling team around them. *"Attention Tactical Team! Meeting out on the balcony right now!"*

Bob found himself wondering about the young man. He and Burt had already been through a lot together and he respected his energy and diligence. Burt was capable of taking charge of a mission, but also was a willing follower when someone else in authority was in charge. Bob admired his cheerful disposition and suspected that maybe Burt wanted to be a little more than friends with Jenny. He wasn't quite sure how he felt about that.

He followed Burt out to the balcony that looked out over the Sanglarka valley to the mountains that surrounded them. He had never been able to find Sanglarka on the map and doubted that he ever would. This valley was protected from radar and other surveillance by some major "dastardly alien tech" that he would have loved to get his hands on. However, he had an agreement with The Dimensional Alliance Council and would never dishonor that, so he mentally drooled over it and his fingers twitched thinking about it, but let it be. He knew they had put some major trust in his word, and he couldn't ever go back on that.

"I know I'm not on your team, Burt. But I wanted to hear what you have to say before I head off to Switzerland," he sent.

"Hmm, don't pack your lederhosen yet, Bob. I hear they have something else in mind for you," Burt said with a smirk. *"Say hi to Merv, for me, will you?"*

"What are you talking about? Who's Merv?"

"Haven't you checked your messages yet? We were given our assignments about 10 minutes ago."

"But I assumed..."

"You should be careful about assumptions. I thought all of you 'sciency' guys knew that."

Bob took out his cell phone, shaking his head. He had been sure he would be on the Science and Technology team. Where else could they possibly put him? But the message on his phone didn't answer his question. It just said, "Please contact Lova for your assignment details."

Bob sighed. *"I guess I'd better check this out. Keep me posted,"* he sent to Burt. *"I'll check in with Lova. Thanks for the heads up."*

He headed back to the situation room and Lova was at her desk, poring over a document he assumed was related to the mission. She looked up over reading glasses as he entered the room. *"Bob! I was beginning to think you didn't get my message. Have a seat."*

In Bob's experience, nothing that ever followed those words ever boded well. He sat down and prepared himself mentally for some bad news.

"Did you get Ignatius settled in? I hope his accommodations in the little atrium upstairs are to his liking."

"He is loving it. A lot more wing space than the workshop for sure. He'll be sad to leave it for Switzerland, I think."

"About that..."

Uh-oh, here it comes...

"I'm afraid you won't be going to Switzerland, at least not yet. We are putting you on a supplemental team. You will still be working on Tech, but at Alliance Headquarters with one of our Top researchers, Mervin Wyliit. He is interested in collaborating with you on an aspect we don't want to release yet to the team, as it may be a key to the mystery of the Fleistians. Although we feel that we have eliminated the spy element from among us, we can't afford to take any chances. I need you to leave right away. You may take Ignatius and Fidget, of course and any of your equipment you brought with you in your MDP. Do you have any questions?"

"Uh...no. Are you kidding? Am I dreaming?"

Lova smiled and shook her head. *"You will be the liaison between both teams. You were the best qualified to connect the dots between both projects. You will go to Alliance HQ to get your orientation. We will keep you apprised of any developments from here. Go ahead and get your bird and your bot and leave from the main gate outside. I have oriented it to your key for this specific trip. You can go unescorted now because of your agent pass."*

Bob couldn't stop grinning as he grabbed Ignatius. He added the few things he had stashed in the room he and Burt had been sharing into his MDP. He knew Lova had already briefed Burt, so he walked to the gate and stepped through to the Alliance Headquarters gate. He knew this was the default setting for gate departures for anyone with an agent key. You had to be escorted by the guardian to go anywhere else.

He stepped through the gate and breathed deeply, taking in the magnificent view from the hilltop. Below him spread the valley city where he would find the Dimensional Alliance Headquarters. Ignatius perched quietly on his shoulder, looking around calmly. He was always surprised at how the macaw seemed to take everything in stride, not a common trait in most domesticated birds. "Stay, Ignatius. I want you to make a good impression on the guards."

The two ubiquitous Trooper guards stood a few feet away from the shimmering scanning field directly in front of him. He had been through the gate before with Jenny and Tarafau but was admittedly a little nervous his first time through on his own. He passed through the shield, feeling no sensation, but he knew from experience it was doing its job. The last time he went through the gate he had inadvertently brought a knife through and it had set off an alarm. The knife had been evidence from a crime scene, and he hadn't known about the sensor field.

"You are Bob Reid from Earth?" one of the Troopers sent in mind-speech.

Bob nodded. *"I am."*

"Come with us."

They led him down the wooded hill to a waiting self-driving hovercar.

"You are expected. The guards at the doors will direct you and your, um, companion to the Private Council Chamber where you will be briefed on your assignment."

Bob thanked them and stepped into the car after perching Ignatius on the back of the seat next to him. One of them closed the door and the vehicle moved forward onto the street that led to the heart of the city. Ignatius sidled slowly closer and closer to Bob. He had traveled in cars before on Earth, but the engine of this vehicle was silent and there were no wheels to make contact noise. Bob could tell his bird was nervous, so he "skritched" him gently on the back of the neck, one of Ignatius' favorite things.

Bob watched the beings on the sidewalks of the street with interest. The size, colors and variety of creatures ambling along the boulevard was somewhat mind boggling. As the primary governmental body of the Gate Network, the Alliance hosted visitors and citizens from all over the dimensions. Some of them carried rebreathers on their backs. These were those who could not breathe an oxygen rich atmosphere.

Others appeared to be parents with children, small duplicates of them following or being carried by them. Bob recognized reptilians, avians, insectoids and humanoids among the throng. He bounced gently on his seat in anticipation. He couldn't believe he would be working and living in this city while completing his assignment and, as exciting as the city would be, the assignment itself was beyond anything he had hoped for.

The vehicle finally halted before a large glass building of perhaps 50 floors. The two guards standing before the gigantic double doors just inside a shaded entry way smiled at him (a somewhat bizarre thing, as they had three eyes and all three of them crinkled with the smile). One held up a hand as Bob alighted from the hovercar with Ignatius on his arm.

"*The Troopers called ahead. Go through these doors and you will see the elevator straight in front of you. Tell the elevator that you want the Private Council Room and it will take you there. Check in with the receptionist and they will take it from there.*"

Bob nodded and one of the huge doors slid back. He stepped through and sure enough there was an elevator with doors as huge as the entrance doors in front of him. As he approached the doors slid open on their own.

"Uh, Private Council Room, please," he said aloud, hoping the guard hadn't actually meant mindspeech. But the doors slid closed and before he could take more than a couple breaths, the doors opened again, and a pleasant voice (female?) said, "Private Council Chamber" and he stepped out into a room with a receptionist desk a few feet beyond the elevator doors. It seemed, he mused, that offices were pretty much the same everywhere you went.

"*Bob Reid?*" the secretary inquired. She was foxlike, covered in soft white fur and her blue eyes sparkled in the soft office lighting.

"*That's me. I hope I'm on time.*"

"*They are expecting you,*" She replied without answering his remark. "*Go right in.*" She gestured at the large dark wooden doors to her left.

Bob nodded and then stopped. "*Is it all right if I bring my bird with me? I don't have any place to put him. Ignatius is very well behaved.*"

"*I am sure Myla will think him charming,*" she said and nodded toward the door.

At the end of the council room on the dais were Ingot, the Chief Councilor, Liliath, his second and Myla, his third. They were a colorful and somewhat bizarre group.

Ingot looked a lot like Arvid, except his clothes were colorful and his hair well kept. Bob was used to the tousled, often wild white hair of Arvid, but he could definitely see the family resemblance. Ingot was Arvid's nephew. Like Arvid, he was clean shaven and about four and a half feet tall. His bright blue eyes were keen and penetrating, but his smile was welcoming.

Liliath, who reclined on a chaise made especially for her was, of all things, a dragon. Bob knew Liliath was kind and very astute, one of Jenny's favorite "people". He also knew that her colors could shift from their current calm blue green to purple and red when angered. And, yes, she could breathe fire when necessary.

Myla was an avian, wings folded sedately behind his muscled arms which rested on his lap. Large and clawed, they appeared to be hands that were used to working with heavy things. His coloring was similar to a sun conure his aunt had cherished. The bird had been terribly spoiled and horrendously loud, he remembered, mentally shaking his head. Ignatius puffed up on his shoulder, as if ready to display in challenge. Bob reached up a comforting hand on the bird's back. He recognized why he was intimidated. Myla stood about seven feet tall, with a huge scoop-like beak and long well-muscled legs.

Bob knew Myla was as gentle as Ignatius, but he wouldn't want to be on the other end of that beak or the claws on feet and hands if the avian was angry.

These three were wise and trusted by all the dimensions in the Gate Network to order the affairs of the Alliance.

In one of the chairs arranged before the dais was a lanky man dressed in jeans, of all things, and an aloha shirt. Were those high-topped tennis shoes on his feet? His skin was pale, and he sported a large hooked nose on a narrow face. His large brown eyes were nearly hidden by his silver bangs and his hair hung below the collar of his shirt. He sprawled more than sat. But Bob felt he was more interested in the proceedings than he appeared to be. Bob realized he couldn't quite place the man's age, which wasn't all that unusual with those from other dimensions. Tarafau didn't look much over forty years old, but he was hundreds of years older than Bob. As he took in this man's appearance, he decided he was probably in his late fifties.

"Ah, Bob," Ingot said with outspread hands. *"Welcome. You know my councilors. Allow me to introduce you to Mervin Wyliit, the head of science and technology for the Alliance. You will be working with him for the next few weeks on a puzzle we have yet to solve that may provide important insights to the Insenium threat. I can't stress enough that this project is not to be spoken of to anyone not on his team or this council. I do not believe they know what we have gotten ahold of and, if they did, we believe it would be extremely dangerous for all of us. They will stop at nothing to prevent us from discovering this secret. I know we can trust your discretion in this matter."*

"I understand, sir. It is good to meet you, Professor Wyliit."

"Oh please, we are colleagues, Bob. Call me Merv."

He extended a long-fingered hand and Bob shook it. *"Whatever you say, Merv."*

Merv nodded to the council and wagged his head toward the doorway. *"We have a lot to do. Let's get you and your bird settled in, so we can get started as soon as possible."*

They turned to go, but Myla sent. *"Wait. You have not introduced your companion, Bob. I think he is feeling somewhat left out. Bring him to me."*

Bob stepped forward and Myla offered Ignatius his arm. Ignatius' eyes pinned and his feathers puffed out. Myla gently reached a clawed finger up and touched Ignatius on the forehead. *"Now, little brother,"* he said in a crooning mind touch. *"Is that better?"*

"Better," agreed Ignatius, wonder in his mind voice. *"How is this done?"*

"A little trick I learned," said Myla. *"Now we can all hear you."*

"Bob?" Ignatius inquired, cocking his head. *"You hear?"*

"I do," Bob sent back in awe. *"This is an amazing gift, Myla. Thank you."*

"Little brother's mind is as beautiful as his feathers," Myla replied. *"Now your bond is strengthened, and you will feel the joy of wings."*

Merv tapped Bob on the shoulder and again nodded toward the door. Bob nodded, retrieved Ignatius from Myla's arm and followed Merv out to a new adventure.

After Merv settled Bob into his suite, complete with a small tree with a bird feeding platform and a small fountain for Ignatius for bathing and drinking, he gave Bob the mental door key.

"Bring the bird," he directed. *"We understand he is your lab partner and we have added a perch with all the amenities for him in the lab. You won't be spending a lot of time in your suite and we don't want Ignatius to get bored or lonely. Will that work for you, Ignatius?"*

"Works for me," agreed Ignatius.

"I had a pet owl once, on one of my sojourns on your Earth. One of the few things they ever got right about me."

"You visited Earth? You look humanoid, so I assumed you were able to pass as an Earthling. How long ago was that?"

"A very long time ago, by your standards. They could never get my name right, though." And he sighed. *"Something about the 'V' in the middle kept getting copied as an 'L.'"*

"Mer-l-in... Wait! Merlin? THE Merlin? King Arthur and the Round Table?"

"The same, although I'm not sure why that is the one thing they remember about him. Silly, that. I am surprised that he isn't more well known as the one who brought the tactics of cavalry forces into play in the defeat of the Saxons. The table was just a slice of a very old oak tree after all. They didn't even bother to remove the bark or sand it. I still have scars from some of the splinters." He said this matter-of-factly, as if it was an old, unresolved gripe, without noticing that Bob's mouth was hanging agape.

They entered a room very much like Bob's workshop on Infinity Loop only much larger. Although many of the gadgets were unfamiliar to him, it had a laboratory feel to it. Clean, tidy and organized. Lights flashing here and there and soft beeps intermittently gave it a feeling of home to Bob. Various individuals (mostly humanoid, but not all) puttered about at different tasks and it had an aura of important work being done.

He let out a breath he didn't realize he had been holding. He realized he was acting like a star-struck teenager and that wouldn't do. He was going to need to work with this man and his diverse team on a professional level, and that meant mutual respect.

"By the way," Merv continued vocally, "We don't use mindspeech much in here unless it is a private conversation or there are too many conversations going on at once. All of my associates speak the Queen's English here, except maybe Hortense over there," he nodded at what appeared to be a tall velociraptor bent over a computer readout. "She can speak it, but when she gets excited it all comes out as hisses and growls, so she confines herself to mindspeech most of the time.

English is such a colorful language and there are some scientific concepts that are just expressed better in that tongue. Will that work for you?"

"Uh, sure, of course. That'll be just fine."

"By the way, her name isn't really Hortense, but it's what we all call her, since her name is unpronounceable by the human mouth."

Hortense hissed, her shoulders shaking with what Bob sincerely hoped was mirth.

"Let me introduce you to the crew," he continued with barely a pause.

"Gather up, folks! I want to introduce you to our new associate," he said in a raised voice and waved at them. "Someone get Argent's attention, please. He has his earbuds in again."

He turned to Bob and said from behind his hand, "Argent is Ingot's great uncle, or something, and he puts white noise into his earbuds to block out 'un-necessary distractions', or so he says. Personally, I think he is listening to another episode of Doctor Who. I should have never brought those back from my last trip to Britain." He winked and straightened to face the crowd.

Up until now, Ignatius had sat calmly on Bob's shoulder, apparently soothed by the familiarity of his surroundings, but now, as the crew gathered around them, he shifted uneasily from one foot to the other. *"Friends, Bob? Friends?"* he sent worriedly.

"Friends, buddy. They're all scientists like you and me." And Bob laid his hand gently over Ignatius's clawed feet.

"Listen up, you lot," Merlin said. "This is Bob and Ignatius. They're here to work on the 'special' project for the blokes upstairs. All hush hush and so forth. Bob has done some significant work on Earth and is well qualified to help us out. His head works somewhat different than ours, so we are hoping he brings a new perspective to our work. Tarafau thinks highly of him, and you all know that is as good a qualification as any we can get.

Bob, let me introduce you to our crew."

He started at one end of the semi-circle of five individuals who were as different as any group Bob had ever met.

"This is Rayard," he said, motioning to a humanoid male of about five feet eight inches tall, with cherry red frizzy, bushy hair, large green eyes and large fleshy ears. He was dressed in a traditional white lab coat, but underneath he wore a bright yellow t-shirt and jeans with some kind of rough looking sandals that showed his 6 large toes with black nails. He smiled and held out his hand. "Nice ta meetcha, mate," he said.

"Good to meet you as well, Rayard," Bob returned, matching his smile. Rayard's grip was firm and he looked Bob straight in the eye.

"And this lovely lady is Inle," he said gesturing to a glistening insectoid who reminded Bob very much of a praying mantis, except her coloring shifted in pastel shades of blue, purple and rose and she had paws similar to a spider monkey. The irises of her opalesque eyes swirled with darker shades of the same colors that patterned her body with long black diamond shaped irises that were opened wide at the moment.

It was odd to hear, "Glad !tchick! to !clicka! meet you, !tchicka! Bob," coming from the beaklike mouth. She also extended a hand to shake, which he did, trying not to flinch at the slick, almost plastic feel of her skin.

"And this is our chief curmudgeon, Argent. He's brilliant, would prefer to have a laboratory on a distant unknown planet where no one can interrupt his brilliance, but he doesn't bite and most of the time, he's right, if he begs to differ."

Argent folded his arms across his chest but nodded. It was clear he wanted to get back to whatever he was working on. Bob just nodded back with a smile. He'd worked with the type before and, if he was honest with himself, he liked peace and quiet to work on his projects as well.

Next, he turned to a greying woman with her hair pulled back in a tight bun at the base of her neck. "This is Clarice. You know her younger sister, Lova. She's been an agent longer than Lova has been a Guardian. She actually had recommended Lova to the former Guardian of the Sanglarka gate."

Clarice smiled warmly. It was easy to see the resemblance now that he knew to look for it. Her startling blue eyes, her build and facial features were an older version of Lova. He knew he would enjoy working with someone like her. If she and Lova were as alike in personality, he knew she would be well organized, mentally quick and imaginative. Bob extended both hands as Lova always did and she grasped them firmly. "We're glad to have you here, Bob. I hear good things about you from my sister."

"And finally..."

"Elves! Elves it is..." Bob breathed.

"Alwen Stardotter," Merv continued smoothly. "Gate science and technology specialist. She is on loan to us from her dimension. Her people have not only visited through the Earth Gate many times through your history, I understand they once had a colony on your planet."

She was tall, nearly six feet. Her gently waved red gold hair hung to her hips held back from her face with two long thin braids. Her violet eyes were slanted ever so slightly in a pale face and the braids holding her hair back exposed two pointed ears. However, there the resemblance to faerie ended. Her white lab coat was open at the front and revealed jeans and a green t-shirt, which seemed to be the uniform of choice in the lab.

She smiled at Bob wryly. "Don't concern yourself Earth-child. It seems my forbears left an impression on your kind so long ago. But, see here. I am not a figment, nor do I have magical powers. I am a scientist like yourself. We will get on well and you will quickly lose your awe of me and my kind. The stories have made us much grander than we really are. Are we good?"

"Good," Bob agreed, still stunned. He grasped her extended hand and shook it.

"Team," Merv said, "allow me to introduce Ignatius. He has mind speech and will be overseeing our projects with diligence. *Ignatius, say hello to the nice people.*"

"*Hello, nice people,*" Ignatius complied cheerfully.

"Now let us retire to the break room and we will brief Bob on the project, shall we?

The break room was not what Bob expected. It was not the stark, business-like setting that was typical in most office buildings. Rather, it was more like a rec center. There was a ping pong table in one corner, a Ms. Pac-Man video game arcade console, an 80 inch television on one wall complete with theater seats and a popcorn machine, and a circle of red cushy armchairs each with its own end table with bowls of M&Ms, of all things, on each. There was a soda machine with many more selections than Bob recognized. A long lunch table sidled along a kitchenette. A dart board graced one wall and there was a huge Lego complex under construction on a large table. It reminded Bob of one of the big tech startup companies.

"Active minds sometimes need distractions while they work on intricate problems," Merv explained. "If there is anything that isn't here that you would like, let me know. Your chair is the one with the perch behind it. We couldn't leave Ignatius out of our councils. Other than our briefing today, however, don't expect interminable scheduled meetings here. We spend 98% of our time in actual research. Random conversations happen frequently over different aspects of our projects, but we don't tie ourselves up in bureaucracy here. That's for the guys downstairs."

They all seated themselves. Some drew tablet devices out of lab coat pockets. Ignatius sat content on his perch behind Bob's chair. At either end of the perch were bird snack bowls, and a water bottle hung above him within easy reach. They had considered everything, it seemed. for his welcome and comfort. Evidently, they had known he was coming long before he did.

"OK," Merv began as they had all settled down. "The deal is this. When they did the Groga raid in South America, one of the officers dropped something on the ground and it wasn't until they were cleaning and restoring the area, they found this..." He handed Bob what looked like a debit card of unknown origin. "Believe it or not, someone almost threw it away. What do you make of it?"

Was this a test? Bob turned the card over in his hand. At first glance it just looked like a rigid plastic card with no markings. However, on closer examination it had the delicate outlines of complex printed circuits. Not what it appeared to be. Not at all. His fingers itched and his brain felt like it had exploded. "You say an officer had dropped it? How do you know it wasn't just one of the grunts?"

"Your drones were in operation the entire time recording the incident from every angle. Thank you for that, by the way. One of the cameras just happened to catch the fall of said officer. He fell hard and the contents of his pockets splattered along with him. We cleaned the blood off and, voila!"

"Well, this is obviously tech I haven't seen before, but it could be anything from a type of memory card to the key to his car," Bob said, shaking his head. "What makes you think it is significant?"

Merv looked around the group then fastened his eyes on Bob intensely. "It's a gut feeling, mostly. But there was very little in tech found amongst the Groga at that encampment. About the only thing was some kind of communications center that was linked to a device on the perimeter guards' uniforms and the portal controllers held by several of the officers in camp. Those we confiscated and Argent is working on them to determine the permutations of the portal addresses they contain and how many of those correspond to gates in the Alliance network."

Bob whistled quietly and Ignatius echoed it. "You're right to be suspicious of something like this. For all we know it is a controller to set off a bomb or trigger some kind of wide-scale attack. What kind of analysis have you done so far?"

Arwen spoke up. "We have tested carefully for radiation emanations, any kind of signaling wavelengths and have magnified and printed out the circuitry pattern for analysis. As you can see, there doesn't seem to be any type of input or output port, so we have to assume a wireless interface of some kind for lack of any better concept."

"We will make all of the reports of our previous examinations available to you." Inle sent. Her mindspeech was devoid of the clicking sounds made by her voice. *"I should give you this. It is your work tablet. You can mindspeak to it directly and it will transcribe it into reports you can make available to all of us. Simply think, 'Bob report', and it will begin transcribing. Then send, 'Bob end report' and it will not record any further mindspeech until you invoke it again."*

She handed the tablet to Bob. It was considerably lighter than any version he had seen on Earth. And mindspeech compatible? His mind was officially blown.

"It will also allow verbal transcription, do calculations and it has dual high definition cameras for including photos of your projects and so forth."

"Thanks," Bob replied. "I can see we have the tools we need to go forward with this. Do I have a workspace?"

"Just look for Ignatius' perch. You may stand or sit at the desk provided; it adjusts automagically." Merv said with a grin. "You sound eager to get to work."

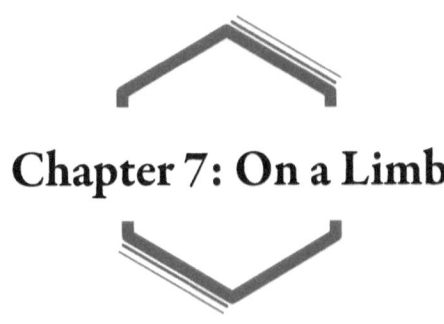

Chapter 7: On a Limb

B urt turned from Bob with a smile on his face. He wished he could be there to see the look on Bob's face when Lova told him about his assignment. He had clued the Alliance Science and Technology team in on Bob and his bird and knew this was going to be a good fit. He had a lot of confidence that his friend would fit right in with that bunch. Geek heaven for sure.

They were all waiting for him on the balcony. Gariel stood at one end of a circular table. Desminda sat next to him, straight-backed and attentive. Brendan, Xao Ting and Arvid had left him the remaining seat. It was a small group, for sure, but the assembled years of experience more than made up for their numbers. He knew they would be calling in specialists from the Alliance from time to time, but for now, this was their core. Burt was the youngest, but not inexperienced as he had joined the Alliance in his teen years. That being said, it humbled him to be included in this council of war.

The moment he sat in the remaining seat, Gariel began.

"First, there are a few things we need to be clear on. We do not fight a war of retribution. This isn't about anger or passion or allegiance to a cause. This is about defending the innocent from terror, torture and enslavement. This is about securing the Gate Network to protect the inhabitants of all dimensions, regardless of individual allegiances. If we approach this task with feelings of retaliation, we will lose the advantage of rationality and purpose that will drive this mission forward.

It is true that the Groga, the Fleistians and the Insenium have inflicted unjust dominion, terrorism and enslavement of innocents and that this must be stopped. I do not dispute this, but we must focus on our desired outcome and the most effective ways to achieve it.

This is a small team for such a large task, but each of you was chosen for specific skills and experience. I know we can work together well, as we have had experience with one another in the past. We mustn't take for granted that we will always have as good success as we have in the last few missions. We must be prepared with alternatives when not everything goes as planned."

Gariel paused, looking somberly into the eyes of each team member in turn. His dark, usually animated beard lay nearly still, just the tips twitching. "I intend to ask much more from each of you than you think you have to give. We will all be stretching to the ends of our abilities on this mission. I vow I won't quit on you and I know each of you will give your utmost. Now, let's get to it."

Every person seated around the table leaned forward in their chairs, eyes and attention fixed on the squarely built trooper. The silence was only broken by a hawk screeching overhead in the crystalline sky.

"The Groga force is intimidating, but, in a direct battle, we have the numbers and weaponry and tech to take them on successfully. If that was the only challenge, we could handle it, although more than likely with heavy casualties on both sides.

However, they are simply the spearhead. The true threat is the combination of the Fleistians and the Insenium. We know little to nothing about them other than their intentions to enslave the multiverse at any cost. They have no care for the lives of their fighting force, nor do they value life in any of its forms except as tools for ultimate domination and power.

So our first priority will be to infiltrate the enemy and gather intelligence that will help us more fully plan our stratagem and tactics and assemble the needed resources to put an end to the threat.

To this end we will be working with the Science and Technology team and the Logistics team to coordinate our efforts.

"Burt let's start with you. Your strengths are all related to covert operations. You have proven your worth time and time again in your service to the Alliance. We will need you to go under cover and retrieve information about our enemies. This will mean separating you from the team. I know you have given the matter some thought, what can you tell me about your potential plans?"

Burt cleared his throat a little nervously, even though he replied in mindspeech. *"I think the key is what Jenny learned while she was held captive by the Fleistians. Besides the Groga city on their planet, there is another nation on the planet. The inhabitants of that nation do not agree with the Fleistian philosophy of conquering for power. They are a peaceful people and I think my first step will be to create a relationship with them. From there I will infiltrate the Groga city posing as a random humanoid slave. The goal will be to find a way to locate the Insenium and report my findings back to the team and ultimately the Alliance Council."*

The members of the team nodded their heads in approval. *"Well said, Burt. This sounds like a worthwhile use of your skills. I would like to suggest you leave immediately. Desminda would you be willing to transport Burt to the Fleistian planet? I believe you were with Tarafau when he freed Jenny."*

Desminda nodded and smiled warmly at Burt. *"I would be happy to. How soon can you be ready?"*

"I came here ready for whatever we decided. Do you wish to leave now or after the meeting?"

"I have already been briefed on the topics that will be covered here and I understand you were also in on the details we will be discussing here today. If you wish, we can leave now. Do you have everything?"

Burt patted the MDP on his wrist. *"Packed and ready to roll."*

Desminda stood and, as Burt did likewise, touched Burt on the shoulder...

Suddenly it was very dark. As his eyes adjusted, he realized he was standing on a knoll looking down on a city whose pale lights shown in the distance. Burt could see no stars and the silence was almost eerie.

Burt had traveled with Tarafau to his home planet in the past, so he wasn't exactly startled by the abrupt change in his surroundings, but it always felt so bizarre to transition so quickly over vast distances.

"Do you require further assistance?" Desminda asked.

"Nope, I'm good," Burt replied. *"Just one quick question...How do I get home?"*

"Oh, I almost forgot." She took a small device, somewhat like a game controller out of her MDP. *"This is attuned to the Earth gate in Brazil and will take you through the Fleistian portal. You can call home from there."*

"But I thought we locked that gate."

"It has been temporarily made available. It is heavily guarded and will remain open until your return."

"OK, great. See you then."

She nodded and faded from his view without another word.

Burt installed the control device in his MDP and sighed. *"Off to see the Wizard. I could use those Ruby Slippers right about now."*

He took off toward the huge city shining softly in the perpetual dark. The ground beneath his feet was springy, covered with an unrecognizable moss-like plant. The only features of the ground before him were rocks and an occasional sluggish stream of what he thought might be water. Fortunately, he wouldn't have to test that as he had enough water stored in his MDP to last him over a month. He didn't like to leave things to chance.

While he had been preparing for this mission, he had seen to it that he could be self-sufficient for weeks, if necessary. He knew he didn't have much time to gather all of the needful intelligence and, if he was actually gone for weeks the mission would likely fail. He only hoped he would be able to get safe access to the Fleistian portal when the time came to get out of Dodge.

He pulled out his quarterstaff and, using it as a walking stick moved forward. Distances could be deceiving, but he guessed the city was about a day's march, or at least an Earth day's march. He wasn't sure about the day/night cycles of this place, but he would have to go by the chronometer in his head.

The walk would have been boring except that his mind kept straying back to the last few months and everything that led up to him being on this mission. And in the center of all of it was...Jenny. There was something about her that he couldn't quite grasp, something that made his mind want to gravitate to her at any of his idle moments. He had felt a strong pull from her within the first few days after meeting her.

It wasn't her looks, although she was beautiful. Sun-blonded curly hair, blue eyes and a glorious smile. She managed to be beautiful even sweating and tousled from a grueling workout, stick fighting with people taller, more muscular and more experienced than her. She never gave up, never backed down and could be so fierce that she could even make Tarafau back down a step. He grinned at that thought as Jenny was a mighty five foot four inches tall and Tarafau loomed at about six and a half feet.

But it was so much more than that. Jenny was smart...not just intelligent. She had a truly organized mind and paid attention to details. She had not sought out her position of authority as The Gatekeeper. Far from it. She had, however stepped up and valiantly yet humbly acceded to the burden placed upon her with more grace and skill than he knew he would have been able.

He was glad when Tarafau had announced she would be going to his planet for training. It wouldn't be a break, exactly. He knew that Tarafau would work her hard to prepare her more fully for her role in all of this. But he also knew that Tarafau's family environment would be strengthening to her for the difficult and dark tasks ahead.

They were about the same age. Burt guessed her to be a couple years younger than him, although he knew everyone still thought of him as "the kid". That was okay with him. He wasn't ready to settle into mature demeanor and he wasn't sure he ever would be. He took his job seriously, but he loved what he did. The adventure of exploring different dimensions and meeting beings from out of fantasy was without a doubt better than anything he had ever expected to do. He had graduated early from high school and decided to explore a bit of life before going on to the university, especially since he had no clue what he wanted to do as a career. He had signed on as an assistant for an archaeologist on a dig in the African Congo when he first encountered Lizzie and Tarafau. At the time, their assignment had been one of those rare occasions where Tarafau was himself on Earth and not Tidbit.

What had ensued had changed his life forever. Since Burt had discovered Tarafau's secret, Lizzie had turned to Tarafau and said, "Well?"

Tarafau had grasped both of their shoulders and he had found himself in front of the Alliance Headquarters building. Tarafau had looked at the three eyed guard and the guard had nodded grimly. Stunned, he did not resist as Tarafau had steered him into a vast elevator, said, "Private Council Chamber," and in two breaths the door had opened repeating "Private Council Chamber" in female tones.

The small, white-furred foxlike creature had looked solemnly at Tarafau, nodded and gestured toward some large doors on her left.

There, seated on a low dais were three "creatures". An elf, a dwarvish creature with a face like a garden gnome, and a dragon.

Lizzie said aloud to Burt, "This is the Chief Councilor of the Dimensional Alliance Council, Danaii. He will approach you and touch you. You will not be harmed."

The elf stood and approached calmly. He touched Burt's forehead. *"Be at peace, Burt. This will allow you to communicate with any being who has the ability of mindspeech. Please be welcome and be seated."*

"Simply think of the person to whom you wish to speak," Lizzie sent. *"No one here can read your mind. They can only hear you when you intend to speak to them. This eliminates the language barrier as it sends in concepts rather than words."*

"Got it. Why am I here, exactly?"

"Chance. I won't say whether it is fortunate or unfortunate, yet. That depends a lot on you."

Danaii looked Burt up and down, his expression neutral. *"Will you please tell us, how you discovered Tarafau and Lizzie?"*

"Who?"

"The two who brought you to our council."

"Oh. Well, I was actually just taking a whizz behind a bush."

"You were urinating?"

"Yes. And I looked up to see these two staring at me and I stared back. Then the big guy, Tarafau (?), put his hand on my shoulder and here I am."

"Why were you in that place, if I may ask?"

"It's no state secret. I was helping Professor Alexander on an archaeological dig, something about ancient aliens. And what do you know? I found some. Not so ancient, I guess."

Danaii actually smiled. *"So what do we do with you, Earth child? Here are your options. First, we can wipe this memory from your mind and your life will go on as before with no difference. Second, we can get to know you better and see if you would qualify to work for us. Our dilemma is that Tarafau must not be known by any Earthling at this point."*

"Yeah, I can imagine. I have noticed he is somewhat...different. What about Lizzie. Is she an alien too?"

"I'm actually originally from the Midwest of the United States, currently living in L.A... How about you?"

"I'm from Toledo. So, okay, you want to keep these folks a secret. What were they doing in Africa in the first place? How do I know this isn't some dastardly alien plot to invade our planet, make us all slaves or turn us into appetizers?"

For the first time the dragon stirred and emitted what might have been a low chuckle.

Burt's eyes widened.

"I am Liliath," she sent, an amused cast to her mind voice. *"I understand humans taste good with ketchup..."*

Burt gulped and essayed a weak laugh.

"I love Earthlings," Liliath sent, *"Actually, I've never sampled that particular delicacy, but I love your vivid and active imaginations. Most humans I have associated with are honorable, intelligent, and fascinating to spend time with. I love the creative ways you express yourself."*

The little dwarfish person stood, Ingot if he remembered correctly from the hurried introductions, *"To answer your question, we are The Dimensional Alliance chief councilors and our intent is benign. Our mission is to protect the universe of every dimension in the Dimensional Alliance. It so happens that your planet Earth has a dozen gates we have discovered, and Lizzie is the Guardian of one of those gates. Her job is to monitor traffic in and out of her gateway and to be an unofficial representative of Earth in the Alliance council, as your Earth has not yet been sanctioned as a member of the Alliance. They are not yet deemed ready to know the gates are there, much less that they will take you to other dimensions.*

However, as there are gateways on your planet, we have carefully recruited individuals who guard the gates and keep your planet from being over-run by 'visitors' from other dimensions. When you are technologically advanced enough and your world government is more stable, we will gently integrate your Earth into the Alliance."

Coming back to the present and looking back in his mind into the past as he grew closer to the city before him, he realized that it was inevitable that he would have joined the Alliance. Here was the life he had sought. That long-ago day had brought him to this point. He was grateful he could be involved in something that had so much potential to create good, not only for Earth, but for all of the other dimensions out there, the majority of which he would never visit in his lifetime. Regardless, he knew that what he was doing was right and that was enough for him.

Burt generally enjoyed walking, but the monotony of the countryside and lack of sunlight made it more of a chore than a pleasure this time. He picked up his pace and returned in his thoughts to Jenny.

He couldn't help but wonder how her trip to Ungoli was progressing. He had wanted to have a quiet conversation with her before she left, but things moved much too quickly for that. He wanted to know more about her and for her to know more about him. At this point, she treated him more like a brother than anything and maybe that was where that relationship needed to stay...

His thought was broken by the first sound he had heard since beginning to walk. A horn? He really wasn't sure of the time. Could that have been some kind of wake-up call for the city or was it an alarm? Had he been spotted? In no time, he realized the answer to his question as the gates in the wall surrounding the city opened ponderously and a group of what had to be about 20 soldiers issued from inside the city. They walked (not marched) in a loose group, which he hoped boded well for a potential friendly meeting.

He stopped where he was and waited. He knew very little about these people, but according to Jenny, they were peaceful, and he didn't want to do anything they might interpret as hostile. As a people they were known as the Cindu and were ruled by a king named Nivi. He hoped he could use mindspeech with them, or this might be even more difficult than he had imagined.

They were humanoid, reminding him of a friend he had known in high school. The fellow was albino, with no coloring in his skin or hair. He had been extremely sensitive to sunlight and had to wear long sleeves and a hat even in the summertime. The group that approached him wore what might be a uniform of soft browns, similar to the old frontiersman styles of the 1700s.

He dropped his staff into his MDP and held up both hands, palms open, in a gesture of peace as they drew closer. The man in the front, stood about six feet tall and had a stocky build. The others in the group varied in size and build, but none of them made any hostile moves and their faces were passive. The leader began to speak in a language that Burt didn't understand. Burt shook his head and held up a hand. *"Can you understand me?"* he sent in mindspeech to the group. No response.

He pointed to himself. "Friend," he said with what he hoped they would interpret as a friendly smile.

"Please take me to see King Nivi," he added, hoping they would at least recognize the name of their king. He spread his hands wide in a welcoming gesture then pointed again to himself. "Friend," he repeated.

Their leader nodded and pointed to himself. "Friend, Cindu."

Burt nodded. "Friend, Alliance."

At the word Alliance their faces relaxed. Their leader gestured for him to come with them and they headed to the gates of the city.

At one point the leader signaled a halt and stood again before Burt. He spread his hands to signify a peaceful intent. He then motioned Burt to place his hands together. Burt understood. Before they could take an unknown person inside those looming walls, he would have to be restrained. Burt nodded and extended his hands which were firmly bound before him, but not so tight as to cause real discomfort.

The gates opened and they proceeded onto a broad paved boulevard. This city seemed larger standing inside than it had seemed looking down from the hilltop. The streets were lit by softly glowing lamps. People bustled here and there, carrying packages or trailing little ones. With the lack of light, the pastel colors they wore seemed to feel closer to white than to actual colors. There were basic wheeled vehicles, carts, carriages and so forth, being pulled by some sort of large goat like creature. The homes and shops that lined the streets were similar to the Victorian era structures of the large cities of the United States. Ahead of them at the end of the boulevard stood a huge building on the other side of a large city square.

The people rushing to and from their various errands didn't give them much more than a glance as they proceeded directly toward what Burt assumed was probably a castle. However, they stopped at a residence at the edge of the square that didn't appear to be much different than the others they had passed, just before they arrived before the palace-like building. Heading down a walkway at the side of the house, they went through a gate that appeared to be constructed of some sort of woven material.

It was someone's backyard, evidently. On a covered patio in one of a number of outdoor benches sat a man in the same type of uniform as the guards who surrounded Burt. He stood and spoke to the leader of the guards and then turned to Burt. "Fleist?" he inquired. "Namal?"

Burt shook his head and pointed to himself. "Alliance. I am Burt. I am your friend."

"Alliance?" the man said and clapped his hands. "Perseus!" he called.

A short, balding man without the pale, albino skin of the others in the city, stepped forward. He was dressed in slacks and an open collared shirt. His brown eyes were narrow, and his mouth and ears seemed too small for his head, but his face seemed open.

"You are from the Alliance?" he sent in mindspeech. "Is something wrong? Who leads the Council at this time?"

"Ingot is the Chief Councilor and Liliath and Myla are his second and third."

"Thank the lights. This is king Nivi," he said, gesturing to the man who had called him.

Burt was surprised. This house seemed like a simple home, not a regal palace.

Perseus turned to the king and spoke for a moment. King Nivi inclined his head.

"Do I bow or something?" Burt asked.

"Not in Nivi's court. He lives simply like his subjects and works at a trade as well. He has organized his government so that he can spend more time relating to his people than dealing with issues of state. He has reigned here for over 200 years and all is well as long as the Fleistians keep their noses out of it. I will translate and you will answer the Kings questions?"

"Gladly. What does he want to know?"

"Where are you from and why are you here?"

"I am from the Dimensional Alliance and my mission is to discover the motives and plans of king Namal with his allies the Insenium."

King Nivi barked a curt command to one of the guards who moved forward with a hunting style knife. Burt held his breath for a moment as the knife was turned upward in the man's hand and he moved close, grabbing Burt's bound hands and cutting his bonds.

Nivi hissed, his pale face and almost transparent brows furrowed, and his jaw tightened in anger. He nearly spat his next words to Perseus.

"He wants to know how we can help? We do not attack them, as long as they leave us alone, but we know they have been meddling in the affairs of other worlds. This is affecting worlds in your Alliance?"

"Yes. They are raiding planets all through the Alliance Gate Network using new technology to create their own fixed portal stations. We also believe they are raiding in other dimensions through the portals that exist on your planet. These are dimensions that are not yet connected to the Alliance Gate Network and are not protected from them. According to our intelligence, their plan is to dominate every dimension they can find and impose their own moralities while enslaving populations for their own gain."

"That sounds like Namal. God of our fathers, I wish they had not split off from us from the beginning. Anciently our people were one. We are all related by blood, although you would never know it to look at us. As our planet started to drift from its orbit so long ago, we discovered the portals. One group wanted to use the portals to discover a dimension planet that was not populated so we could migrate there and save our people from their inexorable fate. The other wanted to use the portals to migrate to an inhabited world rich in resources and life and enslave the beings there for our gain.

There was intense contention over this and eventually it came to war. There were two gates that we could discover, and the war was fierce and devastating. Tens of thousands were killed and eventually millions on both sides. We are but a remnant of our original numbers. In the last war we won access to the second gate, which resides in the large building at the center of our city.

We had to develop a philosophy that we would protect this gate and eventually find a way to disable the other gate, but we could not afford to go to war again unless our brethren attacked us.

It is hard sometimes not to wish to attack them and force them to comply to our morality, but we know that force will not change them. It has been tried before. Occasionally one of them defects to us, but we have defectors as well. I see now that we cannot remain passive at this time. How can we aid you?"

Burt considered. He was surprised at how easy this had been so far and he wondered how much he could ask of this community that had already endured so much.

"First of all, do you know anything about the Insenium? And secondly, I need to infiltrate the Groga city as a slave."

Nivi's eyes went wide. *"The first request is easy. We know nothing about them except that they marched through Namal's portal many years back and went straight to Namal's fortress. They left within a few days and we haven't seen anything since then to indicate they did more than visit. The Groga continue to come and go through the portal, sometimes in large numbers. We assumed it was because Namal continues to search for the optimum planet for them to conquer and enslave.*

Your second request is not only dangerous, but perhaps foolish. Yes, the Groga have many slaves and it might be a simple thing to enter their city disguised as one, but we have yet to detect the escape of even one slave from their city in all of the years since they were first established by Namal."

"*I have a few more resources than any of their slaves,*" Burt answered with a grin.

"*Their slaves are conditioned to hide nothing from their masters. You will not be able to trust any of them to keep your secrets. If you are determined to go on with this plan, you must remember that. We can probably get you close enough to the main road to allow you to slip into a slave caravan and we can get you appropriate clothing,*" he said through Perseus, eyeing Burt up and down and shaking his head.

"*That would be greatly appreciated. I know I may look young to you, but I do have experience in this sort of thing.*" He realized that must sound somewhat disrespectful to the king, but it was a simple statement of fact.

Perseus listened for a moment while the king spoke, nodding his head. "*King Nivi says that he is assigning me to outfit you for your mission. But before we do, he imagines you are probably tired and hungry from your journey. You are welcome to eat with him and his men.*"

"*That will be great. Thank you so much for your help and kindness.*"

At that moment, a small girl ran out into the patio, holding what appeared to be a piece of artwork. King Nivi beamed at her and said something that was obviously praise for her accomplishment. He hugged her and sent her back into the house.

"*King Nivi's youngest grandchild,*" Perseus sent. "*He dotes on her as any grandpa would. She lives with the king and his wife, as her father and mother were killed in a Fleistian raid a few years back. This is why the gates remain closed and few ever leave this city for any reason.*"

The king arose and they all set off out of the garden and onto the street to a large building on the way to the palatial structure at the end of the square. It turns out this large building was for the military. It was basically a several block deep compound with what appeared to be multi-story barracks, a parade ground or assembly area at the center and what could be administration offices at one end.

As they entered the main building, Burt's nose twitched with the smells of something good cooking. They entered an area filled with tables, not different from pretty much every mess hall he had ever seen, regardless of the culture. Men were walking down a line where they were being served by others standing behind long tables with simmering pots on braziers and many different types of what looked like vegetables.

When Jenny had lived at the Fleistian fortress during her captivity, she had described pale, grey looking fungus-type vegetables being served to her there.

"How are you able to grow vegetables in this poor light?" he asked Perseus curiously.

"They have vast underground buildings dedicated to aqua farming with artificial light. The thermal core of this planet is a great source of energy for artificial lighting and other energy requirements. It may not be evident on the surface, but the Cindu are quite advanced, technology-wise. They choose to put out a very pastoral front. They very much wish the Fleistians to underestimate their abilities. It keeps them from raiding them for their tech. As you may have heard, the Fleistians would rather gather their tech than create it. Their slaves know more about it than they do."

"Since I'm not familiar with the food here, what do you recommend?"

"The vegetable stew is good, and they have a very nutty bread that goes good with the cheese."

"Cheese? They have herd animals?"

"No, the wildlife and domesticated animals died off long ago with the exception of what they call the pullers, a goat-like animal that pulls wheeled vehicles. They make this cheese by fermenting a legume. It's quite good."

Burt followed his suggestion and they all retired to a table to eat together. The food was actually quite tasty although very different from anything he had eaten so far in his life. He had gotten used to eating a lot of exotic foods while working for the Alliance. In his training they had emphasized that, unless the food was inimical to human digestion, he should always eat the native food. It was part of the diplomacy part of his job. Most of the time the food was at least passable and, if it wasn't, he had learned to smile and choke it down anyway.

Burt watched Nivi and his men as they ate. He noticed a familiarity that was unusual for a monarch and his troops. Nivi had stood in line with the rest of them and didn't even sit at the head of the table. From time to time someone would come by and say something to the king, not as a toady or servant, but just as one man would speak to another he knew. Often, they would laugh over some little joke together which Perseus would attempt to interpret for him.

He marveled at the casual tenor of King Nivi's court. First, no palace and attendants and now no formality or kowtowing by his men.

"*You seem somewhat confused about something,*" commented Perseus.

"*I've never seen a monarch that was so casual with their people before. Royalty on my planet tend to surround themselves with high security and luxury. Even those who are elected representatives in the republics on my world tend to set themselves above congress with average citizens.*"

"*I've seen this in other dimensions as well. Ultimate power is a heady brew. Most people can't handle it with any grace, regardless how they begin their reign. Eventually, for most beings, it goes to their head and turns their hearts to stone. The Cinduans don't really know how blessed they have been to have a long line of good kings. I think it has something to do with their attitude towards royalty and that all kings are crowned by the voice of the people and held accountable to a type of parliament that represents the will of the people.*

King Nivi's son will likely reign after him, as is the tradition, but only after he has been carefully trained in both an occupation and the responsibilities of kingship. He was schooled right alongside the village children and he apprenticed to a tradesman at age 14. No special treatment."

Burt whistled softly. "*That is some achievement, where government is concerned. I don't think I've ever heard of anything like it before.*"

"*I asked for this assignment, when I was a young man,*" Perseus continued. "*One of Tarafau's people somewhat accidentally discovered the Cinduans and was concerned, as they weren't on the Gate Network, yet they had dimensional portals that seem not to function in the same way as ours. So, they sent me as an ambassador. Luckily I ended up in Cindu instead of Fleist.*" He gave a little shiver.

"*It looks like the Cinduans treat you well enough,*" Burt sent, wondering, at the same time why no one at the Alliance had clued him in on this.

"Indeed, they have set me up with a room at a little inn. I work in their vegetable garden and they feed me well. I learned their language and the king consults with me on a number of different things, although I think it is out of courtesy. He has plenty of wise advisors. On the whole, the Cinduans are good folks. If it wasn't for the Fleistians, I believe they would make admirable members of the Alliance."

Having finished their meal, the king said his goodbyes to the group and Perseus relayed to Burt that they would meet with the King in the early morning before they took Burt to the appropriate place on the road where Burt could insinuate himself into a caravan as an unknown slave.

Burt realized it even sounded like a bit of a shaky plan to him and he could imagine them all shaking their heads about the crazy alien.

Perseus escorted Burt to a storage building behind the barracks. It was a typical military supply operation. A person Burt decided to think of as the "supply sergeant" looked up from what might have been a ledger and barked a question at Perseus. Perseus didn't take umbrage at the man's tone but replied in civil tones in the man's language. He stepped out from behind his desk and looked Burt up and down and then proceeded to rifle through some shelves, setting various items on the counter.

In almost no time he had stacked some loose grey trousers and a shirt that looked like a sack with holes cut in it for the body head and arms along with some rough-looking sandals of the same grey tone.

A grey hat that might have been made of some kind of straw joined them and the supply sergeant added a rough sack. *"That's for your food ration for the day. Every slave carries one,"* sent Perseus. *" The rest is pretty typical slave wear."*

"Looks like I'll be stylin', then." Burt replied, taking the pile. *"Where can I change?"*

"They've arranged for rooms for you. You aren't to change until just before it is time for you to leave."

Burt nodded his thanks to the supply sergeant and carried the clothing outside where he promptly inserted it all into his MDP after looking around to make sure no one but Perseus could see him.

"How will you hide your MDP? That shirt has no sleeves."

"Glad you asked. I had this made special for me in the lab."

He pulled two things out of his MDP and put one on each wrist. They were the same color as his skin and even had arm hairs on them. Both of them made his wrists look somewhat thicker, but when laid over the MDP, there was no betraying bulge.

"*They're made out of a penetrable material. I can still add things to my MDP and take things out, but it doesn't show. I've had to use it several times on missions where the MDP might be noticeable.*"

"*Clever,*" admitted Perseus. "*I nearly never wear mine, mostly because I rarely need it and also because I don't want to encourage curiosity about it.*"

"*I can have the guys at the Alliance whip you up a couple of these wristbands, if you'd like.*"

"*I don't foresee a need for them, really. I may yet be here for a long time and my needs are very generously met here.*"

"*As you wish. Let me know if there is anything I can bring back for you when this is all over. I really appreciate all of your help today. This would have been a lot harder without you.*"

Chapter 8: Linked

Jenny woke in Tarafau's guest room to sunlight streaming through the sheer fabric of the curtains that were so fine as to seem almost misty. She started for a moment at the warm squirmy lump under her covers at her feet until she remembered Chidwi.

Chidwi had been her constant companion since linking with her in the grove two days ago. Since then, she had spent a lot of her time, learning more about the Linklings and exploring Tarafau's home planet. Chidwi spent a lot of time sitting happily on Jenny's shoulder wherever they went. No one seemed to pay her any mind and Jenny wondered how many of them could even see her.

What had surprised Jenny most, however, was how helpful Chidwi had been with her mental exercises. Amenia had been working her hard, three sessions a day. She had been close to a breakthrough during her session the night before and was looking forward to her session this morning. Amenia was a great teacher, patient, but thorough.

Jenny sat up in bed and reached under the covers to pat Chidwi. *"Wake up, sleepy-head. We've got lots to do today."*

"Chidwi is waking. You take a shower. Your feet smell."

Jenny laughed and went into the bathing facility that connected to her room. The room was shared through doors on both sides with Elizabeth's bedroom. Jenny knew Elizabeth would have been up for awhile already. She showered quickly, the warm water falling like rain from the ceiling of the shower. There was a lever to pull to stop it while lathering up and then pull again to rinse off. It was heavenly. Even more so, because the water was recycled for watering the plants outside and the energy to heat the water was solar, so she could take a long, steamy shower without guilt.

She dressed in a clean Gi, pulled her hair back into a ponytail (which Elizabeth had taken to imitating) and went to the kitchen to grab a green drink from the cooler. Chidwi had already let herself out to do her own oblations and came back into the kitchen about the time Jenny finished her breakfast.

Together they went to the workout room and found Elizabeth, Amenia and Tarafau stretching. She joined them while Chidwi perched on a barre at the side of the room, watching the contortions of the humanoids with fascination.

When they sat on the mat to prepare for their mental exercise, Chidwi sat quietly on the floor next to Jenny, imitating the lotus pose of the rest of them. Jenny started mentally relaxing every muscle while doing the breathing exercises she had been taught originally by Lova and Arvid. At this point these had become very complex patterns, but she had been doing them long enough that she fell into them easily.

"Are you ready for deep focus?" Amenia asked the group. *"We will begin today where we left off. Tarafau and Elizabeth will be simply lending support while you and I move past your last barricade."*

All previous sessions had been leading up to this. Based on what Amenia had explained to her, there was a barrier between conscious, subconscious and the deep area of the brain that most humans never touched. Today they would take the final step that would either break through that barrier or would at least tell them whether it was possible for her. Amenia had said she had a strong feeling that Jenny could do this nearly impossible thing. She had told Jenny that Lizzie had not made it that far, although she was very good at defending her mind from attack and had incredible control of her own mind and body.

Amenia led Jenny to the place in her mind they had stopped the night before. Jenny pictured it as a drawbridge over a castle moat. Amenia had explained to Jenny that she would have more success if she could put together a very detailed representative image in her mind. She had said this worked similar to a password or a key and in the future the image she set would play a large part in how she could use this access.

Jenny had decided to picture that area in her brain as an insurmountable fortress to protect her and her mind from unwanted penetration. At the end of the drawbridge was a huge portcullis, heavily armored with sharp outward pointing spikes. At the side of the portcullis was a tall knight in bright shining armor, his spear upright in his hand, grounded on the bridge and the visor of his helmet was up. The eyes of the knight were stern and somewhat intimidating.

"Jenny, I am with you. Move forward, looking the guardian in the eyes. Say nothing. With your will give him recognition of you. When he knows who you are, the rightful Lord of the castle, you will gain access."

Jenny did as instructed. In her mind she crossed the drawbridge at a regal pace, never losing eye contact with the knight. As she got within reach of the spear, she stopped and stood there, her head held high. His steely eyes gazed into hers and he continued to stand there silently, not blinking or even moving.

This was as far as she had gotten last night. She had stood there, erect and unrelenting for a very long time until Amenia had finally called a halt.

Jenny almost felt as if she were pushing on the huge stone walls of the keep. Despite her firm gaze at the knight before her, she still wasn't sure exactly what she was doing. She wondered what would happen if she did break through. Amenia had seemed so sure...

Suddenly she felt the small warm hands of Chidwi on her shoulders. It was odd, since she couldn't even feel her own hands rested loosely on her knees. In this place she had no sensations of the world outside and only her feelings and thoughts.

Chidwi's mind touched hers.

"Jenny is strong. Jenny is the master of this place. Move forward and extend your hand."

Stunned, Jenny moved resolutely within arm's reach of the stern-eyed knight, never taking her eyes off of his. She imitated the confident attitude of her father whenever he had shaken the hand of someone. The man's eyebrows rose slightly, and he held out his hand. Jenny grasped his.

Immediately the portcullis began to rise slowly before her.

The knight withdrew his hand and bowed from the waist. *"Your majesty,"* he said, respectfully. *"I did not recognize you. My apologies. May I help you in any way?"*

"I would like to enter the keep, please."

"And your companions?"

Jenny turned to look behind her and sure enough, both Chidwi and Amenia stood behind her, smiling at her accomplishment

"These are Amenia and Chidwi and they may enter at any time."

"As you say. Please enter. Do you wish a guide?"

"Do I need one? Perhaps not. Please keep these gates closed unless you see me, Amenia or Chidwi."

"As you command." And he bowed again.

Jenny walked with some trepidation under the portcullis and was amazed to see a duplicate of Miriha's village square, just as it appeared the first time she had visited. People bustled around quietly in the marketplace. Far at the end of the square was the large green building where she had first met Miriha.

She sought out Amenia with her mind. "I think I did it, but I'm not sure what to do here."

"Yes, Jenny, you breached your wall. You can now return at any time. If you wish, you can come back to us and we can discuss your next steps. You don't have to walk back out of the gate, simply come back to us in your mind."

When Jenny opened her eyes, she was seated exactly as she had been when she began the exercise and sure enough, Chidwi stood behind her, her little hands still resting on Jenny's shoulders.

Around her, still seated in the same position were Tarafau, Elizabeth and Amenia. They were beaming at her as if she had just won the Nobel Prize or something. Jenny ducked her head in embarrassment.

"That was amazing!" Elizabeth gushed. *"I felt you go through the wall, even though I could not follow. I have never gotten that far, and I have been trying for years."*

"For some it just takes longer, and you didn't have the advantage of a linked one to walk you through It, Elizabeth," sent Amenia.

Amenia looked at Chidwi. *"Thank you, Chidwi. You saved Jenny much needed time on her journey."*

Chidwi crooned happily.

"Jenny easy person. Jenny strong and true. We make good things together."

"Indeed," agreed Tarafau. *"The two of you do well together. At the next session we will show you how to use the power you have tapped."*

"Oh, thank you all so very much!" It was Jenny's turn to gush. *"I don't know what we just opened up, but I feel like something has changed inside me and it feels like a really good thing."*

They all stood up and a group hug ensued with Chidwi happily crooning as she weaved in and out through their legs.

I think a sparring match is somewhat redundant at this point. Jenny has already come off conqueror today. I think we are ready for a walk in the open air. I have an interesting field trip for us today and the timing is perfect."

Tarafau said no more but grinned his catlike grin. Jenny looked inquiringly at Elizabeth who shrugged and at Amenia who shook her head. No information there, she could see.

"Should Chidwi come?" Jenny asked, hoping for another clue.

"Chidwi should always come," answered Tarafau. *"You are linked. She is as much your guard as I am now. We will continue to have your bodyguards assigned to you, but Chidwi is a whole other kind of protection. A mindspeaker of your power can do some amazing things when you are finally fully trained, but Chidwi can be your guide in this more than any of us. It is no accident that she chose to link to you."*

"I think you're right; I have a good feeling about it."

Jenny and Elizabeth went to their rooms to change into their travelling clothes. Elizabeth had bought Jenny a couple of blouses in the native style. She loved the bright colors that faded from shade to shade, highlighting the flowing sleeves and loose swishy lines of the tunics that were nearly long enough to be very short skirts. They moved nicely with Jenny's enthusiastic stride and made her feel pretty. Her dark leggings were not at all out of place here and went nicely with the bright colors of her blouse.

She wore a sturdy pair of walking shoes, since these ventures out into Tarafau's homeland always required a lot of walking. It was no wonder that she seldom saw a portly Daringi. After she had put her hair into braids, mostly to keep it out of her face, she felt ready to take on whatever was next on Tarafau's menu of adventures.

Meanwhile Chidwi had sat patiently on her bed while she accoutered herself. She knew Chidwi found the whole clothing thing amusing. *"You could just grow fur."* she had remarked after Jenny had changed clothes three times in just a few hours the first day they were together.

Jenny had laughed and Chidwi had been somewhat bemused at what was so funny.

They headed out, Chidwi perched happily on Jenny's shoulder. Jenny had seen people carry birds like that and had thought it was pretty cool. Obviously on Earth, Chidwi would have to "turn off" her reflection so others wouldn't see her walking around with what would look like a green monkey on her shoulder.

Today they strode over the hill, past the Apex and into what could only be called some kind of transportation station. There were some kind of pod-like vehicles that people got into after scanning their small tattoos in front of a little screen. There were several colored buttons on the dash and a number pad.

Tarafau rapidly punched in a series of numbers, pushed one of the colored buttons and the city faded from view only to be replaced by a small lakeside station surrounded by a forest with narrow paths leading in different directions.

"You remember Glitha?" Tarafau inquired of Jenny.

"Of course, I do. She's the arachnid who captured Sam. I never got an opportunity to thank her in person."

"Then this will be your opportunity. We are in her forest. We are here to inquire as to the disposition of Sam."

Jenny gulped. She had heard of people gulping when they were scared or concerned, but this was the first time she had actually done it.

"I really thought we were done with her, you know. What more do you think we can learn from her? I doubt seriously that she will have anything nice to say to me or to you."

Tarafau nodded. You are probably right. She will not have anything nice to say. However, I do believe she will let something slip if you follow my lead."

Jenny sighed. She knew he was probably right, but the thought of it made the little hairs stand up on the back of her neck.

"Well, let's get this over with," she sent, her mouth dry and her back stiff.

They moved into the forest that, at first glance had seemed beautiful and peaceful, but now it took on an eerie, threatening cast, colored by the anxiety in Jenny's mind. Chidwi rode on her shoulder, one hand patting her gently on her neck. *"Jenny be calm. Chidwi is here,"* she sent soothingly.

Jenny's mind stopped racing. She fell into the breathing pattern designed to put the mind in a peaceful state. She had nothing to fear. She was accompanied by her friends and the arachnid denizens of this place wouldn't allow Sam to harm her.

The light filtered through the dense leaves overhead was like constellations projected onto the floor of the forest. It wasn't exactly dark, but it didn't let a lot of light in. There were soft noises created by some kind of life, but there was no breeze stirring the leaves, so the deep quiet would alert them of anyone or anything approaching them from any angle.

Tarafau was alert, but that was normal for him in nearly any situation. Amenia and Elizabeth appeared to be having a mental conversation, based on the animation on their faces, but they didn't seem to be worried at all.

Suddenly, ahead of them they heard the measured tread of many feet. Jenny straightened and set her face in a placid, non-committal expression. To their view loomed an immense arachnid-type being. If Jenny had not seen one of them participate in her rescue in Sam's dimension, she might have been frightened. But she knew Glitha's species to be peaceful and intelligent.

The spider, as she thought of them in her mind, not knowing the name of their species, halted a few paces before the group who had paused to wait for it.

"Glitha awaits you, Tarafau, Jenny and companions. Please follow me," was all it said and turned back in the direction from which it had come.

As they followed it down a wide path, Jenny considered what she might say to Sam, or Engoza, as she was named by her parents. Sam and she had been the best of friends, or so she had thought, for over 6 years. They had met in Jenny's sophomore year in college and had been roomies, sharing in all of the many experiences of college life. How could she not have known that she was being played by an agent of evil? Sam seemed to have been the perfect best friend. They had laughed and cried together, hiked all over Southern California with their hiking club and even studied for exams together.

Now she was faced with dealing with a woman who had captured her and tortured her, and the betrayal still stung like fire.

She supposed she would let Tarafau take the lead and wait and see. After all, what more could Sneaky Sam do to her?

They arrived at a sunlit circular clearing. Wildflowers bloomed in the center and, around the circumference, were large boulders regularly spaced a few yards apart. On several of them perched arachnids of various sizes, colors and types. Some were all legs, like the daddy-long-legs of Earth. Some had muscular legs and smaller abdomens, with huge faceted eyes that seemed to dominate their faces. There was one with what looked like a handlebar moustache. And another had feathery antennae that looked a lot like a moth she remembered seeing once.

Surprisingly, Jenny recognized Glitha among them. She had expected them to all look so much alike that she wouldn't be able to tell them apart. Beside the boulder on which Glitha sat stood Sam. She wore her Engoza face, pale with a greyish cast to her skin. She was dressed in loose grey robes somewhat like a nun of Earth, but without the headpiece. She stood there silently; her scarlet-nailed hands folded in front of her.

"*Welcome, friends,*" Glitha sent, her antennae waving gently around her face. "*You have come to see the captive. She awaits your decisions as to her fate. We have been working with her and find her to be an interesting subject. Her changeling abilities are currently blocked, not that it would matter. Her mind is now familiar to us and we would know if she ever attempted or even considered escape. She is aware of our conversation and the purpose for your visit.*"

Tarafau considered and then sent, *"This one has done a great wrong to many, and many innocent lives have been lost as a direct consequence of her actions. Her people are plotting to dominate, torture and enslave the populace of the known dimensions and desire to infiltrate the Alliance for that purpose. It were better for her to have never been born rather to have perpetrated these atrocities. Although I cannot fathom how she could ever make recompense for her actions, I would offer her a slight chance of redemption."*

Glitha turned to Jenny. *"Do you have anything to say?"*

Jenny looked at Sam, who looked sullenly at the ground before her.

"Why?" was the first thing that she could think of.

Sam looked up defiantly. Her mental voice growled. *"Why? Why? I wanted you to believe. Why couldn't you believe? We could have been friends again. We could have conquered the dimensions together. Worlds and universes would have bowed at our feet. You and me.*

With your power and my cunning nothing would have been denied us. Ever. We would have even ruled my parents. You would have been the overlord of the entire Earth. And now you've ruined it all. Now the Insenium will just move on without us. You couldn't possibly dream that you've won, can you? Phah!" And she spat at Jenny's feet.

Jenny was taken aback. She realized her hands were knotted into fists so tight that her knuckles were white and there were tears streaming down her cheeks. She felt Chidwi's hand on her cheek. Elizabeth put her arm around Jenny's waist and Tarafau laid his hand on the shoulder that Chidwi had left vacant. Amenia looked at her, compassion bright in her eyes.

Jenny opened her hands, flexing them to bring the circulation back into them. She shook her head sadly. *"I want none of that. And, no, we know we still have much to do to defeat those grasping terrorists. Which is why we are here. What more can you tell me about them?"*

"Really? Just like that? Why should I tell you a single blasted thing? Right now, I wouldn't even tell you the color of my socks. I really did like you Jenny, but I care nothing about your self-righteous questions or the success of the Alliance.

Give it up. You don't stand a chance against the might of the Insenium. They have so much more power than you can imagine. When they find the final key there will be nothing you can do to stop them. Nothing your interfering little 'team' tries will be effective when the Insenium has access to every gate planet and every universe we can find.

And, yes, I said 'we'. I'm not out of this yet, even with all of your little spidery friends to guard me. The Insenium will rescue me and decimate this little hole-in-the-wall planet that has been so neatly protected all of this time. No gate? That's not going to matter..." And she trailed off, realizing she might have said more, in her indignation, than she should have.

Glitha's pincers clicked and her spinnerets waved agitatedly. Around them similar noises came from the other arachnids. Sam resumed her original position, head down, shoulders hunched, glowering under her brows.

Finally, Glitha sent, *"What would you that we should do with her? We will willingly keep her here. She has no way of escape. She is accompanied by one of us at all times. I would hate to consider the only other option we have. I could bite her and stop her heart. We are currently not meat eaters, but our predecessors were. I am equipped with venom that would paralyze her. There is an antidote to revive her if she is not kept paralyzed for too long. She would be aware and conscious most of the time and could even use mindspeech but would be unable to move or do anything for herself. It would be distasteful to care for her in such a situation, but we would do it, if required of us."*

At this, Sam's eyes widened, and her face blanched even paler than before. Her breathing became labored and she trembled from head to foot. The thought of being paralyzed, completely helpless was much more terrible than simply being imprisoned or even put to death. Jenny could see pleading in her eyes, although Sam would never voice that plea.

Tarafau shook his head. *"No, we could not require this of you. The only other safe alternative would be to euthanize her. For now, we will leave her here with you, un-paralyzed. We will leave those options in reserve. For now, I can see she is secure and perhaps over time you can help her see reason."*

Glitha's two main eyes glistened and her agitation slowed. *"As you say, Tarafau. You are known as a man of wisdom and honor. We will abide your decision. Engoza,"* she said, turning to Sam, *"You are dismissed. You may go with today's companion."*

Sam nodded sullenly and stomped off, followed by a wooly spider, very like Earth's tarantula. Glitha paused until they were out of sight.

Brendan had once told Jenny about a spider found frequently in Australia, called the huntsman spider. It was, with its legs, roughly the size of a dinner plate. Glitha reminded her of that spider. She was the color of a dead leaf. She had eight faceted eyes. Two of them, in the center of her face were huge. There were two eyes above each of the large eyes and one below them. She seemed to look at things through the two main eyes, but Jenny imagined the other eyes gave her amazing peripheral vision. Jenny imagined she didn't miss much.

But, from what Jenny knew of her, despite her fourteen-foot leg span, she and her kind had a gentle nature, with no wish to do harm to any living thing. It seemed ironic to Jenny that Sam had gotten a spider tattoo when they lived together in the college dorms. She touched her own arm where Sam had etched a butterfly into the skin with a dagger, what seemed like ages ago. It had long since healed, but the scar would be there forever.

Glitha turned to them after seeing Sam disappear into the forest with her companion. *"That one is so very lost, my friends. She believes what she says. The shame is that there is so much potential there for good. Spending time with the people of Earth has changed her in some very interesting ways. She fights it, but part of her truly does want to be your friend, Jenny. She admires you and hates herself for it. When left alone in the little cabin we had made for her, she rants aloud and broadcast's mentally to all around her. I don't think she even realizes she is doing it. She has been heard calling your name in her sleep, alternately reviling you and apologizing to you. It is sad."*

Jenny just stood there. She really didn't want to hear this. She wanted to hate her. She despised everything she stood for, but mostly she was just terribly hurt by Sam's callous betrayal of their friendship.

"Has she betrayed any further knowledge of the plans of the Insenium or her kingdom? I think she accidentally dropped an important clue just now. It appears the Insenium is working on some kind of powerful weapon or tech that could prove our undoing if we don't know how to counter it or destroy it."

Glitha responded; *"She does go on and on about how we should turn our dimension over to the Insenium and join in their brilliant plan for conquering the dimensions. She insists there is much to be gained for us to turn traitor to our dimension: Power, glory and ultimate dominion can be ours if we turn traitor. As if that meant anything to us. What would we do with any of that? We have everything we need and want, and we are content. Her war means nothing to us, except their plan to ultimately enslave every intelligent being over all the dimensions. That we must not allow, if it is within our power to do anything to prevent it."*

Tarafau nodded in agreement. *"I knew we could trust you to keep her safely until such a time as we decide how best to help her. But that must wait until we have finished our task. Is there anything you need that will help in doing your part?"*

"No, Tarafau. We are well equipped to deal with her. She is like a child in many ways. Although I would not wish to underestimate her cunning and resolve. We will keep watch over her. Never fear."

"We thank you, Glitha, and your council, for their aid in this matter. If there is nothing else, we will depart. We have work to do."

Glitha approximated a nod. As they turned to leave, Jenny looked around one last time. Once again, she wished she could spend some time with these gentle creatures. She felt she could learn much from them. She didn't think she would ever think of spiders in the same way again.

Chapter 9: By the Seat of His Pants

B urt crouched nonchalantly by the fire, poking it with a metal stick. He was careful to appear to be completely engaged by the flickering flames. Groga and other slaves milled about at their work, ignoring him for the moment, which was exactly what he had hoped. He had sneaked in just before daybreak, if you could call the slight lightening of the sky daybreak. It was more like the beginnings of false dawn on Earth. He had sidled up to a tent and then, stretching, as if he had just awakened, he grabbed a bundle of something that had been left on the ground beside the tent and had moved off, as if he knew where he was going.

Over his years working in intelligence for the Alliance, he had learned a number of important principles. One was to always act like you knew what you were doing and where you were going. When he had noticed the fire, he realized that people would generally gravitate to light, so he laid his bundle on a nearby table and picked up the stick. From his vantage point he could get a pretty good idea of what he might be up against.

The camp was not the orderly place he had expected. These Groga, unlike their counterparts in the South America camp they had shut down, were somewhat slovenly and there didn't appear to be a clear chain of command.

Two types of slaves were in the camp. The first type looked as if they had been slaves for a long time and knew exactly what they were doing. These had free rein in the camp, going about their duties with quiet subservience.

The second group was obviously newly captured, being transported from the portal to their new home in the Groga training city near Fleist. There they would be broken in and trained to serve the Groga city here and on the Groga home world.

The Groga were very loose with their communications, often broadcasting in mindspeech to no one in particular. They very seldom spoke aloud. This was probably due to the disparate groups of slaves they captured from different worlds. It would have taken far too much time and effort to teach their slaves to speak in their language. This was a fortunate turn of events. One of the things Burt had worried about was how to communicate. It was evident that at least some of the Groga had been trained in how to transfer mindspeech to another. This surprised him, as so far, none of the Groga he had had the opportunity to interact with had been very bright.

But he knew that at least some of them must be intelligent enough to lead their men, as both of the fighting forces he had encountered on Earth had been led by other Groga, with none of their masters in evidence.

As he continued to poke absently at the fire, he noted what sounded like a disturbance on the other side of the camp. It seemed that many of the prisoners were objecting vehemently to their treatment and were being disabused of their thoughts of rescue or escape.

Burt knew they were close to the Groga training camp under the rule of the Fleistians. He would ignore the incident, although a part of him wanted to rescue all of them from their enslavement. However, it was probably time for him to find another occupation. He noticed a group of slaves engaged in disassembling the tents, preparing to move out. He dropped his stick, sauntered over to the group and took one end of a piece of canvas to aid in folding it.

"I don't recognize you, friend. How did you end up on this detail?"

Burt shrugged. *"They noticed I had finished my chores and sent me here. I'm Burt. What's your name?"*

"Linga," the man replied. *"Have you been a 'trusted' long? I don't recall seeing you before today."*

"I am pretty new," Burt improvised. *"Do you have any tips for a new person?"*

"Just do your work and stay out of things that don't concern you. The easy way to get into trouble is to be lazy and nosy. None of that type last for very long."

They finished folding the canvas and stacked it in a box along with the ropes and tent stakes. You would think that, with all their technology, the Groga would be better equipped than with these ancient rigs. They secured the box, made of some type of plastic and finished tidying up the space the tent had been occupying. The box was on a type of flat dolly, towed by a rope. They moved to the next tent without further conversation. Linga hadn't seemed like he was in the mood to talk and Burt didn't wish to rock the boat at the moment.

They worked like that for a couple of hours until it seemed like everything was packed and stowed. In one area Groga soldiers had assembled in two hollow square formations. In the center of the first were the newly captured slaves. Some of them had been bound and looked as if they had been thoroughly beaten. The others looked down at their feet, shuffling or rocking or sobbing. There were children among them also. Burt didn't want to think what would happen to them once they got to the city.

His new "friend", Linga, walked unconcernedly into the second square, where an aisle had been established for the "trusted" slaves to enter. Once they had all assembled, someone barked a command and the formations started to move. They didn't exactly march. It was more like a coordinated walk at a fairly good pace. There was no synchronization to it. They did maintain the square shape and the hollow in which the slaves walked. Other than an occasional sob or shuffle or the cry of a small child, quickly hushed, no one spoke. It was somewhat eerie. The only sound was the shuffling of hundreds of feet.

Burt guesstimated that there were about 200 slaves in the newly captured bunch and another 50 or so in the "trusted" group. He didn't try to strike up a conversation with anyone. This was obviously not the time, unless he wanted to draw attention to himself, but he paid attention.

Even without speaking with any of them, he could tell it was quite a mixed bunch. Many of them looked resigned and tired. There were those who looked like they might be the bullies in the bunch and a few that held themselves with dignity, also resigned, but not bowed.

They all wore the same basic uniform. Even the women wore the leather-like breeches, a rope belt and the flour bag style shirts. They were all shod in simple leather-like sandals and they were all dirty and unkempt. Burt imagined that bathing and basic hygiene supplies were not high on the priority list where slaves were concerned.

The Groga weren't much better, he realized. Their simple brown uniforms were not adorned with patches, medals or even rank, as far as he could tell. They didn't seem to need to comb their hair, which was shaven close to the scalp in a very short, dark stubble which did nothing to enhance their greyish mottled skin. Of course, in the low light, nearly everything gave off greyish colors. Those he had seen in the hot humid Louisiana swamp and in the hot, moist sun of the Brazilian rain forest hadn't seemed that much different in color from an Asian, if a little less yellow and a little more grey.

Weirdly, their eyes were all black. He assumed they actually did have irises of color, although he hadn't noticed one way or the other before. But the constant darkness seemed to make all of the pupils of everyone around him much larger and, in some cases, they obscured the color of their eyes.

They didn't stop at what Burt might have thought was lunchtime but kept moving. He could see that some of the adults of the newly captured had picked up children and were carrying them either on a hip or piggyback. He could only see them from the back through the gaps of the troops walking ahead of him, but their postures were slumping farther and now and again one of them stumbled, only to be shoved back into formation by one of their captors.

As the city drew nearer, Burt considered his next moves. His desire was to be transported to either the Groga planet or the Insenium as a slave. This meant he would have to get as much information as possible about the "trusted" and their duties. It was obvious to him that he wouldn't get any information until he got into the city proper, where he would have to devise a reason to get away from this party and move more freely through the city. It was a big challenge, but not the first sticky situation he had found himself in. In every city there was an underground, which usually consisted either of the dishonest or those with a mission to overthrow tyranny.

He hoped to discover the latter and see what he could do to aid them, perhaps to get them in touch with King Nivi's people, but he would take what he could get for the moment.

He hated to think what Jenny would think of his decision, but, although she had already been through some really difficult and terrorizing experiences, she was still on the naïve side. She had been rescued, somewhat miraculously on two of those occasions, although she had acquitted herself well when faced with a violent attack by three Groga masquerading as home repairmen, not to mention torture and pain at the hands of Engoza.

He hadn't known Jenny well at the time. He wasn't sure how she managed to attract people to her as she did. Personally, he was a bit of a recluse and preferred to do his job as a solo act. Although, he had to admit, he enjoyed working with Jenny's team, especially Bob. There was a special rapport and a feeling of unity that he hadn't experienced before. It was like they were all mentally compatible, even though they came from so many differing backgrounds and specialties.

For now, however, once again he was on his own with only his own instincts, training and experience to aid him, not to mention an MDP full of gear and supplies. He loved the skin flap he now used. It meant that his MDP was as secure as it was possible for it to be.

He trudged along with the rest, his head down. He was surprised, therefore, when he started to hear the cacophony of a large city not far ahead. They were nearly there. Someone at the front waved the wagons that were being pulled by a large hulking breed of slaves, nearly 7-foot-tall to go ahead of the square columns.

The first square marched to the side toward what appeared to be cattle pens. There, the captives were driven into a fenced-in pen about the same size as the inner part of the marching formation had been. Several began to moan and cry and some of them tried to charge the soldiers in denial of their fate.

This availed them nothing but another beating, however.

The rest dispersed in through the city gates. Burt had positioned himself in the center of the "trusted" and casually followed them into the city. Once inside, most of them headed toward a large barracks-style building, while others rushed off, apparently on errands of one kind or another. Burt followed their example, walking at a steady pace in the first direction that occurred to him. He had conjured a bundle from out of his MDP after ducking down a narrow, deserted alleyway. He also retrieved his quarterstaff. It would serve as a walking stick, and if his plan worked out, he would probably need it as a weapon.

From the mouth of the alleyway he blended into the foot traffic on a broad street lined with shops and workshops. As he strode along, he nodded to passersby in a friendly way. Most of the people on the street were slaves of different races and planetary origin. Most were humanoid, which seemed to be the preferred type of slave. Burt had heard that most of the raids had taken place on humanoid planets with very few exceptions. He also noticed that most of them were beyond the stage of their slavery where they were timid or half-hearted. You would have thought you were on a normal village street pretty much anywhere in the multiverse.

Although many of the slaves wore the baggy pants and sack-like shirt he wore, most of them were dressed in simple but serviceable clothing, mostly clean. They didn't look dirty or scruffy and went about their duties as if it had become normal to them to serve their Groga masters. Burt realized that each of these was a survivor of a huge disaster and had come out of their hardship with their minds and attitudes intact. This probably meant that, once the Groga had initially acquired and trained their slaves, they were not necessarily onerous taskmasters.

He heard occasional discussions in various languages, none of which he recognized, but also saw the evidence of mindspeech being used to make transactions and various group interactions. So, it wouldn't be unusual for him to approach someone with mindspeech. This was going to make his next moves a lot easier.

He noticed a small man, taller than Arvid, but about a foot shorter than himself, sitting in front of a shop working a piece of leather with an awl, under a lamp extending from the shop wall into the street. He was punching small holes along the edge of the piece, occasionally looking up and nodding to different ones, obviously enjoying being out among people as opposed to working quietly alone in his shop. He would do.

He put a puzzled look on his face, turning to the right and left, then walked up to the man and asked, *"Excuse me friend. Where can I find a decent meal and some serviceable clothing in this town? Is there an inn or tavern you can recommend? I'd just as soon forego the slop they feed us in the mess hall, and these aren't exactly my style,"* he sent with a grimace at his slave outfit.

The man looked him up and down. He knew that even in the lamplight he looked somewhat scruffy with a two-day old beard and his current attire. He made a mental note at the first opportunity to change into something more appropriate from his MDP or potentially purchase native clothing that would not make him stand out. He had years of disguises and clothing in his MDP, but it wouldn't hurt to acquire more.

"Do you have any coin?" the man asked skeptically, but not unkindly.

"No, but I have some things to trade," he answered, pointing at the bundle under his arm.

"Then, first I would suggest you go to the marketplace where old Gaffer and his lady trades in used goods. Depending on what you have to trade, I am sure you could get enough for a meal or two. Who is your squad commander?"

"Don't know. They haven't assigned a new one yet. My old commander died. Tripped and hit his head on a rock."

"Ah, I see. Then I suggest you look for The Broken Sun tavern on Langer Street. Low prices. The food is basic, but it's good. Stay away from their ale, though. It's good, but very strong. New guys don't all react to it in the same way."

"That's good of you, friend. I appreciate it."

"I was the new guy once. I suggest you get a bath and a haircut. You'll look a lot less like a new-comer."

"Thanks, I will."

He gave the man a vague salute and walked off in the direction of the market.

It seemed so odd to know that it was late morning and yet it still appeared to be twilight. The perpetual glow of lamplight was just not the same as the morning sun. He supposed one would get used to just about anything. People bustled about intent on their errands. He found the street that led to the market square quickly. It looked like a giant flea market from home.

Tables, long and wide, ranged in rows, making wide aisles between for the shoppers. The vendors stood behind their tables, some crying their wares, others silently waiting for customers and still others actively engaged in mostly silent haggling. Burt smiled. It reminded him somewhat of the market square on Miriha's planet. Blast it! He missed her. She had been a friend and mentor when he was training as an agent for the Alliance.

He approached a stretch of tables containing what were obviously used items. Not in bad shape, really, just not new. Most of these were items of clothing, tools or household items. The household items were of a number of different cultures and levels of technology.

He surreptitiously reached into his bundle. Once his hand with his MDP was well inside, he withdrew some tradable items from the MDP, leaving them inside the bundle.

"I have some things to trade," he said to the woman minding the table. He noticed that many of the merchants minding stalls were women. She was nearly his height, curvy, wearing a dark kerchief over her straight grey locks. She tilted her head at him, eyeing him up and down without expression.

"A new one then? No coin and needing a start." She sighed. *"Let's see it then."*

Burt looked to his right and left, as if concerned that someone else would see. She reflexively did the same. He knew this automatically would up her curiosity and potentially up his price. He brought out his first item, a New York Yankees ball cap in good condition and handed it to her furtively.

Her eyes widened. *"What is the purpose of this?"*

"It is a cap, meant to shield eyes from the sun and proclaim your loyalties. In my homeland these caps are regarded with respect for the power of the symbol."

"And what mean the runes inscribed thereon?"

"It gives one power to win, when one puts all of their strength and skill into a challenge. You could sell the pattern to one of the local tailors or seamstresses and contract to make a profit every time they sold one. It is considered very good for business where I come from."

"And what do you ask for this?"

"I am unfamiliar with your coinage. What do you think would be a fair price for something that would make you many future profits?"

She fingered the fabric of the cap, noting the emblem stamped on the inside, the embroidery of the NYC Yankees symbol on the front and the elastic cinch in the back to adjust the size of the cap. Her brows furrowed. He knew, if he could look into her mind, he would see a calculator running up columns of numbers. He had seen that look before as he traded with merchants on other worlds. It meant he had made a sale, but now the bargaining would begin.

He walked away later with two full outfits of native clothing in good repair and enough coins, she said, that would allow him to eat well for a month. (Not that he knew how many days that would mean on a planet that seemed to always be in night.)

He didn't expect he would be here for a month or even a week, but it would mean he wouldn't have to expose himself to the slaves in the barracks, which meant less of a chance that his true purpose would be discovered.

He found the inn the old leatherworker had recommended and rented a room for a couple of days, including a bath. Once he had bathed and shaved and changed, he went down into the common room for some food. He let the serving woman choose a meal for him and then looked around him.

The inn was tidy but plain. He had noticed that there were no wooden structures in the town, which made sense. Most of the local buildings seemed to be made of a kind of adobe or possibly stuccoed brick. Only the official buildings were built of mortared stone.

The inn wasn't crowded this time of day, although he still hadn't determined what time of day it might be. But in his guise as a slave new to the planet, he could eventually get the answers he needed. Most of the slaves in the inn seemed to be dressed similarly to himself. It made sense that the Groga would allow the slaves to create their own part of the city, as he was sure many of the goods they made were given to the Groga as tribute. They were allowed to trade among themselves. The coins didn't seem to be made of any metal Burt recognized, but he decided they were mostly just trade markers with no value in and of themselves. They weren't stamped with any emblems, but simply numbers, which he hadn't known how to decipher.

The trader woman had schooled him in the basics, as to which ones would buy more as part of their bargain. She had also invited him to come back and trade again. Burt found himself wondering how soon he would start to see Yankees ball caps become part of the everyday wear among the slaves.

At various tables around the room were men and women in small groups. He was the only one sitting alone. The drawback of mindspeech was that it had to be directed to you in order to hear what people were saying, and those who conversed in their own languages might as well have been speaking Chinese. No help there.

When the serving girl brought his meal, he asked her, *"What is there to do in this town, when we aren't working?"*

She shook her head, *"I'm not sure what you mean. I suppose there is the arena. We have no minstrels and dancing is not allowed. Only contests of strength are encouraged by our masters."*

He nodded, thanked her, got directions to the arena and ate his meal in silence, listening to the chatter around him and the noises coming from the kitchen. He couldn't help but wonder how long that young woman had been a slave. She had the air of one who didn't find her life at all unusual. How many generations of slaves were represented here? He tipped her what he hoped was considered a generous tip and left.

At the arena, he hoped that most of the mindspeech would be more of a crowd mentality, broadcast as opposed to being directed at any particular individual. Also, this was potentially a good place to make some contacts and perhaps draw out more information about the situation in the camp.

The arena suited its name. Tiered stone seating surrounding a packed Earth enclosure, it was surprisingly packed with men and women, some shouting in various languages at the competitors battering at one another in the ring.

He paid the small admission fee and joined the crowd, sitting next to a happy looking fellow who was alternately jumping up and down from his seat and occasionally to his feet to howl something unintelligible at the competitors.

In the center of the ring were two men, one wide and burly and the other wiry and tall. The burly one had a thick rope with a knot at the end of it, nearly the size of a fist. The wiry one had what looked like a tree branch with a worn knob at the end similar to what the Irish called a shillelagh. Burt imagined it had come with him from his native planet. It was obvious that once the slaves of a place had been subdued, they were able to bring at least some of their belongings with them, or at least those that weren't collected by the Groga for their own use. It was also obvious that the slaves were allowed to have some basic defensive weapons, which spoke volumes of the confidence of their Groga masters.

Both men seemed to know what they were doing, and it seemed they had been at it for awhile as both were covered with the sweat of exertion.

Burt only watched the match out of the corner of his eye, however. He was much more interested in the people around him.

As he had expected, few were directing mindspeech to single individuals, which made sorting various conversations out somewhat like trying to put two jigsaw puzzles together at once when the pieces had all been dumped into the same box.

"and then, you know what he did?" ... *"You can't expect anyone to find anything in all this darkness."* ... *"I would have never imagined she would be attracted to Simon, after all..."* ... *"do you think they'll let us..."* ... *"Did you bet anything on this match?"*

With a start, Burt realized this last had actually been directed at him from the happy fellow next to him.

"No. I just came to watch. New in town and haven't been given an assignment yet."

"Well, then! Welcome to hell," he paused, waiting for Burt.

"Burt, and you?"

"Jui's the name. Glad to meet ya, Burt. I only asked if you had any money on this match, as it's over and you didn't seem like you were all that interested."

"To be honest, I don't know much about how these matches go or how they are scored. I'm guessing the loser of this one is the big bloke with a huge bump on his head being pulled out of the arena by his feet?"

"Well guessed," Jui agreed cheerfully. *"The next one is the one I came for. It's a freedom match. You have to work your way up in the rankings to play at that level. You get three chances to win. If you win, they set you loose, somewhere on this planet. You have three days to find your way to civilization, otherwise known as King Nivi's people. If they catch you after that, you get extra duty for a very long time.*

The fellows competing today are pretty good. This is a no weapons match, so just their hands and feet, since, once they turn you loose, you get no weapons to carry with you."

The crowd all stood up suddenly and called and yelled at the two men currently entering the ring.

They appeared to be about evenly matched, neither overly muscled nor tall. Actually, there wasn't much difference between the two at all except the color of their hair. One was blonde, his hair glinting in the torchlight and the other's hair was a blue black. Both had the short haircuts that most of the male slaves usually wore.

They gave a hand-to-breast salute to the Groga guard who had escorted them out onto the ring then turned to one another and did the same. The Groga smacked two large hands together and then stood at parade rest as the combatants began to circle one another.

"How do they score the match?" he asked Jui.

"Score? Dear fellow this match is to the death or unconsciousness, whichever comes first. Obviously, this means strength, cunning and skill and maybe just a tad of luck. These matches occur seldomly considering the price of failure. In the last bout it was to unconsciousness, but when the loser came to, he was unable to function, so the Groga killed him anyway."

"Fudge nuggets! And the rest of you bet on the outcome?"

"Not I," Jui protested, *"I only bet on the regular matches. But there are many who do. Most of those are second generation slaves."*

"Do you have many slaves ever escape?"

"None that live to tell about it," Jui admitted. *"We have learned over time that it isn't possible. After you get over the trauma of being forcefully moved from home and kindred and "trained" to be "trusted" it isn't such a terrible life. But I do miss the dancing."* And he sighed at that.

The crowd was loud now both mentally and audibly. The two men had finally grappled one another around the shoulders, each trying to lever the other into a position that would allow them to dominate the other. The black-haired fellow pivoted on one foot and leaned the other backwards over his hip. The blonde man let loose of the other's shoulder using both hands to grab the wrist of his opponent and pull it back. Back and forth they struggled until the blonde actually managed to get his elbow into the gut of his opponent. The black-haired man doubled over and the blonde shoved him roughly to the dirt, dropping onto him.

Burt turned from the contest. He wasn't squeamish, but he had no desire to watch this grim event. He had always said he wouldn't have made a very good Roman during the time of the Roman circus spectacles. Fighting was sometimes necessary and sometimes people died, but this seemed so cruel and purposeless.

Instead he turned to Jui. *"Any tips for the new guy? I would certainly like to avoid any, um, complications, if I can."*

"Never look a Groga in the eye. Always respond immediately to all commands. Curfew at sundown..."

"Wait! Sundown? How can you tell?"

"The first bell rings at a few marks before. You can't miss it. The bells ring about 4 marks apart. If you aren't off the streets by third bell, you get put in the stocks for two days, no food or water."

"OK, I'll pay attention. Anything else?"

"Yes, be careful who you talk to. The better the clothing, the more likely you are talking to a 'devoted'. These are those who have proven their loyalty to the Insenium by 'special' services, if you know what I mean."

Burt nodded grimly. He most certainly did. In nearly every society or culture there were the toadies, the hangers-on who thrived by ingratiating themselves to the powers that be.

At this point it was obvious that the blonde was going to win. The choke hold he had on the other man was turning the man's face purple. Burt got the feeling he was trying to go for the unconscious option, but sometimes it was hard to gage what was too much pressure. At the moment the other man's eyes were bulging huge and bloodshot out of his purple face, his fists opening and closing, his kicking growing more and more feeble.

Burt turned away. *"Thanks, Jui. Are you staying in the barracks?"*

"No, Burt, I live with my wife and 4 kids in an apartment in the city. Do you have a place to stay or are you going to the barracks?"

"I've found rooms. I'll see you around."

Jui nodded and turned back to the spectacle.

Burt left without turning to see the outcome of the match. He wandered up and down different streets, noticing that regardless of the fact that these people were slaves, there didn't seem to be a slum or a poorer section. The buildings were pretty much of the cookie cutter variety. Most apartments seemed to be over top of workshops or those selling goods. There were no parks, with or without trees. Also, no children playing in the street. From time to time there were small play yards with children under kindergarten age playing with balls or small cloth dolls supervised by one or more teenage children.

Like all slave masters across the multiverse, the Groga encouraged childbearing. It was in their best interest. The larger their army became, the more slaves were required to oversee the day-to-day needs of their masters, so the Groga could focus on training and raiding. Slaves acquired by breeding were much less troublesome and expensive than those acquired by raiding. At that thought, Burt decided it was time to move closer to putting his plan in motion. He had thought he might actually take a few days to get to that point, but the arena wasn't the place to accomplish his plan.

So far it looked like the intelligence he had received in King Nivi's company was good. It all added up. It was unlikely staying any longer would make much of a difference based on what he had already seen and what he could surmise from past experience. He was used to making snap decisions based on a combination of discoverable facts and his gut. So, he turned his steps toward the Groga side of the city.

According to his sources, the arena on the slave side of town wasn't the only one. On the Groga side, there was a training arena that also involved the slaves. This one was for training Groga to fight non-Groga. Burt needed to get "invited" into that arena and the fastest way to get there was to pick a fight with a Groga soldier. This wasn't smart, he knew, but sometimes stupid was the only way to get where you wanted to go.

Chapter 10: Off to See the Wizard

Bob stretched forward, working the forms of the meditative exercise that all of the scientists in his lab participated in every day at their lunch break. It was almost a dance, done in unison on the soft blue-green grass in the park on the rooftop of the Alliance Headquarters building. It was cool up here, a gentle breeze fluttering the leaves of the small trees that bordered the park.

Mervin led them. His wiry frame almost seemed boneless as he moved gracefully from one form to another. He insisted on this exercise halfway through their day of working in the lab. So far Bob had been playing catch-up on their research but today was the day he would be briefed on the current most urgent project. In the three days he had been there, he had come to enjoy the interaction with the other scientists and inventors. Generally speaking, most of his life in the sciences had been pretty solitary, one of the reasons he had invented Fidget and enjoyed the company of Ignatius. The two of them were great company and Fidget was quickly developing the skills necessary to make him an able assistant in his work.

At this point, Fidget was proving very useful, fetching and carrying and tending to small tasks that didn't require a lot of understanding. This being said, he had filled Fidget's database with all of the notes he had ever made on every project he had ever personally worked on. Fidget was a walking encyclopedia of everything Bob knew. The other scientists had dubbed it the "Bobpedia".

It was good to be back into serious research with a definite end in mind. It was like a massive treasure hunt or a grand adventure. This was what Bob DID. This was what he excelled at and loved more than just about anything. Except maybe peanut butter and jelly sandwiches and cold root beer on the patio with Lizzie. He had loved that. He still missed her terribly. Even with Jenny in his life, he missed her aunt sorely. It was a great joy to him, therefore, to have put Lizziebot into production. He still had some upgrades to install. The Alliance had given him permission to install some "dastardly alien tech" into the bot the next time the opportunity presented itself, with the caveat that Jenny should never use Lizziebot in the presence of a non-Alliance Earthling.

They finished their workout and went down to their personal suites to shower and change. They would then lunch together in the lab in the break-room while Bob got his orientation to the super-secret project, he would be working on with them, the reason he had come to headquarters in the first place.

Fidget was waiting for him there, having straightened up the place and gotten out a fresh t-shirt and jeans. He hadn't originally intended Fidget as a manservant or valet, but he performed these duties admirably and saved Bob precious time that he could devote to this urgent project.

After he dressed, he and Fidget proceeded to the lab where the rest were already assembling themselves. He knew all of them had servants who performed all of the things Fidget did for him.

Ignatius was already on his perch in the break room, daintily picking at the snacks that had been provided for him. Ignatius was thriving with all of the attention the others gave to him. And interestingly, he was becoming more and more articulate in mindspeech. His saucy personality and quirky sense of bird-humor had made him a hit of the lab.

He was a little leery of Inle. She was certainly imposing in her insectoid way. But everyone in the lab accepted Ignatius as part of the team and coddled him to the point that Bob was concerned that his bird was getting seriously spoiled.

They sat around the table and, as usual, Argent was the last to stump in with his habitual scowl. Bob had his number, though. He had realized in the first day that Argent was dedicated, but not as sour as he appeared. You just had to get to know him.

As Argent settled down into his seat, Mervin looked from face to face in the circle. Finally, he said, "Bob, there is no easy way to tell you this, but we have failed. We have failed again and again to unlock a secret that should be simple. You have had an opportunity to read our notes and theories, none of which seem to apply, but at least we know how much ground we've already covered. Unlike your Edison, we don't have time to fail a thousand times. The timetable is very short and even with our extensive resources, we feel like we are running out of options.

We would really like to have your thoughts on the issue."

Bob leaned forward. "First of all, why this card?" He indicated the card that sat in the center of the table, the center of everyone's focus. "Why, of all the things we recovered, is this so important? I saw no such reasoning in any of your reports. Lots of experimentation, but nothing to tell me why we are putting our focus here."

Mervin shook his head. "I wish I could say. It's more of a scientific hunch. Something about it is hinky. It was just so very out of place. In all the detritus we collected, this was the only card like this; actually, the only card-shaped thing at all. It occurred to us, when we viewed the tapes, that this officer, instead of fighting, was heading frantically towards the portal, the proverbial beeline. He didn't have a blaster in his hand or any weapon we could find, and, unlike the other officers, he wasn't yelling commands or chivvying any of the grunt soldiers at all. He was just running pell-mell towards the gate."

Bob nodded thoughtfully. "I see."

He straightened up in his chair ticking off his thoughts on his fingers. "It isn't a bomb or a detonator. Neither of those make any sense. Firstly, because these raids all seem to be about collecting tech and slaves. Bombs are messy and could destroy the stuff they're trying to acquire.

It isn't a computer module, although that is definitely circuitry embedded into it. From what we know of the Groga and their overseers (admittedly not as much as we'd like) they aren't avid users of tech even though they are avid collectors of it. Most everything except the portal transceivers that we collected from them was really low tech. I'm guessing the Groga don't have the capacity to understand or use more than basic tech, and Sam's folks are somewhat disdainful of it, based on Jenny's reports.

We must ask ourselves, why was it in the Groga camp? Had they retrieved it in one of their raids? Based on the fact that they raid for tech, could this be what they were looking for all along? Do they know what it is? And maybe it is none of the above. Just maybe they invented it and there was a specific reason it was in that place at that time."

"Our thinking as well," put in Argent in his least grumpy voice. "We have come to the conclusion that, whatever it is, they will be most unhappy about it when they realize it was lost. Hopefully they don't know that we have it or we could see some fighting right here in Alliance Headquarters."

"OK," said Bob. "So the conclusion I would like to jump to is that this has to do with dimensional travel."

Everyone just sat there, stunned. "No," said Alwen, a stricken look on her face. "Please, Creator of All Things, no."

Merv nodded. "This is why you are here, Bob of Earth. I dread to think it, but I believe you have trod the path none of us were even willing to consider. And if this is true? Do we destroy it or do we continue our research in hope we can use it somehow to win this war?"

"Something tells me that the unknown material this is made of would resist all attempts to destroy it, and can we afford to take even the tiniest chance that there is another one somewhere out there? We have a very short window, unless I mistake. We can't afford for this to fall into the hands of the enemy and we absolutely must know what this does. It may be a red herring, but my gut tells me it isn't."

Merv scanned the group. Each of them nodded in assent.

"We are agreed, then. Based on this new theory everyone will study it from this aspect using the tools of their own discipline, do your research and come back in the morning, while we are still fresh, to put forth your hypothesis. Bob, I want you to take the card and examine it with your own resources. If you need any type of scanner or other equipment, let us know. You are now the head of this project. You may choose any of your teammates to assist you. You are right about our timetable. I am guessing we have about two weeks to figure this out. And THAT!" And he snapped his fingers, "For Edison and his camel-eating light bulb."

"Camels eat light bulbs?" Ignatius asked in wonder.

This made them all laugh. Bob explained patiently to his indignant bird that it was just a turn of phrase and not to believe everything that any of this crew said.

Ignatius unruffled his feathers and took the arm Bob extended to him to move him to his perch in the lab. The perch had become even more lavish than the original one. Manzanita branches for him to gnaw on, various gears and other parts painted bright colors hung in a mobile for him to peck at. He loved to tap the metal parts and make them move and ring like a cacophonous windchime. No one in the lab minded it, as it was intermittent. There was the usual snack tray and instead of a water bottle, there was a water fountain that Ignatius could turn on and off with a tap of his claw. The first day that had been installed, he had spent an hour just turning it on and off and chuckling to himself.

Bob settled him on his perch whereupon he rang his chimes just once. It had become a "thing". No one took any notice.

Bob sat at his lab table on the tall stool that gave him the option to sit or stand. He pulled out the card. Talk about your dastardly alien tech, he thought shaking his head. This was beyond anything he had ever theorized or imagined. Dimensional science was considered a pseudo-science by most Earth scientists, especially since no two of them could ever agree exactly what that meant.

For some it was the onion theory that basically said that the dimensions were basically in layers that touched one another, and each dimension was just an iteration of the ones above and below it in the structure. So the same person was born in each dimension, but as that person made differing choices, the history and future of the different dimensions could differ wildly.

Other scientists felt the dimensions were more about differing realities within the same space and simply unseen, each dimensional culture using the same space and time completely differently and each completely undetected by the others. They used this to explain phenomenon such as ghosts and spirits.

But, as he understood it, dimensional science as experienced by the Dimensional Alliance was a lot more like a bunch of branches interconnected by dimensional fields; each one a universe of its own. Each one unique even to the point where the physics in some dimensions were very different than any Earth scientist would ever believe.

Bob had seen a tumbleweed once. It was devoid of leaves, a skeleton of rust colored branches. The various branches made a tangled, ball-shaped structure, all attached to a center stem. All were connected although many of them had ends, but traveling the various paths made by those tangled branches you could get to any one of them including the main stem. He doubted that the dimension where the Alliance Headquarters resided was the stem. It was just another branch and potentially a fairly obscure one. The difference between that tumbleweed and the dimensional network was the vastness of it. While the branches of a tumbleweed had thousands of potential unique paths and destinations, the branches of the dimensional network was beyond counting by any numbering system Bob was aware of.

So how had this seemingly inconsequential piece of whatever, become the center of their hopes for winning this conflict? It looked like plastic although none of the techniques they had used had yielded any recognizable elemental structure. That alone was suspicious. They knew so little about the Insenium, which was really holding things up. Was this an Insenium invention? He had expressed his doubts with good reason, but what if he was missing something? They definitely couldn't afford to make unfounded assumptions about anything at this point.

How did this card tie into this horrendous war and what could they possibly do about it? They could struggle for weeks, probing and prodding, examining and turning this problem inside out without any progress. What could he, Bob, do about it? What gave them the slightest idea that he could do more than the combined minds of the Alliance's best scientists and "tinkerers"?

Unconsciously he stroked the agent gate pass at his neck. The infinity symbol that formed the pendant of the necklace was keyed to the Gate Network, but he needed a Gate Guardian or the Gatekeeper to access a gate. The Guardians and Gatekeepers' pendant was in the shape of a key, each key unique in its design and each one sending off a signal that would open the gateroom to which they were assigned. The Gatekeeper's key could open any gate. He remembered that both Lizzie and Jenny would also often touch the key around their necks with an air of wonder.

He understood Jenny's awe. It was such a privilege to be accepted into this community of peace-loving scientists and cultural leaders. Regardless of their internal politics, their one focus within the Alliance Council was to maintain the integrity of the dimensional network, to prevent the incursions of the last war and to keep the dimensions safe. These portals or "gates", as the Alliance designated them, were naturally occurring phenomena and before the Alliance, it wasn't unusual for different dimensions to accidentally "leak" into one another. Without the gate mechanisms, they were open for anyone or anything to wander into, potentially at the great detriment of both dimensions or of all of them.

He turned the card over and over in his hands. He needed the key to this problem.

He froze and his mind began to race. A KEY. Could it possibly be that simple?

"I need a key!" he shouted. All faces turned to him, some dismayed, some curious and some irritated at being interrupted.

"A what?" Argent shouted back. "What in the name of Ingot's saggy drawers are you talking about?"

"Tell me what you know about the keys the Gatekeeper and the Guardians wear. It's important."

Understanding began to dawn on Mervin's face. "It's the whole sword in the stone thing all over again," he said softly.

"Exactly," Bob replied. "You get it. It's about the connecting vibrations. The sword and the stone were set to react to the minute vibrations of a specific DNA key, right? Am I right?"

Merv nodded. "How did you get to this conclusion so quickly?"

"We're not there yet," Bob said, stroking his moustache as he often did when deep in thought. "This could be a red herring too, like all of the other theories you've pursued, but you've eliminated most of the obvious paths. This one was serendipity, if anything.

What would happen if the Gatekeeper was destroyed or lost with her key? Surely there is a backup," Burt asked urgently.

Merv considered. "I would think so. We should consult The Council in private session. Fidget, please transmit to the Council room that we need an emergency meeting."

"Complete," said Fidget. "Anything else?"

"That will do," Merv said. "Let's go. I knew we needed this Earthling. They think differently," he said smiling and tapping his head. "Oh, and by the way, sorry about coopting your bot. A bad habit of mine."

"Not a problem. He is fair game inside the lab. If you'd like I have a couple new ones in my MDP. Right now, they're just sitting there collecting dust, so to speak. I actually don't think there is any dust in that environment, although, when we get some time I'd really like to find out."

Merv laughed and shook his head. "Not without permission from the council, although, if you pull this off, I don't imagine they would deny you anything. As far as an extra bot is concerned, if they are all as amazing as Fidget, I might consider it."

They entered into the elevator. In any other elevator they probably wouldn't have fit, but an elevator scaled for dragons made it actually quite roomy. The disembodied voice said, "Private Council Chamber" almost instantly and the door opened into the reception area. The foxlike receptionist nodded to them and said, "You're expected."

They entered the Council Chamber and, as usual, the Chief Councilor and his second and third sat beside him on the dais. Ingot stood and spread his hands. *"Please, be seated,"* he sent. *"I understand this is urgent. How can we help you?"*

Mervin stood and explained Bob's theory. All three of them showed indications of excitement. Ingot's eyebrows shot up, Myla's feathers ruffled, his eyes pinned, and small tendrils of smoke trickled from Liliath's nostrils, a clear sign she was agitated.

"I need to know if there is a back-up key to the Gatekeeper's key. If, because of an accident or an attack she was destroyed with the current key or if, in the process, the key was lost, what would you do?" asked Bob from his seat. *"Do you have the ability to create a second one? I would assume this has been taken into account at some point."*

Ingot grimaced and looked at his great uncle. Argent met his eyes but didn't say anything unless it was in private mindspeech. He sighed. *"I was afraid this might come up at some point. The answer to your question, Bob, and I assume the rest of you as well, is yes. There is a backup, but not in the way you imagine it. You see, no one in the general Alliance Council know about this, unless they are former Chief Councilors. It is a very deep secret. There is not only a spare key, but there is also a spare Gatekeeper, so to speak. She is protected by Liliath's people in her dimension. She is aware of Jenny and her situation and everything that has come about in the last few months."*

"So when Miriha died, why didn't you put this alternate Gatekeeper into the position instead of an untried young girl with very little training?" Bob asked, his face flushed, and his arms folded firmly against his chest. He could feel his fists tightening in anger.

Ingot made calming motions with his hands. *"If Miriha had not passed the key to Jenny directly, we would have done just that. Jenny's presence at the time of Miriha's death wouldn't have necessarily meant she would be created as Gatekeeper on the spot. Had Miriha passed without giving the key to Jenny, it would have fallen off and disintegrated, so that no unauthorized person could have touched it or used it. Miriha must have thought Jenny up to the task, or the key would not have been passed. However, once it was passed, it was out of the Council's hands."*

Bob felt his arms relax and his fists unclench although he was still breathing roughly. He nodded in apology to Ingot. *"OK, that being said, how can we get ahold of the backup Gatekeeper? We need to get her key in proximation to the card,"* and he held it up for them to see. *"It is our opinion that this is some type of portal access device that can access any natural portal anywhere or something of that nature. By extension of that theory, it may even allow an individual to travel interdimensionally WITHOUT a portal."*

Ingot gasped and once more Myla and Liliath showed agitation.

"Exactly," Bob agreed. *"This could be the most dangerous thing anyone has ever seen in any history in any dimension, especially if it fell into the wrong hands. 'One ring to rule them all,' if you take my meaning."*

"You and Mervin will leave at once," Ingot said with a sigh. *"You are right of course. I will notify Sanglarka that you will be pursuing your research elsewhere, but not any of them will know where or why. We can't afford a leak about this. It also means that the rest of the scientists will temporarily be sequestered in the floors between the suites and the roof, for their own protection. If any word of any of this leaks out, it would be catastrophic."*

Merv nodded and, turning to Bob said, *"Pack your bags, kid. We're off to see the Wizard."*

Chapter 11: Teamwork

Strategy and Tactics: Brendan shifted in his seat. They had been at it for hours. Gariel had lost no time getting right to work. Desminda, Brendan, Xao Ting and Leonora sat around the table on the balcony overlooking the valley and up into the majestic snow-covered peaks that surrounded it. They were about as disparate a group of people as Brendan had ever worked with. Each had their specialties, but their commonality was that all had some kind of combat training and every one of them was dead focused on defeating the Insenium and their allies.

There were several issues on their plates, organization of the forces and resources they would be putting into play, discussing possible tactics for actual warfare, with what they knew so far about their enemy, and putting together a usable command structure including lines of communication and modes of travel. In all of this, they would be working with the Logistics, Resources and Communications team in Puerto Rico and the Science and Technology teams in Switzerland and at Alliance headquarters. It felt a little to him like walking a tightrope, juggling china teacups, while hopping up and down on one foot and whistling "Yankee Doodle" with a crocodile waiting underneath for you to fall.

It turned out that Alliance forces were in two parts, first the Troopers, an elite group similar to Special Forces in the various Earth armies and second the individual armies of various dimensions in the Alliance network who were volunteering to aid the Alliance in this vital mission. This latter turned out to be a force beyond Brendan's imagination. Before becoming a Gate Guardian, Brendan had been a fighter pilot for the Australian government. Like the others on the team, he was not a stranger to troop movements and tactics. His last mission entailed surveillance and reconnaissance in Somalia to combat piracy in the area.

But this was so much bigger than anything he had tackled in his military career. It wasn't the fate of a single country or even the planet. Billions of worlds in billions of dimensions were potential targets of the Insenium coalition. Based on latest intelligence, the Fleistians and the Groga were just a taste of what the Insenium had in store. Information retrieved in Groga mind dumps hinted at forces held in reserve by the Insenium that they hadn't even faced yet. According to Lova, Bob and Burt were both on fact finding missions at this very moment. She couldn't give them the details yet, as their reports would be somewhat sporadic, and even then, security was a high priority, due to the nature of their assignments.

The latest from Bob had been that he had integrated with his team and they were on the verge of something big. Vague as that seemed to be, it gave Brendan a certain amount of comfort, as Bob wasn't prone to exaggeration.

Burt was on a reconnaissance mission that would hopefully give them some targets and enough information to get started with, but even before that, there was so much that had to be organized.

Desminda had been extremely valuable to the team in this regard. She understood the current command structure of the Alliance Troopers and was herself, a commander in the Daringi forces, which included several other intelligent species of their planet. There was an arachnid force that originated from Tarafau's planet and sounded formidable. Brendan wasn't fond of spiders. With over ten thousand species found in Australia, over a dozen of them venomous to one degree or another, Brendan knew that spiders cause much more damage and fear just by their presence than almost anything he could think of. But blow them up to 12 and 14 feet and you have a whole new dimension of terror.

Desminda had a business-like air about her that only served to enhance her beauty. Her vivid green eyes could stare a hole through a steel plate, however, when she was vexed. Fortunately for all, this was seldom. She had a presence and self-control that Brendan found admirable.

Xao Ting was an expert in stealth fighting and had a formidable talent in the use of herbs and chemicals. Brendan had no illusions. This war would require some tactics that would be, putting it mildly, distasteful. Bio warfare had been banned by most of his planet's governments, but he didn't think for a minute that the Insenium would stop at anything to achieve their goals of domination, torture and enslavement. Xao Ting's presence was a calming influence.

He had a gentle disposition and spoke softly and seldom. When he did speak it was always after careful consideration and always added a new dimension to the discussion. Also, he was one of the few team members who were working for two teams simultaneously. He was also attached to the Science and Tech team in Switzerland where they were currently working on a delivery system for his potential chemical attacks.

Leonora was a stocky, squarely built woman, who had served in her military as well. She might have been a farm wife, with her stolid features. She kept her black hair cropped only a couple inches long and she was very matter of fact. She was impatient with busy work and was extremely athletic. She had a sharp, organized mind and could see holes or discrepancies in any pattern. She kept them on their toes, often seeing potential issues far before any of the rest of them.

Gariel was the Chief Commander of the Alliance forces and brought about 80 years' experience to the mix. Technically Burt was also a member of the team, but his current mission meant they would have to catch him up later and vice versa. Brendan felt like this was a team he could work with easily. He was their aerial combat specialist, and there had been hints that some off-world flying opportunities might present themselves. This had been a lifelong dream of his, to fly out of the bounds of gravity. He would have rather it had been under other circumstances, but if the opportunity presented itself, he would not turn it down.

Gariel stood. *"Now that we are up to speed on all of the reports, based on the most current intelligence, I wish to add one additional item to consider. There are two major things that will very much impact our planning. One is that there has been a breakthrough on Bob's team which is being assertively pursued. It could have a great influence on which of our resources will be most likely to lead the attack on the Groga and the Insenium. Secondly, Burt is on the verge of infiltrating either the Groga planet or the Insenium dimension, either of which will be very important to our strategy.*

Therefore, I want us to keep in mind that planning a single strategy will probably not be enough. Our plans could change very quickly and perhaps radically, based on what Bob and Burt discover. This is why it will be very important for us to plan for every eventuality that seems possible and perhaps a few that may seem impossible, based on current intelligence."

He looked seriously around at the faces of his team. *"Each of you has your specialty and will see the possible choices from a different point of view. Xao Ting, I have never been a fan of biological warfare, but if there is anything we can do to slow them down, make them non-functional or even kill large groups of their forces without impeding our own, I will take responsibility for any moral imprecations from any of our allies. There will be no gentle taps involved in this war. This is no-holds-barred conflict. They will not hesitate to do anything necessary to destroy us and our forces.*

Please report to Lova for instructions and departure for Switzerland. Since their first task is delivery systems for anything you come up with, that will be your first priority. I need you to report frequently on any progress."

Xao Ting stood and bowed to Gariel, turned on his heel and left for the situation room.

"Leonora, you have a keen understanding of long-distance munitions, as I understand it?"

Leonora nodded. *"If you give me access to barrage weapons and missiles, I can deploy them in ways that make sense in pretty much any situation. I will need a team of weapon masters and a list of the equipment and weapons available."*

"Gariel nodded. I think I will pair you up with Desminda for now. She is very familiar with the weaponry that will be available to you."

"I would like to take exceptions to atomic weaponry, or at least express my distaste for using them," Leonora added quickly.

"Agreed. We don't have access to anything that primitive in our arsenal. I think you will find the Alliance is in agreement."

Desminda stood. *"Are you fully packed in your MDP, per earlier instructions, Leonora? If so, I would like to depart immediately."*

Leonora nodded and stood. Without another word, Desminda laid her hand on Leonora's shoulder and they faded from view.

Brendan shook his head. Going through a gate was one thing, but he was doubtful he would ever get used to this ability of Tarafau's people; kinda scary in a cool way.

Gariel turned to Brendan. *"You're with me. You're packed? I want to introduce you to your fleet."*

Brendan goggled. *"My what?"*

"We have a large fleet of flying things. I understand that's your specialty. We are about to introduce you to your crew. Let's go." His beard wriggled agitatedly, and Brendan didn't hesitate another moment.

SCIENCE AND TECHNOLOGY Team: Adelle escorted her team to the conference room. She was excited about this opportunity to spend time with other intellects in the pursuit of new uses of technology and, like Bob, she was not a little intrigued by the potential opportunity to use alien tech.

Her laboratory and her gate were part of an isolated observatory in an unfrequented part of the Swiss Alps. She seldom had visitors. Most of the scientific world had forgotten it was here. She had basically inherited it with her Gate Guardian key, as each new Guardian did. It was difficult to get to, except by helicopter, and even then, in the winter and during spring storms it was nearly impossible to fly in.

Of course, Adelle had no issue with that. For one, she was an avid gardener and had a year-round aquaculture facility in the basement supplemented with grow lights. She also raised chickens and cattle. She had been a farm girl and had never really felt like anything but that, even during her time in the Swiss military and at university.

Even if she had not been so prepared, she could easily get supplies at Sanglarka or the other Earth gates. Luz sent her crates of fresh mangoes from time to time and Arvid was generous with large baskets of her favorite mushrooms.

She had happily shown the team around her little homestead which was currently getting ready for winter. The rest had settled in and they had enjoyed a nice lunch of garden-fresh salad, cheese and dark rye bread with fresh churned butter.

Now they settled into the conference room with full stomachs and clear heads. They hadn't spoken of their current task at lunch. Adelle insisted on leaving "sciency stuff" out of mealtimes so they could relax their minds before tackling the projects before them.

Adelle stood, smiling warmly at the group. Dhakira, Megan and Elgyra smiled back, attentively.

"Welcome to Starlight, also known as Sternenlicht," she said, gesturing in a sweeping motion, *"the Switzerland gate and my home. I am grateful to have this opportunity to work with you all, even if it must be in such dreadful circumstances. There are computer stations in each of your rooms and we have very reliable, fast broadband satellite Wi-Fi connection courtesy of the Alliance. You will also find workstations throughout the lab for anything you need. You may use any software you prefer after it has been duly scanned by my own personal virus intrusion software.*

We have several tasks to do, but we will be approaching each of them in a team format, one at a time, for now, as there are priorities we have been given by the Alliance. Our first priority will be to aid Xao Ting. We need several potential delivery systems for biological weapons. We need several options, since we don't yet know the environments or circumstances where they may be needed to be deployed.

Each of you has been chosen for your skill, intelligence, creativity and experience. This is not about experimentation and discovery or even recognition. This is the science of invention. For that reason, every possibility any of you bring forth will be explored as thoroughly and efficiently as possible, as we are also working under a deadline. Some of you work better under deadlines, stress and pressure than others. This is why you should know that we have several break areas and even soundproof rooms to allow you to retire from the group to think, meditate or even work out, if that is what works for you.

Documentation of every step in our individual processes is going to be vital; therefore, we also have a number of video cameras from different angles to record every discussion and every process as we work on our tasks. This encrypted footage will be streamed to the Alliance cloud where it will be made available to the Tactical Team and the Science team at Alliance headquarters. By streaming the feed constantly, we have a backup, if, heaven forbid this unit should be attacked or destroyed.

There is a break room kitchen stocked with healthy snacks, the makings for a salad or sandwiches for during the day. This will allow each of you to eat on whatever schedule works for you, but no food or drink will be consumed in the lab for obvious reasons.

So, for now I would like us to work in pairs. We will begin by each reading the notes of the intelligence collected so far about Groga and Fleistian physiology and any intelligence we have on either of those races. Although we don't have any hard information on the Insenium, we have an agent working on that, as we speak. You will find the current intelligence already installed on your personal Alliance tablets. You have until tomorrow morning to ingest the report information, at which time Xao Ting will be joining us. Feel free to eat as you will and rest or workout as you need to. We will begin working in pairs on our task after breakfast in the morning. Any questions?" she asked, finally.

She noticed as she looked at the three before her that each had immediately reached for their tablets. They shook their heads and as their screens lit up, each began to read.

Logistics and Communications Team: Luz bustled around the kitchen, listening to Juan greeting their guests. Aliki, Leland and Mustapha had arrived moments ago. Lova had sent them directly to the Puerto Rico gate as soon as she had sent Jenny and Tarafau on their way.

She smiled as she picked up the tray of her famous fruit punch made from tropical fruit, with a base of mango juice. She loved the opportunity to play hostess, knowing that in truth, she was so much more than that. Most people didn't know she was Juan's Guide when he had first come into his Guardian position. She liked it that way. It meant she could observe more easily with less discomfort from the other Guardians and agents. She and Juan had fallen in love as they had progressed in his training and she loved the idea of the Guide and the Guardian being married. They would soon celebrate their 10th wedding anniversary.

She carried the tray into the dining room where the dining room table had been coopted as a conference table. This had always been the case with the lodge at Sanglarka, as well. The open French doors at one end of the dining room let in the tropical breeze and the sweet aroma of both the jungle and the sea air blowing in from the coast. The large windows surrounding the house let in so much sunlight that during the hot part of the day the shades were often drawn to cool things down and spare eyes from the glare.

Aliki, Leland and Mustapha were already seated and graciously accepted the cold punch from the tray. After Juan had taken his, and Luz had been seated, Juan stood and cleared his throat.

"Since we all speak English, I have decided that we will ignore mind-speech and use vocal communication during this project. It may seem like this team is the least important of the teams who will be searching out and destroying the Insenium threat, but actually, none of the teams involved can function without us. Our job is to see to it that everything from every team is coordinated, that they have everything they need in order to complete their tasks and that communications happen seamlessly.

In addition, as a precaution, all communications from all teams, including those at Alliance Headquarters, will be streamed here and digitally stored as a backup, to be sure that, for instance if the headquarters building were attacked, little, if anything would be lost and the mission could proceed.

We will be also coordinating all necessary types of transportation as well as seeing to it that timetables are coordinated for all the stratagems put in place by the Tactical Team. When all is said and done, we are the lynchpin and we must not fail. Each of you has been chosen for your experience and skill and the ability to work closely in a coordinated team effort. Since failure is not an option, we have to get this right the first time. I don't think any of us can begin to imagine the chaos and destruction that awaits every dimension in the multiverse if we do not succeed.

Reports and requests will be coming in daily from the tactical and science teams based on their needs. It will be our job to see to it that these needs are met. An Alliance liaison will be joining us in a few days to aid us in making this happen.

We have been given access to empty MDPs that have been coded to the members of this team and will eventually be given to the supply and logistic specialists of the various military components with all of their supplies and equipment stored inside. We must see to it that all of the elements are not only assembled for easy retrieval, but that a manifest is created for each of the MDPs to be uploaded to the supply specialists' and commanders' tablets.

We will also be responsible for re-supplies and special requests. Keeping all of this straight will be a major undertaking, since the numbers we will be dealing with are beyond anything any of us have experience with.

Any questions so far?"

"Am I guessing right that this task may require some foraging and potential trading?" Leland asked.

"Absolutely. One of the reasons we, as gate Guardians have been enlisted for this is that some of the things we need may not be immediately available at Alliance Headquarters. I have given each of you a list of cooperating dimensions that have offered their support for supplies and equipment. For large orders or equipment, it will require us to take our own MDPs to where the supplies or equipment are being held for us and transport them through the gate, then offload it into the warehouse and distribute them through MDPs to the waiting forces and teams. The nice thing about this is that we won't be using trucks or other transport to get the supplies to or from where they need to be. Since each of the MDPs supplied to us are keyed to this team, we will need to key them to the various supply specialists and commanders as we release them."

Leland nodded his head with satisfaction.

"And what about communications? I'm assuming we will be using the Alliance satellite network from Earth to coordinate communications between different units. How, exactly will we be able to hide the increased activity? Earth communications networks have advanced greatly over the last few years. Won't they notice something is going on?" asked Mustapha. His somber face appeared even more serious than usual.

But Juan was ready with his answer. "It won't be a problem. The Alliance recently funded several new satellite startups that will be putting up huge amounts of data all of a sudden. Our signals will be relatively small in comparison. We also made sure that these new satellite companies are under constant scrutiny by various governmental organizations. They won't have the resources to expand their surveillance efforts enough to notice our signals, which have been blending into the other more mundane satellite communications which have been vetted as not much worth paying attention to. And finally, we have altered our dimensional signal vibrations to a point that it would be highly unusual for anyone to pay them any real attention or to be able to de-cipher them if they did. To their ears it will be just so much random noise."

Mustapha nodded, seemingly satisfied.

Aliki had been sitting there unusually silent and serious for all of this time. Finally, he said, "How secure are we here?" looking toward the open doors. "I know that there was concern about a security breach when Jenny was last here, something about photos?"

"There has been no follow up surveillance to our knowledge. We have an extensive security system, put in place by my Luz," and he nodded smiling at her. "Her previous work was in Alliance security and she has added a few special surprises of her own. The likelihood that we will have to worry is slight. That being said, our orchard workers serve a second purpose. Every one of them is a trained jungle fighter and can handle anything short of a good-sized armed force. If it came to that, I could have an Alliance Trooper battalion on the grounds at very short notice, based on our current state of affairs."

"Then I will not worry," he said, almost magically reassuming his usually cheerful air. "By the way, my lady, the punch is amazing. I must get the recipe for my Liana. She is always looking for something new to serve our guests at community celebrations." He smiled at Luz, his straight white teeth bright in his nut-brown face.

Luz smiled. This was such a interesting assortment of individuals. Both Juan and Aliki were animated and generally cheerful, although they could get serious as needed. Mustapha was not unreasonable and extremely helpful, despite the fact that he seldom smiled. He was extremely dependable and very efficient. She also knew he could be very dangerous when he had to. The thing was she also knew him to be a gentle soul, but seldom demonstrative.

Leland was pugnacious and often times you couldn't tell whether or not he was kidding as he had a dry sense of humor. Regardless, she knew him to be a man of integrity. You could count on him in any situation to be there as he was a team player. Juan had worked with all of them in the past on one project or another, and they worked well together.

Juan now looked at Mustapha. "You are our communications expert. I will rely on you to coordinate with Sanglarka regarding what additional communications equipment and arrangements you will need based on the Strategy and Tactics team's needs. I have set up a communications room in the library for your use. Right now, it is just equipped with the regular Alliance set up; however, you can commandeer anything else you feel is necessary for your use. If you need additional team members to assure 24-hour monitoring, merely put in the request with Lova and she will send you as many as you need. We have more than adequate accommodations to house and feed as many as we need to.

As far as supplies are concerned, as you fill various orders, some will be needed to be sent immediately through the gateroom and some will be processed by Leland who will be organizing necessary MDP storage requirements.

Aliki, I need you to be in charge of all transportation equipment that will be going to the various battle-staging areas. You will also be coordinating with the Strategy and Tactics team through Lova. This will require you to work with Leland as well, since he will be handling all MDP storage and organization.

We are not yet aware of what the full range of transportation requirements will be. Some of these may be interstellar transport and some will be ground based. Your job will be to coordinate delivery and storage when necessary, but we won't know specifics until we get back the surveillance and intelligence gathering reports of agents in the field, such as Burt. You have also been authorized to request help with your mission from intradimensional agents who can deal with the various supply centers for transport in the Alliance.

Your workspace will be in the harvest barn behind the mango grove. That should be an adequate amount of space, but, if it turns out not to be, we have added an additional work and loading area in the gate room. Find the black door, third from the end. There is about 15 acres of space there and we can transport any needed thing directly there. This would probably be the best assembly area for anything too non-terrestrial."

"Leland, you have been issued a couple dozen MDPs to start with. These are currently unlocked and immediately available. We will all be given the keys to these and I understand you have been trained in how to lock them and transfer the locks to specific persons. This means security of those MDPs will be one of your primary responsibilities. As with Mustapha and Aliki, as you need assistance, you can send those requests through the Sanglarka base. As you and the team you acquire will be doing the loading, you will be working in the same space as Aliki."

"I will be overseeing the operation as well as assembling the supplies for physical troop requirements, such as food, medications and first aid supplies, housing, clothing and personal weaponry. As I said before, the sheer numbers we will be dealing with will require each of us to be on our toes. This means that at the end of every day and at any time during the day when it becomes necessary, I will need reports on your progress. Please use the tablets to record every step you take in your process, so that, if something unforeseen should happen to any of us, we could quickly be up to speed on where you are in your process, so the work can continue. For this reason, not only are all of our tablets connected to my main networking tablet, but they are all streaming to Sanglarka and Alliance headquarters. This may sound like callousness, but we all know that we can't afford to be interrupted in our work. Too much depends on us.

Be absolutely sure that you have enough help to do what needs doing. Lova assures me that we can have as much help as we require and that our team is an Alliance priority."

They all nodded solemnly.

Luz gathered their empty glasses and walked over to Juan, her tray in one hand, and put her arm around his waist, looking up at him. He smiled warmly at her and kissed the top of her head, unabashed at the others in the room. *"How'd I do?"* he sent to her in mindspeech.

"Brilliant, as usual, my love," she sent back, beaming up at him. He gave her another squeeze around her waist and said to the others aloud, "Let me show you to your workspaces. We will have lunch in about an hour and supper will be at around 6 pm. Around here, breakfast and supper are the main meals. Feel free to eat lunch and snacks as you will. There are plenty of choices in the pantry and refrigeration unit. Our hacienda hands will be

in and out of the house. They are trustworthy and you need not fear to ask them for help at any time when it is something outside of your appointed work areas. They have been given instructions to stay away from the library and the harvest barn. They have their own apartments and supply buildings in a separate compound near the gate and the mango grove."

Juan led them to the library, continuing to talk to them as they went, making sure they knew what facilities and resources were available within the hacienda. Luz had her own chores to see to. Putting the glassware into her dishwasher and wiping off the table, she left to give instructions to her workers. It had begun, and she also had her own instructions to perform.

Chapter 12: Here There Be Dragons

Bob and Mervin stepped out of a gateway and the view immediately took his breath away. Merv had warned him not to step off of the gateway platform, and Bob was grateful for the warning, as they had stepped through the gate onto a platform the size of his master bedroom at home. This would have seemed like plenty of room, but it was on the side of a cliff that dropped off into a chasm that, from his viewpoint, looked bottomless. A forceful wind whistled through the pass to one side of them, but not quite hard enough to blow them from their seemingly precarious perch.

"You'll want to stay well back, against the cliff face," Merv said with a grin. "Our transportation will require some room for us to be able to board." He put a silver whistle to his lips that made nearly no sound as he blew through it. Like a dog whistle, Bob thought.

Sure enough, in a few moments, there was the sound of very large wings flapping in their direction, approaching like an oncoming city bus, only with a wingspan that would have encompassed his entire home workshop. The blue green dragon glided the rest of the way, finally tucking in his wings and landing almost daintily onto the platform.

On the back of the dragon were two saddles, one behind another made of some type of pale leather. Down the side facing them was a rope ladder that reached almost to the ground.

"Bob, meet Anente, our host. He will, um, escort us to his home where we will prepare to meet the alternate Gatekeeper and her family."

Anente turned his huge head to Bob, looking at him from that side of his head with one huge eye of green and orange with large, vertical, black-slitted pupils. "Greetings," he said vocally. His voice was surprisingly soft, like Liliath's mindspeech voice. "Let us get you to the lair and we can chat in comfort."

Bob followed Mervin up the rope ladder gingerly, not wishing to injure this beautiful creature by a misstep. Anente chuckled. "You need not be so gentle. Dragon hide, though soft to the touch is actually quite tough. Are we all belted in? Then let us depart."

Anente turned toward the edge of the platform and, bunching power-ful legs, sprang off into nothingness. The air pulled at them, leaning them back in their saddles. Bob was very glad for the straps that held them in their seats. With a loud crack, Anente spread his wings and they glided to a more level flight and then, with slow flaps of his beautiful blue veined wings, they sped as straight as an arrow towards what looked like the epito-me of a fairytale castle on the top of a mountain peak. From their height, in the sunlight that streamed from a bright blue sky, he could see a road that wound round the mountainside towards the castle.

Under the castle appeared a huge cavernous entry way into which they glided, with nary a sound. Anente landed softly, without jarring his passen-gers.

Bob looked about him in open wonder. The cavern sparkled and glowed from the light coming in from the entrance. Impressive stalactites and stalagmites reminded him of the decorative columns of an ancient tem-ple. The stone floor was agate-like and polished, he imagined, by eons of comings and goings by the huge dragons. The ceiling was embedded with crystals and another tunnel-like opening in the ceiling flooded the area with additional light.

As they dismounted, a few people who had been waiting at the en-trance ran forward to unstrap the saddles and remove them to a huge rack that was adorned with several more saddles of differing sizes, shapes and colors. From the back of the cavern a delegation approached of several men and women in flowing garments of what might have been silk, in an array of subdued colors. The woman at the front of the group moved ahead to Merv and Bob.

"Welcome, Mervin and our new friend, Bob Reid of Earth. I am Elwithe Starbringer. This place is Winethia and you are on planet Donali of the dimension Totania. We are glad to have you here and we stand ready to aid you in such a dire and compelling cause. We won't keep you waiting for a welcome banquet at this time, but you will be escorted by Melitta to meet with the Gatekeeper."

A young woman in light blue robes came forward and held out her hand to shake. *"Please follow me,"* she sent. She beckoned and turned, leading the way up a well-lit tunnel into the back of the cavern. The lighting that was a continuous strip along the ceiling of the cavern almost appeared painted onto the smooth rock. The incline was gentle until they came to a flight of stairs leading both up and down. They ascended the wide stairs to a landing and up another flight until they came to a tall, wide set of double doors.

The great room they entered was the size of a tennis court. The floor was a gold and white polished marble and the ceiling was high. Occasionally along the walls were cushioned chairs and love seats interspaced with small end tables. Double doors on the opposite walls were open and appeared to lead into a long wide hallway.

High up on the walls on one side were tall windows about 6 feet tall and ranging all along that wall. The light that spilled unobscured from those windows made rainbows on the floor and the opposite wall due to the prismatic glass that edged each of them. Pastoral scenes of forest glens, meadows and lakes travelled around the walls below the windows. On the wall beside them was a carpeted stairway that led up to another level.

Melitta continued up the staircase and, gesturing to her right, led them into another room. This appeared to be a sitting room, furnished with cushioned divans of burgundy plush fabric. This room was also lighted by sunlight streaming through windows similar to those in the great hall.

Portraits of various persons and dragons hung here and there. In the center of the rectangle framed by the divans and chairs was a woven carpet depicting a flower garden. Obviously, this was a place of rest, but not necessarily a place to be casual. It was what in the 1800's on Earth would have been called a "drawing room", or even earlier, a "with-drawing room". On the inner wall was an ornately carved wooden door with a brass-colored handle.

Melitta motioned for them to be seated and left the room. Bob sighed as he sat. He hadn't been prepared in any possible way for this. He wasn't sure what he had expected, but this wasn't in it. Merv sat back in a cushioned chair, not quite sprawling in his casual way.

However, they both stood when a petite young woman walked through the door. As small as she was, she held herself with quiet dignity, calm brown eyes in a face the color of mahogany, curly blue-black hair that hung unbound to her waist. She wore a loose gown of burgundy subtly piped with gold around the modestly scooped neckline. And there, on her neck was the Gatekeeper's key, identical to the one Jenny wore around her neck. Every Guardian had a similar key, but the design of the Gatekeeper's key was unique, a flower petal pattern that spiraled into the center, the petals getting smaller and smaller until they disappeared.

"Greetings, I am Anela." she sent with a gentle smile. *"Please sit. Let us speak in comfort. I understand you come from the Alliance on a mission of great urgency. Therefore, let us not stand on ceremony. Speak freely. I would do anything within my power to repay the kindness and vigilance of the Alliance in behalf of our dimension."*

"Thank you, Gatekeeper." Merv sent in reply. *"This is Bob Reid, my companion in this quest, and I am Mervin Wyliit. We come from the Science and Technology team at Alliance headquarters. We are here because we may have made a discovery that could change the way we approach the war ahead of us. It involves your key."*

Her hand went up reflexively to her neck.

"My key? Whatever for?" she sent in obvious confusion. *"I don't understand."*

"Gatekeeper, are you aware of your counterpart? Did you hear that Miri-ha is no longer the main Gatekeeper?" sent Bob.

Her face went still; her eyes large in her face and sorrow in her eyes. She nodded. *"I understand she gave her life for the Alliance. I loved her like a sister. She is one of the few who knew of my existence. I have yet to meet the new Gatekeeper. I understand she took on the key under very trying and unusual circumstances. She has my sympathy as I also know she has only the bare essentials in her training."*

"Exactly." Bob sent, wanting to sympathize, but his concern for Jenny was making it difficult. *"We may have discovered something that will make her task even more dangerous and could mean the eventual triumph of the Insenium. If we do not figure this out and quickly, it may not matter what other forces and resources we have at our command. My suspicion is that this discovery may make the Gate Network obsolete and render it useless in defending the dimensions connected to it."*

"I understand you have facilities that we can use to work on this?" Merv had straightened in his seat and leaned forward, eyes on Anela.

She nodded. *"If you don't mind working with a somewhat grouchy dragon. Cornelium is particular about who enters his private domain, but we have made arrangements with him and, in this case, he is as interested as you are in this potential threat.*

We have arranged for quarters for you near the laboratory. I assume I will be needed, as I can't detach the key from my neck?"

"Yes. We would have used Jenny's key, if it hadn't been for the fact that she is intrinsic to all of this and we can't afford to interrupt her training at this key point. Everyone on all teams is working around the clock to see to it that we don't get caught unawares when the Insenium finally makes its move. You might consider changing into more casual clothing, as I am not really sure what we will have to put you through," agreed Bob.

"Very well. Melitta will escort you to your suites and then to the laboratory, where you may acquaint yourself with Cornelium. I will be along soon, after I change into something more appropriate." With that, she rose, motioning to Melitta, who had been seated in a chair along the wall waiting for Anela's next request.

Melitta gestured for them to follow and took them back down the stairway into the great room and through the double doors into a long corridor. Once again, paintings and what might have been needlework adorned the walls as they walked along the carpeted hall lighted by the light-strip they had seen in the tunnel coming up to what Bob could have only described as a castle. About halfway down the hallway a stairwell presented itself and they ascended two floors to yet another corridor. This one however was short with only a few very large doors down its length and a set of huge double doors at the end.

"These two rooms are for you," she said, unlocking each door with a finger touch, followed by the snick of a lock disengaging. *"Please press your finger on this metal pad for me."*

They did so and there was a soft chime. *"These doors are now attuned to your personal vibration and will only unlock for you and the servant who will attend to your needs."*

Bob whistled in appreciation. *"Nice tech."*

Melitta grinned. *"Cornelium will be gratified to hear you appreciate it. About twenty turns ago, he had all locks on the doors in the castle removed and replaced with these special locks. They are attuned to the unique bio-vibrations of each user of that space. I imagine he will attune you to the lock on the laboratory as well, but for now, we will have to knock. Do you wish to go straight to the lab or freshen up a bit first?"*

Bob looked at Merv pointedly, and Merv nodded. *"We'll take the first option, please."* Merv sent. *"Bob will probably have a seizure if he has to wait another moment to get to work."* As urgent as this all was, Bob had no desire to kick his heels in his room. And the chance to work with a dragon and a wizard (even if he wasn't really magical, although he knew Merv had done some pretty magical things) was almost more than his excitement could handle.

Melitta nodded and walked with them to the double doors and knocked with a knocker on the huge wooden doors three times.

The lock in the door snicked and Melitta opened it, waving them through.

Bob gasped. The room was huge, as it had to have been, since towering before them was a brown dragon with gold highlights to his scales. The huge eyes were amber with green flecks and the black slits were narrowed. It was true that it was sometimes difficult to tell a dragon's mood by their facial expressions, unless their teeth were bared and smoke was coming from their nostrils, but the eyes seemed to say, "Who are you and why are you disturbing me?"

To his astonishment, the dragon spoke vocally in slightly accented English, "So these are the Alliance technicians?" There was a certain amount of disdain in the voice and the use of the word "technicians", instead of scientists, was intended to be demeaning. Bob couldn't help himself. He grinned. In the university he had been assigned as a lab assistant to a professor who was like this and she had been one of his favorite teachers.

"You know me, you old lizard," said Merv, also grinning up at the huge dragon. "Cornelium, allow me to introduce you to my friend, Bob. He is an Earthling and is the one who put up the theory that this," he held up the card, "is a threat to the entire Dimensional Alliance. We'd be honored if you would join us in exploring the potential threat and advising us as we work on a solution to the problem."

Cornelium nodded to Bob and Merv. "OK, so, Merv, you know the rules. Bob, there will be a space available for the two of you to be able to work in peace. I may peek in from time to time to see if you need any help. No food in the lab, no pranks and keep your area clean as I don't allow servants in here. I recognize you must solve this conundrum and why," he sighed, the metallic smell of his breath stirring the hair on Bob's moustache, "you MUST use my facility. However, I will not stand for any hijinks. Do you understand?" At this, he looked intensely at Bob, and Bob nodded quickly in agreement.

"Well then, let me get you settled in. I do have a break room that doubles as a conference room, not that I often have invaders in my lab, but from time to time I do consult with other like-minded beings. He led them through the wide spaces between tables that were as high as Bob's nose. On the tables were machines that blinked, buzzed and whirred, as well as screens with indecipherable symbols on them. On a couple were cages with small creatures in them. Science experiments or pets, Bob wondered to himself. They went through a wide arch into a huge space that included a chaise, similar to the one Liliath used in the council chamber and several regular chairs in varying sizes from troll sized to Arvid sized.

A low table (or at least low to the dragon) stood in the center, devoid of any detritus. Two levels of counters ran along one wall with what looked like a glassed-in lab sample refrigerator with numerous types of what Bob assumed to be food displayed in neat rows of shelves. A cupboard that might be a pantry or supply cupboard ran along one entire wall of the space and a couple desks, one dragon sized and one that would have accommodated Bob or Merv, stood on the third wall.

"This is our meeting and break space. We've provided a variety of foodstuffs and snacks here, as most of the time we are loath to leave the lab for the general dining room of the castle, especially when we are in the midst of a breakthrough. I insist on a time out for every being working in my lab at least 2 times a day. More frequently is up to you. Non-compliance means an enforced," and here he grinned, showing his impressive rows of white teeth and fangs, "break of at least 2 hours away from the lab.

I keep the lab available all hours of the day or night, but once again, a sleep break of whatever is normal for you is required at least once in a day. Any questions?"

Bob and Merv both shook their heads.

"I understand the Gatekeeper will be attending us here in a few minutes. I understand her key is central to your project. I will insist that she be treated with respect and honor. She has a quick mind, and she visits the laboratory from time to time as part of her ongoing education. She is an able student and I won't tolerate any ill-handling of her. Is that understood?"

Once again Merv and Bob nodded solemnly.

"Well then, let me show you to your area of the lab."

Sure enough, there was a human sized area with tables of a normal standing height and stools for things that required seating for stability as they worked. The tables were equipped with familiar lab equipment, including monitors they could sync their tablets to for a larger display. Everything was pristine and orderly as any good lab should be, in Bob's humble opinion. He got the feeling he could work here with confidence. He would miss Ignatius, but he knew his partners of the lab at the Alliance would take good care of him. He had explained to Ignatius in mindspeech what he was about to do, and Ignatius had just told him to "be good."

He invoked Fidget from the MDP. "This is Fidget, my lab assistant. Fidget, meet Cornelium."

Fidget looked up at the huge dragon. "Hello, Cornelium. How can I assist you today?" he said.

"Hurrrummm, little bot. You may assist me by keeping these gentlemen well occupied and out of my way, unless necessary. Can you do that, Fidget?"

"Indeed, sir. I am sure they will be very busy with their current task and when it is completed they must urgently return to Alliance headquarters. Will that do?"

Cornelium cocked his head and then said. "That will do nicely, Fidget. Bob and Merv, allow me to introduce my lab assistant. Flitter, come here!"

Into the room flew a lizard (not big enough to be designated as a dragon) about the same height as Fidget. Flitter was cobalt blue with a ruff like a raptor and leathery wings like a dragon. His black eyes blinked and his head tilted in what Bob felt might be curiosity. *"Yes, Cornelium?"* he sent in mindspeech. *"How may I help you?"*

"Flitter, these are Bob, Mervin and Fidget," Cornelium replied, pointing at each one in turn. "They will be using this lab area for an indeterminate amount of time. Please be aware of them and assist them whenever I am not employing you at some task. Bob, does Fidget communicate in mindspeech?"

Bob stared. How could a robot, regardless how sophisticated use mindspeech? "No, Cornelium. I was unaware that was possible."

"Would you mind a slight upgrade? As long as you don't share the technology, I would be happy to 'tweak' Fidget a bit."

Bob stood there in shock. "Of course; that would be gratifying. It would be very helpful in my work with the Alliance. But may I ask one thing? The current Gatekeeper, Jenny Japhet has a second version of this bot for her use and support. May I have your permission to pass on this upgrade with her next update? I promise not to ever do that without your express permission, but this would be extremely helpful for her as well."

"I would agree to that. Of course, it is my honor to do anything I can to be of assistance in protecting and aiding the Gatekeeper. I can see how this little tweak would be helpful to someone of her particular skill. It's based on the unique vibration of mental communication. It isn't anything all that mysterious, just a little trick I stumbled upon years ago. We moved past robotics a century or so ago, but the science is still good for something."

"Say thank you to the nice dragon," Bob said to Fidget.

"Thank you, nice dragon," Fidget said compliantly. "How soon can we begin?"

Chapter 13: The Rock and That Hard Place

B urt sprang up from the dirty street, his quarterstaff twirling even before he was completely on his feet. The club whistled again over his head. He couldn't believe he had let the troll-like Groga officer trip him like that. He had ducked under the club, swinging and connecting to the creature's back and had heard the satisfying crack of what was probably a rib, and then found himself on his back on the ground.

The Groga grunted in surprise and grimaced in pain, switching his club to the other hand. Burt smiled. He HAD connected. Good. As he sprang to his feet, he watched the Groga's eyes for a signal of what was coming. Burt circled with the Groga.

The watching crowd consisted mostly of slaves. Unlike in the arena, none were cheering. It was almost eerily silent in the circle around the two combatants.

The Groga swung at Burt's head. Burt ducked the roundabout swing and pivoting on his right foot, landed another loud crack, this time on the Groga's side. The resulting crunch of bone on the same side as the already damaged back was satisfying and the effect was evident from the loud roar of pain from the Groga. His pig-like eyes were scrunched up, which gave Burt another opening. Two rapid back and forth whacks connected with both shins. The Groga howled and flailed blindly with his club, his eyes streaming with tears of pain.

It was obvious that he hadn't broken those legs like small tree trunks, but shins were very sensitive to pain. Burt didn't relax. His eyes were focused on the Groga's face to see him telegraph his next move. Which is why he didn't see the Groga he hadn't realized was behind him, grab his arms and twist them behind his back. Man! That hurt!

The Groga he had been fighting dropped his club. He roared something unintelligible to the one who was holding a still struggling Burt firmly while he secured his hands with some type of flexible mechanism that clicked shut around his wrists snugly. The Groga then shoved Burt to the ground and replied in the same guttural language.

Finally, the Groga who had captured Burt turned his attention to Burt, who was glaring up at him, his chin thrust out and his brows furrowed.

"He hit me first!" Burt sent with his best playground swagger. He doubted the Groga would believe him or care, but he wasn't going to give them any reason to think him cowardly or intimidated. Neither would fit his plan.

"Puny human slave. You have earned the wrath of the Groga. You will be taken to the Groga-ha to report this grievous assault. Do not press it further or I will let Nonar use that club on your head." Nonar grinned at this, showing bloody teeth. Burt wanted to grin back, as the first contact his staff had made was to Nonar's mouth. But he stood sullenly, his head erect and allowed himself to be marched to see the Groga-ha, which he assumed was the commandant of the camp.

The still silent crowd parted to let them through. Some of those faces looked dumbfounded, others shot him encouraging glances. He doubted many of them entertained thoughts of going one-on-one with a Groga, but they didn't seem upset to see one do so. They were probably fairly certain that Burt was going to his death or worse, but they couldn't help but admire Burt's attempt even though many probably thought it extremely foolish. He would have had to agree with that assessment.

They frog-marched him along the city streets, drawing curious eyes. At one point they went by the leathermaker's shop. He nodded acknowledgement from his usual seat and then shook his head sadly. Burt grinned at him which made his eyebrows shoot up in astonishment. They passed the market square and over to the Groga encampment. The Groga going about their tasks completely ignored the three of them. Evidently, they had learned to keep their nose out of the business of other Groga. Probably a good decision, when he thought about it.

They marched past barracks and a training ground where several Groga were practicing with their blasters at moveable dummies on ropes and pulleys. The slaves to the side who ran the pulleys never looked up from their task. Finally, they came to the first permanent structure he had seen on this side of the city. It was made of black stone bricks chinked with grey mortar. There were no windows, which seemed a bit ominous to Burt's way of thinking.

The brute who had tied his wrists together shoved him in ahead of them. Burt didn't even bother with a withering look as it would have been lost on this grunt. Rather, he looked about him intent on gathering every bit of detail his mind could absorb. Later he would use his dastardly alien tech to suck the memories out of his head without erasing them. They had been stored and would be transmitted as soon as he was somewhere connected to the Alliance communications network. This was typically how he wrote his reports which, to Burt's ongoing amusement, had been praised for their detail and accuracy.

The room looked pretty much like any command center he had ever been in. Maps on the walls, tables strewn with documents, and Groga at desks apparently writing reports seemed so familiar. A Groga writing? He had in no way ever imagined such a thing. Of his previous observation they were without exception, brutish and slow. However, he agreed it must have made sense for at least some of them to be literate, else how could they get their orders and send in reports to their superiors? The frowns of concentration on the two clerks' faces, however belied any great intelligence.

They marched him through the reception area without any of the clerks even looking up from their work. Through a door on the other side they entered a dim hallway. The reception area had been lit fairly well with lamps, but this hallway was only lit with an occasional wall fixture. They halted several doors down. The guard that had brought them here scratched at the door jam. There was a sound that sounded like they were being gruffly invited in.

They entered a small office with one desk and no chairs besides the one behind the desk. The head Groga gave what Burt imagined was a salute to the Groga behind the desk, his fist resting on his head with his clasped fingers facing the front. Burt guessed this must be the Groga-ha. He returned the salute sloppily and glared at the three of them, obviously waiting for an explanation of this interruption.

The Groga shook Burt roughly by his shoulder and proceeded to choke out some kind of explanation of their purpose in the growling Groga language. When he stopped his tirade, he folded his arms and the beaten Groga hung his head in reluctant shame, shooting the tale-telling Groga a vicious look under his brows. "I wouldn't go down any dark alleys any day soon, buddy. It looks like your friend here means business," Burt thought, hearing an evil laugh in his head.

"So, miserable little humanoid slave. You think to insult the great Groga Empire with your puny attempt? This we will NOT allow. You will eventually suffer an ignominious death at our hands, but first we will humiliate you. I see Nonar has brought your insignificant little stick with him. Very well. You will get your little stick back soon. In the meantime, you will be held in the dark room while we arrange for your defeat." The Groga-ha put his hands behind his back, rocking on his heals and nodding. He was confident he had subdued the pride of this gnat of a human.

He barked an order to the Groga still holding Burt by his bonds and waved them off, beckoning with the other hand with an ominous look to poor Nonar. Frankly Burt was grateful he was going to a cell, rather than to be in Nonar's place.

The cell he was shoved into by the gloating Groga was about five feet square. No windows. No lights. Wooden door reinforced with steel bands and the lock was on the outside. He waited until the door was fully closed and pulled a small flashlight, a water bottle and a ration bar out of his MDP. There wasn't even a chamber pot or anyplace to sit. He sat on the floor to wait.

Jenny awoke with a start. Something was wrong. She had no idea why, but she had dreamed of Bob and Burt in completely different circumstances. Not only did the dreams seem real, but the places and people she had dreamed about were completely unknown to her. Chidwi's usual warm lump lay by her feet. She realized she was sweating as if she had been on a five-mile run in the jungle. She got up in the darkened house, managing not to wake Chidwi, turned on a light and put on her bathrobe and slippers, grabbed some clothing and quietly made her way to the shower.

She felt an odd tingling across her shoulders and the back of her neck. It made her shiver and she couldn't help but wonder what had been happening to her. It was nearly the end of her time with Tarafau's family. She had seen many wonders and she had learned so much. In her most recent exercise, she had been practicing mindful seeing. She had realized soon after making her major breakthrough that her vision was changing. Not as if her eyesight got sharper, more like she was noticing things that had been there all along, but she didn't know to pay attention to them.

She let the hot water run for a long time grateful she could do that without guilt. Tarafau often said that the planet gave everything you could need if you helped her instead of ripping what you wanted from her. Jenny was beginning to understand what he meant. The Daringi and the other species on the planet lived very well in harmony with the resources and wonders their planet provided. Of course, it didn't hurt that they understood the principle of reaping.

You only get back what you put in, she thought, agreeing. Her dad used to laugh and say, "So many people are waiting for their ship to come in. Unfortunately, they never sent a ship out in the first place."

She toweled off thoroughly and dressed, feeling much more awake. She decided that, since most of the household were probably sleeping, she would go down to the workout room and breathe for awhile, hoping to center herself before the rest of the household arose.

She was startled, however, when she got there and realized that she wasn't the only one who had come down to the workout room in the middle of the night. Amenia was working the forms, quietly gliding from one stance to another with perfect grace. At the sight of Jenny, she stopped, not even breathing quickly.

"Why Jenny! What are you doing up at this beastly hour?"

"I could say the same about you, Mom." Jenny had taken to calling Amenia Mom when Elizabeth had encouraged her to do so. It was nice having a second mom and Amenia seemed happy to answer to "Mom" when Jenny called her that.

"I have an early appointment with a client," she answered. *"What about you?"*

"Bad dream. At least I think it was a dream..." Jenny hesitated. *"Maybe you could help me sort it out? If you're finished with your forms, that is."*

Amenia smiled and sat on the mat, gesturing for Jenny to join her.

"Your dreams? Hmmm... strange dreams are pretty normal at the stage you're in. Tell me about them."

Jenny complied, telling her first about the dream of Bob working with Merlin the Great Magician to start. Something about a card and Jenny and another Gatekeeper. And then...dragons and castles and the other Gatekeeper. She described the beautiful young woman and Amenia just nodded and waited for her to continue.

"Then there was Burt. He was in the Groga city near the Fleistian fortress. He had sneaked in and was gathering intelligence and then, for no reason I could fathom, he picked a fight with a Groga guard with a big old club. He beat the Groga, of course, but another one grabbed him from behind and tied him up and now he is in a small, black prison cell, waiting for his doom. Some dreams, huh?"

"May I come into your mind? I need to see something. It's important. Something you said..."

Jenny nodded and assumed her relaxed breathing posture, falling into her breathing patterns and her own mind more easily than falling asleep.

In her mind, she waited at the portcullis of the keep, on the drawbridge. Amenia appeared before her. "May I approach?" she said aloud in English. In their sessions it was always this way. Because she was already in her mind, they could communicate directly, each moving their mouths in regular speech patterns.

"Enter, milady." Jenny replied with a grin. The armored knight who stood beside the portcullis saluted as they entered the keep.

"So where do you keep your dreams?"

"My what?"

"Everyone has a place where dreams are kept. Even the ones they think they've forgotten are all in there. Where do you keep yours, I wonder?"

Jenny thought about this. If this was a place where thoughts and memories were all kept, as she had been taught, then there would be a physical-seeming representation of that. Jenny had always been a voracious reader. She had the Dewey decimal system memorized. She could always find a book without any help and as a professional ghost writer she had often ignored the search engines and went straight to her local library. There was something about the peace of the place that invited thought and creativity.

"Come with me," she said with growing confidence. She realized she knew exactly where to go. The library building in her keep was larger than any other building she could see, even larger than the huge, Hollywood style mansion down a scenic drive lined with fountains, flowers and trees behind the market square.

They entered the doors carved with the white tree of Gondor. "All that is gold does not glitter, not all those who wander are lost," she quoted softly. And as she did, the doors slowly opened. Inside was what Jenny would consider to be heavenly. The smells of old books, printers' ink, and paper oiled by many fingers, leather and wood, all mingled to make the aroma that was like no other.

"They won't be in the stacks," she told Amenia. "They will be in the vault." She walked confidently into the administrator's office. Every library had one. There, behind the wall at the back of the reception area was a large room containing a vault, much like a bank. Jenny didn't hesitate. This was *her* library, after all. She used the verbal key, "Frodo lives." The door swung open and there, inside, were rows and rows of security boxes as far as her eye could see. Sure enough, right by the door was a box labeled, "Last Night's Dreams". "Curiouser and curiouser," she said aloud as she reached for the box.

Amenia laid a hand on hers. "Don't open it. Just let me hold it for a moment."

"Hmm," she said aloud. "This IS very curious. There is not a shred of anything in your dreams last night that sounds like anything you told me." She laid the box down and held up a finger, forestalling Jenny's objections.

"Do you have any idea what this means?" Amenia said, her eyes wide. "You, Jenny, are a Nexus."

"A what?"

"A Nexus is a communications link."

"I'm familiar with the word," Jenny interrupted.

You are a Nexus, capitalized. That means a person who can go beyond mind speech. You didn't dream those scenarios. You reached out across dimensions and pulled them from the minds of Bob and Burt. You must care for them very much to be able to do that your first time out."

"My first time...what are we talking about again?"

"I knew you had abilities we hadn't discovered yet. I just had no idea they extended this far. You, when you learn how to access this deliberately, will be able to communicate across dimensions in real time. I still think there is more to you, but for today we should focus on this one thing. You need to return to Sanglarka in two days, and I don't want to let you loose until you have at least mastered the basics of this new gift. I'm rescheduling all of my appointments for today. Cut the connection and go get Chidwi. I think she will be a great focus for this little trick of yours."

Jenny came to herself still sitting on the floor next to Amenia who leaned over and gave her a huge hug. *"You never cease to amaze me, Jenny. Go get Chidwi, get some food into you, as I see the sun has come up. Then meet me back here. I will let the rest of the family know what is going on and they will give us the privacy we need to see to this. I can't wait to see Tarafau's face!"* she sent, beaming.

Chapter 14: A Fine Kettle of Fish

Burt laid his ration bar with the paper folded around it on the floor next to him and took a big swig of water from his water bottle. The Alliance had developed a nutrition bar that was not only high in calories and all of the nutrition a humanoid might require in a day, but they were seriously filling and satisfactorily chewy. They even tasted pretty good. Burt had stocked up with his favorite flavor, salted caramel. He put his water bottle into his MDP and reached down for the bar he had laid down moments before only to find it gone.

"Huh?" He pulled out his flashlight and once more scanned the room. He was alone and all that was left of his ration bar were a few crumbs in the shape of the outer wrapping on the floor. He scratched his head. Was there any chance he had eaten it and not noticed it? But if that was the case, what had he done with the wrapper?

He examined the floor more closely and discovered another pile of crumbs, this one, in one corner of the cell, was slightly circular, as if it had fallen off of a plate. Burt had been around in the dimensions enough to know that not everything was as it seemed. He walked nonchalantly back over to his place on the floor. Out of his MDP he pulled a bag of kettle chips. He liked these particularly because of their loud crunchiness. He opened it with a pop and then proceeded to toss chips one at a time, spaced out by 5 seconds each time toward the corner where the circle of crumbs lay.

To his surprise, the chip closest to the corner just disappeared, followed by a crunching sound. And then, even more surprising, a purr, similar to a cat began. One by one the chips nearest the circle of crumbs disappeared from sight. More crumbs were now in evidence around the spot.

"OK, give it up! Whoever or whatever you are, the jig is up. I know you're there. Come on out. I won't hurt you." A flat round spot peeled itself away from the wall and then swelled, changing color to a squished golden-brown orb with two huge eyes and a huge mouth to go with it. It was about the size of half a cat. "What the heck! Where'd you come from? How'd you do that? Are you kidding me?"

The little golden orb person just blinked at him.

"OK, settle down," he told himself. "It doesn't understand you. You're scaring it. Maybe mindspeech."

"Hello, little guy. Where did you come from? I couldn't see you."

"Come from walllll. Eats and eats. Food good. Person kind. Feed BaaGah. Feed BaaGah more?"

"Wait. You were in the wall?"

"BaaGah was the wall. Now BaaGah is BaaGah."

"You were IN the wall?"

"BaaGah WAS the wall. You see?"

"I didn't see you until you peeled off. Can you do it with other things? Not just a wall?"

He set the chip bag down. Suddenly BaaGah sprouted two chubby legs under his round body and walked to the chip bag. He sort of melted into the bag. The bag didn't seem to be any thicker or heavier when Burt picked it up to examine it.

"You still in there, BaaGah?"

"BaaGah not in bag. BaaGah is bag. Now sit bag down, pleasssse?"

Burt sat the bag down and bemusedly watched BaaGah melt away from the bag, leaving it intact.

"BaaGah eat bag? Eat bag pleasssse?"

"Sure thing. You earned it with that stunt. I'll pour them out for...uh...never mind."

Too late. BaaGah had eaten the chips, bag and all.

"Can BaaGah do that with my pant leg? The becoming thing, not the eating thing..." He pointed at the leg of his pants.

"Yes! See? BaaGah show."

Once again, he sprouted short stubby legs without any discernable legs or toes and got close to Burt's leg. Burt didn't feel the pant leg change at all in texture or weight, but BaaGah became the pant leg.

"And you can communicate to me while you are something else? That's amazing. It might be good to have an invisible companion who is easy to tote along. What do you eat, anyway?"

"BaaGah eats stuff. All kinds of stuff. You have stuff?"

"I do indeed, BaaGah. Lots of stuff. Friends?"

"FRIENDS!!!! FRIENDSSSSES!" BaaGah shouted into Burt's mind. The little golden melon-shaped creature was quite beside himself. *"BaaGah never had friends before! BaaGah will be friends with..."* he trailed off.

"Burt. Friends with Burt, BaaGah. Do you want to be BaaGah again or would you rather be my pant leg?"

" Friend, Burt, has warm leg. BaaGah stay, for now. Tell BaaGah when to change?"

"Yes, I will. I wonder, if someone or something hit my leg, would it hurt you?"

"BaaGah no hurt. BaaGah is between spaces. BaaGah no hurt or jiggle or burn or cut when BaaGah is something else. BaaGah safe. Safe being something else, always."

"Ah, I see. Well, for now, be safe. I don't know when..." he trailed off as he heard a key rattle in a lock.

Burt put his flashlight and water bottle into his MDP and stood. He would not have his captors see him cowering in a corner of his cell. Even though the Groga had taken no thought for his comfort or necessities, he had been fed, watered and entertained the entire time and he had no idea how long it had been since they first locked him in.

The door swung open and Burt feigned being shocked by the sudden light, though dim, that streamed into the tiny cell. The Groga that stood framed in the door gestured for Burt to come out and he complied. He didn't make any sign that he might wish to escape. First, an unarmed prisoner would stand no chance against even one Groga (well, Burt amended, maybe *most* unarmed prisoners wouldn't stand a chance) and second, his plan was working out exactly as he had planned, with the exception of the little creature riding along as part of his pant leg.

They emerged out of the black stone building into the dark of night. Well, maybe it was night. Coming from a lighted building, this planet always seemed like it was midnight. It appeared they were heading for the training ground.

There was quite a crowd gathered to watch whatever was about to happen. The guard shoved him through the gate in the fence surrounding the grounds. The Groga-ha was standing imperiously just a little forward of the practice dummies that were stacked haphazardly on the ground where before they had been the moving targets for Groga blasters.

"This bag of dragon manure seems to think he is up to beating a Groga with just a stick!" he broadcast to the crowd. There was a roar of derision from the waiting troops.

"This dung heap slave would have us believe he is a great hero of legend. We know that this is not possible because only the Groga could have that title. We will prove this on his miserable puny body. Who will be the first to challenge him?"

A unified chant came up from the watching crowd, "Orgu! Orgu! Orgu! Orgu!"

The crowd went instantly silent when a beast of a Groga stepped forth onto the training ground. He stood about 7 feet tall, one big giant muscle of a creature. Now, Burt had seen trolls before, of course. There was a planet of very nice ones in one of the dimensions. However, this looked more like something out of a wild tale. His piggy eyes glared in bloodshot hatred. His round head was covered with black bristles and his nose looked like a spoiled mushroom had been casually stuck off center of his face. He didn't walk as much as stomp across the grass to stand beside the Groga-ha.

"Our champion stands before us. You all know the rules, but for the benefit of he who is about to be gloriously defeated by Orgu the Vast, here they are: Fight using anything available to you, ("including sticks", he added with a snicker). Stay on the training ground. This fight is until death or unconsciousness. Are we clear? Even if we aren't, you may begin when I exit the training field."

He handed Burt his "stick" with another chuckle and strode out of the training ground gate, turned and nodded.

Burt did not wait to see what Orgu was going to do. He used his staff like a vaulter's pole to get some distance between him and the hulking brute. The watching crowd laughed in derision at this evident display of cowardice. He turned to face him. The big guy plowed forward fists knotted and arrogance written all over his face. He wasn't going to dignify Burt's challenge with weapons. He was just going to pound on Burt until he was dog meat.

Burt had no intention of being some hound's dinner. He waited patiently for Orgu to reach him then, neatly sidestepped while pivoting for a strike against the monster's giant calves. He knew it probably only stung, as Orgu stumbled when he didn't encounter his target and moved slightly out of the full power of the swing. However, Burt stepped forward and, leaping, rapped his enemy hard on the back of his head before he could turn to face him. The crowd roared its displeasure and deprecations.

As Orgu turned to face him, his expression livid, Burt grinned at him, intentionally angering him further. He needed to get this beast really, really mad. At that point, Burt would have him exactly where he wanted him, unconscious. He didn't want to kill him, even though he was sure he could. He wanted this overgrown Groga humiliated as much as possible. This would hopefully move him into the position he desired.

Orgu roared and charged again. Again, Burt leaped aside and caught him, this time, on his buttocks. As Orgu yelped and then turned, Burt was already several yards away, having immediately cartwheeled back to Orgu's original position. He was going to stay away from those massive fists as much as possible. As he waited for the behemoth to turn back to him, he realized he was feeling a funny tingling moving from his pantleg up his body.

"BaaGah? What're you doing?"

"BaaGah safe. BaaGah make Burt safe."

Burt thought, safe? What was that about? But in the nano second all of that took place in his mind, Orgu was charging again. Obviously, he was a slow learner. This time Burt stepped to the opposite side and with full force swung for Orgu's gut. It was a chancy move and he paid for it. He connected and Orgu responded with an OOF and then caught him a glancing blow to the chest with his clenched fist as he doubled over.

It knocked Burt back and the crowd cheered, but surprisingly, it didn't hurt. The force of the blow should have at least cracked a rib or bruised him, but all it had done was to push him backward onto the grass. *"Burt safe. See?"* came BaaGah's voice in his mind.

Burt was so blown over by this that he almost missed Orgu's new tactic. He was clomping up to him slowly, as if to sneak up on him. His beady piggy eyes were slitted with concentration, intent on Burt's smallest movement. He still had not picked up anything to use as a weapon, although there was detritus perhaps deliberately left around the edges of the field. If it had been Burt, he would have grabbed a rock to throw at him.

Burt watched him come, not willing to distract himself with another conversation with his little friend, but he was sure going to have a long one with him, as soon as he worked his plan.

He held his staff in the guard position, watching Orgu's eyes and hands attentively and putting a big grin on his face. "Come here, little Groga man," he said aloud in the voice one would normally use to call a shy dog or cat. He beckoned as he said it. "Nice little Groga. I promise not to hurt you too much..."

"Nice little Groga" didn't seem too pleased with Burt's condescending air. He growled, still stomping slowly toward him. Burt danced back, twirling his staff in a flashy move, Orgu's eyes watching intently as he continued to come to Burt. Burt continued to back up until his heel touched the four foot high fence that ringed the grounds. He stopped and it was Orgu's turn to grin. He had Burt right where he wanted him, trapped. Burt grinned back. He had Orgu exactly where he wanted him, over-confident and deceived.

Orgu swung his clenched fist overhand, as if it was a hammer, right at Burt's head. Burt ducked and as he did, jammed the end of his staff again into Orgu's gut. The blow Orgu had begun, glanced Burt's shoulder, which was apparently not protected by his BaaGah shield. It hurt, but he didn't think there were any bones broken. Unfortunately, the force of the blow did knock him down. He crawled quickly under Orgu's bent over form and scampered away, rolling his shoulder as he went. Orgu retched and then slowly straightened up and turned to face Burt. There was death in his eyes.

Burt had seen that look before and it meant he had achieved his goal. The crowd's angry cries faded from his senses. As he focused his mind to include every possible nuance of Orgu's movement he reached that state where time slowed down and every microsecond seemed an eternity. Burt had planned to make his stand near the practice dummies to give his opponent visual clutter to deal with on top of his insane anger. He stood between two of them as if they were two guards who had decided to take a nap in the middle of a battle.

He had seen a bullfight once. It had disgusted him so much that he had left before the end, but just before he had left, he had seen the bull, now bloodied and maddened past any rational thought, charge the matador like an oncoming freight train. This reminded him of that. Orgu stood hands on his hips for only a moment and then charged with every ounce of his strength, weight and speed focused on Burt.

Burt was ready. His staff was held loosely in his hands. As he feinted a move to the right, he instead jumped aside to the left. Orgu had built up enough speed as to not be able to respond with more than a slight turn to the right, so when Burt again hit that tender gut and followed up with a blow to the back of the neck, he didn't stand a chance, but when he fell, twisting around his hurt belly, he fell right across Burt, knocking him under his fallen body. Fortunately, the two dummy guards had done their job. Orgu's body straddled the two of them with Burt wedged between the three of them like a pimento in a cocktail olive.

"Burt safe?" came a timid voice in his mind.

"I'm safe, BaaGah. Thanks. I just have to get myself out from under this putrid, stinking Groga wimp." Burt thought to BaaGah.

Sound had returned at the climax of the fight and now he heard the clamor of angry voices, both outside the makeshift arena and approaching his feet. He lay still and waited to see what they were going to do. Evidently none of the Groga relished the task of raising the now unconscious champion from the ground. Burt was sure they assumed he was dead from the impact of Orgu on his "miserable puny body", so they ignored him as they trussed both of Orgu's arms with heavy ropes and hauled him up via the pulleys used to animate the target dummies.

He felt the weight of the body lift and waited until it had cleared the dummies and then jumped up with his arms and staff in the air and shouted, "TaDa!"

The Groga holding the ropes that were holding Orgu up dropped them and ran, resulting in Orgu hitting the ground in a thud that vibrated the ground under Burt's feet. The crowd, now dead silent, stared in astonishment, just for a moment. Then, the shout that burst from them made the ground vibrate even more. The Groga-ha had come through the gate and he held up his hand. Once again, the crowd fell silent. *"Attention!"* he mindshouted. *"Orgu has been defeated by the trickery and cunning of this dishonorable slave. We WILL have the secrets of his magic."*

At a signal from the Groga-ha, a net was cast at him, tangling his quarterstaff and pulling his arms close to his sides. He didn't struggle. He just stood there grinning at them. He knew they would be infuriated by this and he would probably pay again. This didn't bother him much. He was escorted, still wrapped in the net and none too gently back to his little cell. Once the door was closed and he was back in the dark, he summoned a small knife from his MDP and cut the net from his body. He didn't care much what they would think of this. If they wanted to think he had magic, he would allow them to continue that train of thought.

Chapter 15: Alternate Reality

Jenny was glad they would be going back to Sanglarka tomorrow. Tarafau had relayed the reports from Sanglarka to her daily while she was there, and at this point she was pretty much caught up with it.

She and Amenia had worked on learning how to be awake and receive from her friends as she chose. She still hadn't learned how to make a two-way connection yet, but she knew that Bob was making good progress on his project and she also knew that Burt had been taking some heavy risks. She was both proud of him and worried about him at the same time.

She had also peeked in on Juan's group and Adelle's group. She was amazed at how all of the moving parts were so well coordinated, and it seemed like when the two big breakthroughs Bob and Burt were making came through, they would be ready to do something about it. That being said, she also knew that there would be much more work to be done and what she was learning was also a part of it. Amenia had said that now that she could do the first stage of this talent, Amenia would work with her long distance to allow her to practice. Since Amenia was already aware that Jenny could do this, she would likely be able to create that two-way connection that would make Jenny's new skill a game-changer.

She dressed in one of her new outfits that she and Elizabeth had picked out on a final visit to the Apex. She wanted to look especially nice today, as there was to be a farewell celebration and she would be going to meet with some important people about the Daringi role in the Alliance offense. Although it was hard to think of it in that way, Jenny knew that a defensive war would not allow them to defeat the Insenium. Only all-out offensive tactics would bring them close to eradicating the Insenium threat. This meant people, many people, on both sides would die. Jenny's insides squirmed at the very idea.

Jenny had come from a military family and so many of the friends she had grown up with were in the military on Earth. She knew the grief of families when a soldier died in combat. She understood the cost of an all-out assault in lives, resources and sorrow. She was not looking forward to this, but she knew it must be done. The alternative was unthinkable.

Chidwi sat on the bed, observing as usual. She thought the whole changing clothes thing was absolutely fascinating. Jenny had offered to get her an outfit also and Chidwi had laughed until tears had actually come from her eyes. Jenny didn't mind entertaining her with her daily clothing rituals, though. Chidwi had become a dear companion in the few days since she and Jenny had bonded. Already, Jenny couldn't imagine her life without her. Chidwi loved Lizziebot as well, remembering Lizzie when she was alive.

Chidwi had commented to Jenny that she wished she could speak with Lizziebot. Jenny understood but told her that this was not possible. Chidwi had a hard time with the concept of impossibility. Her mind told her that things were only impossible until they weren't anymore. Jenny seemed to remember something about this when she peeked in on Bob, but she shook her head. Surely, she had remembered that incorrectly.

Chidwi often spoke of Lizzie, a tenderness in her mind voice that bespoke the huge influence Lizzie had had on the Linkling community. Jenny had gotten to go out into the grove a few times since bonding Chidwi and enjoyed visiting with the Linklings. They were very bright and curious and just fun to be around. They told the silliest jokes that made no sense, which was why they were funny. They would tell a joke and watch Jenny's face to see if she got it in such an expectant way that it made Jenny giggle just thinking about it. Jenny realized they probably thought her a little slow on the uptake, since there was always a pause before she laughed uproariously. She didn't mind that either. It actually made them even sweeter to her.

Chidwi jumped up onto Jenny's shoulder, her favorite perch, one hand holding lightly on Jenny's earlobe. Fortunately, Jenny wasn't one to wear much jewelry and had never even considered piercing her ears, or anything else, for that matter. She just wasn't much of a "girlie girl" as her dad used to call many of her friends who primped and worried about their appearance. For Jenny, if she was clean and had done something to her hair, the rest was just whatever it was. She seldom looked into a mirror except while brushing her teeth or combing her hair for the day.

The family was already stirring. Most of the time they were up bright and early, bustling about in the kitchen. Elizabeth had taken time out of school and Tarafau was around most of the time, doing whatever family business was needed, including taking his turn in the garden and chores. Amenia still saw clients different times of the day, but she was currently very focused on getting as much training in with Jenny as possible.

Today they would be meeting with their version of a congressional assembly. Tarafau told her she needn't be intimidated about it. She did well enough when she had to speak to the team, and she was up to speed on all of the arrangements that were being made at the command center in Sanglarka. Also, he emphasized that he would be right at her side to guide her through the process. As Gatekeeper this was actually one of the jobs she was supposed to be training for and as her Guide, it was his job to help her get through this successfully.

She ate a quick light breakfast of fruit and some flat bread that was Elizabeth's recipe. Elizabeth was in class this morning and would meet Jenny and Tarafau at the Apex in the council chamber. Evidently, as a student she could observe from a balcony seat at any proceeding at any time. The Daringi felt strongly that all citizens should have transparent access to every legislative decision and the discussions that preceded them. There were few new laws in their society, but the congress often met to discuss how different situations in the law applied to their current laws and to make arrangements for help whenever there was a need in the community.

In their case today, the laws weren't changing. They would just be deciding the extent of their aid to the Dimensional Alliance in manpower and resources.

Tarafau assured her that historically, aid to the Alliance was approved as a matter of course, but to make sure that every citizen was apprised of what was happening, they had to formally apply to the congressional body and be formally approved with every detail of the request.

She finished her breakfast, cleaned her dishes and the table where she and Chidwi had eaten together. She then retired to the workout room. She wasn't in workout clothes, because today the workout would be strictly mental. Amenia wasn't willing to waste a single minute of her time with Jenny, in hopes they would be able to make the additional breakthrough that was needed before she had to leave.

Amenia was also dressed in a nice outfit in the intense colors she preferred. Today she and Jenny were a close match with blouses that fluttered, long open sleeves and a loose-fitting bodice that flared down to the hip. Her calf long skirt was of the same fabric and a similar fit. Jenny thought they looked like two beautiful butterflies.

They sat on the mat and immediately fell into the trancelike state that was induced by the complicated breathing techniques. Jenny let Amenia into her mind and into the keep beyond the guarded portcullis. They didn't go to the library. Rather, Jenny had imagined into her fortress a communications building. It was full of equipment with blinking lights and screens, which meant absolutely nothing. It was just an appropriate background to prepare Jenny to use her mind in communications mode. She and Amenia sat across a desk with a computer and she typed into a search bar on the computer, "Juan at the Puerto Rico gate."

The computer screen and the entire communications room faded from sight. Now she was in Juan's living room. Luz was seated in a chair crocheting, something she liked to do in her spare time or when she needed to think. Jenny had always wished she had learned, but she never could sit down long enough for it. Her mother would have been happy to teach her. Next to Luz, with a book, Juan sat, apparently deeply engrossed. None of the others were in the room. Jenny had to assume they were working in their respective workspaces.

Jenny knew she could walk around in the room as long as Juan, the designated search person was within her sight. Amenia had assured her that this would eventually change, that she would be able to wander from room to room and person to person. But for now, this was just fine. She could almost feel the gentle breeze that wafted through the open French doors at one end of the room. Luz looked so peaceful and probably deep in thought. It might actually be easier to try her as she wasn't focused on anything that required intense concentration. The hook flashed in and out of what looked like it might become a shawl.

As Amenia had taught her she sent a soft message in mindspeech. *"Luz? It's Jenny."*

Luz looked around and Jenny was hopeful, but she nodded to someone who had entered the room from behind her. She tried again, *"Luz, can you hear me?"* No response.

She decided that maybe because she had deliberately put Juan's name into the imaginary search that she had focused mentally just on him. So, with a mental sigh she tried that theory. *"Juan? Can you hear me? It's Jenny."*

Juan didn't stir. He continued to read with the focus and concentration of a typical bookaholic. Luz had once complained to her that you could set a bomb off under his chair while he was reading, and he wouldn't even notice. Jenny's mom had been the same way. Jenny let go of the connection and the communications center faded back into view. Amenia could tell by the disappointment in Jenny's face that it had been a no-go. Jenny sighed.

"Please don't get discouraged, Jenny. It may be you need to try it again with someone you have a stronger connection with. Who, in the Alliance or your Earth team are you closest with?"

Jenny thought about it. She didn't want to accidently break Burt's concentration at a crucial time, though he had been the first one she had connected with originally. But she definitely felt closest to Bob and he probably wasn't in the middle of something that would cause a small shock to put him in a dangerous situation.

She typed into the search bar: "Bob Reid, Winethia".

Once again, the room melted, and she found herself in the dragon lab. Bob was bent over what looked like a debit card and was taking notes. *"Bob? It's Jenny. Can you hear me?"*

"Jenny? Where are you? I thought you were with Tarafau. You probably shouldn't be here right now."

"I'm still with Tarafau's family. I go back to Sanglarka tomorrow."

"Then how are you doing this? This is cross-dimensional communication. What are you using to do this? I hadn't heard of any tech like this at the Alliance. This will come in very handy for our mission."

"No, Bob, it isn't a mechanism. It's my mind. Amenia and I have had a breakthrough."

"I'll say! I had no idea someone could do this with their mind. This is a superpower, if ever there was one. We'll need to come up with an alternative identity and find some spandex or at least a cape for you. This is amazing!"

"This is the first time I've been able to do two-way communication. Before now I could only observe. I was able to watch you fly on a dragon! How cool is that?"

"Very cool indeed. Is this visual on your side? I can hear you, but I can't see you."

"I can see you in your lab. Fidget is standing next to you and in the background, there are huge tables, I'm imagining they are for the dragon scientist you are working with. I know about the alternate Gatekeeper. She is beautiful and seems like a nice person."

Bob sat up straighter, not really sure where to look, much like when a blind person would, with their only clue the direction of your voice. His brows furrowed and then rose. Jenny could see the gears turning like mad in his head.

"Jenny. You need to be careful. Did you realize you are now a weapon? I know you would never use this gift this way, but please listen to me. The Alliance needs every edge they can get in this fight and your ability could very well be one that will make a huge difference. Please, please be careful and don't allow yourself to be pushed into anything. Listen to Tarafau. He has your best interest at heart. You can provide a serious tactical advantage, but it won't help anyone if you get yourself hurt or worse. Do you understand me? Who else knows you can do this?"

"Well, as of this moment, you, Amenia and I. This is the first time I managed two-way communication and, at least for now, I can only do it with people I am really close to. I can peek in on anyone on our team, but so far, I haven't figured out how to make it work both ways except with you. I promise to be careful. I get that this has potential to be dangerous if anyone on the other side figures out I can do this. That being said, I have to do my part."

"And that is so like your Aunt Lizzie that it's scary, Jenny. She would have said the exact same thing." He sighed, shaking his head. *"Very well, I will continue to work on my part and the sooner I figure it out, the sooner we may be able to end all of this for good. I'll get back to it. Tell Tarafau I said to watch you like a hawk."*

All of a sudden Jenny was startled by the voice of Chidwi piping in. She was sure she had left her sleeping in her bed! *"Chidwi will watch better than hawkses or anything else. Chidwi is with Jenny."*

Bob jumped up off of the stool he had been sitting on. *"What the heck is a Chidwi? I thought you were the only one who could do this?"*

"Chidwi is Linkling, Bob, sir. Chidwi is Jenny's. Chidwi can do anything Jenny can do. Chidwi and Jenny are linked. You are Bob. Jenny loves Bob. Chidwi loves Bob too."

"*I'll be snookered. I can hardly wait to hear about these adventures you've been having with the Daringi, Jenny. It sounds like your training is finally kicking in big time. But for now, I have to set up my next set of experiments on this darned card. I think if I can get the key to open it up, I might be able to replicate it in some way, even improve on it.*"

"*Now it's my turn to tell YOU to be careful, Mr. Reid. Expert tinkerer or not, don't you go getting yourself killed or injured. I need you...*" she trailed off, tears welling up in her eyes. "*It isn't every day a girl gets three amazing dads in her life. And my dad can't be here for me in this situation. I need you and Tarafau so much. Be careful, please.*"

"*Don't worry, Jenny. I'm as careful as it's possible to be, I promise. I don't have Burt here to get me into trouble.*" And he grinned. "*I don't suppose you've learned how to give a hug through this connection? So, virtual hugs will have to do.*" He wrapped his arms around himself and squeezed. "*There you go. I'll get back to this. Don't be a stranger. Drop in whenever you can.*"

"*Thank you, Bob. I will. I will be working on this every day for awhile and connecting with you regularly will give me the practice I need. Once I get on Earth, we can calibrate times so I'm not waking you up in the middle of your night or catching you in the shower.*" And she blushed at that thought.

"*I should say so!*" he agreed emphatically, his silver-black moustache twitching in amusement. "*I'll look forward to hearing you again soon.*"

He waved and Jenny cut the connection, fading back into the communication room. She looked at Amenia who was grinning like her face would break. She threw her virtual arms around Jenny and squeezed.

"*That was amazing, Jenny! You figured it out! I'm so proud of you I could burst.*" She looked at Chidwi who now had appeared in the communications room as well. "*And YOU! You amazing creature. I had been worried about when Jenny would be doing this on her own, but now she needn't ever be alone and you can continue to guide her, can't you?*"

"*Chidwi is always here for Jenny. Always and forever here,*" Chidwi said with a nod of her furry little head. Chidwi had an adorable way of smiling that crinkled her eyes and showed her little teeth, the tiny pink tongue contrasting nicely with her pale green fur.

"I think we have done enough for now," Amenia said, still grinning. *"We still have the council meeting to attend and a few other things, I'm thinking, before we sleep tonight. We're going to use every minute we have left with you on this visit. We'll let you go back to Sanglarka after breakfast tomorrow, but for now, I think we've made enough breakthroughs for one day."*

The communications room faded and once again Jenny was seated on the mat with Amenia and now Chidwi who stood behind her, both hands on her shoulders as she often did when Jenny practiced. A group hug ensued, and they went upstairs to report to Tarafau and get started on their day.

Tarafau was pleased to hear about the progress Jenny had made as the four of them, Tarafau, Jenny, Chidwi and Amenia walked to the Apex. He told her that he agreed with Bob that Jenny should be accompanied by him or her guards, who were currently awaiting their return to Sanglarka, or someone who was assigned to her at all times. He also told Jenny to never go anywhere without Chidwi who could protect her in many ways she had yet to experience. Of course, Jenny also had Lizziebot, who rode always in her MDP.

Inside the Apex the main floor was bustling, as usual, with shoppers, shopkeepers on their break, vendors and entertainers of all kinds. Elizabeth was waiting at the entrance and gave Jenny an enthusiastic hug and sent: *"You are going to be great. I'll be up in the observation balcony with Mom and we will be cheering you on."*

Tarafau led them to an elevator where he instructed the elevator to take them to the council assembly chamber on the top floor before the observation deck. Jenny had already decided that regardless what happened with the Congress, she would like one last look from the observation deck so she could gaze at the far reaches of the Daringi lands. The beautiful container gardens had such a calming effect and there was something exhilarating about being up so high in a benign environment. The air even seemed different up there.

They entered the council assembly chamber and Jenny was amazed to see how large it was, more like an amphitheater, if anything, rows and rows of tiered seating with most of them already filled. Elizabeth and Amenia split off to the observation balcony and Jenny was about to tell Chidwi to go with them, but Tarafau put a hand on her unoccupied shoulder.

"Bonding with a Linkling is considered a high honor in our society. It will be good for them to see you and Chidwi together. It will give weight to what you have to say. You may notice you are not the only one accompanied by a Linkling, although this is actually a rare thing. You are the first of our family to have achieved it, besides Lizzie."

Jenny was surprised by this. She hadn't realized that she had achieved something so unique. It bolstered her confidence to know this. She reached up and patted Chidwi and Chidwi reached down with one small hand to pat Jenny's cheek in affection.

They walked around the edge of the chamber and up some stairs to the dais, where were seated a couple dozen beings. Jenny was surprised. She had naturally expected to only see Daringi. *"Is this normal for a council to have representatives from the other species on your planet?"* she sent silently to Tarafau. She noticed the arachnids (Glitha among them), a furry almost gorilla like species, an avian species, not quite like Myla and a beautiful winged insectoid very much like a butterfly with a six-foot wingspan. The gorilla-like being was dressed in colorful robes and held a decorative staff and seemed to be the leader of the delegation.

"Yes. This council represents our entire planet." He gestured to the crowd behind him. And indeed, Jenny saw representatives of each species scattered amongst the seats. The arachnid species and the butterfly-like species had their own sections, Jenny assumed, because of the difficulty they would have had with the bench seating in the rest of the auditorium.

They approached the main area on the dais. The representatives all stood, and Jenny found herself trailing Tarafau in a sort of reception line. Tarafau introduced her to each of them and Jenny knew she would never remember all of their names and hoped that wouldn't cause a problem. Without exception, she noticed that each being gave their respects to Chidwi and Jenny realized what Tarafau had said was true. Having Chidwi on her shoulder raised her up a notch in their opinion. This definitely served to bolster her confidence.

The Chief High Councilor greeted her with a slight bow. *"Welcome to you Jenny, honored Gatekeeper. My name is Ingwili Liger. We look forward to hearing your proposal. We have a few things to start with and I will invite you to the podium to speak at the appropriate time. The entire council is assembled here today from all over our planet to hear what you have to say. Please be seated and we will move forward."*

He indicated a chair next to him and Tarafau took the seat on the other side of her. Ingwili stood at the podium and mentally broadcast to the audience. *"Greetings, representatives and citizens. This council meeting is being broadcast planet-wide to all who wish to attend. We have in our midst honored guests. Tarafau, as you all know, has honorably represented our dimension to the Dimensional Alliance for many years. His companion this day is the new Alliance Gatekeeper. Jenny has already proven herself as capable even though this position was thrust upon her unprepared and only newly ascended as a Gate Guardian.*

Although we are not included in any dimensional network, to our knowledge, we are still affected by this latest dimensional calamity. The enemy who has attacked the Alliance has technology that allows them to establish portals similar to the natural gateways included in the Alliance network. This does not bode well. It puts every dimension at risk, as this evil conglomerate is intent on conquering and enslaving every dimension, they can find access to.

This we cannot allow. We have resources and trained troops that can be made available to the Alliance, if we can come to an agreement today."

He paused, scanning the silent crowd. He was impressive. A few inches taller than Tarafau, his waist long blue-black hair was plaited down his back. He wore a colorfully embroidered headband much like the Samoan beaded ceremonial headbands of Earth. His ankle length loose caftan appeared to be somewhat formal, tightened at the waist with a black sash. The caftan itself was as colorful as the headband in bright bold stripes that ran down from his shoulders. This was a being to be respected and yet, Jenny knew that he hadn't been in the office long. As Tarafau had explained, every Daringi took their turn in their leadership and each was trained to be able to take on any office as a representative of their people.

"However, I will not attempt to persuade you to one side or the other of this proposal. I will, instead, allow our guest, Jenny Japhet, Gatekeeper of the Dimensional Alliance to address you."

At that he turned to Jenny and gestured to her to come to the podium. Somehow the podium, which had been chest high on Ingwili, lowered silently to accommodate Jenny's stature. She stood as tall as she could manage and stepped to the podium breathing and centering herself as she approached. Tarafau had expressed confidence she could do this. At this point, all she could do was her best. Her hands stopped shaking and her stomach stopped churning. She paused for a moment, scanning the crowd. Looking up toward the balcony, she saw Amenia and Elizabeth, who were seated right in the front row, smiling encouragingly to her.

Taking one last deep breath, she began. *"I bring greetings from the Dimensional Alliance Council and, unfortunately, a message of warning and a plea for your help. I would have preferred to meet you in better circumstances, but sometimes we must deal with what is, not what we wished it would be.*

In the dimensional network a great evil has presented itself. There is another alliance, one who would, if they have their way, conquer and enslave every planet and every intelligent species they can discover. The really bad news is that they are no longer restrained by the boundaries of the Alliance Gate Network. They have devices that will allow them to establish portals outside of the network. They did this on my home dimension on the planet Earth. We have disabled that portal, but we now know that they are also doing this to other dimensions, raiding and enslaving every species they come across.

I have it from their allies that their intention is to not stop until they have conquered every culture and species within their reach, which has now grown. The good news is that this technology is still in its infancy and not perfected. They evidently have to already know about a dimension, sometimes discovering new ones by accident, in order to use their technology. But the fear of Alliance scientists is that they may have discovered a personal portal device that may be capable of allowing their forces to do as your people are able to do naturally. They will be able to individually and instantaneously transport to any dimension, anywhere, including, potentially, yours."

There was a hushed murmur of voices and minds as the assembly took this all in.

Then, to her incredulous mind, she began to hear mental cries of, *"How can we help?" "What do you need?" "Our forces are yours." "We stand with the Alliance!"*

The entire dais stood, hands to heart, or at least those who had hands. The others stood silently and then, as one, the entire audience stood silently, in solidarity with their leaders. Jenny couldn't help herself. Tears streamed down her cheeks. She had expected questions, debates and even arguments, but not this. No wonder Tarafau and his family were such amazing people, if this was the culture they were raised in. Her own congress, even in this type of circumstance would have never achieved this kind of unity on this kind of a proposal this quickly. It would have required, at the least, several hours of debate and potentially even weeks.

Tarafau had stood and walked up on one side of Jenny, his hand on her unencumbered shoulder and the Chief High Councilor stood at her other side. He held Jenny's hand up and with his other hand made a broad sweeping gesture at the crowd. *"We are unanimous. We shall meet with your representatives as soon as possible to counsel on what specific aid they require. Our resources are at your disposal and we will not quit until this threat is eliminated. We would rather never fight or injure another being, but we will also not stand idly by while any being is threatened by evil from another, if it is within our power. You may depart in peace in the morning to relay our message to your council, Gatekeeper."*

Jenny would remember in later years the feeling of extreme relief and exultation she felt as they made their way home several hours later. She had attended a private meeting with the High Council only, followed by a reception in a great hall with hundreds of beings in attendance. She shook hands. She hugged. She even rubbed foreheads with the butterfly-like creatures called Leilua. Their featherlike antennae tickled, and they found her giggle amusing.

She felt a bit overwhelmed at the sweet acceptance she found among these beings who were so much different than her imagination could have conjured. There had been dancing and music and she discovered that Linklings liked to dance. Chidwi and the few other Linklings among the crowd performed to their own crooning music. They were so graceful and the music so exhilarating that the entire hall stopped to watch them. And Jenny had also gotten her opportunity to walk around the observation deck, accompanied by several of the High Council, before they departed.

Now, walking back to Tarafau's home, where they would spend the rest of the day, a bittersweet sadness had begun to set in with Jenny, as she contemplated that she would probably not get another chance to visit here soon. Truly, if it wasn't for the need for her training and delivering the message to the congress of the planet, she would probably not have had an opportunity to come in the first place.

They ate a lovely meal that had been prepared in their absence by Elizabeth's brothers and their wives and children. Then they retired to sit around the firepit near the grove. The Linklings were in fine fettle this evening, crooning happily in their grove. Chidwi sang along from Jenny's shoulder.

At last, Tarafau stood and beamed at his family surrounding him. *"We will soon bid farewell to Jenny for a time. As is traditional, we gather together as a family for this. Jenny once asked me if all of our people transformed into cats. I didn't give her much of an answer then, as I had hoped we would have the opportunity to do what I have planned this night. Jenny has her own gifts, but I know this thing we do fascinates and delights her. Therefore, we will have some fun. Jenny close your eyes."*

She complied with a thrill of anticipation. *"Now open."*

Standing around her was a complete menagerie where before her Daringi family had stood. Tarafau was no longer a black cat, but a magnificent bird. Standing beside him was an identical bird which Jenny assumed was Amenia. The two birds were about the height of Jenny's waist in colorful plumage, although, Amenia's was somewhat muted, as was common with female birds. The tops of their heads were crested with silvery feathers, while the rest was a gradient of colored iridescent feathers from deep reds to other jewel tones as if someone had fully intensified every color of a rather spectacular rainbow. Elizabeth was an auburn colored deer-like animal with tapering curled horns, huge brown-gold eyes with large black irises and dainty ivory-colored hooves. Her brothers were large lizard-type animals with shiny black scales. Not dragons, more like some of the more graceful dinosaurs of Earth. Their wives were smaller versions of the same. The children were as varied as their elders, cats, dogs and one duplicate of the Leilua she had met earlier today.

Jenny clapped her hands in delight. *"You are all magnificent! I feel like I am in a fairy tale of epic proportions! I never in my wildest imaginings ever thought I would have an experience like this week has been. Perhaps, when my life settles down, I will become a fantasy novelist in addition to my Gatekeeper duties. After all, Lizzie found the time to write boxes full of journals. I wish I could take a photo."*

Chidwi sprang from her shoulder and backed up several paces from the group. *"You all stand together and see me. I take picture."*

Jenny couldn't believe this. She took her place in the center of the amazing group and waited. Chidwi smiled happily at them and made a sound very similar to the shutter of an Earth camera. *"Lizzie teached us about photoos. Now I have photoo for Jenny and this family. You keep in head, ok?"*

To Jenny's astonishment a picture appeared in her mind of the group of them standing together and amazingly, Chidwi was perched on her shoulder in the "photoo". How'd she do that, Jenny wondered?

"Thank you Chidwi. It is beautiful. I will store it with my most precious memories." She decided she would mentally frame it and put it on the wall in the communications room of her mental fortress.

For most of the evening they continued to show her different forms they could take. It was the best entertainment she could possibly have asked for. At one point they all became cats. Amenia was a large tortoise shell cat. Elizabeth a white long-haired cat with a smooshed face and a long fluffy tail. The others took on various cat forms of different sizes and even alien cat species, but the most impressive were the huge jungle cats by the two brothers. Their feral grins made Jenny shiver and she was glad those weren't the shapes they had chosen to display first.

She went to sleep that night with a warm regret that she couldn't spend the rest of her life here with the Daringi. But duty called, she had a dear family on Earth, and off to Sanglarka she would go in the morning to do her duty or die trying.

Chapter 16: Sciency Stuff

Bob looked up from his lab table to see Anela approach. He hadn't noticed the door to the lab open, but then, his area was behind dragon height tables which didn't afford him much of a view of the entrance, as large as it was. She was dressed in her usual breeches and a colorful linen shirt, their version of jeans and a t-shirt in her culture. It seemed that she only wore those flowing robes to parties or when receiving off world dignitaries.

Her key was barely exposed by the gentle scoop of the shirt's neckline. Today they were going to do something that might be a bit dangerous and he hated that she had to be attached to the key in order to do it. He had inquired about the possibility of removing the key, but everyone he had consulted had agreed that only death or terminal illness would allow the removal of the key.

He had gone over all of his research so far about the card with Anela. She had a sharp mind and evidently served as an additional lab assistant with Cornelium from time to time as part of her training. He was beginning to realize, based on his conversations with Anela that Gatekeeper training was as rigorous as multiple PHDs and never fully ceased. Anela had been trained in the sciences, technology and engineering, along with diplomacy, multiple dimensional languages, physics, literature from multiple cultures, crafts and even music. It was a pleasure to not have to go into detailed explanations of the concepts that were necessary to get her up to speed on his current research.

She sat on the stool next to him, acknowledged Fidget and said, *"Are we ready?"*

"Yes, I just want to do a quick review with you, so you are aware of the risks and to see if you have come up with any new considerations, if that's ok."

"That will be fine. Let's do this."

"So, you remember that we have currently subjected this piece of tech to multiple types of scans in a protected environment. We have detected no known power source, so we feel that a specific type of power, that is outside of our understanding, must be applied for it to do anything. It may also need a specific interface in order to function. We have applied several types of known power very carefully with no current (if you'll pardon the pun) results. We have subjected it to different forms of radiation and have measured it in every way we are able with known technology. Nothing we have tried up to this point has had any effect or demonstrated any noticeable readings.

Our thinking to this point is that perhaps, because the Gatekeeper key is connected to the Gate Network and actually allows the Gatekeeper access to whatever force it is that allows transport from one dimension to another, that deliberate exposure of the key to the card may elicit some response. Cornelium has shown me that this table is embedded with technology that should allow us to measure any response of your body function, the key or the card. Do you understand and do you have anything to add?"

"I understand that there is some potential risk either to me, the key or the card when we do this. I also understand that we will not know if this is the threat you think it is unless we try this. Otherwise we may find ourselves facing a bigger threat to the Alliance and it's member dimensions than was previously thought. Is that about right?"

"It is. Do you accede to this request to potentially put yourself in danger then?"

"If I am not mistaken, the danger is not only to me or even yourself; it is to trillions of beings across the dimensions, if we do not proceed. I not only accede; I wholeheartedly agree that this must be done, and I am willing."

Bob nodded ruefully. He didn't feel any better about subjecting Anela to this experiment than he had with Jenny. But one way or the other it had to be done. Had there been any other way... But as his grandmother used to say, "If wishes were fishes, no one would be hungry."

"There are two ways we can do this, either you can lean over until your key is in close proximity or you can lie down on the table and I can bring the card close to the key."

"I would prefer to lie down. I think it will allow for better control as I won't be able to flinch or accidently overbalance if there is a response."

She stood and used her hands to lift herself to a sitting position on the table and then lay on her back. She smiled up at him. *"Let's do this. I'm ready."*

Bob nodded. He pulled the card from his shirt pocket. He held it between two fingers and slowly lowered it to within an inch of the key. *"Are you feeling anything?"*

"No. Usually the key responds to stimuli by warming slightly against my skin and sometimes it sends a tingling sensation, but so far, nothing."

Bob lowered it to within a half inch arching his eyebrows in a question. Anela shook her head.

"Should I touch it? We still don't know what it will do."

"Go ahead. I'm ready." Her eyes remained calm and her lips curved in a gentle smile. Bob realized she must be doing her breathing exercise to be as calm as she seemed. He sure wasn't calm, breathing or no. His heart was racing.

Very carefully he lowered the card the last fraction of an inch. When it finally touched, he thought his heart would burst.

"Wait... Don't move it. I think I felt something. It is very faint and not the tingle or the warmness. It's more like a really subtle vibration. Not quite a buzz. Are your instruments showing anything?"

A screen bloomed over top of the table. Most of the meters were nonresponsive, but one that was used to monitor the outputs of a gate had the slightest variation from a flat line. If he hadn't been looking for it, it would have not been noticeable. The pulsating rhythm was definitely something, but what? He calibrated the meter to a higher sensitivity. Now the line was definitely broken up with a pulsating zigzag. It wasn't even, but it was a repeating pattern with definite highs and lows.

"I'm not sure what it's doing, but it's doing something. How do you feel?"

"I'm fine. Besides the slight vibration, I'm not feeling any physical symptoms of any kind except a kind of mental focus that is more than what my breathing would cause. Are you recording this? Cornelium will be back from his break in a few minutes and he'll want to see this for sure."

Bob pulled the card away from the key and heaved a sigh of relief. The readings went flat.

"OK, young lady, go ahead and get up. We'll wait for Cornelium before we move any farther."

He helped her jump down from the table and she resumed her seat next to his.

"What do you think that was about? It only showed on the one meter and that was to measure gate energy. I could just barely feel it. What kind of power source would it need to activate and how would you interface with it? I have a little understanding of how the gates work, but it is very basic. The problem we may come up against is that even the most learned gate engineers don't know as much as they should. The original builders of the gates didn't leave much behind in the form of theory or even the history of how or why they stumbled on the gate physics or connected them to a network. We do know how to detect working natural gateways, but the technology is old. They haven't made much in the way of advances."

"The young lady is right," said Mervin, popping in from around one of the dragon sized tables. *"One of the big frustrations of the gate techs is that we have all of this technology we use every day and have no idea what we would have to do to fix them if they stopped working or all of a sudden went wonky on us."*

"It's about time you got here. What have you been working on? I thought you were here to help me out."

"Nah. I've got a project of my own. It's related, but not pertinent to your focus at the moment. It might, however mean that we can move you forward faster, when you're ready. It looks like you got some kind of response there," he added, looking at the readout above the table.

"We have no idea what it means, however," Bob replied, his brows furrowed in thought. He rubbed at his salt and pepper moustache as he often did when contemplating a problem. *"I wish I knew more about what these readings were designed to measure. I mean, it's something, at least. It's the first reaction we've gotten of any kind in all of our experiments and it definitely has something to do with gate energy. Any ideas?"*

Merv studied the results for a moment. He scratched his head and sighed. *"I miss my beard,"* he grumbled. *"It was handy to stroke it when I was thinking. It made me look very wise and inscrutable."* And he laughed. *"It was fun being a wizard. I wish I could make this seem like magic. That being said, this meter was meant to measure a sort of 'distance' from one gate to another, based on the amount of gate power that was needed to transport from one gate to another."*

Bob's jaw dropped. *"Say that again. We just might solve this without Cornelium's input."*

"I just said that the meter was used to measure gate output from one gate to another."

"Which was why this output was so minimal. We weren't connecting to another gate. We only had one side of the equation!"

"Zounds, man! I wished human's lived longer!" Merv exclaimed, shaking his head in disbelief. *"This is why I wanted you on the team in the first place. You can be so non-linear. When you do what you do, you can jump higher than any superhero in the multiverse. So how do you expect to input the other gate location?"*

"I might be able to help with that, my friends," Anela inserted. *"Gate travel is not location based. There is no such thing in dimensional travel. We happen to know there are even gates that exist off-planet, in other words, in the blackness of space. All we have been able to discover is a single key vibration, produced by all natural portal vortexes. The technology we use to access natural gateways, or portals, evidently can sense an additional unique vibration that these portals make. I know your scientists are studying the science of how wormholes and black holes work. This isn't quite like that, but it is close.*

Dimensional travel takes place in a layer between universes, but rather than some kind of spiraling hole, it appears to be more like a plane. And that isn't quite right either. It simply has no discernible shape or mass or substance that we are able to recognize. Just like some creatures can see colors or hear sounds that other beings cannot, this dimensional reality is not discernible by any of the senses we have yet to discover. The best we can do is to measure the vibrations of a particular natural portal, once we discover it, and then make it into a gateway with our gateway normalization device that automatically connects it to the network." And as she spoke, she gestured expressively with her hands and face as she had launched into this explanation.

Bob again shook his head. Anela was not just a pretty face. "*This is really all like Disneyland to me. So many smart people and all of the equipment beyond my dreams and a project to work on that really means something. You give me hope that we will find a solution. So, do either of you have any suggestions how to complete this part of the puzzle? I simply don't have enough information yet to make a firm hypothesis on how to connect this, now that we know something of what it might do.*"

Merv shrugged. "*The multiverse is fundamentally statistical by nature. Patterns are formed by every phenomenon we have been able to figure out over eons of scientific research. It is usually such a pattern that sparks discoveries. Ancient Earth scientists noticed patterns in life on and above the planet. They only had primitive tools to measure with, but it was those patterns that engaged their imaginations and helped them to make huge leaps in understanding the universe. Your scientific community is yet so young that they have no idea of their limitations. It is why they seem to make so many 'golden leaps'. This was what I was hoping for by bringing you on the team. You have already demonstrated this even more than I expected. There will be a breakthrough and soon, I can feel it.*

For a very long time on your Earth I was considered a 'wizard'. Everything I did was considered magical. But the true magic was the creativity and intuitive guesses made by your people. I have been popping in and out of Earth gateways from before they were part of the Alliance network. Your species has always held great fascination for me.

You are a young planet, but you are and have been progressing so much faster than many older ones who had a huge head start on you. The reason for this is the gift given to humanity of intuitive pattern recognition and the ability to, as you put it in modern times, 'think outside the box'. I think it is time we gave this a rest and got you out into the fresh air. Put the card in the vault and let's 'blow this popsicle stand'". This last was said with a twinkle in his eyes. He really loved using what he called "Earth vernacular".

Bob realized that Mervin was right, after all. Some of his best ideas had come on a walk or while fishing. It wasn't surprising that Archimedes, Newton, and others had inspiration outside the laboratory that changed the world. So, he put the card safely in the vault and followed Mervin and Anela out the double doors leading to a change of scene.

Chapter 17: Together

J enny, Tarafau and Elizabeth dropped in briefly at Alliance headquarters for a quick debriefing. And, when Jenny stepped through the gate to Sanglarka, it was like waking from a dream. It had only been a week by the reckoning on Tarafau's planet, but so much had happened that it felt like months. It was cold here. The crisp mountain air practically sparkled. Lova was there, hands out-stretched with Jenny's three bodyguards, Lyra, Nona and Mynn all three standing at parade rest, eyes front, hands behind their backs, their backs straight.

Jenny grasped Lova's hands. *"Welcome, Jenny, Tarafau and Elizabeth. We are glad you are back. We have much to discuss and we hear you have a few revelations for us as well."* She turned to the three "girls" as they were fondly called. *"All right, you three. We're all very impressed. Get the starch out of your backbones and come welcome Jenny. No more of that parade ground military nonsense here."*

Then Jenny was surrounded by enthusiastic hugs and grins that made her heart want to sing.

When they entered the lodge the smell of fresh baked cookies greeted them. They immediately proceeded to the huge dining room with its long wooden table and many chairs around it. There, at the table, were every Gate Guardian and team member, except Burt and Bob, Jenny realized with a pang. They all greeted her with smiles while Arvid passed around his famous spicy sugar cookies and mulled cider.

Jenny's heart swelled within her when she realized how much she had come to love and care for these people and how much depended on each of them. All were in danger of one type or another just by doing what they normally did, but now each of them was embroiled in something so vast and terrible that she shuddered to think of it. None of them were really safe until the threat was eliminated.

Jenny started to rise to speak to them, but Tarafau put his hand on her shoulder and then stood himself. *"As the leader of our motley crew, I wanted to thank each of you for your current efforts. The reports we have received tell us that you have been as busy as we were this past week. We will not go into great detail in this reunion. We will, instead adjourn to the Alliance Headquarters private council room to report one and all. Please finish your tasty cookies and cider and we will gather at the gate in fifteen minutes. You won't have to bring anything with you, unless it is pertinent to your report. Jenny, did you want to say something?"*

Jenny stood and scanned the smiling faces before her. *"I just wanted to say that as much as I missed all of you, I am only now beginning to see how big the task is before us. I thought I understood, but now I know that it will take everything we have, every talent or ability, every idea, every backbreaking task and every ounce of commitment and courage we can muster. I can't tell you how much I look forward to hearing your progress on each of the teams. I know I can count on every one of you and that is the one precious thing that gives me hope to move forward. Thank you all so much."*

There were nodded heads, smiles and many determined looks from her friends, her team-mates and those who had also become her family. She sat and for the next few minutes she just enjoyed watching them interact, all munching contentedly on Arvid's famous cookies.

She didn't strike up a conversation and her friends seemed to know that she was enjoying just being with them for the moment. "The Girls" didn't chat. They simply sat there grinning at her. She was going to have to get used to having them with her everywhere she went again, which was not as big a deal as it used to be. They had defeated enemies together and had gone shopping together, not to mention discovering the 5 MDPs left to her by Lizzie. She knew she could count on them to do their best to keep her safe. And now, as she was growing her mental abilities, she would need more protection than ever.

Jenny had arrived with Chidwi turned off and she could imagine their delight at her new companion. Jenny wanted Chidwi to be able to see her team in action before subjecting her to the attention she would receive when Jenny revealed her. A few already knew about her, but for now it was better to keep her out of the mix. But she knew that her guards would devise ways of making Chidwi part of her security team.

The group began to rise and head toward the entrance, heading for the gate. Jenny's guards didn't move until Jenny rose and also headed toward the entrance, stopping only to thank Arvid for the cookies and cider. She hugged him to his surprise, and he hugged her back sheepishly. For all of the brusque manner he put on with everyone else, he was a toasted marshmallow, crusty on the outside, but soft, sweet and gooey on the inside.

Once they had all gathered, Tarafau bringing up the rear with Lova, they went through the gate one at a time and passing the attentive guards one-by-one, they headed down the hill to the waiting vehicles. These were the same hover cars but different in that they could hold a dozen passengers at once. They had prepared two of these.

When they arrived at the headquarters building, instead of getting out in front of the main doors, they were driven into a parking garage with a huge elevator and finally got out at the security station a few levels from the private council chamber. After a security scan in addition to the one at the gate, they were escorted to the main elevator. They entered the reception area and the white foxlike receptionist just waved them on in.

There were plenty of chairs set up in a circle and the councilors were already waiting, not on the dais but in seats at the top of the circle. In addition to Ingot, Myla and Liliath there were three beings in lab coats and a uniformed Trooper. Ingot waved for Jenny to seat herself next to him with Tarafau at her side. Her guards did not sit but stood at the back of the room, each sweeping the room constantly with their eyes. It seemed a little much to Jenny, considering where they were, but she wasn't going to tell them how to do their job.

When all were seated, Ingot began without getting up from his chair. *"Welcome, my friends. We have been looking forward all week to this meeting. Although we've heard bits and pieces, we felt it important that everyone was up to speed on everyone else, so each of us can have the big picture of what is going on and hopefully we will be able to spot any deficiencies or new ideas to help us move along. My gut tells me that our time is even shorter than we originally thought, but enough of that. Let's start with our Logistics Team and see where they are in their process."*

Juan stood at his place and smiled his usual smile. Jenny found herself randomly wondering if he had finished his book. *"We are doing well, I think. We have been assembling equipment and supplies for several ground units in the MDPs provided. We are also putting together specific supplies for the space carriers and their flight crews. We may need a few more MDPs as I get the feeling there may also be a potential navy as well. I know we haven't yet discovered the lay of the land where the Groga planet and the Insenium are concerned, but I would like to assemble the appropriate equipment and supplies to hold in reserve, if the council agrees.*

Mustapha has set up an admirable communications hub in one of the libraries in my house. I think the equipment is all up to date, but we may need some contingency plans if the enemy finds a way to block our current system."

He sat down at his last word and waited.

"Very well done," Ingot said. *"We will send specialists back with you to take a look at your set up and see what you are lacking. Every resource will be made available that we have access to. We don't know if the Insenium has better tech than we do, but for now, it looks like we are ahead of the Groga and the Fleistians, not that this is anything to brag about. How about our Science Team?"*

Adelle stood. She looked first at her team, nodded and looked around at the assembly. *"My team has been working on two separate issues; one is a method of delivering some of Xao Ting's potions and concoctions to the armies of the Insenium. One is actually intended to simply put them to sleep and the others are much more deadly. We have considered several possibilities including aerosols that can be inserted into any type of central heating or cooling unit, a type of smoke bomb that serves double duty, both obscuring the vision of the enemy and spreading the chemicals and a kind of drenching bomb similar to what is used in firefighting on Earth. The belly of a plane would just open up and dump the chemical diluted properly for the correct dosage on the enemy. This has a disadvantage of not being able to penetrate a building or bunker and it will pollute the soil for a very long time.*

We also examined different ways of using drones for administering the chemicals in both gaseous form and liquid for smaller groups of the enemy or in tight places.

We are working under an assumption that much of it may need to be delivered by air, which Brendan has assured us is entirely possible.

Our last choice would be to put chemicals into their drinking water. We hesitate because there may actually be innocents in the Insenium and also the Groga planet. We would like some guidance as to your preferred methods before we should proceed further."

She sat down abruptly to punctuate the end of her report.

"I appreciate the summaries, brief and to the point," Said Ingot. *"The full reports of each team have been assembled and will be added to your tablets at the end of the briefing including any conclusions we come to by the time we have all had a chance to report. Strategy and Tactics?"*

Gariel stood, the hairs in his animated beard waving calmly. Jenny had the stray thought that the beard never seemed to grow. Did he trim it or was it naturally a certain length? She gave herself a mental shake and returned her attention to the conversation.

"...and I appreciate the work of this team under difficult circumstances," he was saying. *"We have so little to go on. We have an operative in the field and no real way to communicate with him. Burt has set himself to infiltrate the enemy and I have confidence in his ability. We have a backup agent prepared to also attempt this, if we don't hear from him soon. That doesn't mean we haven't accomplished anything.*

Brendan and I and an elite group of the Troopers have been preparing space-going vessels to use in the attack of the Groga and Insenium planets. We seldom have to use these for anything but occasional rescue operations, so we have had to gear them up for war. This has required attaching weapons and equipping each of the cruisers with a fleet of space to ground small fighter vehicles capable of both space and planetary flight. Brendan is training the pilots for these and has performed admirably, I must say.

Our strategy for now is simple. Get as much intelligence as we can, make sure communications and logistics are kept up to speed, take advantage of every resource we have and not to take any shortcuts. This will be an all-out assault, but since we don't even have guesstimates of the numbers or technology we will be up against, for now we are keeping it simple. We are reviewing classic winning battle strategies. We will be preparing interruptions in their communications, supply lines and picking tactical targets for guerilla attacks where possible. Right now, lack of information and a ticking time clock are our most vicious enemies."

He sat and Arvid looked at Jenny. *"As Burt and Bob aren't here to report, can we get yours, Gatekeeper?"*

Jenny stood and realized that a lot of her report was good news. She told them about the agreement of the Daringi congress to support the war effort with resources and manpower. Brendan whistled at that news. She then told them about her breakthrough and the things she had seen of both Burt and Bob. Finally, she told them of her new ability to do two way communication, cautioning them that she had only had one successful attempt so far.

There was silence in the room, both mental and verbal. Then, they all began to talk at once, both among themselves in mindspeech and to Jenny wanting to know more details.

Tarafau stood, holding up both hands to quiet them. *"Jenny has taken the time to put all of this in writing and she has left nothing out. I wanted to keep this meeting as to-the-point as possible, simply because Gariel is correct. Time is our enemy. Please put any clarifying questions you have into writing and Jenny will post the answers on the team communication forum. Some of you caught it, but most of you didn't make the connection of the fact that there has been a great deal of information that must remain classified secret to all but those in this room, not counting Burt and Bob.*

The other thing you may not realize is how much more danger our Gate-keeper is in at this time because of these breakthroughs that have the potential to give our forces a great advantage. In order for her to pursue this and increase her abilities, Jenny will continue to work very hard. That is not to say that she will be separating herself from the team, but it will require a lot of time and effort on her part if we are going to be able to use it to our best advantage. Am I clear?"

All heads immediately nodded. Gariel raised a hand. *"May I ask one question that will be helpful for all of us?"*

Tarafau nodded and Gariel continued. *"Jenny, how often can you get reports to us as you continue to monitor Burt and Bob's progress? I don't desire to put any pressure on you. But both of those missions are vital..."*

"I will be doing a report three times a day when I can, but definitely every evening before I retire. I know how vital this is to all of us and I especially am concerned about Bob and Burt as well as the missions they are pursuing. I think you will agree that my report gives us reason to hope on both fronts."

Gariel nodded somberly.

Ingot stood and asked Myla and Liliath if they had any questions. Both shook their head, but Liliath spoke up.

"I want Jenny to know that Bob is in very good hands and in no discernible danger. My people are on constant watch of the gates in our dimension and they have some formidable abilities that most people, even in legend and myth, do not realize. I can't vouch for Burt, but I wanted to relieve your mind some-what."

"Each of you has done an admirable job in a very short time. There will be more assignments as we receive more intelligence about the enemy, and I have no doubt you will be successful. Mustapha will be facilitating communications and will keep your tablets updated as each new report comes in. Jenny will be staying with Juan for the next week or so and will be coordinating with Mustapha as we will need to encrypt communications. We have no illusions that our system is unbreachable and, if it was breached, we would need to be sure all communications are secure from prying eyes.

Jenny's guards will be traveling with her, but Tarafau will be working at Sanglarka until Jenny's new assignment is complete. The rest will continue your work and check in daily as you have been. If there are no questions, we will adjourn, and you may return to your team sites."

They all stood, and Jenny was suddenly completely encircled by her team, each of them holding the hand of another. *"This is what you must picture each day as you commence your mind exercises, Jenny,"* said Tarafau, looking straight into Jenny's eyes. *"You are surrounded by the support of this team family. There is not one of us who would not willingly give our life to protect you. Never, ever consider yourself replaceable. Cherish this thought. Take a moment and look around you. Look into our eyes and see our intent and our commitment."*

Jenny slowly turned on the spot, halting at each face, looking into eyes that radiated determination, respect and kindness to her. Each nodded in turn as she looked to the next face and the next. Without exception, each of them bared their heart in their eyes. Blue ones, brown ones, green ones and even alien ones. When she came full circle to Ingot, she crouched before him, looking deep into his eyes and saw tears brimming there. She hadn't thought of anyone crying over her. Her eyes welled up as well and she hugged him and then, standing, said simply, *"Thank you."*

Hugs ensued all around and the Earth Division of the Dimensional Alliance Defense Team departed to their assignments with a united and renewed commitment to the cause that had brought them together.

Chapter 18: Into the Den of the Beast

Burt was jerked to his feet just after the heavy wooden door opened. They had left him there for what seemed like ages, probably deciding what to do with him. He had been asleep, and in his dream, Jenny was calling to him, *"Burt, can you hear me? It's Jenny."* Of course, it was Jenny. He would recognize that mental voice among a crowd. The thought of her face, sweaty and flushed from her staff workout, tendrils of hair escaping from her ponytail flashed into his head. He knew she probably would have been a bit embarrassed to know that this was the picture that came to mind most easily. But he did find her attractive in that state, for sure.

But before he could respond, he had been rudely wakened by the flash of light and creaking from the door opening. They hadn't paused to address him or allow him to recognize them. They had yanked him up by both arms, secured his hands in those flexible cuffs and dragged him out of the cell. He was grateful he had taken the precaution of cleaning up his food and water, stowing them in his MDP and telling BaaGah to go back to his pant leg. So, he stood there blinking in the dim light of the army headquarters of the Groga, facing the Groga-ha.

He looked none too pleased, which was not surprising. Burt slapped a grin on his face, as sleepy as he was, and waited, tapping one foot.

The Groga-ha growled, baring large square stubby teeth as he did so. *"You, slimy ugglewurm, have now grinned your last grin. When the Insenium get their claws into you, you won't be so smug. As a matter of fact, your time has completely run out. We are sending you through the portal right this minute, and from there you will be their problem and good riddance."*

He turned on his heel, jerking his head at the two Groga who still held Burt's arms, somewhat painfully, as if they didn't expect him to be able to manage on his own. More than likely, they were fearful that if he had any access to his arms at all, even with his hands tied, he would use his alien magic to destroy them all. Actually, if it hadn't been that they were taking him exactly where he wanted to go, he could have done just that, even with them holding both arms in a death grip.

But he walked along, a cocky grin on his face, as if the Groga surrounding him were an honor guard. They were joined by a full platoon, who made the now familiar hollow square formation, with him and his three guards in the center and the Groga-ha at the head of the formation. At a command from him they all moved forward in an un-organized shuffle out of the city. They passed curious on-lookers, constantly looking around themselves as if they expected some kind of dramatic rescue attempt. For the most part, however the slaves and other Groga just stared. Burt had to assume this wasn't a common sight, that many armed Groga escorted one bound humanoid prisoner.

Burt grinned and nodded to every person he could visually connect with, sure that he was stirring things up. The guards on either side of him occasionally gave him a slap upside the back of his head, growling, as they did so, but Burt ignored it. He did think, however he might have a pretty good headache in the morning if he kept it up, but it was worth it.

If his arms hadn't been bound and his arms held firmly by his guards, he would have waved too. They exited the city gates and he stopped his grinning and nodding, as there was no one to see. He was sure his guards already thought him somewhat insane, one more reason for them to fear him. Why else would he act in this manner?

He should have been frightened out of his wits. If he had to be honest, only with himself, he wasn't as confident as he seemed. He was about to get the first glimpse of the really big bullies of the multiverse. He had no way of predicting what they would do with him, but he would get as much information as he was able, get some readings on "location" of the dimension (although location wasn't the right word) and get it somehow to his fellows in the Dimensional Alliance.

It was a long tromp along with the hundred or so Groga with Groga-ha puffing along ahead. The first thing Burt did when they got outside the gates was to mindspeak to BaaGah. *"Hey, buddy. Could you do me a favor? I need you to protect the covering for my MDP. On my wrist is a flesh-colored material that keeps people from being able to see it. Can you go into those spaces and keep anyone from looking under it?"*

"BaaGah is buddy. BaaGah help Burt. MDP has food in it? BaaGah take good care. Put hand in pocket."

Burt managed to get his hand into a front pocket, covering the gesture by pretending to stumble forward. The mild tingling sensation moved up Burt's pant leg and into his pocket and then disappeared.

"BaaGah protect MDP and food. Buddy, BaaGah."

Burt grinned. *"Yes, BaaGah is Burt's buddy. I will give BaaGah food when we finish our task."*

So, the way to BaaGah's heart was through his stomach? How hard could that be? He wasn't much bigger than a football. Surely keeping Baa-Gah fed was the least of his worries.

As he walked along, he realized he had absolutely no clue what to expect. This was a somewhat novel thing to him, as usually on expeditions like this he at least had some idea of what he would be dealing with. He imagined the beings of the Insenium to be fairly intelligent, as they had a manifesto of a sort and they had been able to recruit a vast force from at least two dimensions.

It also followed, since they had either found or had invented the portal creation and access mechanisms, that they had some understanding of technology. Whether they had invented these themselves or only had the intelligence to find the tech and use it were yet to be determined, but either way, probably more intelligence than the Groga or the Fleistians.

As far as their appearance or any special talents, he would have to wait and see. None of the Groga or any of the beings he had met so far, including King Nivi, had let any hints drop. Jenny's teacher among the Fleistians, Mynah, had spoken only of their philosophy and their hunger to put the dimensions in order under their rule.

He had an uncle who was famous for this. Uncle Art was the most meticulous soul he had ever met. Dust motes were afraid of him. He had never married, because that might have changed some of the order in his world. He had the spices alphabetized in his cupboards. You could have eaten off of his floors, but no one would have dared. His furniture was placed by measurement and a carpenter's square to be exactly in their appointed places and every placemat on his table was in perfect symmetry. Why he had more than one, Burt couldn't figure, as he never had visitors.

This would have been fine enough, but as he walked down the street, he carried a bag to pick up trash as he went. He straightened cans on grocery shelves and muttered about lazy, disorganized people. He once announced at a family gathering that, if he'd have his way, every child would be put through a boot camp that would teach them how to keep their lives in order. Burt chuckled. He also remembered that the kids would take turns while his back was turned talking to other adults, re-arranging his carefully laid out silverware. It made him crazy.

He came out of his reverie with a start. The column had stopped. At a signal from the Groga-ha, his guards dragged him forward, not that he made them work at it. By this time his fingers were beginning to tingle from the grip they had on his arms. The Groga-ha stood there in front of a wide stone portal arch with one of the gamepad-like devices in both hands. He twiddled with it and pointed. The Groga hauled him through the portal...

...to bright sunshine. Behind him the Groga-ha followed. All paused, blinking and allowing their eyesight to adjust to the beautiful light. But they weren't outside. The room in which they stood was cavernous and white. Light streamed in from huge windows high on every wall and through clear dome-like openings in the vaulted ceiling. Every wall was white, and the floor was polished white quartz with gold veins and crystals sparkling just beneath the polished surface. Sparkling chandeliers hung in the circular edges of the room that intensified the brightness even more.

The portal arch they had walked through appeared to be of some kind of ivory. And next to it was what could only be called a throne and, on the throne...

...Burt couldn't help it. He gaped. He had always been very good at controlling his facial expressions. It had been a requirement of his assignments. But this was a first. The being that sat regally upon the throne all dressed in silver was tiny, not like Arvid, but about the size and build of a five year old child. His hair was white and curly, and his face was serious. His huge violet eyes that reminded him of the big eyed children paintings of Margaret Keane on Earth, had surprisingly large pupils when you considered the amount of light in the room. His complexion was pale, but not white and his tiny rosebud mouth (as his grandmother would have called it) was neither smiling nor frowning.

He turned his head to look at all of them, *"Well?"* He arched his faint thin brows and waited. His mind voice did not sound like a child. *"Your message said this was urgent and all I see before me is a country dullard surrounded by enough guards to dominate a great warrior. What is the meaning of this? Are you bored? If you are, I can FIND something for you to do."*

The Groga-ha actually cowered before this tirade. He was reminded of European royalty. It wasn't so much about accent as it was about attitude. This tiny person radiated regality. He managed to sound threatening, regal and bored all at once.

In the meantime, Burt had regained his composure, if perhaps a beat too late. He grinned at the creature and sent, *"Greetings your magnificence. My name's Burt. What's yours?"*

The personage on the throne looked at Burt with, if possible, even wider eyes. But he answered. *"You have the honor of addressing His Most Potent and Excellent Imperial Majesty, Peril Inseni the 11th. You may address me, when I give you permission, as Imperial Majesty."* He turned to the Groga-ha.

"And I ask you again. Why is he here? I can't play nursemaid to your every need. The Fleistians have that dubious honor."

"Your Imperial Majesty," The Groga-ha began, but Peril cut him off.

"To be honest I don't even want to hear it, but now that he's here I have some questions for him. You may go."

The Groga-ha jumped and bowed and turned on his heel, adjusting his little gamepad. Burt's guards dropped his arms as if burned and followed their commander through the gate.

"*Be at your ease, Burt. You cannot harm me, and, at this point, I have no desire to harm you.*"

He clapped his hands and several small people just like him popped out from seemingly nowhere and brought a stool. It was low to the ground and the seat was small, but Burt assumed they didn't have much call for larger. Burt sat compliantly and waited. He didn't look around. He put on a neutral expression and waited. Everything about this situation was unexpected, even with all of Burt's experience traveling the dimensions he had not expected the big bad guys of the universe to be kindergartners.

Suddenly he realized he was hearing a grumbling of mindspeech that didn't belong to the Emperor. It was BaaGah and this surprised him. So far BaaGah had been quiescent, simply riding along. Now his mind voice was wordless, but very agitated.

"*Are you all right, buddy? What's the matter?*"

"*Bad, bad, BAD! Burt is in danger. These bad thingygummies. Make bad. Hurters!*"

"*It will be all right, BaaGah. I will keep you safe.*"

"*No safe! NO safe! Burt go far away.*"

"*I must stay, BaaGah. Will you leave me then?*" The thought of that saddened Burt for some reason.

There was a mental sigh. "*No, BaaGah stays. BaaGah always stays.*" And he went silent.

In the fraction of a second in which this conversation took place, Burt had settled on the little stool, his knees bunched up in front of him. Not comfortable, but it beat bowing or prostrating.

"*I have heard of the dimension from which you come,*" Peril began. "*We had troops there not long ago and your people defeated them. It was an unfortunate misunderstanding and I would hope to make it right. Can there be reconciliation between our peoples?*"

"*Sire, I am not authorized to do this, but I am sure it would be preferable to war between us. I cannot speak for the Alliance, but I would offer myself as a liaison. Would this suffice, for now?*" Burt said this in an even tone, looking straight into those huge eyes. Inside, however, his guts were churning. This was opposite in every way to what he had been expecting. He was expecting the Insenium beings to be these monstrous, horrid things, to be subjected to cruelty at the very least and yet here he was facing this almost angelic child creature who was speaking to him civilly. He would have to be careful. However, the slightest little niggle of hope began to warm up his emotions. What if they could actually find some common ground with these people? Lives could be spared, and a major conflagration might even be avoided.

He tamped down that whisper of hope. He needed to be careful and not assume anything. This was a fact-finding trip and he must be unbiased if he was going to give the Alliance solid information.

The emperor cocked his head in thought, his big eyes focusing contemplatively on Burt's face, obviously trying to detect any deceit in Burt's earnest words.

"*Very well. Let us proceed on the assumption that you are, as you say, a representative of this Dimensional Alliance. We will spend some time together and learn from one another. For now, we should allow you to refresh yourself. Adequate clothing will be provided and a place to sleep. When you are ready, ring the bell in your room and an attendant will bring you back to me in a more informal setting. I would be pleased to show you our city and help you see what we are doing here.*"

He touched an area on the arm of his throne and a servant came rushing over. He was dressed in livery, silver and black. He bowed to Peril and waited. "*Please escort this, um, gentleman to the best guest suite. See to it that he is allowed to refresh himself and provide him with suitable attire for a day in my presence. When he is finished with his oblations, he will call, and you may escort him to me in the sitting room.*"

The servant bowed again, *"Yes Your Imperial Majesty. Please come with me honored sir."* He gestured to Burt to follow. Burt nodded to Peril and followed his guide out of the vast chamber down a long hallway, past what must have been a dining room, judging from the smells issuing from it. His stomach growled in protest. *"May I have your name, friend? I don't want to just call you, 'Hey you.'"*

"I am Penchant, Burt. I will be your attendant while you are here. If you have any needs, you may simply ring the bell I shall show you. And here we are."

They stopped in front of a white carved door with a brass handle. He took a key from a ring on his belt and opened the door, gesturing Burt to precede him into the room.

Burt had been in some very nice hotels during his service in the Alliance, not to mention his elegant suite in the Alliance Headquarters building, but this was beyond anything that made any sense. Inside the door was a huge room with an additional door he assumed led to the bedroom and bath. At the far end of the room were large glass doors that opened out onto a balcony that was big enough to hold a party on. The furniture was actually human sized, which surprised him. Evidently, they did have visitors that were his size or similar. Something worth noting.

"Sir Burt," Penchant began.

"Just Burt, Penchant. I have no title to speak of. This is very nice. Do you often have visitors, um, my size?"

"From time to time. Our Empire stretches throughout our galaxy and beyond. Ambassadors and monarchs from other worlds visit on occasion." He said this with an air of pride; another thing worth noting. This man was definitely not someone he would want to engage in anything that might be suspicious or that might undermine his Empire. He was faithful; an admirable quality, but not useful for Burt, at the moment.

"A tailor will be with us shortly. I took the liberty of ordering you some food from the kitchen that you are welcome to eat out on the balcony. This will allow you to admire the city at your leisure. The main afternoon meal will probably be too long for you to wait." Penchant walked over to the bedroom door and opened it, leading the way inside.

"*You will find adequate bathing facilities through this door,*" he said, pointing at a door on the other side of the lavish bedroom with all the amenities. Burt realized he might get tired of white while he was here, however, as there was nothing of color with the exception of a few pastel decorative touches.

Penchant opened the bathing room door into a lavishly appointed tub large enough for Tarafau to have stretched out in. There were large fluffy towels, a robe and an array of soaps and shampoos along a shelf within reach of the tub. Penchant twisted a nob or two, showing the one for hot and cold. While the tub began to fill, he asked, "*Would you like some bath oils or anything else sir before I leave you to it?*"

Burt shook his head, somewhat relieved that Penchant would not be attending him in his bath. "*This will do nicely, Penchant. Thank you.*"

Penchant turned and left the room. Burt sighed and shut and locked the bathroom door. He had an itchy feeling about this. It was all too perfect. He spoke to BaaGah as he sat on the changing chair. "*Hey, buddy. Don't come out but climb off into my pant pocket. I have an idea how to feed you.*"

He casually put his hand into his pocket. He felt the immediate tingling as BaaGah obeyed. "*So here's how we will handle this. I will put my clothing into a messy pile, then rummage around in it as if I'm looking for something. That will mean I can get food out of the MDP for you and you can eat quietly under the clothes while I take a bath. When you're finished, just climb back onto a pant leg. When I'm finished bathing and I pick up the clothing, you can climb into the bath robe and from there into the wristband. This way, even if there is surveillance of some kind going on, they will have no idea you're there. OK?*"

"*Burt feed BaaGah? Ooh, Burt has spaces thingygummy. Thingygummy full of lots and lots.*"

Burt paused. "*Wait a minute. You can see into my MDP? You can see into the place where I store things? How is that possible?*"

"*Thingygummy is between spaces. Thingygummy has room for many things.*"

"*BaaGah, are you inside the...thingygummy?*"

"*Yes, Burt. It is in the spaces. BaaGah do wrong? Not go into thingygum-my?*"

"*Yes, please, BaaGah. We will talk about it later. Right now, eat the food I got out for you and let me take a bath, OK?*"

There was a mental sigh. "*OK, Burt. BaaGah is Burt's buddy. BaaGah will do this thing for Burt.*"

Burt thought about this new development while he soaked his aches out in the bath. He was so tired. It would be good to sleep in a soft bed tonight. But this thing with BaaGah? Burt had always been under the impression that you couldn't put anything living into the MDPs, or at least he had never heard of anyone doing so.

It was almost like a virtual storage place, where nothing existed in its actual physical state, like the molecules were just encoded there, but perhaps there was more to it than that. After all, it must have been named a Miniature Dimensional Portal for a reason. Was he actually carrying a gate around on his arm all of this time? A one way gate, to be sure. As far as he knew the gate only went to the storage area. He would have to have a long conversation with BaaGah before he went to sleep tonight, but for now, he had to prepare to meet with Peril.

Chapter 19: The Key in the Lock

Bob shook his head. It was late and he probably should have been in bed, asleep. But he had this feeling that he was so close to solving this puzzle. He'd never been one to give up easily. His dogged determination had been the result of many breakthrough patents in the world of AI and robotics and he knew there were few puzzles that couldn't be solved if you looked at them from enough different angles and with a lot of research and testing. He wasn't frustrated. He knew that multiple educated failures eventually brought results most of the time and he hadn't been working on this one for long enough to be discouraged.

Bob was no stranger to burning the midnight oil and although the rest had already gone to bed, he just needed a little more time on it right now. He stared once again at the metered readings they had done with the card and the key. They had tried a number of things, including having Anela hold the card while touching her key, trying to have her give a command to the card via mindspeech while touching both the key and the card, among other things. None of these had produced any noticeable results after that first small success.

Then at one point, there had been a noticeable reaction. But Bob couldn't figure out what had happened. The gate vibration meter had gone wild for a fraction of a second and then subsided. He was sure that was some kind of a breakthrough, but what?

This was why he was standing here in the lab while everyone else was comfortably sleeping in their beds. He decided to put up the video surveillance footage one more time, slowing it down considerably with the idea of pinpointing the event where the meter responded and seeing what he could glean from that perspective.

As he watched, Anela very slowly touched the card to her key and held it there. There was the slight variation they had already seen in previous times. Bob had hoped that by her holding the card and touching the key at the same time and simultaneously giving a mental command for a specific gate, that it would work. They had her sitting on the edge of the table, instead of laying down since they had already determined that the contact didn't seem to affect her in any way they could tell. However, he remembered that at this point Merv had entered the lab. Anela had turned and unbalanced. Bob had reached out to steady her and...THERE! He paused the video. The meter was peaking nearly off of the chart.

Bob examined the picture carefully. He had already looked at the screenshot of the meter for that time from every angle he could think of, but this was the first time he had viewed the footage of the entire scene.

They were frozen in that moment. Anela had her head turned and he could see Merv in the background, just coming around the end of one of the huge dragon tables toward their lab station. Bob was grasping Anela by one hand and the opposite shoulder to steady her. But what was different? The card was still touching the key at her neck, but not at any particular angle that he could recognize.

He picked up the card and held it up next to the still photo, positioning it exactly as it had been in the photo, noting the area of the card that was touching the key and how much of the key was showing. Bob remembered that Anela had not been focusing on a gateway at that moment, as she had just sent a mental message to Merv in greeting. So, what could have been stimulating the card or key or both in that particular instant?

He took a screenshot of that frame and sent it to his tablet to examine later. He really felt strongly that this was a breakthrough, but of what?

Now it was time to sleep on it. His brain often found solutions while he was sleeping after he had done all possible research and then posited the problem. Fidget followed him out the door as he secured the lab and went to his room. He had hardly noticed the surroundings of the suite they had so generously provided.

He missed Ignatius. The silly bird usually rode his shoulder to his room at the end of a long day of research when they were at home or at the Alliance headquarters, and he missed the bird, who had often been his sounding board while he was doing his research, before and even after Fidget was completed. Ignatius was a good listener and from time to time, some random exchange between the two of them had triggered something that led to a new direction in his research.

He didn't even bother to undress. He just plopped down on the bed. He didn't need a blanket as the temperature was pretty much perfect for sleeping. Fidget went "to sleep", shutting down for the night with the exception of his security sensors. Who needed a bodyguard when he had Fidget? He hadn't yet briefed Jenny on the new security features he had installed in Lizziebot's most recent upgrade. There had been no time. He made a mental note to tell her about it in his next mental communication with her.

He was amazed at her new talent and could see some very interesting applications. His most recent upgrade of Lizziebot, delivered wirelessly, included the mindspeech adjustment Fidget had received. The two things together presented some intriguing possibilities.

He turned that line of inquiry off for later and centered himself on the issue at hand. He knew there was an answer to the puzzle and his mind would work on it as he slept. Sometimes the result was the complete answer, when he did this, but most often it was just another piece to the puzzle. He would see.

As he drifted off to sleep, he could see on the screen of his mind that intriguing photographic instant, seeing the entire scene as clearly as the original photograph.

He didn't often dream, but this one was vivid. He was in his workshop laboratory at home. Ignatius sat on his perch, as usual, supervising whatever he was working on. On closer inspection it was a plastic puzzle with a piece missing. The piece was in the shape of an old fashioned keyhole. He looked and looked, on the floor, under the table and several unlikely places without finding it. As he was ready to give up, Ignatius cried out, "Bob, can you hear me?"

"Of course, I can hear you, you silly bird."

"Bird? What are you talking about?"

Suddenly Bob realized it wasn't Ignatius's voice.

He was wide awake. *"Jenny?"*

"Yep. I wanted to talk to you about something I now know about the Insenium. I've passed this on to Lova and the Alliance, but I thought you should know right away. Burt is in the Insenium and, although it doesn't make much sense, the Inseni look very much like small children, around 5 or 6 years old. I will know more soon, but something really interesting happened. You may not know, but I can hear mindspeech between two people, if I'm connected to one of them.

Evidently Burt has acquired a companion. Not a Linkling, but some kind of little creature shaped like a spaghetti squash and about the same color, with little orange knob-like protrusions on its skin. He's a cute little guy and somehow Burt ended up feeding him accidentally and the creature bonded to him. Anyway, it turns out the little guy, who calls himself BaaGah, can infiltrate solid matter such as a wall or floor or even cloth and completely conceal himself by blending in.

BaaGah calls it being in 'the spaces'. That is amazing enough, but it also turns out he can insert himself into an MDP, which shouldn't be possible, should it?"

Bob sat up with a start. *"He WHAT????"*

"That's what I thought," agreed Jenny. *"I keep forgetting the MDPs are portals too. Lizziebot tells me that no documentation exists on the science behind them and if the machine that creates them ever broke down there would be no more of them ever again."*

"Oh, I can guarantee there is documentation somewhere. No scientist ever does anything without keeping notes. The problem is that they are also very stingy with that information and often keep their notes in vaults or other hidden places. Many of them also put them in their own personal code or encryption. Thank you so much for sharing this with me. It may be the piece of the puzzle I'm looking for. I've been breaking my head on this thing. I've had some lucky breaks, but I haven't been able to connect the dots yet. This is a lead worth following. Can you do more than just watch Burt yet?"

"*So far, I've only been able to make a two-way connection with you, Amenia and Tarafau, but I'm working on it. It feels a little creepy watching him without his knowledge. And I have to take breaks, so I miss things. Being able to have an actual conversation with him would be a lot better. I really need to rest at this point, but I needed to tell you about this, or I wouldn't have been able to sleep.*"

"*Well done, Jenny,*" Bob said, wishing he could see her face. "*Any chance you might be able to make an image along with the verbal communication any time soon?*"

"*Amenia seems to think I'm close, but she doesn't want to work on it until I get the hang of connecting to more people. It feels a lot like magic to me, although I know there is science behind it. Every time I turn around, it seems like I have something else on my plate. No break in sight, though. I just hope we still aren't working on this, months from now. I don't know if my nerves can take it.*"

"*I don't think we have months or even weeks to figure this out, kiddo. If ever there was a 'rush-job', this is definitely it,*" Bob sent back. "*Keep me posted if you find out anything more about this. I'm happy to wake up in the middle of the night for any report you have to make, or even if it's just to say, hi.*"

"*Thanks, Bob. I'll let you get back to sleep, if you can. For now, I'm gonna get in a workout session, take a shower and get to bed myself. Take care. I wish I had a way for you to let me know if you needed to talk, but I don't see how.*"

"*Oh, that reminds me, before you go, I didn't get a chance to tell you about Lizziebot's new upgrades.*"

"*Upgrades? How did you do that?*"

"*Oh, they weren't physical, just software. I uploaded it through the Alliance communication network...THAT'S IT!*"

"*What? What's IT?*"

"*How I can communicate with you. DUH. I can send updates to Lizziebot and she will tell you I need to speak with you. I won't even have to send a message. Just tell Fidget and he will ring Lizzie and then you can get in touch with me soon as it is possible to do so. I promise not to overuse it.*"

"*Bob, you never cease to amaze me. Does that brain of yours calculate 24 hours a day? That's brilliant.*"

"Couldn't have done that one without you, kiddo. OK, let's both of us get some sleep. You saved me many hours of tearing my hair out by our little talk tonight. Big virtual hugs and sweet dreams."

"To both of us," Jenny agreed. *"I'll talk to you again soon."*

And then she was gone.

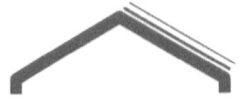

Chapter 20: The Little People

Burt came out of his bath refreshed and ready to face Peril, well, except for clothes. He didn't dare pull any out of his MDP, since that would reveal more about his resources than he cared to. However, when he got out of the bath, a towel wrapped around him and the bathrobe over that, he was surprised to find he had visitors. Two tiny men stood in the bedroom with Penchant, looking up expectantly at Burt.

In their arms were draped some cream colored clothing, a white shirt and some brown sandals. *"We apologize profusely for the footwear,"* sent one of them, looking abashed, his wide eyes cast down. *"We have very little in your size and no measurements to go by. These clothes were made for another diplomat who did not pick up his order and we were hopeful that they might fit you for now. Please try them on. The sandals will have to do until we have measured you as well. Once you are dressed, we will get your measurements and withdraw."*

Burt took the clothing, complete with under garments and put them on. Mostly they looked ok, although his wild hair possibly clashed a bit with the lordling outfit. The cloth was soft and breathed well and it fit a little loosely. When he went out to the living area, the two little men went immediately to work with knotted cords, measuring and noting their measurements on a small tablet strapped to their wrists.

They bowed to him when they were finished and retreated, not saying a word. Burt turned to Penchant; his brows raised. *"So, OK, what's next?"*

"Do you wish to eat? I can have food brought to the balcony as I said if you wish it."

"No, I'm good. I'd like to move forward as soon as possible.

"In that case, I am to escort you to the sitting room of the Emperor, milord. Please to follow me."

Burt was glad he had taken a moment while dressing to transfer Baa-Gah to the wristband covering his MDP. He was sure no one would have noticed, had BaaGah become some of the bedding or a part of the curtains, but he preferred, especially since the latest revelation about BaaGah's new trick, to keep him close at all times. He only wished he could somehow communicate with the Alliance about this. He was pretty sure this had some real potential in battle strategy, if he could figure out what BaaGah was doing and how he was doing it.

Penchant led the way down the wide hallway. At the end of the hall there were two large white doors with intricately carved polished brass handles. Penchant halted in front of the doors.

"I will enter first and announce you. When the Emperor bids you enter, pause just beyond me, bow and wait until he beckons you to sit. You may address him as 'Your Imperial Highness or High Lord Peril' as you choose."

Penchant knocked softly and opened the doors, stepping just inside. *"Your Imperial Highness, may I present, per your request, Burt Scout, representative of the Dimensional Alliance."*

Burt stepped forward as instructed, bowed and waited. Emperor Peril sat on a low cushioned chair appropriate to his size, his feet up on a small ottoman. He nodded in return to Burt's bow and beckoned him forward. Burt sat carefully in the chair indicated, but not in his usual sprawl. As flip as he tended to be, he did know how to behave in a business situation, and this was definitely the time to put on his best manners.

"Welcome, again, Burt Scout. I must say, you do look refreshed. Did my servants meet your needs?"

"They did indeed. I apologize for the sandals, but they didn't have any shoes to fit."

"That is not your doing, and I apologize for the lack. Shall we discuss why you're here?"

"I am here at the request of Your Imperial Highness. How can I serve?"

"I believe you will not be convinced of our honorable intentions without an opportunity to meet our people and observe our culture. Perhaps then, you will be able to go back to your Alliance council and give them a more accurate picture than you have heretofore received?"

"I promise to keep an open mind, sire." Inwardly, Burt knew that regardless of how open-minded he could be, that there was little to nothing that could explain away what had already happened across the dimensions where the Insenium was concerned. But he smiled and nodded.

"In that case, I would like to offer this: I will allow you an eight-day to explore The Insenium, unfettered or tracked. You may speak to anyone you choose, go where you wish. Nothing will be held back from you by any of the people in my kingdom."

"Even your military? Even your scientists?"

"Scientists? I don't know the term."

"What do you mean? Someone must know how your portals work, how your weapons work."

"Ohhh, you mean our wizards. Of course, if you wish to understand the magic. Have you the gift?"

"Alas sire, I am as you see me, a humble ambassador, but I do have an interest in the craft." Burt felt like he was in the middle of one of his favorite fantasy novels. Wizards? Really? He should introduce him to Merv. He almost chuckled at that thought but managed to maintain a straight face.

"I dare say you are probably hungry. I thought perhaps instead of the fare of the palace you might prefer to take a meal at my favorite inn. They have a hunter stew there that is superb. While we are there, I will procure a room for you and introduce you to some people to get you started on your quest for truth."

"Thank you, sire. That would be great."

The emperor stood and gestured for Burt to rise. Burt followed him out of the sumptuous little parlor, out the double doors held by a servant he had not noticed was there. Did the man stand by the door all day at the rare chance that the emperor might need to leave the room? Burt couldn't imagine that.

As they strolled down the wide carpeted hallway, Peril said, *"Before we leave the palace, I need to give you this."* He held out his little hand and in it was a silver medallion on a chain with the likeness of the emperor engraved on it. *"When you wear this, it shows you are on my errand. No one will deny you anything. You can get anything from any shop, and they will send me the bill. You can talk to anyone and they must take the time to speak with you. This should facilitate your exploration and prevent any misunderstandings."*

Burt took the medallion from Peril and placed the long chain around his neck. To his shock and surprise, the chain instantly shortened to just below the neckline of his high-necked shirt. *"Thank you, Your Imperial Majesty,"* he sent, trying to keep the sarcasm from his mental voice. *"I appreciate your generosity."* He realized he had just fallen into a potentially deadly trap, even if he didn't know the extent of it and wanted to fume, but he kept his face impassive.

Peril seemed to notice his dissatisfaction with the situation, however. *"I assure you; it is a simple thing to remove the chain. The spell on it simply is a precaution to keep you from accidentally losing it."*

"How thoughtful of you, sire."

They came to the entrance of the palace out into bright sunlight.

The door opened out into a wide bricked courtyard surrounded with long rectangular planters filled with pale pastel flowers and sculpted topiary in the forms of what Burt could only assume were native beasts. There was no statuary and the courtyard was empty. At the far end was a trellised gateway of what he assumed was wrought iron painted white. They passed through this onto a street paved with what might have been smooth, pale concrete. There were no vehicles on the street, but there were many people coming and going into what he assumed were shops and other commercial buildings.

The people were mostly Inseni, with the same huge eyes and diminutive size. They all seemed to be clothed in pastels of many hues. It was almost like someone had taken a movie and desaturated all of the color. The only bright color in the picture was the sky, a bright aquamarine almost too intense until he realized that this was not a sky, but the ceiling of a dome that stretched as far as his eyes could detect and so far above them that the curve of the dome was almost invisible to the eye.

He had been in domed cities before. Most of the time, people constructed domes because the surroundings were inimical to humanoid life. Oftentimes a domed city meant that the population had not originated on the planet but had colonized the world for various reasons.

In addition to the Inseni, there were some Groga and a few humanoid slaves, some of which followed their masters, carrying bundles. Some of them, however, purposefully strode along on their errands. Their clothing was generally white or grey. Burt assumed this may have meant a difference in rank among the slaves, but for now, he withheld judgement.

The shops along the street bore no signs, but each had a designating icon above their door indicating what they did, similar to ancient towns on Earth he had visited in Europe. Finally, they came to a larger establishment with plate and bed over the door. Peril led the way through the door and was greeted with bows and led to a private booth on one side of a common room filled with tables and chairs. The serving person was male, a white apron covering his belly and a blue skullcap on his head. He was, like all of the male Inseni he had seen so far, clean shaven, rosy cheeked and quiet. His mouth set in the same impassive position as all he had seen.

He had noticed in the streets that none had used verbal speech at all. They appeared to be a totally non-verbal culture that showed their emotions only through the expression of their eyes.

The server greeted them. *"Your Imperial Majesty and guest, we are honored by your presence here at the Wayfarer Inn. How may I serve you today?"*

"First, could you make arrangements for a good room for my guest, Burt Scout? You will notice he wears the Imperial Pass around his neck and you will offer him all hospitality in whatsoever thing he requires of you."

"Of course, sire. Is there anything else? Do you require we bring his things from the palace?"

"He has no things to bring as his visit was...unexpected. However, we would like one of your fine meals, as he has not yet eaten this day. You may serve him what you serve for me. Also, please arrange for a guide. He will be exploring the city and for the first few days he may need some aid in this."

The servant nodded, bowed and bustled off, appearing to give mental commands to other servants and hurrying to the kitchen.

"This is a very nice place," Burt commented. And indeed, it was. The room had a beamed ceiling and a white tiled floor. Every surface gleamed clean and white, reminding Burt of a diner he had visited on Route 66 in the states one time. The serving bar was of some blonde polished wood with a beautifully patterned grain. The tables and chairs seemed to be of the same material. Light streamed in from windows high on the walls supplemented by crystalline ceiling lamps.

The smells emanating from the kitchen were appetizing and the lunch crowd here was quiet and mannerly. All in all, a genteel place for a business lunch indeed.

"I do enjoy it. I come here from time to time with a guest to enjoy the cuisine and the atmosphere. Very different from the formality of dining in the palace. Relaxing. You may dine anywhere you choose in the city, due to your pass, but I believe this is the best establishment around."

"I noticed your city is under a dome. Are all the cities on your planet protected in this way?"

"Yes, although there are few cities on this planet. The Empire is spread throughout this galaxy. Most of the planets we have colonized have an atmosphere more hospitable than here in the center of the Empire. Most of the domes on this planet are for farming and industry. You can arrange to visit any of these you would like. I truly wish you to experience life in the Insenium Empire, that you may take back a favorable report to the Alliance."

"So, the Insenium began on this planet?"

"No, we originated elsewhere, but we had to retreat from that place. It became inimical to life. Fortunately, our wizards are very clever and determined a way for us to escape that situation and to come here. Once we were firmly established, we made it a priority to settle on more than one planet as a safeguard, if it ever became necessary to relocate again."

"When may I meet these wizards? I feel I can learn much from them that will be helpful in my report. Obviously, these are the scholars of your culture."

But Peril did not reply, as the server had come with their food. It consisted of bowls of some kind of stew that smelled appetizing, a basket of rolls and what looked like some white sliced cheese.

"And there will be Your Imperial Majesty's favorite nectar cakes for dessert, of course," The server said as he handed each of them a linen-like napkin.

"Thank you, that will do," sent Peril and the servant bowed again and re-treated.

What happened next completely changed Burt's perspective on this mild seeming tiny man. The little cupid-bow mouth hinged open into a huge opening, to envelope an entire roll. The exposed teeth reminded Burt of a great white shark. Then the mouth closed back to its original tininess, while Peril's jaw worked, chewing the roll contentedly.

Burt realized this was a test and he tried not to show his surprise. Instead, he grabbed a roll, opened his mouth as wide as he could and stuffed the entire roll into his mouth, closing it as best as he could to chew. It was tasty and light, so it compressed pretty quickly, and he was able to chew it without choking.

"Tasty," he sent and put his most insolent grin on his face, wiping the corners of his mouth daintily with the cloth napkin and placing it back on his lap.

It turned out that the bowl of the soup spoon concealed under the stew was more like a ladle. Burt tried not to watch Peril eat, his head down, concentrating on eating from the ladle spoon without spilling. At least with mindspeech he didn't have to worry about talking with his mouth full.

"You'll want to get some clothing and some shoes that fit," Peril sent while masticating the chunky stew. *"You can get transportation to the other domes at the station. Your guide will be happy to show you."*

"Thank you, sire. I am looking forward to it."

At this point, Burt realized that the emperor had already finished his meal and was wiping his mouth with his napkin. *"I must leave you now. Much to do. You can send a messenger to the palace if you need anything you can't find here. I will arrange a meeting with the wizarding guild in the coming days. Please enjoy your stay in the Insenium. We will speak when you are ready to return to the Alliance. There will be no barriers to your return by any of our people either here or in Fleist."*

He stood and without any ceremony left the table and went out the inn door. Burt just sat there for a moment. Then, he decided to take his time with his meal while he considered what to do next. As it was, he expected the baby-faced emperor with the mouth of a shark wasn't the only surprise awaiting him. And he had another surprise to consider. He sighed. One step at a time, but quickly. He needed to be both thorough and speedy, if he was going to carry this off and still get all the information he would need to help the Alliance successfully put down the Insenium threat.

Chapter 21: Fidgeting

Jenny wiped the sweat from her face with the towel she kept at her belt. She grinned at her bodyguards and plopped onto the bench by the workout room wall with a happy sigh. It had been a good workout and she was ready for a shower and a change of clothes before she began her mental workout.

This had become her new routine. First, basic breathing exercises and stretching, then her martial arts workout, rotating through staff, hand to hand and now sword practice, something she had never thought she would ever do or even be very good at, but it turns out her work with the staff had taught her the balance and stance that worked with sword practice as well. She knew she would probably never win any prizes, but she could defend herself better than anyone would ever suspect she might be able to, which might give her enough of an edge to defend against an opponent if the situation ever came up again. She suspected it probably would, but for now, the physical workouts were her least challenging.

However, every day, after showering and changing she and Chidwi went to the warm little room Lova had arranged for her and sat down on the carpeted floor, Chidwi in her usual position behind her. The room had been well insulated from noise and distraction. As she sat there, she went through the more complex breathing and relaxation routines that Amenia had taught her.

Once she was deep into the trancelike state those exercises induced, she mentally entered the fortress she had erected dividing her conscious mind from the deepest and least accessible part of her subconscious mind. A guard met her in front of the spiked portcullis and saluted. There, on the drawbridge, next to the guard stood Amenia.

"Hello, Amenia. What will we explore today?"

"Let's retire to the communications room. We will be reaching out again, but slightly differently than before. We will be working on enhancing your two way communication abilities. I have a plan." She smiled warmly at Jenny and Jenny smiled back.

"Whatever you say, Amenia. I know this will be useful. I had another session viewing Burt last night and I think he may be in more trouble than he realizes, but he also holds a key he doesn't understand and I think I can help him, if I can finally figure out how to communicate with him."

They entered the communications room, Chidwi on her shoulder. There was a new addition to the room that Jenny had installed per Amenia's suggestion last time they were there. It was a contraption, which was all Jenny could think to call it.

"This," said Amenia, pointing to the contraption, "is a cell tower. I heard about them from Tarafau. If I understand it right, it relays a signal from one cell phone device to another far away and allows two way communication. Is that right?"

"Um, yes, but what does that have to do with my block?"

"Actually, it is a focal point, much like a magic wand in your Earth fairy tales. Anytime you encounter 'Magic', as you call it, it is one of two things. Either it is very complex and practiced trickery, or it is mental abilities disguised to make those abilities more acceptable and at the same time very mysterious. Slap a label on it, such as sorcery or magic and all of a sudden, a common thing becomes very mysterious and entertaining.

This cell tower is a focal point for two way communication. Right now, you are receiving information, but not broadcasting. This means your signal needs a boost. This will give you one. Of course, in order to communicate with someone on a cell phone, you must know their number, correct? What if you had a phone number for everyone you wanted to communicate with in your mind?"

Jenny considered this. She knew that a large part of her abilities had to do with creative visualization, which was why there was a fortress and inside the fortress there were buildings that served various purposes such as the library where she stored memories and thoughts and the communications center where she went to communicate. She had yet to visit some of the other buildings in her fortress and, as of yet, had no idea what their function was. Amelia had explained that this would come in time.

But for now, she realized that Amenia may be right. Perhaps, like shaking the guard's hand or typing a name into the search engine on the computer in the communications center, this was another visualization she needed.

She realized that Chidwi had placed her hands on her shoulders in the real world, as she often did when Jenny was working on her abilities. Her soft, tiny hands were warm and seemed to be capable of spreading calm throughout Jenny's soul. She had a hard time remembering what it had been like to be without her. In the short weeks since their bonding, Chidwi's companionship was more like adding a missing part of her than meeting a new friend. It was like they had always been intended to be together, even across dimensions.

Now, returning in her mind to the control room, Amenia instructed her to turn the cell tower on. Sure enough, there was a big red button on the tower platform. The spire of the tower reached up through the ceiling where a hole had appeared conveniently enough, just the perfect size opening. When she pushed the button, the thing started a quiet hum and small LED lights sparkled along one side.

"OK, it appears to be running. What next?"

"You need numbers, as I said. Go ahead and do a search for Luz's number."

Jenny obeyed. Up on the screen popped a series of numbers related to Luz Roman. She looked inquiringly at Amenia. "Don't I need something to input these numbers into?"

"I never thought you'd ask," Amenia replied with a grin and held out her hand with the latest smartphone, copied, as Jenny thought from her own. "There's a special app on there. Just click on Chidwi's face."

She laughed and touched the icon that represented Chidwi. A new screen popped up that said, "register mind contact information". It was similar to the contact screen on her phone. She obediently entered the number for Luz and pushed save.

Now a new button was available that said, "Luz Roman".

"OK, Jenny. Your roadblock is removed. You may call Luz and, this time, she will hear you and be able to respond."

Jenny nodded and dutifully pressed the link. She found the room melting around her as before. This time, Luz was in her large sunlit kitchen, preparing a salad. Jenny said, "Luz, can you hear me?"

Luz looked around, a puzzled look on her face.

"*Luz, it's Jenny. I'm not in Puerto Rico. I'm in Sanglarka. I can see you preparing a salad in your kitchen.*"

"*Jenny? How is this possible? Do we have some new tech I should know about?*"

"*No, it's just me. It seems all of these mental workouts have shown me I have some new abilities and I am practicing. How are you and Juan?*"

Luz's expression had changed. Her eyes crinkled in a big smile. "*You have come a long way. I miss you, but Juan and I are being kept busy with all of the preparations for an assault on the Insenium. We just wish we had more to go on. It's hard to make arrangements like this without more information than we have.*"

"*Then you'll be glad to hear that I have a connection with Burt, and he has discovered a lot of new information, as he is currently on the Inseni homeworld and by an interesting and dangerous subterfuge has been given free rein to do as he pleases. He is in the process of discovering everything he can about the Insenium and their plans.*"

Jenny spent the next half hour telling Luz what she had discovered so far and what Burt was up to. By the time she was finished, Luz was nearly dancing on the balls of her feet.

"*I'll be sure to fill Juan in. Can you connect directly with him also?*"

"I am sure I can. I've had a major breakthrough today. Up until now, the only person I have been able to communicate with other than just watching what they were doing was Bob. He is very close to something significant as well. I believe in the coming week we will have a much better chance of putting this whole thing to rest once and for all. Amenia has been working me hard and this new ability is exciting, but she tells me I haven't yet reached my full potential. Not sure what that will mean to our mission, but I continue to learn new things every day.

The Sanglarka headquarters aren't even aware of this new thing yet. For some reason I thought you would be the easiest to make contact with, so you are the first."

I'm honored." Luz beamed. *"I wish I could see you. You say you can see me?"*

"It's as if I am standing in front of you in your kitchen. Amenia thinks I may be able to manifest a live image of myself at some point, but for now, I can only use mindspeech. Bob says it is somewhat disconcerting to have me in his head without being able to see my face. He says he doesn't know where to look while he's talking to me."

Luz laughed. *"Bob is right, you know. Usually when we use mindspeech we are in each other's presence, so this is definitely a new experience."*

"Well, I hate to leave you, but I need to move on to make some other connections. According to Amenia, once I have made two way contact with you, I can find you wherever you are to update you or even just to chat. How cool is that?"

"Jenny, do you have any idea how amazing you are? Every person on this team already looks up to you. You are accomplishing things you never imagined a year ago and you are just beginning. Lizzie made a really good choice when she passed the L.A. gate to you. And I don't think it was a coincidence that you were there to receive Miriha's key. The Alliance had no idea how much they would need you and your abilities. Please take care. You are precious to us."

Jenny felt tears welling up in her eyes. *"Thank you. That means a lot coming from you. I will get back in touch soon. Give Juan a hug for me?"*

"Will do, gladly. Goodbye, Jenny." And she made a gesture as if she were reaching out to hug her.

Luz's kitchen faded away and again she was in the communications room.

Amenia was grinning like the Cheshire Cat. "You did it, Jenny! That was amazing."

"I couldn't have done it without that little visualization trick of yours."

"Once you get the hang of it, you won't need the cellphone anymore, but for now, let's see if we can program in a few more. I know you've already done two-way with Bob, but I have a thought. Bob said Fidget has mind-speech. Let's see if you can make a direct connection."

Jenny obediently typed in "Fidget" into the search bar. It brought up a number which she programmed into the phone. She hit the send button.

Once again, the communications room faded, and she found herself in the living area of the suite Bob lived in at the palace. Fidget was standing next to Bob, who was eating what looked like supper. One of the things she didn't have any control over at this point was relative time. It was morning where she was and obviously evening there. The room was lighted with lamps as it was twilight outside the windows of the suite. From there she could see mountains that would dwarf the mountains surrounding the Sanglarka valley.

"Fidget? It's Jenny. Do you hear me?"

"Indeed, Jenny. It is a pleasure to see you again."

"See me? You can see a visual representation of me?"

"It is, as Bob would say, a figure of speech. Do you have the ability to make yourself seen?"

"Not yet. I'm working on it. How is your project coming?"

"Which one? We now have two and perhaps a third, if we can work out the science of it."

"Well the one I was thinking of was your MDP experiments."

Bob continued to eat, oblivious of the conversation going on in his presence.

"We haven't gotten back to it, but I think Bob has something specific in mind related to the card. He thinks the science that allows the MDP to do what it does is intrinsic to the individual portal device. He is very concerned that the portal card technology will be very dangerous if there are more of them out there, especially if the Insenium is farther along in its research than we are."

"I can see where widespread use of this technology would be devastating." Jenny said soberly. "I find myself grateful every day that Tarafau's people are so responsible and peaceful. What they can do could be very scary if possessed by a warlike people. According to what I learned while I was on his planet, they didn't discover their dimensional travel abilities until after the peace movement had been successful, and they never considered using it for insidious purposes."

"I agree," Fidget replied. "We will be doing some exploring in the MDP later this evening. You would be welcome to come along. I could use your viewpoint. Humans see things differently than I am currently able to do. Although, I am learning and growing daily. Speaking of which, have you noticed the new upgrade on Lizziebot? I sent it earlier today."

"Which means it happened while I was asleep. So, what have you done to Lizziebot then? As far as I know she is functioning very well."

"It isn't to correct error. Lizziebot is practically perfect in every way, but as I get new tech, we have permission from the Alliance to also install it on Lizziebot and any other of Bob's bots that will be used strictly in the confines of Alliance projects. If you activate Lizziebot when you are finished with your current project, you will find she now has mindspeech like myself."

"Wow! I can hardly wait to try that out. And obviously, based on the fact that I can communicate with you, others should be able to communicate with her as well. Thank you, Fidget. That will make a lot of things much easier and may be important in later endeavors."

"Bob wants to make sure you have every edge he can give you. He mentions you a lot. I think you are pretty constantly in his thoughts, at least when he isn't focused on what he calls 'sciency stuff'. He is in a very favorable atmosphere, at the moment, for achieving his goals."

"Well, thank you, Fidget for the conversation. You will hear from me again. How long before you go back into the MDP?"

"Bob usually spends some time reading after supper, before he heads back to the lab. It's a requirement of Cornelium that he take adequate breaks. So, maybe about two hours Earth time."

"I will return then, Fidget. Goodbye. Don't tell Bob we talked. I want to surprise him."

To her astonishment, Fidget chuckled. *"Goodbye Jenny. My lips are sealed."*

Bob's living room faded from view and she was back with Amenia in the communications room.

"That was extremely informative, Jenny," said Amenia with an exultant grin on her face. "Communicating with such as Fidget is highly unusual. How do you think that works?"

"I'm not sure, but did you notice the chuckle? A robot with a sense of humor? How...wait. Come to think of it, Lizziebot has been known to tell a joke and to be amused at something. What is Bob doing? Lizziebot was doing that before she was Lizziebot. Even the AI in the tablet seemed to have Lizzie's personality.

Bob always seems so humble and inobtrusive about his work. He is definitely not a show-off or a praise-junkie. And yet, some of the things I have seen so far from him are beyond any tech available on Earth. I tend to think of him as my kindly neighbor across the street, but he is really brilliant beyond anyone I have ever met without being absorbed with himself, which is almost as rare as his intelligence and inventiveness."

"But you realize, Jenny, that this shows me your ability is the most unique I have come across. We are just touching the surface. As Fidget inferred and as Luz stated, this means we must be extra careful to keep you safe. You have become a rare and priceless asset to the multiverse.

I don't want to overwhelm you with my speculations of where your abilities might take you, but, if it wasn't for your very grounded and generous nature, you would be frightening to contemplate. Another reason we must continue to work on the guardianship of your mind.

Like any muscle, this must be continually exercised to keep you safe. I know that while we are working together, you are very disciplined with your practice, but the time will come when you will have to work alone. Never forget that these gifts do not come without a price. Only you can determine whether you are putting in the work that is needful. You will eventually get to a point beyond my ability to guide you. At that point, you will need to guard yourself.

I was considering sending Elizabeth to you as extra protection. Would that be distracting, or would it be helpful?" Amenia had cocked her head, waiting for a reply.

"Yes, please do. I have worked out with her enough to know she is not only strong, but canny, and I and my guards would profit from her expertise. Besides, I love her, and it would be a comfort to have her with me, as it is to have you teaching me. I'll be honest. I miss the family and your people. It was a joy to visit there with you all."

Amenia gave her a hug, which she was actually able to feel. "How is it I can feel that hug?"

"This environment is similar to a dream. In a dream, your mind convinces you that you can feel pain and pleasure. Because we are currently existing in the realms of the same place where your dreams come, it feels real to you until you come back to your waking rational mind. When you pushed the button or held the phone, you could feel it in your hand. In this way, you can be completely engaged in your mental experience. This could also be a danger, if anyone ever got past the guard at the portcullis leading into your realm."

"Well, then, let's take a quick break. After all, I have a date with Fidget in about an hour and a half and I mustn't be late. When do you think Elizabeth will be able to come? I would love to have her here when I'm Fidgeting, and I could use a good physical workout before I do."

"Oh, didn't I tell you?" Amenia's eyes crinkled in amusement. "Elizabeth just got there. She's waiting for you in the dining room."

And Jenny severed the connection while she and Amenia were both laughing together.

Chapter 22: Game Theory

Burt sat on the edge of his bed in his small bedroom in the inn. To anyone observing his behavior or trying to listen in, he was just sitting there and staring out into space with his hand in his pocket. Actually, he had gotten BaaGah to locate the small cellphone-like device he used for detecting surveillance equipment.

The device had found nothing, but now he was considering the fact that although most principles of known physics applied in nearly all the dimensions the Alliance had dealt with over the time the Gate Network had been in place, it still didn't account for the different levels at which different cultures used that technology.

In the case of the Inseni planet, they still called science magic and he had yet to speak to the "wizards" of the Insenium. So, he was trying to decide whether it was safe to bring BaaGah into the open or not.

Finally, he decided not to chance it yet. He just didn't know enough for it to be safe. He wouldn't be able to bring anything out into the open from his MDP, even in the so-called privacy of his room. Therefore, he stacked the two pillows on the bed one on top of the other, took off his sandals and leaned back, his hands behind his head.

"BaaGah? How're you doing, buddy?"

"Buddy is just fine, Burt. I hide from the bad guys still. You have chocolate?"

Burt grinned. *"Sure. I will let you go get some in a minute. But first, I want to talk to you about something you did earlier. How can you manage to go into the MDP? It isn't like a sleeve or a floor or a pant leg. This is advanced tech that none of us understand and you just went in there like you were opening a door."*

"It's in the spaces. Burt not understand spaces. I know because he never uses them."

"You're right, buddy. I don't know anything about them. Can you explain it to me?"

BaaGah did the mental equivalent of shuffling his feet uncertainly. *"BaaGah will tell Burt what he can. Is big words that BaaGah doesn't know how to say. Will try. Burt not be mad?"*

"No, BaaGah. Just do your best. When we get back home, I will let you talk to a friend of mine. Bob will be very interested in you and what you know. He will help you find words that will work, OK?

"OK, Burt. I will try. Spaces is everywhere. Spaces in you and me and dirt and rocks and even food. Everything has tiny things that make big things and all of those tiny things hold hands to make things hard or large or scary. Even when those tiny things hold hands, there are spaces. All of us can see them and move between them."

"'All of us'? There are more of you? More like BaaGah?"

"Ah yes, of course. BaaGah is Mookookie. Mookookie all like me. Mookookie live in the spaces. Bad guys hate Mookookie. Bad guys hurt Mookookie. Mean bad guys. Scary bad guys. Mookookie hide."

"Peril says they came to this planet from somewhere else. Did they bring your people with them?"

"No... Mookookie here first. Mookookie are happy here until bad guys come. BaaGah help Burt. Chase away bad guys. Make them leave and never come back. Burt can stay, though."

"I would like to meet the Mookookie someday, BaaGah. So how do you use the spaces and what does that have to do with the fact that you can use the MDP?"

"Your thingygummy is just spaces. Only in it, the spaces join hands like the tiny things. It is like Burt's pants, with holes on top of the holes."

Burt realized BaaGah was talking about the weave of the fabric of his pants. He knew he would have to contemplate this for awhile to put it all together and probably consult with Bob.

"Also, there are roads between the spaces."

Burt sat up with a start, remembered his ruse, stretched as if getting the kinks out and lay back on the pillows once again.

"*Roads? What kind of roads? They wouldn't be made of yellow brick, by chance?*"

"*Brick? BaaGah doesn't know brick.*"

"*Sorry, just me being silly. What kind of road?*"

"*Sparkly road. Roads on top of roads like spaces on top of spaces. All holding hands. Roads to many places. Roads to empty places. Roads to the dark place and the bright places. Too many roads for counting.*"

Burt was flabbergasted. It just didn't seem possible that these complex ideas were coming to this simple creature? Obviously, he had underestimated him. What else might he have missed if he hadn't fed the little guy? It was obvious he and BaaGah would be having some extended conversations.

"*Well, BaaGah, tomorrow looks like it will be a long day. Let's get some rest.*"

"*Chocolate?*"

"*Oh, yes. Chocolate. You may get a chocolate bar from the food stash. Only one. I don't want to make you sick.*"

"*OK, one. More tomorrow? Wrapper too?*"

Burt couldn't help but laugh. "*More tomorrow and wrappers too,*" he agreed. "*Now, let's get some sleep.*"

The room was warm enough that Burt didn't even bother with the blanket. He pulled one pillow out from under his head and slept in his clothes. He knew he would look a wreck tomorrow, but perhaps he could steam them in his bath in the morning enough to pull out the worst wrinkles.

As he drifted off, he realized he must be more tired than he had thought. With all of the events of the day, he knew that normally he wouldn't have slept a wink.

In his dream he was at his favorite fishing place. It was a small eddy off of the Merced River in Yosemite. His mom and dad had taken him there once on one of their infrequent vacation trips. He had been about fourteen at the time and he and his dad had found this place, a bit off the beaten track.

The water in the little pool was so clear that at first, they thought it was just a few feet deep. However, it had turned out to be more than 12 feet deep when Burt had decided to jump in to cool off. The fish had scattered, and he had gone under way over his head, without actually touching the bottom. The stones that lined the bottom were of different colors and shapes all smoothed by their long term residence in the water and could be seen so clearly from the rock that they looked like you could just reach down and grab one.

Trees surrounding the pool filtered the sunlight and there was a soft breeze. He hadn't thought of this place in years. He sat down on the big flat rock hanging over the pool that he used to sun himself on all those years ago, to enjoy watching the fish.

All at once there was a shadow that didn't belong to him. He looked up to see Jenny. She had her hair up in two ponytails. She was adorable. She smiled down at him and his surprise.

"Hey there, Burt. How are you? Having fun in the Insenium?"

"Uh, what do you know about that? Uh, wait. This is a dream. Of course, you would know."

"Actually, although you are really dreaming, this is really me. You see, I've learned a few new tricks since the last time we talked. Amenia has been schooling me in a few new abilities. The nice thing about visiting you in a dream is that it takes up nearly no real time and it means it makes us appear to be talking naturally instead of mindspeech because we are actually already in each other's minds. May I sit?"

"By all means Jenny. Wow, I don't know how many more surprises I can take. First the Inseni, then BaaGah, now you."

"How has BaaGah surprised you, besides the fact that he can eat pretty much anything and can hide in your pant leg?"

"How did you know about this? Mind completely blown. Start from the beginning."

So, Jenny told him about her previous viewings of him and how that had come out of her visit with Tarafau. She told him about what Bob was engaged in and the breakthrough with Fidget. He listened with absolute fascination both with the narrative and the opportunity to watch her face as she spoke. She was so earnest and animated. In this setting she seemed different somehow. She was dressed as if she was at a picnic, clean blue jeans, a t-shirt and sneakers. He had heard she was an avid hiker, but up until now, he could never picture her that way. The last time they had been in an informal setting together it was in the Amazon jungle, both of them dressed in camo and boots and really sweaty.

"So, as you see, I am up to date for the most part on your situation, but I couldn't get through to you to tell you what was going on at home. I have been passing on reports to the appropriate people soon after you started your mission. I hope you don't mind. I was just discovering my abilities and you were one of the first people who came to my mind."

"I'm flattered," he said and realized he meant it. "So, let me catch you up on the newest with the Insenium and BaaGah, so you can have a complete picture to give to headquarters."

And he reported everything that had happened since she last peeked in. She listened attentively and a couple of times he almost lost his place in his narrative, realizing he was looking deep into those amazing blue eyes and being somewhat swallowed up in them.

"Wow, I think that BaaGah trick has some real potential," Jenny commented. "I'll pass it on to Bob. I'll be visiting him at his lab next. I have a date with Fidget."

"Lucky robot. What exactly was his pick-up line so I can file it for future reference?"

Jenny laughed. "It was his electric personality, I suppose, and he offered 'sciency stuff' and some amazing 'dastardly alien tech'. Not to mention, dragons."

Burt shook his head. "How's a guy to compete with that?

So, how do we make best use of this handy new skill of yours? You can drop in on me, but I have no way of notifying you if I need to talk to you."

"Well, for one thing, I can get Lizziebot to calibrate a time zone for you, so I know when you are awake and when you are asleep. Do you have an idea of how long your days are there?"

"Not yet. I'm going to teach BaaGah how to read my chronometer so I can do some measurements. I don't dare bring any of my tech out where anyone can see it. But his new little trick with the MDP means I may be able to set up a little office in there for him and make him my personal assistant."

"What a great idea, as long as you can convince him not to eat the office supplies. At any rate, once we figure out how our day and night cycles coordinate, I will be able to make some appointments with you for two-ways. With your permission, I would like to be able to continue to monitor you and your activities. I always felt a little concerned about invading your privacy."

"Well, so far you haven't observed me in my bath, so I don't suppose it's a big deal."

At this she blushed bright red and ducked her head. This was so adorable that he didn't continue to his next thought.

"OK, then," she said briskly. "Chidwi just gave me the signal that it is nearly time to visit Bob. Anything you would like me to tell him?"

Burt thought about this. "Nah, just let him know I'm safe and I'm on the trail. I'll try to give you a heads up when I'm going to meet with the 'wizards', so you can observe and report. Thanks, Jenny. I was really feeling more alone than usual on this mission. Knowing you're there will make a big difference."

"Well, you do have BaaGah, remember. So, you're not completely alone, are you?"

"You always put such a positive spin on things. It's one of the things we like about you."

"We?"

"You know, all of us on the team. I mean, we all are really glad you are part of the team. You are really making a difference, you know?"

"Oh, thank you, Burt. That means a lot coming from you. I hafta go, but I'll be back in touch soon. Now that I have made this connection, I will also be able to converse with you in the waking world, although I have to admit you picked a good spot for today's meeting." She smiled sweetly at him and faded away like she was made of mist.

Burt just sat there, dabbling his feet in the water, pretty much stunned when he realized just how much he was looking forward to that next "meeting".

Jenny came out of Burt's dream with a slightly fuzzy feeling. Something about the meeting seemed a little awkward. She wasn't quite sure what that meant, but she needed to figure it out at some point. But for now, she dialed Fidget's number from her special phone in her communications center. She was alone there at the moment. Amenia had other appointments and she assumed she was going to have to do a lot more of this on her own as time passed.

In the real world, in Sanglarka, Elizabeth was camped out in Jenny's suite, chatting with her bodyguards out on the balcony. In her little meditation chamber, however it was just her and Chidwi. She wasn't sure how many more individuals she could add to her personal retinue without starting to look like a traveling show. But for now, she had work to do. She had discussed what she was doing with Lova and she had said that a visit to Alliance headquarters might be in order. So, as soon as she was finished with Fidget and Bob, she would be headed out. Maybe she would grab a bite in her suite at headquarters before she came back and started in on whatever they decided she would need to do next.

It all came down to the fact that they were running out of time. If they were going to have any advantage in this conflict, they would need every edge they could get and for now, Jenny's new ability would definitely enable the kind of progress they needed to make.

Fidget came into view. He was standing next to Bob in the huge laboratory. There, it was also night. Jenny knew that Bob did some of his best work in the quiet of nighttime, so it wasn't unusual for him to sleep-in in the morning. Surprisingly, there was also her counterpart, Anela, Mervin, and Cornelium, the beautiful dragon scientist were all gathered around the lab table.

"Fidget, I'm here. Can you do simultaneous translation for me? I haven't expanded my ability to group speech yet."

"Jenny's here, folks. She wants me to be the conduit for her communication. Will that work for the rest of you?"

"Hi Jenny! That will work well for us. You know of Anela, Mervin and Cornelium.

Anela, Mervin and Cornelium, Fidget will be Jenny's voice for us today. Jenny, your timing is perfect. We had just all gathered, and I hadn't had the opportunity to brief everyone on what's going on here this evening. I promise, I won't take you all on too many late-nighters, but this is crucial, and we have had a major breakthrough that I believe will help us to finally resolve at least one of the issues we are dealing with.

"Hey there, everyone. OK, Bob. Shoot."

"Great. Well, thanks to a nice bit of serendipity, we now have some new information that well may help us finally crack this, and I thought Fidget would be our lynchpin. Turns out, there is a second lynchpin. Burt has made the acquaintance of a little fellow called BaaGah. And this little guy can enter an MDP and survive it without anyone directly putting him in it. He entered Burt's MDP out of curiosity and was able to communicate with Burt from inside it."

There were gasps and even little tendrils of smoke coming from Cornelium's nostrils, which seemed to happen when his kind got agitated.

"You've got to be kidding me, boyo," exclaimed Merv. *"And they called me a wizard! Now THAT's magic for sure."*

"BaaGah's race call themselves, Mookookie. Evidently, they have a number of interesting quirks," inserted Jenny. *"They not only can blend in with solid objects, becoming a part of them for indeterminate amounts of time, but they also have the ability to sprout random appendages, arms, legs, etc. They call their blending ability, going into the 'spaces'. As I understand it, they are talking about the spaces between atoms. BaaGah basically explained to Burt, like he was explaining to a Kindergartner, that no matter what the density or seeming density of mass, the spaces are there, and they form what he calls 'sparkly roads.'"*

"That's amazing," enthused Merv, *"So, what are you thinking, Bob? That if these little guys can manage to enter a miniature dimensional portal, that they might have the ability to go between dimensions like Tarafau's people do and that maybe there is a connection between the MDP, the 'spaces' and the card?"*

"I'm thinking that we actually might have been barking up the wrong tree all along. It well may be that we don't need a Gatekeeper's key or a pass at all to access and manipulate this device. Between Fidget's exploration and BaaGah's abilities, we may just have opened Pandora's box here. We need to consider how much of this and at what level, we can communicate to anyone. This is big and it's really scary. This is the bogeyman, Sauron and the Borg all in one neat little package."

They all stood there in complete silence. Jenny could almost see all of those brilliant minds cooking at light speed. For a long moment, no one moved or spoke.

"Right, so now that you know somewhat about what we're up against, this is how Jenny factors into this. She will be riding along with Fidget into the MDP. It's the only safe way we can send anyone there at the moment. We may be able to use some kind of environmental suit, but we still don't know, with the exception of BaaGah, how going into the MDP will affect organic tissue. In future tests we will find ways of seeing what we need to know. Fidget and Jenny, are you ready?"

"Ready, Boss, both of us."

Bob touched the MDP on his wrist to Fidget and Jenny lost connection with him for a brief second, then they were in a huge space with a high domed ceiling. This space was large enough to house a harrier jet and a 20 story building with adequate headroom and space for much more. It was a lot like the large warehouse stores in square footage size. It wasn't quite as big as the Apex in Tarafau's dimension, but Jenny was impressed, nevertheless.

The first question that came to her mind was, "Where are we?" This was a physical space, not virtual reality. There were shelves and items on the shelves as well as Bob's entire Infinity Loop laboratory. He had obviously left nothing behind. It showed the commitment he had made to this cause. The Alliance couldn't have made a better choice than when they invited Bob to become an Alliance Agent.

"Fidget, make a noise and measure how the sound carries," Jenny instruct-ed. She wanted to see how things worked in here and they might be able to tell the dimensions by measuring the "bounce" of the sound waves. She had a basic understanding of science and physics from her college days. She knew that when you were evaluating an environment, you needed to do var-ious kinds of tests.

Fidget obediently made first a high hooting-like sound and then a whirring noise. There was no echo, but the sound seemed to carry different-ly than if they had been in a sound-deadening space.

"Let's go on a tour. Please proceed to the outside edge and let's see if we can circumnavigate. When you get to the wall, make a mark on the wall, so we will know when we return to the same point. This will do more than simply mea-sure the circumference, it will allow us to see what's actually inside an MDP and maybe locate a door to the space or some windows we can look out of. It appears the space is lighted artificially, but you never know."

It looked like time was going to be hard to measure here. It took a lot longer to get to the edge than Jenny had judged it might.

"Fidget, set your chronometer to measure time in Earth hours."

"Jenny, I am already doing that. I am videotaping the entire encounter and the timestamp on the recording is in Earth time units for ease of compari-son. You may not be able to hear it, but I am digitally reproducing our conver-sation to appear on the recording in real time."

"What a clever bot you are, Fidget! And look, we have found an edge. Make your mark and let's move in a clockwise direction."

Fidget made a big red mark on the wall. The building material of the white wall seemed like either a heavy duty plastic or metal. The floor might have been some kind of concrete. It was grey and solid, with no seams. There were no shelves attached to the wall, nor was there anything stored flush against the wall to impede their progress. As they rotated around the circumference Jenny had an even better idea of the storage capacity of this space. The area was divided into sections; about a third of it was free-stand-ing shelving. The rest of the area appeared to have been set aside for storing large objects, such as one of the boats they had used on the Amazon River Basin excursion that now seemed very long ago in Jenny's mind. Bob also had a hover car, sporty version, and, was that a bulldozer?

Of course, there was his little army of bots. Jenny had no idea he had manufactured so many of them. A rough estimate said there were about a hundred of them standing in neat rows like little soldiers. There were also stacks of boxes of what were labeled as rations. At one end, Bob had even stored kitchen appliances. She imagined that if she examined the shelving further, she would find many of his favorite treats as well.

They continued around the edge of the huge circular space and had found nothing that looked like a door or a window so far. The only sound she could hear was the quiet contact Fidget's wheels made with the floor. Fidget had feet and legs, but his feet had small rubber wheels that could extend a couple inches below the sole of his feet, meaning his stride on this smooth floor was much like roller skating.

Suddenly Fidget gave a shudder and stood still. His vision went black.

"What's going on, Fidget?"

No answer.

"Fidget?"

Nothing.

For a moment, Jenny nearly panicked, thinking herself trapped. She had gotten used to riding along in Fidget's head to the point that what he saw out of his eyes were as if she were seeing out of her own. Confining spaces had always been a bit of an issue for her and, although this space was huge, she couldn't see any of it. The darkness felt as if it was closing in on her. For a moment her mind flashed back to the dark room in the place where she had been tortured by Sam. Then she remembered she could just cut the connection and sighed mentally in relief. Maybe this was only an update or Fidget was calculating something. She decided to wait and then...even the blackness disappeared.

She immediately cut the connection and found herself back in her mental communications room. She hurriedly dialed Bob.

"Bob? Something's wrong with Fidget, can you get him out of there?" she blurted as soon as the laboratory came into view.

"Jenny, what happened?"

"We were measuring the circumference of the storage area when all of a sudden Fidget just stopped and wouldn't respond and then everything went black."

"Just a moment," Bob said and retrieved Fidget from inside the MDP. *"Fidget?"*

Fidget didn't move.

"I'll reboot him and see what's going on. Did you notice anything that might have caused this?"

"Nothing. One minute we were moving along and the next minute he just stopped, and everything went black. Maybe he needs a charge?"

Bob chuckled. *"He's not likely to run out of battery any time in the next several years. I have had the opportunity to make some very amazing alterations to his power situation. We'll be doing the same for Lizziebot next time I get my hands on her."*

Now let's see what's happening here."

He opened a panel in Fidget's back and fiddled with a few things and his brows contracted. He shook his head, closed the panel and took out a tiny remote, similar to a car's automatic locking mechanism. He pushed a couple of buttons. They beeped in his device, but Fidget didn't respond.

"Well, the old standby is; when all else fails, reboot." He sighed and pushed the last button twice. *"That will take a few hours, folks. So, Jenny what have we learned so far, minus the actual measurements."*

"How long was I gone? It seemed like at least an hour. That will give us relative time measurements. Fidget was running a chronometer on the video footage, but I wasn't watching the numbers."

"You've been gone for about 45 minutes ET."

"ET? Extra Terrestrial?"

"No, Jenny. Earth Time, which generally means Sanglarka time. We've had to be specific as we have several time-sets to deal with here. Earth Time, Alliance Time, Fleistian time, Insenium Time and local time. It makes every communication and coordination for projects, especially our current one, interesting at the very least."

Jenny knew that Bob used the word "interesting" as a substitute for problematic.

"Time is just one of the variables in the massive datasets represented by my bots, most specifically Fidget and Lizziebot. This means, a complete reboot thorough enough to leave all of those datasets in place and, at the same time, scan for viruses and other invasive elements, will require a lot more time than to reboot a personal computer system. Without seeming arrogant, I can honestly say that the massive data sets involved in making the complex AI in these bots are beyond any supercomputer or quantum computer currently on Earth, and this doesn't even take into account the new tech I've been able to add to them with DAT.

But I digress from the initial question. Do you think time may run differently in the MDPs?"

"I don't know. But basically, all we did was explore the a part of the perimeter and other than to tell you that the place is huge, there isn't much new to report. If we were in there for 45 minutes, we hadn't yet come back to our starting point and guesstimating that I think we were walking at about 5 miles an hour, this seems less like a room and more like enclosed acreage."

"Fascinating. So, it is a physical space, not some kind of dimensional shift or the items sitting around with their atoms scrambled until we call them back. This is one of the issues I've been wondering about. If the MDPs are a physical space, it means they exist in an actual place that can be tracked and traveled to. It also means that there may be more than one potential use for them. But, above all of that, for purposes of our project with the portal card, assuming we can determine portal coordinates, we now have an address.

This is probably why the card responded to the proximity of the MDP. All of this time, we've been wearing a place on our wrists as solid as the lab we are standing in...well at least most of us are standing here. Jenny, did you see any potential exits from the MDP area or maybe, even better, a window?"

"Sorry, no. That being said, we didn't make it all the way around the circumference of the room. We were specifically checking for some kind of egress, besides just measuring the room."

"*Just because you couldn't see one, doesn't mean they weren't there. I happen to know that many alien building techniques allow for invisible entrances and even virtual windows that must be invoked to see through them. It is one of the spaceship designs of one of my former colleagues. She created space-going vehicles that appeared to be solid objects until the camouflaged openings were invoked.*" Merv said, speaking up for the first time.

"*So, anything else you noticed before Fidget blacked out?*"

"*When Fidget made loud noises per my request, there was no echo or dampening of the sound either. I'm not entirely sure what that tells us, but I figured it might be worth noting.*"

"*OK. Well, I understand we have a meeting at Alliance Headquarters. I'll meet you there.*"

Jenny faded back to her meditation room, Chidwi's warm little hands still on her shoulders.

"*Chidwi, would you like to meet the folks at Alliance Headquarters? I have to go to a meeting.*"

"*Chidwi will go anywhere Jenny goes. That's the rule.*"

Jenny grinned. She walked into the living area of her suite to get her retinue. She had a meeting to attend.

Chapter 23: Return and Report

Tarafau looked at the team assembled at the dining room table. The faces before him were a mix of emotions and attitudes. Jenny was thoughtful and her team, including Chidwi sitting on her shoulder, was attentive. Lova looked concerned. Juan's team was an odd mixture of optimism and serious focus. Adelle's team was practically bubbling with excitement.

Tarafau's kinsmen were present, each sitting with the team they had been assigned. Of course, Bob and Burt were away in their respective missions, however, as he understood it, Bob would be meeting them at Alliance Headquarters to report some interesting and potentially helpful findings. Jenny would be reporting on Burt's behalf. In the meantime, Tarafau, Lova and Gariel also had some vital developments to report. The moment he stood; every eye was on him.

"We will be leaving in a few minutes to report to Alliance Headquarters and get a briefing on steps going forward. But before we leave, I wanted each of you to know how much we appreciate every single contribution so far. In the short time since we began this mission all of the teams have made significant progress. I don't think a single one of you has slacked or held back their best efforts. Therefore, I want you to know that I feel honored to associate with each of you.

I assume you have all of your things packed in your MDPs, as we may stay overnight, depending on how long each of you need to give a thorough report on your activities. Arvid has agreed to hold down the fort, so to speak, while we are gone. If there are no questions, let us depart. They are expecting us."

No one spoke, so he gestured toward the door. Jenny and Elizabeth walked up to him, the girls trailing watchfully behind. *"So, have you spoken with Amenia lately? She has had appointments during my last few sessions, one of the drawbacks of infinite varieties of timelines on each planet in the Alliance network."*

"I went home for a few hours yesterday. She is very excited about your progress. She says you will soon have to make progress on your own, as she isn't sure how much more she can teach you. She will eventually turn your training over to Liliath. She is one of the strongest minds we are acquainted with in the Alliance."

"Trained by a dragon? Really?" Jenny's eyebrows shot up and her eyes went wide.

"Eventually. For now, just continue on the path Amenia set you on. You are exceeding the expectations of all of us. We knew you had some talent, but this is beyond our hopes."

The group was met by the usual Alliance Troopers standing at the gate. They were escorted down the hill where waited three multi-passenger hovercars. They were let off in front of the huge double doors of the Alliance headquarters building. The huge automated elevator took them nearly instantly to the private council chambers. It always baffled Tarafau how they could manage such a rapid trip and not have any noticeable feeling of motion or stopping at the floor.

The white foxlike being who was the receptionist, greeted them respectfully, noting that they were expected. The chairs were assembled in a circle, one of Ingot's favorite configurations as all participants could easily see the faces of the others. Seated at the top point of the circle were Ingot, Myla and Liliath; each in their special chairs.

Liliath's seat was actually more like a chaise, so she could recline and bring her head closer to eye level. Myla's was a lot like a nest and Ingot's chair seat was slightly higher than the rest, with a little footstool that doubled as a step to allow him easier access to the chair.

"Welcome, friends! We are so excited to hear what you each have to report, but before we get to that, I think we must wait just a bit for Bob to arrive. He had a last minute task to do that is pertinent to our meeting today. Regarding that, we want complete reports, so we have not set a time to end the meeting, but instead we will break as necessary and return. If we need to we will take a couple of days to be sure every voice is heard. As urgent as our situation is, I still feel it is important not to miss anything in our planning. Therefore, there are suites available for each of you who don't generally come for more than one day to headquarters. Those of you who already have suites know where you will be."

Surprisingly, Mynn, one of Jenny's guards interrupted, *"I apologize, but I must know, have there been arrangements made for Jenny's security? I am sure her suite won't accommodate us, but we will be glad to sleep on cots in the living area of the suite."*

Ingot smiled. *"It is gratifying to me to see your diligence in keeping our Jenny safe. Actually, we have opened up the room next to her suite with an adjoining door and it will accommodate up to 4 people. Will that satisfy?"*

"Yes, sir. Thank you, sir."

"Any time I can do anything to help Jenny's 'girls', as she is vital for our success, both in her role as Gatekeeper and because of her rare gifts, which we will discuss soon. And, good, we're all here now," Ingot said with an including gesture.

Bob came through the door, Fidget at his side. The grin under his salt and pepper moustache made it clear that he had some important news to announce.

"Bob, if you will be so kind, I'd like to begin our briefing with your news first; if you don't mind?"

"I'll be happy to, Ingot. First, for those of you who don't know him, this is Fidget. He is not only my AI assistant, but he has helped me make a huge breakthrough with many implications that will affect our tactics and strategies in the coming war."

Tarafau had learned to respect the short, middle-aged man for his integrity and his brilliant, inventive mind. He knew Bob from when he was Lizzie's Guide and knew him to be a kind person, fit to be a Dimensional Alliance agent as anyone he had ever met.

Bob beamed around at them. *"Say hi to the good people, Fidget."*

"Hi to the good people, Fidget. Ha, ha, ha! It's a joke, get it?"

The group sat there for a moment stunned that this robot had just addressed them in mindspeech and then laughed! Then they all chuckled too. A bot with a sense of humor, what next?

"He has mindspeech? I never saw the like," said Ingot. *"Whose doing was this?"*

"It was a gift from Cornelium. It makes him a much more efficient lab partner; I can tell you. It also means that Jenny can communicate with him cross-dimensionally, which could come in very handy at some point."

There was a gasp from many of them and Tarafau would have also been shocked, if he hadn't spoken to his wife just this past night. Amenia continued to be astounded at the rate at which Jenny was progressing.

"How extraordinary," said Liliath in her soft dragon mind voice. *"I must speak with Cornelium about this gift of his and I would like to consult with Amenia, when she can make it here. I think I can help with Jenny's progress."*

"We were hoping you might say that," Tarafau agreed. *"Amenia will be happy to visit. I think she has the next few days free. Perhaps while she is here you and she can do a session together with Jenny."*

"Done!" exclaimed Liliath, a little smoke trailing from one nostril as it often did when she was agitated, angry or excited.

There was a quiet moment while Bob waited to see if there was going to be any more discussion. *"Well, then, I guess our little surprise went off without a hitch. Now I have more to share. Please hold your questions and comments until the end. And, Ingot, if you agree, I think Jenny's report should follow mine."*

Ingot nodded and Bob continued.

"OK, then, let's jump right in. I won't go into any more scientific detail than I must, but we have been working on something extremely hush-hush that could turn the tide in a battle with the Insenium. On the other hand, it also represents a clear and present danger to every being in the multiverse, if our worst fears are realized.

At our South American encounter with the Groga, which led to finding the Fleistians and rescuing Jenny from their clutches, we discovered something puzzling as we were doing the cleanup. It might have been overlooked, which could have been disastrous. The reason it stood out was that the item we found looked a lot like an Earthly debit card, which would have been completely out of place in the pocket of a Groga officer. Unlike a debit card, however, it has no lettering or symbols on it and visible printed circuits of some kind. Mervin and his team kindly pulled me in to consult on discovering what this item was.

They were suspicious from the beginning since, it was the only such card discovered in the remains of the Groga camp and the Groga aren't tech users or inventors, generally speaking. What we know of them is that they steal tech from dimensions they raid, but the only other tech they seem to use, other than the portal devices the Fleistians provide for them are blasters and the blasters are simple tech. Point, aim and pull the trigger. Anyone with hands could do that.

So, we poked and prodded and theorized, finally decided that this might be a device that created a portable portal that anyone could use to go anywhere, but it didn't have a recognizable interface or any way to input coordinates."

Adelle and the science team were all sitting forward in their seats with anticipation. Up until now they had all had to wonder what Bob was doing in his separate urgent mission. They had obviously caught the potential implications and were waiting to hear the conclusion. Bob wished he could give them a more finished presentation, but they were close enough now that this project could bear a set of fresh eyes and these were some of the most intelligent people he knew.

"We came to the conclusion that perhaps this might be related to, or respond to a Gatekeeper's key. So off we went to a special secret laboratory to explore that possibility. I can't divulge how we were able to have access to a Gatekeeper's key, but we did discover that the key is only one part of the puzzle. Interestingly enough, this led us by a rather roundabout route and through much serendipity to the MDP.

Remember that the MDP you wear on your wrist is not just a trick for storing stuff. The letters stand for Miniature Dimensional Portal. And I can see you are already connecting the dots," he said with a grin when Adelle gasped and more than one of her team smacked a hand to their foreheads.

"*Now before you get over-excited, you should know that there is more re-search to be done, but we are now so close we can practically taste it. This is way bigger than we thought. That being said let me butt into those wheels that are turning in your heads for a moment with a serious caveat.*" He paused and looked seriously into every face before he continued to be sure that he had everyone's attention.

"*The card cannot be allowed to come into use or production. It cannot be shared, and we will not use it. Think of it. There are none of us who would wrongfully use a personal dimensional portal and you are probably thinking that, for example, Tarafau's people haven't gone all 'Master of the Multiverse' on us, but it only takes one being with nefarious purposes to put this into mass production and our collective goose is cooked.*

We need to know how it works and we need to destroy it, but not before we know that the Insenium isn't making these somewhere in a factory and giving them out to their minions by the case. I'm of the opinion that they are no closer to getting this to work than we are, since they appeared to be trying to get ahold of a Gatekeeper before now. If, or when, they figure it out, it's all over but the shouting. This is the One Ring all over again only worse. This is why our next step is not to figure out how to work the stupid thing, but to find out if it is the only one and if not, to destroy every single one in existence. Then we will de-stroy the original.

The Chief Council is in agreement with me. So this is our main mission. If we can isolate the Insenium soon enough, we may even be able to prevent a massive blood bath, the very one we seem to be rocketing headlong to engage. We have Burt deep in the Insenium and thanks to Jenny we can communicate with him directly without any tech and without the Insenium intercepting those messages.

It is my hope that we can find the information we need and that we will discover that we hold the only one. However, if there is any point to a military solution it would be to do whatever we need to locate whatever of these cards still exist out there and destroy them.

Part two of my discoveries can wait for now. I will brief the Science Team, both Earth and the alliance Science team about part two in private session. I'll need all of your heads on this. After that, I will brief the Strategy and Tactics Team and the Logistics Team on our group findings so I can give them the most complete picture possible. I will take questions at the break, so please write them down. Thank you for your kind attention."

Tarafau was impressed with Bob even more than before. He gave credit where it was due and was no braggart. He didn't get dramatic or act the know-it-all. He was direct, said what he needed to say and without fanfare, sat down between Jenny and Mervin and waited patiently for the next presentation.

Jenny stood up immediately. She had matured so much in the past months since the beginning of her unasked-for adventure. She had once told him privately that speaking in front of so many people who were older, wiser and leaders in their respective field made her stomach squirm, but you wouldn't know it to look at her. She stood there as if she had been doing this all of her life, scanned the faces before her and began:

"So much has happened since I was inducted into the Alliance," she began, unconsciously touching the tiny key at her neck. *"And then the Gatekeeper responsibility came before I could even get trained for my Guardian position. Since then I have experienced things beyond my imagination, both good and bad. I am not the same person who had that key placed around my neck on that first day. Little did I realize that the person I thought of as a sister, my best friend, who placed the key around my neck would turn out to be the first of many enemies I would face.*

I still have had a lot less formal training than I had hoped for and I know that my situation is unusual. Having said that, each one of you has played a major role in helping me become what I am today. I still have much to learn, but I no longer feel like the lost, confused kid I started out as such a short time ago. I know what I am. I can't imagine yet who I have the potential to become and none of this would have happened in such a short time without the help and support of the dear friends...no...the dear family I have acquired here.

I only say this now to introduce my report topic. Thanks to Lova's training, recently I had the opportunity to also train with Tarafau's wife, Amenia. Her skills in the disciplines of the mind are amazing. She helped me break through some barriers I didn't realize I had, into a whole new level of mental abilities.

I won't go into details here, as that isn't the best use of our time right now. But it's important for you to know that we have discovered I have some gifts, which is the only word I can use to describe this, that allow me to do some things with my mind that none of us expected.

Mindspeech has always come easily to me from the first time I found that such a thing was possible. But, like the rest of you, I could only communicate mentally with people I had some proximity to. However, I stepped over that barrier while I was staying with Tarafau's family and I continue to explore this new discipline. You see, I can communicate not only across long distances, but interdimensionally with anyone I know.

I have already had the opportunity to visit with some of you, but for the rest of you, I will be dropping in from time to time, so don't think it is some kind of supernatural occurrence. It is, as Amenia puts it, 'the science of mental ability', no less scientific than the workings of your cell phone, just not visually obvious or trackable by any tech we are aware of."

Tarafau watched the faces of the surrounding team members. Expressions ranged from shock to intense interest to shaking or nodding heads. He assumed the ones who nodded had already had a communication with Jenny.

She continued, *"This goes beyond mind speech, as I can see or visualize the person I am speaking with including their environment at the time. Just so you know, I'm not sure I can turn the visuals off, or at least not at this point.*

What this means to our current mission is that I can communicate with all of the people of our team, even when they aren't conscious. Recently I not only was able to observe and communicate with several of you in your waking state, but also in your dreams. This is secure communication that, as far as I know at this point, cannot be intercepted by any enemy force, which gives us a distinct advantage over them."

The excitement in the air was palpable. Every eye was riveted on Jenny and most of them leaned forward in their chairs. Tarafau even saw tears glistening in the eyes of some of them.

"*This most recent breakthrough means that I have been able to observe Burt in the Insenium and establish two way communication with him. The limitation of this is that Burt can't contact me. I have to initiate the contact. I know we have much to discuss while we're here and time is short, so I have written a report of my most recent communications with Burt and uploaded it to the network so you can access the information on your tablets.*

Liliath, Amenia has suggested that you and I spend some time refining these skills and I will make myself available whenever you have time.

In addition to communication with Burt, evidently, I have the ability to do this with any being that is capable of mindspeech. This means that I can also take advantage of Fidget and Lizziebot's new abilities of mindspeech connections. I'm not completely clear on how that's possible, but it does work. Because of that, I was able to participate in an experiment related to the card which led to an encounter inside Bob's MDP. The outcome of that is still being determined, but this also bodes well for future strategies in our conflict with the Insenium. I will leave it to Bob to brief us all in detail later in this planning session.

I know you all have questions, but for now, I would like to hear the rest of the reports so we can put everything into context, if that is ok with the Council?"

Jenny turned to Ingot who nodded. She sat down without further comment. Tarafau knew that heads were probably spinning at this point.

Ingot stood. "*I'm sure I'm not the only one who can see the many possibilities that have already been opened up for us. There are more reports to be made, but for now, I want to give us all some time to read the written reports and absorb the impact of the first two verbal reports. Let's break for refreshment and give you all a chance to visit your suites. We will meet here again in 2 hours, which should give each of you time to prepare for the remainder of the reports. We will try to keep you all for as little time as we can and still complete the briefing.*

After we refresh ourselves, we will return here to hear the report of the Earth Science team and the Logistics group. Thank you for your attention and your patience with this process. I know each of you are anxious to move forward on your various missions, but these reports will help each of us to be as prepared as possible when the time comes to eliminate the Insenium threat."

Chapter 24: The Legacy of His Imperial Majesty

B urt strolled along the street alongside his Insenium guide, Mechi, down the street that led to the inn where he stayed, courtesy of His Most Imperial Majesty, Peril. Mechi was loaded down with packages, mostly clothing, also courtesy of His Most Imperial Majesty, Peril. Burt was really getting tired of the long, drawn out use of Peril's title, but he played along. They were returning to the inn, so Burt could change, especially his shoes. Then they were headed out to visit one of the surrounding farming domes.

Mechi was the perfect servant, attentive, respectful and efficient. He had practically run them between the various needful shops, taking the shortest routes to the best shops for their purchases, so, what would have taken Burt an entire day of random wandering had allowed them to get everything he needed in a few hours.

This was also designed to not give Burt a lot of time to investigate anything. However, this wasn't his first rodeo. He quietly observed the people around him and how they interacted with Mechi and how they reacted to Burt's medallion. It was obvious to Burt that Peril's people had been well trained to respond to the wearer of the medallion in very specific ways. And he might have been fooled by their kindly, respectful answers to the few questions he had time to ask, if it wasn't for the fact that he was looking for the telltale signs, a quick glance aside, or a hugging motion with the arms, nervous fidgeting with the fingers or words that sounded well-memorized.

To the casual observer, the whole thing would have seemed somewhat magical and idyllic, but for Burt it was like fingernails on a blackboard. The word "FAKE" practically screamed at him every time he spoke with one of these people. But, if they continued the charade, so would he.

He went up to his room and changed. He didn't have to transfer Baa-Gah to a pocket or pant leg as he had taken up residence in the arm band that hid Burt's MDP. Last night Burt had set up some rules for BaaGah regarding this thing. On the one hand, it was comforting to know that Baa-Gah was always with him, regardless of what he was wearing. On the other, BaaGah, by his nature was a potential recipe for disaster when it came to all of the things stored in his MDP. Burt had discovered that BaaGah could not only eat chip bags, he happened to like to eat electronic wires, bungy cords and even metal tools!

So, Burt had delineated an area that was fair game for BaaGah, but Baa-Gah had agreed to always ask permission before devouring random things or eating up all of Burt's food storage. When BaaGah had meekly agreed to the rules, Burt didn't worry about him anymore. The one thing he was learning about BaaGah was that the little creature was intensely loyal and scrupulously honest. One of the things BaaGah thought made the Inseni people "evil" was that they couldn't be trusted to do what they said they would do. Evidently, dishonesty wasn't a Mookookie trait.

He took his time dressing. There was something somewhat satisfying about making Mechi wait. He was, however, very interested in his first exploration expedition. So far, the only transportation he had seen on the streets were small carts being pulled by slaves and people's feet. It made for very quiet streets, as mindspeech was used universally here and only the Groga wore boots. From what Burt could see so far, most families in the Insenium had at least one slave servant. The slaves followed their masters seemingly docilely, but Burt would have given a lot to have had an unsupervised conversation with these beings.

Not all of the slaves were humanoid. Humanoids were in the majority, for sure, but Burt noticed a few lizard-like creatures that walked on their back legs, some more apish furry creatures and even a few insectoids, similar to those he had met in Alliance Headquarters.

After changing, into the pale grey breeches and white linen shirt that reminded Burt of something out of a pirate movie, he put on the stockings and the moccasin-type shoes that everyone seemed to wear in the city. Burt was pretty sure they wore something quite different in the trades and farms, but these would do for now.

Mechi was waiting for him in the common room, placid and stoic, and Burt put on his cockiest grin when he saw him. *"So, what do you think?"* he asked doing a slow turn. *"Is this more appropriate?"*

"Quite, Sir Burt. Shall we depart?" Something in the mental tone told Burt that Mechi thought him a clown, which suited Burt just fine.

"Absolutely. Lead on."

They went back out onto the street. He noticed a change in the looks he now received from the passers-by. His clothing changed his status immediately. In their huge eyes his status had changed from Mechi's servant to his master.

Mechi led the way down several streets they had already passed through earlier that day. Finally, they turned into a different area of the city. This appeared to be a residential area. No individual homes. But there were blocks of two-story apartment complexes, each surrounding an inner court that you could see between entrances on the street. These were little park areas. There was nothing resembling playground equipment there, however.

At this time of the day, there was little traffic on these streets. Apparently, those who lived there were all off pursuing their various occupations. Other than shop-keepers and crafts folk, Burt hadn't seen any other trades persons, so far. He guessed some of that would be part of today's expedition.

As they walked, they neared closer and closer to the edge of the dome. Finally, they approached what appeared to be a bus station. Long sleek vehicles stood in rows, mostly empty at this time. In addition, there were shorter, more van-like vehicles. Mechi approached a uniformed attendant, gesturing toward a set of sealed doorways. The attendant nodded, never taking his huge eyes off of Burt.

Mechi escorted Burt to one of the waiting vans. No driver, but the van knew where it was going. They passed through the domed walls.

"My hoommme," BaaGah's voice buzzed wistfully in Burt's head. *"They took it, but they could not break it. It still belongs to the Mookookie who still live. BaaGah's family."*

"Do you wish to go home, BaaGah?"

"BaaGah is Burt's buddy. BaaGah stays with Burt. BaaGah keeps Burt safe from mean, nasty, ugly thingygummy, evil..." he trailed off as if he had run out of negative metaphors strong enough. *"BaaGah stays with Burt."*

The sky was a deep teal green with no discernable clouds. The next dome's pale blue outline was visible several miles away, but between them was only a rolling plain with the one road stretched far ahead. The engine made no sound, presumably electric, so the only sound in the vehicle was the wheels on the smooth road. Mechi stared straight forward with those huge eyes of his, evidently lost in his own thoughts. Burt assumed he didn't consider polite conversation part of his duties as a guide, either that or he didn't know anything interesting to tell him about the surrounding countryside.

"So how many of these domes are there? I am fascinated about the idea of domes as opposed to terraforming a planet to be hospitable to humanoid life."

Mechi glanced at him sideways, a slightly irritated look crossing his face for the merest fraction of a second. *"There are a few hundred of them, each with different specialties. Some are for the training of slaves, some dedicated to Groga breeding colonies. Most are for the production of goods and foodstuffs. You will see."* And with that, he continued his contemplation of the road ahead.

The little van drew ever closer and within less than 20 minutes they were exiting on the other side of the gate into the dome. The attendant waved them on, as they got out of the vehicle, noting instantly the medallion on Burt's chest.

This dome was not filled with buildings. Most of it appeared to be crop land. Some kind of grain crops stretched along the sides of the road they walked along. Farm-workers appeared from time to time going about their everyday tasks. Eventually as they walked along, the grain fields ended and orchards with interesting looking fruits began. Hidden by the orchards was a small town consisting of a main street and a few side streets. As usual people were walking to and from various errands. Most of them were slaves. Only a few Inseni walked the street here. Burt assumed these were overseers and managers of the farming inside the dome.

"I would like to speak with some of the slaves, please."

"Ah, yes, as you wish. Choose any you would like, and we will invite them to speak with you."

Burt considered. He chose a young female, tall and willowy, wearing the usual breeches and sack shirts of the newer slaves. Her brown eyes were serious, and her bearing did not appear to be broken or cowed.

Mechi beckoned to her and she immediately stopped and walked over to them.

"Yes, sires? How may I be of service?"

The words were all correct and proper, but Burt saw in her eyes that almost invisible attitude of defiance. Mechi appeared not to notice. Perhaps the faces of their slaves were so inconsequential as to be beneath their study?

"Hi, I'm Burt. What's your name?"

"I am Enial, Sir Burt."

"It is good to meet you, Enial. And you may call me Burt. I'd like to know where you came from before you were brought here."

"The place no longer exists for me, sire. There is only today and all of the tomorrows to come and those are all here with the Insenium."

"I see. And what do you do here, Enial?"

"I take care of and instruct the younglings, sire. While the parents are working for the glory of the Insenium, I teach them their duty and see to their needs."

The painful look in her eyes and her body posture told Burt she would like to have said more. She shifted her feet for just a moment, as if she would like to be anywhere but here.

"And how are you treated by your Inseni masters?" Burt tried to convey with his eyes that he was hearing her facial subtext. He wanted her to know he was not here as an Insenium inspector, but just the opposite. However, he also could tell that if she didn't toe the politically correct line here that there would be potentially severe consequences.

"Our needs are met and no one who is productive has any fear. We are encouraged to breed and be healthy in our minds and bodies. We do not lack for any necessary thing."

Mechi nodded approvingly. Burt was shocked at his complacency. Couldn't he hear Elian nearly shouting that the lives of the slaves were meaningless, tightly controlled and without hope?

"So you are a school teacher?"

"I teach the children how to serve and be obedient and productive. It is my task. I would never consider shirking. It behooves me to ensure the well-being of my family and community."

Wow, this woman was very good at walking around the truth in a way that clearly said what she actually meant. Nothing she had said could have been construed as anti-Insenium, but Burt understood her, and he felt she knew that he heard her intention clearly.

"Thank you for taking the time to speak with me Elian. My counterparts in the Dimensional Alliance will be very interested to hear that your needs are being met by your masters. I don't want to impede you from doing your duties. I hope the others we speak to today will give us as much useful information."

Her eyes widened almost imperceptibly, and she nodded to Burt, turned and left them. He knew she had received the message he was sending.

He and Mechi moved on, stopping various slaves in the street. All had similar statements as Elian. They were careful about their wording and still managed to convey discontent and wary trust in Burt. The way they spoke to him said so much more than their words. Burt noticed there were no children on the street or any old people. He wasn't sure why, but this bothered him immensely.

"I'd like to go see one of the schools in the community, please," He sent to Mechi.

Mechi only nodded and gestured for Burt to follow him. As he did so, he wondered how he might find a way to communicate with some of these people without his "guide". He was beginning to consider a plan that might save many lives, free these people and put a serious monkey wrench in the intent of the Insenium to dominate the multiverse. He needed to continue to gather information, but he also knew he had to tread carefully if he was ever going to get enough useful information for the Dimensional Alliance forces to eliminate this threat once and for all.

Burt had no illusions that the Dimensional Alliance had some kind of lock on perfect societies or philosophies. Very much the opposite was true. There were many cultures he had experienced in his time as an Alliance agent that were pretty repulsive to him. But they had come to agreements that meant that none of them would force their ideas or ideals on anyone else. They had learned to agree to disagree on pretty much everything but exercising forcible dominion on another.

One of the many purposes of the Alliance was to protect unknowing dimensions from the bullies of the multiverse. This had seldom come to outright conflict, but those who understood the purposes of the Alliance were not naïve enough to believe that it might never happen. Thus, the on-going training of forces to deal with conflict if it arose remained a priority, lest they be caught unawares.

They arrived at a long low building with nothing resembling a playground, rather there was a yard paved in the same material as the road they had arrived on, about the size of half a football field. On it were children of many ages ranged in ranks before an adult slave. Abruptly they all turned in complete unison to face Mechi and Burt. Mechi puffed out his little chest with obvious pride.

"As you can see, these younglings are well trained. Their instructor has done very well with them. We will enter the building to see them in training."

"After the tour, may I speak with the, um, 'instructors'?"

"Of course, of course. Let us go inside."

They entered through the double doors at one end of the building into a broad corridor flanked on both sides with doors leading into what Burt assumed were classrooms. However, looking in through the windows in the doors, Burt didn't observe any books in evidence or any writing. Rather, the children stood in rows or sat in rows on the floor, busily working on various types of machinery or weaving or sewing or doing various types of crafts.

"In addition to these disciplines, we also provide training in building, agriculture and various necessary crafting skills that would normally be performed out of doors." Mechi was saying proudly. *"Every slave is trained in a useful skill."*

"I didn't notice any books," Burt sent, interrupting what he was sure was a well-rehearsed litany.

Mechi blinked a couple of times before answering.

"Why would a slave ever need such a thing? That is reserved for wizards and slaves have no magic."

Burt nearly laughed out loud. It seemed so obvious to Mechi that this should be the case and he could see absolutely nothing wrong with anything he had said. He was seriously trying to impress Burt with this tour and had no idea how ignorant it all seemed to Burt.

"Of course, how silly of me. I look forward to meeting some of your wizards. I'd love to know what kinds of books they are reading these days."

"You can read?" Mechi asked incredulously. *"Truly this must be why His Imperial Majesty, the Emperor, has honored you so very greatly. You are a wizard from off world. We seldom get to interact with wizards who are not Inseni. I am honored to be your guide."*

Mechi bowed slightly and beckoned a bemused Burt forward. He would have to be careful from here on. He had just increased expectations that he might not be able to live up to.

In the meantime, Mechi escorted him to what would have been a faculty room in an Earth school. There, some "instructors" including Elian were seated in a semi-circle in front of two chairs, one Inseni-sized. Burt sat in his proffered chair facing the three. Two women and a man in typical "trusted" slave attire sat before him.

Suddenly, Burt had a feeling he wasn't alone. *"Jenny?"* he sent.

"Just tagging along, Burt. Interesting situation. We should talk when you get back to the inn later. In the meantime, proceed. No one can hear our conversation and I won't interrupt again."

In the fraction of a second it took to have this conversation, Burt realized that the slaves before him looked a bit anxious and just a tad expectant. He leaned forward with his most engaging body language. He knew how to build trust with those who were receptive.

"Hello. I understand you are the instructors for the young people here. What are your names and what do you teach?"

A young woman with blonde hair with just the tiniest tinge of green in it replied, *"I am Tinye, of Glimmerheight. I teach body mechanics, giving each slave the ability to work longer with fewer injuries."*

"Glimmerheight is your home?"

"This dome is my home. Glimmerheight is where I was born." This last was said with a slight sadness in her eyes, although she continued to sit stiffly as if at attention.

"As you know, I am Elian. I teach process management; how to work efficiently and do things in proper order in any situation."

Then, to Burt's intense surprise she sent directly to him, blocking the rest from the conversation, *"And I know you carry another in your mind, perhaps two. Can they connect to me?"*

"I don't know," Burt sent directly to her and to no one else. *"Jenny?"*

"I am here, Elian. Shall we talk later?"

And without a seeming halt she continued broadcasting to the group, *"The students I teach are very adept at following precise instructions and efficiently moving any project forward to a satisfactory conclusion."*

The double entendre in that statement almost knocked Burt over it was so apparent to him, but Mechi nodded cheerfully in agreement, completely missing the sub-conversation.

"I am Ingerd," continued the man at the end of the row. *"I teach physical prowess, weightlifting, strength, stamina and flexibility to allow our workers the most efficient use of their physical resources for the glory of the Insenium."*

Burt nodded. *"How old are your students?"*

"They are younglings, old enough to feed themselves and maintain proper personal hygiene and too young to yet work in the fields or work crews. As they are older, they are apprenticed into various disciplines to allow for more specific instruction. They are evaluated from year to year to determine readiness, those who make it."

"Those who make it?"

"Those who do not die due to mishap or...unhealth. These are fortunately few, less than one in ten."

Ten percent? Burt was dumbfounded. Fortunately? It was all he could do to turn calmly to Mechi and send, *"I think I am done here, for now. Thank you for an enlightening tour of your educational facilities. Can we continue to the workers?"*

Mechi nodded curtly to the instructors, who shuffled out the door ahead of them. *"I have Elian dialed in, Burt,"* sent Jenny. *"I will get back to you after I have had a conversation with her. For now, I will continue to ride along, if that's ok with you."*

"Great by me, but how can you be so calm? Did you hear what they said?"

"I did. But remember that we are in a position to help these people. Keep doing what you're doing. You are amazing and you will make a difference for these people. My Aunt Lizzie always said to focus on what you have, not what you wish you had. But you know that, don't you?"

Burt sent a mental nod and continued to follow Mechi out the doors of the school into the filtered light of the dome.

"Where to next?" he sent to Mechi, putting on his typical grin, as if he hadn't a care in the world.

Chapter 25: What Meets the Eye...

Jenny leaned back in her chair in the council room, Chidwi adjusting automatically to her unconscious shift in position. It had been a long day and she was ready for the next break. Nearly all of the teams had given their reports and she had spent her earlier breaks in communication with Burt. She had told Elian she would be back to speak with her and had reported her visit with Burt during his tour of the first Insenium slave dome.

This had elicited a lively discussion of the potential implications of his observations. One of their concerns had been confirmed. There were many innocents on the Insenium planet. Add to that the fact that the Inseni were not localized on the single planet and their task was even more complicated than they had considered.

Desminda had been of the opinion that they still needed more data, but that with careful planning and a lot of hard work, they could develop a strategy that would be less destructive to innocents and the Alliance forces, but she wasn't willing to commit to a specific list of tactics until all of Burt's reports were in. Gariel had emphatically agreed.

Actually, most agreed with Desminda. Desminda and Gariel had taken copious notes on all of the reports and follow-up discussions, and Jenny had a feeling that she wasn't the only one who would be spending the next "break" hard at work. The group was stimulated by the opportunity to compare notes and be together. There was an energy here that was conducive to collaboration. To Jenny, it was one more reason she was glad to be part of this effort.

Bob stood, *"Welcome back from break, folks. Arvid has asked me to do my extended report now. After hearing all of the progress everyone has made on the various teams, I feel like we are well on our way to a winning strategy in this mission. Now I want to tell you the rest of the story about our discoveries as we attempted to unlock the circuited card with Cornelium and Anela."*

Bob recounted the accidental discovery that the MDP storage was in a physical place and that they were truly wearing dimensional portals on their wrists. He did not speculate, simply telling the story as it unfolded, including the sudden blackout of Fidget.

"Before we discuss the implications of this, I would like to tell you that after a reboot, Fidget had more to report. I'd like to turn the time over to him."

"Thanks, Boss," Fidget said, from his place beside Bob. *"As you know, human time and bot time are very different. We can make billions of calculations in a fraction of a second, so what seems like a short time to you can seem like a very long time for us.*

In the fraction of a second before my circuits powered down, I received a transmission from an alien source."

There were some gasps from the waiting teams and the science team was practically bouncing in their seats. Jenny could almost hear tiny gears whirring in their heads and see the excitement in their eyes.

Fidget continued, *"Evidently the MDPs are not as uninhabited as we originally thought. There is a race of nano-creatures who reside there. These little guys call themselves, 'Protectors', and their primary task in life is the care and protection of the MDP environments.*

They tell me that many eons ago, they were dying. The planet on which they lived was becoming inimical to their life form. As the only intelligent life on the planet, but without the resources they needed to escape their situation, it was apparent that their race would perish. However, at some point, corporeal beings such as yourselves, entered their planet via a dimensional gate. The Protectors eventually were able to communicate their presence and their dilemma.

The kindly beings came up with a solution. (It is just speculation on my part at this point, but I posit that these corporeal beings were actually the forerunners of the Dimensional Alliance scientists who established the Gate Network from the beginning.) The beings built a process that created many spheres that could be launched into the planet's orbit. The sphere processing and launching plant they created was run by robots that are controlled by the Protectors.

Now the Protectors live in the MDP spheres, a safe environment for them. As new MDPs are created, new spheres are launched.

So, when they saw me rumbling around, as they said, inside their MDP sphere, they decided to investigate. They are familiar with robots, so they paused my operation, explored me to be sure there was no threat and then communicated all of this to me with the intent that I report it to you. I now have several of these creatures living in a special compartment in my body. They are intelligent. They can communicate and they are in alignment with the goals of the Alliance. End of report."

Jenny was sure she wasn't the only person stunned by this report given so matter-of-factly by the bot standing placidly before them. A new unknown species and the potential origins of the gate makers? But the implications of what this could mean to the current situation seemed beyond her. She was sure the scientist's minds were buzzing right now.

Bob stood. *"I know you all have questions and there are some long discussions that will want to take place in the various teams about this. To prevent this particular session from going into prolonged overtime, I would like to suggest that we do a session devoted entirely to this particular revelation tomorrow just before we split into teams again. It will mean the information will be fresh in our minds and it will also give the information we currently have, time to percolate a little. Agreed?"*

There were reluctant nods from the group.

Then, Arvid stood. *"It appears we now have a great deal more to go on. Jenny, you are meeting with Burt again later today and with your new contact, Elian, correct? I won't tell any of you that you can't continue these discussions through the remainder of the day. I do ask, however that you confine those discussions either to your suites, the private lounge that has been set aside for this conference or the lab, in the case of our science team. Agreed?"*

All nodded their assent. *"Then, let's break for now. Since all of you have given your reports over the last two days, there is so much more to consider. Please keep in mind that our window of opportunity could close at any moment. Brandon, I would like you to continue to assemble a space fleet. It looks like we may need them. Our logistics team is working out the plan on how best to deploy them in a different dimension, but they have some good ideas.*

Adelle, I am encouraged by the progress your team has made with the delivery models you have created for potential chemical alternatives to typical military approaches. I like the fact you are taking the aftermath into consideration.

Gariel, I will be introducing you to the military leaders of the dimensions who have agreed to provide military support to your operations.

Everyone get as much rest as you can, as I need your minds sharp for tomorrow when we get the latest update on Burt's covert operations. Let us adjourn."

As Jenny rose with the rest, she could tell there were already intense discussions beginning by the animated expressions on many faces. She wished she had the ability to listen in on all of them at once, but both Amenia and Liliath had agreed that this wasn't possible. She might eventually be able to do interdimensional and long distance group conversations, but she couldn't process multiple conversations among different groups, or at least, no one had ever been able to do this as far as either of them was able to tell.

They adjourned to the lounge, where a meal had already been set up for them. The advantage of mindspeech is that the conversations didn't need to pause while they ate and so, the conversations continued. Jenny didn't join in much. Her mind was on her next contacts with Elian and Burt. She had an idea how her new abilities could make a huge difference in the coming conflict and she had a feeling that she and Elian would be spending a lot of time together, making it happen.

She finished her meal and waited for "the girls", which now included Elizabeth, to finish. Then they headed for her suite. So far the conference had been different than any she had ever attended during school or in the pursuit of her profession. Unlike those conventions, every single person on every team was fully committed to getting every possible benefit from their time here at Alliance headquarters.

So, no casual off topic discussions or recreational breaks here. These teams were anxiously engaged in finding every potential advantage over the Insenium. They knew the stakes and they weren't going to quit until they had a solution that meant the Insenium threat was permanently incapacitated or eliminated.

In her suite, Jenny took off her shoes and wiggled her toes in the soft pile carpet. She couldn't figure out what it was made of, but it made angora seem coarse. She allowed herself a deep sigh.

"I'm going to take a nice soak in the tub and then I have some appointments. Will you be good here? Elizabeth, can you spot for me? I'm going in solo, but it would be nice to have someone feeding me good vibes."

"Sure, I'd love to. I definitely need to rest my brain after all of that. The sessions today were really intense."

"Awesome, I have an idea of something I'd like to try. If it works it could be very helpful and I'll need you, in order to make it work."

Nona frowned. *"Something you want to try? Should we be worried?"*

"No, I promise not to do anything dangerous. But I do have to stretch this ability, if I am to be as useful as possible in the coming conflict."

"I don't think I like the sound of that," chimed in Mynn.

"You'll be within shouting distance, if I need you, but I promise I won't be doing anything that will require a staff or any martial arts. OK?"

The three of them stood there, implacable and determined to defend her from anything real or imaginary. The five of them had become close and in many ways, they were a complete consolation for her loss of Sam. They settled into the living area of the suite reluctantly, while Jenny and Elizabeth retired to the bedroom area of the suite. Elizabeth assumed a meditation position on the spacious bedroom floor, while Jenny went into the bathroom to soak in the garden tub.

When every muscle was warmed and relaxed, she dressed in her Gi and joined Elizabeth on the floor. These days she really didn't need to assume the posture, as she could fall into the required state nearly anywhere in any position, but this was a comfort thing. Chidwi stood behind her in her usual place, her tiny warm hands resting gently on Jenny's shoulders. She fell into the deep state almost immediately. *"Are you ready, Elizabeth?"*

"I am. Just tell me what you want me to do."

"For the moment, just hold yourself in relaxed readiness. I have a visit I need to make, and she seems to have the ability to sense a second mind."

"She is a discerner? That is really rare."

"I think I could learn to do it. Perhaps I will get her to teach it to me, if she even realizes she is doing it. At any rate, after I have made contact and gotten her permission, I will try to bring you into the conversation. There is an important role for you to play in all of this and, if what I sensed in her is true, it could be a major help in lessening casualties and could potentially put the Inseni at great disadvantage."

"I'll be ready when you call, sister Jenny; always."

Jenny knew this to be true. She only had the one brother at home, and he was four years older than she, just enough that they never quite fully synced. She loved him and he her, but they had never been close. She had always wanted a sister and Elizabeth was a perfect fit. Even with the huge gap in their ages, their attitudes, likes and desires were very similar.

Jenny focused her mind and entered her mental fortress. Inside the communications room, she picked up the cell phone visualization and dialed the number for Elian. She could already do this without the imaginary cell phone for several of her contacts, such as Burt, Bob and Luz, but the visualization helped her make a strong connection the first several times she made contact with someone she added to her list. She couldn't reach out to someone she hadn't met, so the contact Burt had allowed her to make with Elian had been crucial to this attempt.

She dialed the number and her surroundings faded. She was in a room that looked a lot like a barracks. Elian was sitting on a cot cross-legged. She was the only person in the room at the moment, which was good for Jenny's purposes. Jenny noticed she was stitching something, possibly doing some mending, a task that seemed to be universal anywhere you went. Sometimes men specialized in it, but women definitely seemed to be attracted to the peaceful movements of a needle in and out of cloth.

"Elian? It's Jenny."

Elian jumped and then put her finger in her mouth. She had stabbed herself with the needle.

"That was unexpected, but I suppose it is difficult for you to be more subtle. Are you in the dome?"

"I'm not even on your planet. I reside in a completely different universe than you do. I am contacting you because I want to help your people. A friend of mine died and her people were kidnapped by the Inseni and I want to fix that. She was a good woman and her people were peaceful and kind. None of you deserve to be there."

"That is kind of you, but what can you do where you are? Sir Burt was here in person and I assume the two of you know one another, but he is just one man and the Insenium is a vast empire. What can you possibly do to change our fate? I would do anything to save my people and the other slaves of the Insenium, but I can't see how it is possible. And who would possibly expend the resources and risk the lives of their people to save us? We are nothing in the grand scheme of things."

"Keep sewing. If anyone comes in, we don't want them to see you staring off into space. I think I can do something interesting and I need to see if it works. Can you wait there for a moment while I check something?"

"Of course. I don't have anything better to do."

"Elizabeth, please join me. Here is what I want you to do. Can you sense a dimensional direction, a location when I take you with me to meet Elian?"

"Hmmm, I don't really know. I would be excited to try. I'm with you."

"Elian, can you sense that there is someone else with me?"

"I sense three of you; you and two others, who are dissimilar from one another."

"Elian, that is amazing. I have with me, Elizabeth and Chidwi. Elizabeth is a humanoid friend of mine and Chidwi is a Linkling, a creature of yet another dimension."

"Sir Burt also carries an additional mind with him that is not humanoid, but the mind is somehow familiar. I don't know how I do this. And it seldom happens that more than one mind is present in single communication. I find this intriguing. I greet you, Elizabeth and Chidwi, but I still don't understand what we are doing here."

"Elizabeth, can you possibly sense a location?"

"I think so. I would like to test it, though. Elian, do you expect to continue to be alone for yet awhile?"

"Everyone else is at mealtime. I wasn't hungry. I doubt there will be anyone here very soon."

"OK, then, here we go..."

Before Jenny could object, Elizabeth disappeared from her mind and suddenly she was standing in front of Elian who gaped, dropping her mending onto the floor beside the cot. *"Come with me,"* she said quietly and grasped Elian by the shoulder and they both disappeared.

Chapter 26: Insurrection

Burt was relieved to dismiss Mechi that evening when he returned to the inn. He requested his meal be brought up to his room. Everything was as he had left it, including the little notepad he had blatantly left on a corner of his nightstand. Or at least, that was what they wished him to think. The tiny hair that had lain under the notebook had been moved. If it hadn't been for that, he would never have known someone had been in his room. He had requested to do his own housekeeping and per his instructions, his bed was made exactly as he had left it.

There was a scratching at the door jamb, and he let the servant with a tray into the room. He deposited the tray on the nightstand and left without pausing to receive a tip. Refreshing, Burt thought.

He kicked off his slippers and pulled off his stockings, wiggling his toes with a sigh. An awful lot of walking in a day with nothing better than the moccasins they wore. They must have really tough feet, he thought. There was a lot about these Inseni that was disconcertingly different than what it appeared to be. Although this was often the case with the many alien races he had encountered, something about the Inseni grated on Burt's instincts of self-preservation.

For one thing, everything was entirely too orderly and organized to suit Burt's idea of healthy living. Every moment appeared to be planned and every experience precisely measured to the status and desired aptitude of both the Inseni citizens and their slaves. It was like this guy he knew in high school. His name was Victor, but everyone called him "the crease". Everything about him was perfection; never a hair out of place. His handwriting looked like it had been created by a computer and he never even had a zit or a hangnail. Burt thought him creepy. The Inseni reminded Burt of him. Victor would have fit in well here.

Burt flopped down on the bed. *"How's it going, buddy?"* he asked Baa-Gah.

"Buddy is fine, but hungry. Buddy eat chocolate?"

Burt laughed. *"Sure, go ahead. While you're at it, have a bag of chips, the really spicy ones. You've earned it today."*

BaaGah had kept up a running commentary at any time they were traveling which alleviated the boredom and gave him information that Mechi didn't seem inclined to hand out. He was good about staying quiet when Burt was talking with all of the slaves on their trip, but Burt never felt alone with BaaGah hanging out with him. This surprised him, as he had never been a "pet person".

The closest thing to that was when his family hosted the school guinea pig one summer. It was the only time they ever volunteered for that particular honor and it didn't make him at all sad when they took "Barty" back to live in the school science room again.

Burt nibbled on his meal distractedly. So much to think about and he was not sure if he had learned anything he had not already expected, except that the Inseni seemed to be completely oblivious to the undercurrents running through their slave population. It seemed somewhat bizarre to him that Mechi had been so proud of his guided tour today. He didn't seem to notice how many carefully worded innuendos were communicated in Burt's interviews with the various slave populations inside the farming dome.

The populous was ripe for revolution and the Inseni seemed to feel they had completely and thoroughly subdued them. They seemed to understand nothing about the spirit that pervaded every single being Burt had encountered today. Even if the Alliance never got involved, the Inseni were heading for some big trouble down the line. It would only require the right spark to bring their carefully planned and orderly existence down on their heads.

On the one hand, Burt knew he was probably about to ignite that very spark. On the other hand, he also understood the inevitable cost of a revolution. He had seen the consequences of such action in various dimensions he had visited since becoming an Alliance agent. Oftentimes the resulting devastation took centuries for a culture to recover from.

He sighed and thought of the coming days. Mechi had scheduled a trip to a production dome where various industries produced necessary goods and finally a trip to the planet where their wizards resided.

As he considered this, Jenny's mind voice came to him. *"I have a surprise for you. Do you think they have any kind of electronic surveillance on your room?"*

"So far, I have yet to see any tech that resembles video surveillance. Why do you ask?"

"Are you willing to take a chance?"

"Uh, what are you up to? OK. Hit me with it. We'll deal with the fallout, if there is any."

Suddenly, before him were three women, Jenny, Elizabeth and Elian.

"We're not going to stay. I just wanted to show off a little. Previews of coming attractions. I have to put Elian back now. She is officially an Alliance agent at this point. You and I can talk after you go to sleep this evening. See you then."

And with that, they quickly faded from the room, leaving Burt sitting on the bed, his mouth agape.

He hadn't even gotten to say hello or get one of her amazing hugs. She was just there and gone again. Oh…and Elizabeth and Elian too, of course.

And now she wanted him to go to sleep? She had a twisted sense of humor, for sure. Well, the good news was that he had some chamomile tea in his MDP.

He gave instructions to BaaGah as to where to find the tea, a cup and the cool little bit of alien tech that would heat the water without worrying about a silly inconvenience like electricity. BaaGah brought it all to him with great pride. He could easily get used to that sort of thing, but he worried about turning BaaGah into nothing more than a convenient servant. True, he fed the little guy and praised him, which seemed to be all BaaGah cared about, but he despised those who took advantage of the meek and childlike.

After finishing his supper and his chamomile tea, he did the breathing exercises that helped him relax further.

As he drifted off he heard BaaGah's mental sigh of, *"Chocolate gooooood."* He chuckled to himself.

In his dream, he was back at the pool in Yosemite. There, waiting cross-legged on the big flat rock that overhung the deep little pool was Jenny. She looked up at him as he sat next to her, dangling his feet over the edge into the water.

"Show off," he told her. "You really know how to make an entrance."

She giggled. "I knew we didn't have a lot of time. I had already brought Elian to the council chamber for all of 15 minutes and I didn't want to have her discovered right out of the box."

"And you got her back safely?"

"Yes. Her barracks room was still empty when we put her back."

"So how did you work this bit of magic, Jenny? I know about the Daringi ability, but don't they have to know where they are going before they can transport from dimension to dimension?"

"Absolutely. But I had been thinking long and hard about this 'thing' I do. I always have this feeling like I am physically 'in' a place whenever I contact someone trans-dimensionally. It's not something I can really put my finger on.

Since the Daringi have this cool natural 'beam me up' ability, I had wondered if Elizabeth might not be able to get coordinates or whatever they call it to a place I brought her to mentally. Evidently, she can. She says she had never heard of anyone doing this particular thing, but, as far as I can tell, the trans-dimensional communication ability is pretty rare just like the Daringi ability is almost unheard of in any other species in the dimensions. The fact that more than one species on their planet can do it is mind-boggling."

"I would say so. And so, she was able to go to Elian and transport her to Alliance HQ. Now we have a person on the inside of one dome, but these domes are pretty isolated. As far as I know only the Inseni overseers have any way of communicating with the main dome or any of the others. Rebellion in one dome is unlikely to cause much of a ripple in their system, as far as I can tell."

"Gariel and Desminda agree. However, assuming we can get over that hurdle, Elizabeth has communicated the coordinates of the Insenium planet to all of the Daringi. As I understand the process, all Daringi now have the ability to come and visit the Insenium at this point. Their next experiment will be to see if they can bring some special Alliance tech with them to pinpoint coordinates to allow them to create a networked gateway.

Did you say that the 'wizards' of the Inseni are on a separate planet from this one? I will definitely want Elizabeth to ride along on that encounter. In the meantime, what did you discover when you visited the rest of the dome?"

"Everything isn't as it seems there, but the Inseni aren't seeing it. Elian isn't the only discontented slave in the compound. They have become very good, however at hiding this from their masters. Inseni have no sense of the subtleties of humanoid body language or facial expression, relying on words and tone and their own prejudices to interpret what is said. I think we can use this against them. The slaves who farm in the domes allow their masters to think them content with their lot, but I am sure a frank conversation with any of them would tell us very clearly that the opposite is true."

"I wish I could figure out how to do group broadcasts to people in different locations," Jenny said with a grimace. "I've scheduled some sessions with Liliath. She seems to think I may be able to do this. She also intimated that I may have other abilities that aren't limited entirely to communication. I have so much to learn that some days I feel like I'm going to explode. Accessing the additional area in my mind does help but learning how to maximize it without it being over-whelming still eludes me."

"Don't kid yourself, Jenny. You're doing more than any of us ever imagined a human could do. Don't you really understand how amazing you are to all of us? You stepped into a situation that no ordinary person would have been able to handle. It isn't like you were seeking any of this. It got heaped on you at a time when most people are still 'finding themselves'.

Yes, this situation is dire. Yes, a lot is at stake. But don't you see? All you can do is all you can do. You can't be more than what you have the resources, intelligence and will to become. You've already exceeded all expectations. Give yourself a break."

He threw a pebble into the little pool. Through the ripples they watched it sink down and down until it lay amongst the other colorful pebbles at the bottom.

"That's just it, Burt. It isn't about expectations. It's about doing what's right. I'll take a break as soon as it's time. I'll take a break when the job is done. It would be so tempting right now to just go home to my nice little house on Infinity Loop with the koi pond and the bougainvillea, but I could never be happy there until I know this threat doesn't hang over our heads, or the heads of the others who are being enslaved and destroyed by the Insenium and their followers."

"In that case, we'd best get to work. Now I know what to watch for. We need a way for the slaves to communicate with one another. We need to know if the 'wizards' have duplicated or even figured out the card and we need to lull the Inseni into a false sense of security. I think I can do that. Tell the council I meet with the scientists or 'wizards', as they call themselves, in a couple of days. I doubt they'll come right out and talk about it, so I may have to come up with a strategy. I was thinking there might be some way I could enlist BaaGah's help, but..."

"BaaGah help? Help, Burt?"

"*Maybe, but I don't know how yet. Why aren't you asleep?*"

"*Sleeping is thingygummy, man stuff. Mookookie don't know sleeping thing.*"

"*Mookookie don't sleep? How's that possible?*"

"*Mookookie rest in between the spaces. Lots of spaces between stuff and times. Lots and lots.*"

"*Someday I need to meet your brothers and sisters, BaaGah.*"

"*No brothers. No sisters. Mookookie are one and then many. All in one and one in many.*"

"*Can you speak with Jenny, BaaGah?*"

"*Yes! BaaGah speak with Jenny. Hi, Jenny! I'm BaaGah. Buddy of Burt. You buddy of Burt too?*"

Jenny laughed in delight. Suddenly BaaGah appeared between the two of them. She started and then reached out gently with her hand, something that Burt had actually never tried to do. BaaGah didn't back away, but leaned into her hand, a snuggling motion that made Burt laugh and Jenny blush.

"*Yes, BaaGah, Jenny is Burt's buddy too. You are such a good helper to Burt. I hope I can meet you someday in person.*"

"*Jenny meet BaaGah outside the spaces? That be happy day for BaaGah. You bring your buddy too?*"

"*My buddy?*"

"*Fuzzy buddy. BaaGah sees her between spaces, like you.*"

"*Chidwi? Chidwi, really?*"

Chidwi appeared on her shoulder. "*BaaGah can see me when my reflection is off. Very clever little person. I like him. He takes care of Burt for us. I take care of Jenny for Burt and BaaGah. We take care of each other. It's a very good thing. You do well, BaaGah.*"

Burt and Jenny sat there gawking at the two creatures that had come into their lives so unexpectedly. And then they looked at one another and burst into waves of laughter, holding their sides.

When Jenny had wiped the tears from the eyes of her dream-face and Burt had stopped wheezing from laughing so hard he could barely breathe, she sighed.

"I have to go, Burt. Looks like you and I have an insurrection to plan, among other things. I will relay this information to the council. We meet for two more days, enough time for you to visit at least one more dome and the wizard planet. Can you think of anything else I need to tell them?"

Surprisingly, Burt blushed. "Actually, tell Merv I have a bit of a problem. You see, I let down my guard the very first day and..." he trailed off and tugged at the medallion hanging around his neck. "I hate to admit it, but I didn't see this coming. I'm not sure if there are any special properties in this thing, like a gate key or agent pass, but Peril made sure that I couldn't get this off without his cooperation. It means I may be stuck here for at least as long as it takes for the Alliance to get here and remove him from his tiny little throne."

Burt was grateful to see that Jenny didn't laugh. She nodded seriously. "I can see where that might be a problem. I'll let Merv know. I need to get back, since I think they are about to start the next session. Please be careful, Burt." And she laid her hand gently on his for just a moment and then faded away.

Chapter 27: What She Does Best

Sam fiddled with the leaf she was supposed to be focusing on to "learn peace", as her captors put it. Bah! Peace was for people with no vision. Peace was for people who didn't mind being at the bottom of the pile. She would have nothing to do with it. Hot feelings of rebellion and disgust for the pacifists on her list coursed through her like the backdraft of a raging fire.

Nevertheless, she put on a placid face and downcast eyes. Her arachnid mentor, Sully, was beginning to relax her guard around her and even sympathized with the pathetic whining story of her supposed repentance. Sam, as she continued to think of herself, was very good at putting on an act. After all, she had fooled them all over the many years since her parents had sent her on this glorious mission, to represent the Insenium in their quest to put the multiverse in its proper order.

Self-righteous indignation welled up in her. How was it that they couldn't see? How was it that, as intelligent as she was, Jenny could be so obtuse about this? She had thought when Jenny had been instructed that she would have gleefully fallen in with Sam's plan. After all, wasn't she offering her the rulership of her planet and infinite power and dominion? What more could she possibly want?

She controlled her hands that wanted to tremble with her inner distress. She must appear to be calm. She must not even let a glimmer of her impatience and irritation show to her captors. Most of them were beginning to believe the charade. Most of them were beginning to let up on their constant surveillance, allowing her to do simple chores around the community and participate in group events, such as the evening "singing". Although how they could call that music, she had no idea.

Every evening they would gather in the clearing and make spider music, either low thrumming sounds with their legs or eerie low-pitched vocals rather like the monk chants that Lizzie had been fond of on Earth. Sam detested it. Her people were not fond of music in any form. Her father had called it a waste of valuable time to pursue the musical arts, much less sit around long enough to listen to music of any kind. Legend had it that at one time the arts had been supported by the throne and even encouraged, but her father and mother preferred stark asceticism and so it was that Sam had been raised with no appreciation for anything that didn't increase their kingdom's quest for ultimate power.

Thus, when the Insenium had come along with their offer of an alliance to reach into every corner of the multiverse for control and domination, her father had immediately fallen right in with the Inseni as a firm ally.

Now, here she sat, captive by these pitiful peace-mongers, unable to complete her mission of the complete domination of the Earth gates and the elimination of the gate keeping system. She had been greatly praised when she had turned Guaray, the guardian of the India gate. His assassination of the Gatekeeper and subsequent acceptance into the ranks of Alliance Earth guardians had been a major coup for her and had earned her much praise from her parents and the Insenium.

To blazes with that Jenny and her milksop interference! How ironic that she had been the one to stumble upon the dying Miriha after all Sam had done to set that raid up. It should have been HER! Sam should have been the one with the Gatekeeper key around her neck. Sam should have been the one to have brought her Groga to every Earth gate to prepare for complete domination of Earth. Instead, here she sat.

She suddenly realized she had crushed the leaf in her hands into green goo. Sully clicked her pincers in remonstrance. *"We shall try again later, Sam. I think you are too distracted to continue."*

Sam put on a repentant expression. *"I'm so sorry, Sully. I was just thinking about how many regrets I have about how things have turned out. I made some poor choices and now many are paying for them. I am so very sorry."* Not a word of that was false. She WAS sorry that she had made so many bad choices and for the consequences of those choices, but not for the reasons Sully would assume.

"The past is the past, Sam. You must learn this. You must forgive yourself before you can move on. Perhaps you would like to go for a walk? That often seems to soothe you."

"I would like that, Sully. Shall we go now?"

The big arachnid unfolded to nearly her full height and preceded Sam out the wide cabin door, although she had to duck to get out of it. The little cabin was evidently one of a number of guest houses for humanoids who occasionally visited the arachnid city. Sam exited without bothering to close the door. She had no possessions here and there was no lock. The day was sunny, and the open door would allow the cabin to air out. The spiders had a somewhat spicy scent that irritated Sam.

Actually, nearly everything irritated her these days. She had been such an utter failure. She had been sure she was on the brink of a great victory and still couldn't figure how she had gone wrong. It all should have worked. She hadn't counted on Jenny's strength or cunning or the extent to which her compatriots would go to rescue her.

She sighed and strode out, her long legs hidden by the long folds of the robes she was required to wear here. They had taken her clothing and burned it, a symbol of a new life, or so they said. She just thought they simply had really poor taste in clothing. Not surprising, since they didn't wear any adornments or clothing of any kind.

These walks usually consisted of a long trek around the edges of the small lake near the clearing. It was monotonous, also designed to increase her inner peace and harmony. She was glad to be out and moving, but rather than meditating on that harmony, as she walked, she generally spent her time plotting potential escape. She had been making preparations and, if all went well, today would mark a successful attempt.

Not that she hadn't tried several times in the beginning of her captivity, but the arachnids were fast and strong and had no compunction about wrapping her securely in web strands when she resisted recapture. They were surprisingly gentle creatures, very unlike the arachnids of Earth. She often found herself regretting the spider tattoo on her right arm. It seems so sappy now, compared to what it represented to her when she lived on Earth. These arachnids were nothing like the predators on Earth she had so admired.

So for now, she strode alongside Sully, her face once again a mask of serenity. Sully made no further comments, which suited Sam greatly. She wanted to psych herself up. This was going to work. It had to.

She knew the arachnids had done something to her when she first arrived. It had short-circuited her ability to morph. At first, she had raged with them about this. Over time, however, as part of her ruse, when she had realized she would never escape using brute force or any of the ploys that would have worked with humanoid captors, she decided to change her tactics. She had made "friends" with an arachnid named Ziggin. He was young and a lot less boring than his counterparts. He dreamed of adventure outside his dimension and he felt a bit constricted by the quiet lifestyle of his elders.

She would be meeting him later that day as he took his usual turn guarding their "guest". He was very tarantula-like and was fascinated that Sam had a spider tattooed on her arm. He took it as a personal compliment. She would complete her walk around the lake and then would be turned over into his custody.

She hadn't been wasting her meditation time. She knew some things about her gifts of which the arachnids were completely oblivious. When she finally realized that throwing fits or sneaking in the dead of night wouldn't get her what she wanted she fell back on what she knew. In a way all of the unsuccessful escape attempts had played into her hands. The arachnids were overly confident in their ability to keep her in place and she had acted the part of a defeated, lost little girl perfectly.

Sam had found her gifts early on in her training by her parents to be an agent for her family. They had praised her for it, a rare occurrence where her parents were concerned. As a result, she had outdone her trainers and moved far beyond the goals they had set for her.

The day she had discovered her ability to manipulate her body in creative ways, above her mental abilities in communication and subtle manipulation of others, had been amazing. She could still feel that euphoria when she realized she could do something her instructors and her parents could not. It meant she was special. It meant she was better than any of them.

So, in the past couple weeks she had spent her meditation time going into that special place in her mind that would allow her to manipulate herself and others. She started slowly and carefully, not sure how much of it would be recognizable by her captors. She knew they could sense her moods, when she didn't control them and, although they couldn't actually read her thoughts, they had set some wards against any thought she had of escape, relying on the idea that escape would require elevated levels of adrenalin.

So, instead she worked on two things, strengthening her mind shields to allow herself to appear to be blasé about her escape plans and untying the virtual knot they had put in her morphing abilities. In her mind she could see it, the huge, complex knot in her ability. Behind the knot her face was frozen in its current state. But she knew that this knot could only last as long as she was in range of her captors, so she ignored it. Of course, the knot wasn't real. It was a representation of the blockage they had placed on her ability. But they didn't know as much as they thought they did and that was about to work in her favor.

Ziggin liked to hear Sam's stories about other dimensions. At one point he had expressed a desire to see them for himself. Sam had sympathized with him, encouraging him to express his discontent as often as possible. Having found this weak spot, she romanticized her stories, stressing the idea that she wished she could help him, but there was no possible way for her to leave here. She had coordinates of many dimensions in her head, but it was useless without a portal, especially here. She was careful to tell no lies; those might be detected. She only used the truth to entice him more and more every day.

He had told her he looked forward to the times when he was assigned to watch over her and that he couldn't see why everyone was so upset by her. She was a nice person who had only been in the wrong place at the wrong time and she had sincerely repented, hadn't she?

She had assured him in complete honesty that she had repented of the mistakes she had made, without telling him which mistakes she was actually sorry about. By not elaborating, she could be totally honest in her emotions as she expressed remorse.

So, she walked around the lake with a lighter heart, knowing she would soon be able to put her plan into action. Ziggin would be her escape route. She would use his trust, something she had become very good at. Sully noticed her quiet and calm demeanor.

"I told you, you would feel better when you took your walk. Feel that calm, remember it so you can call it up again when you are distressed. You will feel so much better once you have mastered this."

"You're right. I'm much calmer now. I think I will be able to get in a nap before supper. Thank you."

"I am gratified to hear that. I think we are making progress." Sam could feel the smugness in the reply, but replied meekly, *"Thank you so much."*

They finished their walk without incident and Sully walked her back to her cabin. There, waiting nearby was Ziggin. *"Here you go, Ziggin. Your shift should be quiet. Sam has decided to take a nap before supper. Be vigilant."*

"Yes, Sully, as you say. Nothing much to do but wait."

Sam entered her little cabin and lay down on the straw mattress. Lumpy as it was, she had shaped it into something that molded fairly well to the contours of her body. The canvas cover was worn, but serviceable and kept her from being poked by stray pieces of straw. As she lay there, staring at the rough beams below the roof of the cabin, she calmed herself further. She might as well get some actual rest before she started out, she reasoned. When she awoke, she could sense Ziggy at his post.

"Ah, you're awake, Sam. Are you ready?"

"I am. Are you?"

"I've been ready for this for most of my life. Where will we be going?"

"Well, first I want to see my parents and from there we can go pretty much anywhere you'd like."

"I just need the coordinates. No one is watching and I've left the clues you suggested for them to find. They will think you have gone back to Earth, with me as a hostage. That should keep them all busy for quite awhile."

Sam gave Ziggin the coordinates to her parent's portal and he touched her with one fuzzy leg.

It was dark, blessedly dark. They were standing beside the portal and she could see her parent's fortress before her.

"We can get there a lot faster if you will let me ride on your back. Is that alright?"

"Sure."

Ziggin squatted, lowering his body to a point where Sam could climb on his back between his two forelegs. As he arose and moved forward at a breath-taking pace, Sam was very interested to see how the eight legs worked together. The undulations of his back were very different from a four-legged creature. Sam had ridden a horse a few times while on Earth, not her favorite experience, but something the hiking club had done once a year.

Sooner than she had expected her parents' fortress loomed over them, its black stone walls barely distinguishable from the perpetual black twilight of her home world. He allowed her to dismount and they went through the huge doors, flanked by two large trolls, side by side.

The cavernous entryway was flanked by torches high up on the walls. The light of each set of torches barely extended to the light of the next set of torches. The long walk from light to light was familiar. Sam sighed. She knew this would not be a happy reunion. She had much to atone for and that would not be pleasant, but she also had a hostage that could potentially give them the coordinates of Tarafau's home world. Surely that would be worth something.

She felt only the slightest twinge of guilt for what awaited the being at her side. It was the cost of war and she was willing to pay it, especially if it meant paying it with the blood of another, no matter how innocent. Betrayal came as naturally to her as breathing and what was one more betrayal in her career of stealth and deception? So she took another deep breath and moved forward.

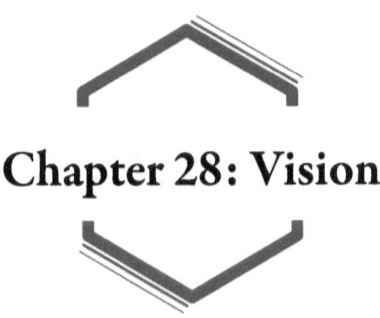

Chapter 28: Vision

Jenny woke in her suite at Alliance headquarters with anticipation. Today she would be working with Liliath. Liliath would be instructing her in a new way to look at her mental abilities. She could barely get her head around the fact that her newest instructor would be a dragon! Jenny had always considered herself a rational and practical person. Her bent for writing and a sharp imagination had always been guided by her sense of reality. She loved stories about elves and dwarves and dragons but had never had any illusions that they were anything except fantasy.

Now, of course, she knew better. It didn't make it any less amazing. The reality of her new life often nearly overwhelmed her. When she considered that less than a year ago the most exciting thing she had to look forward to was the next excursion with her hiking club, she sometimes had to pinch herself to be sure it wasn't a dream.

She had been invited to Liliath's quarters at the top of the Alliance headquarters building. Liliath had scheduled 6 sessions with her over the next couple days and then would be practicing with her long distance while she was in Sanglarka or elsewhere. Today they would be making the connection that would allow them to communicate at will. Evidently Liliath had similar abilities to Jenny and she was going to help Jenny explore areas of her fortress that she hadn't yet considered.

The elevator opened out to a corridor nearly 20 feet wide and equally tall. Jenny felt miniscule in this huge environment. Looking up and down the hallway, Jenny saw four dragon sized doors, equally spaced. Jenny knew Liliath wasn't the only draconian inhabitant of headquarters but hadn't thought about them actually living in the building.

As instructed, she went to her right and pushed the button by the door on her left. She heard no buzzer or chime, but the door slid open and she heard, *"Come in, Jenny."*

Jenny entered with a little shiver of excitement. She was not disappointed. The room had the appearance of a large, well lit, cavern. Light shimmered on one wall, reflected from a small pool fed by a tinkling fountain. The floor appeared to be some kind of quartz, smoothed and polished to a gleaming glow, the small crystals in the quartz also reflecting the light from the windows and skylights in the room. The room was open to the outside, leading out onto a balcony that overlooked the city.

Liliath reclined on a stone shelf on one side of the room that appeared to have been created specific to the contours of her dragon body. Liliath gestured to a round plush cushion on the floor in front of her.

"Please be seated, Jenny. I would like to speak with you for a moment before we begin. I know this hasn't been easy for you, being plunged into your position as you were. You barely know any of us and yet you have shown so much trust, courage and loyalty to what we do. You are to be commended. Not many of your age and experience could have risen to the task you have agreed to take on.

Historically our species has been fascinated by the humanoids of our acquaintance. I'm afraid we didn't get off onto the right foot with your race in the early days of your planet's existence. For this reason, I am excited to mentor one of your kind, and not just because it is necessary to our cause to see you get the best possible training.

I think you are something unique, an element of humankind we have seldom seen in the history of your race. It is seldom we see your kind of talent combined with such integrity and valor. I just wanted you to know that you have my respect. I think that is important, especially in your case, since you tend to undervalue your contribution."

She paused, her reptilian eyes gazing calmly at Jenny. Jenny could feel the warmth of that expression, even if it was so alien to her.

"*I suppose I've never thought of myself in that way before and it is all so very much and so fast. I worry that I am holding the rest of you back, keeping you from getting things done as well or as quickly as you need to. I feel like the little kid who has been invited to play with the big boys on an unfamiliar playing field.*"

"*Oh, Jenny. Never consider yourself that way. I don't think it was an accident that you ended up as The Gatekeeper so unexpectedly and at such a young age. I believe your background, coming from a loving family and well-educated and having done so much traveling already in your life has well prepared you.*

For now, let's just get the awkwardness out of the way. I am a dragon. You are a humanoid being. It wouldn't be the first time our races worked together, but that is beyond living memory for your kind. So let us decide to embark on this journey as friends and equals, shall we?"

"*Yes, Liliath. I would like that. I am so looking forward to working with you. It feels very unreal to me. I have so many protectors and mentors now. I worry it will make me feel invincible and perhaps more entitled than I am.*"

"*Which is precisely why I am confident that won't happen to you, Jenny; you are so aware and willing to take responsibility for your actions. That is a very rare thing in one so young, even among dragons.*"

Jenny sat up a little straighter, looking directly into Liliath's eyes. "*So tell me what to do and we can get started, shall we?*"

"*Go into your regular deep-thought breathing pattern and allow me into your fortress. Amenia has briefed me on your progress so far. Today we will explore some new options for you.*"

The large round cushion that Jenny sat on was extremely comfortable. It reminded Jenny of the memory foam mattress and pillows she had purchased when they had refurnished the bedroom that had been trashed by those thugs what seemed like ages ago, but it had been merely weeks. She'd only gotten to sleep in that new bed a few times, but this cushion reminded her of that.

She relaxed into her breathing patterns and within a few breaths was meeting Liliath on the drawbridge before her mental fortress. "This is Liliath, Sir Knight. She has permission to access the fortress as she chooses."

The knight who guarded the portcullis nodded. "Of course, my liege. Please enter."

Liliath turned to her and Jenny was surprised to see her lips move as she spoke aloud. Her voice was soft and not sibilant as Jenny had supposed it might be. She had forgotten that in her mental fortress they could speak directly without the appearance of mindspeech.

"This is impressive, Jenny. I can hardly wait to see what you have built here."

"I think it is a combination of all of the fantasy books I read as a kid and my visit to Miriha's village. I was fairly surprised at it, myself. I've only visited the library and the communications center so far with Amenia. I really don't know what the other buildings represent, yet."

"Let us go to the observatory I see in the distance, shall we? I am fascinated to discover what prompted you to put that there. Nothing is here by accident, Jenny. Every bit of this was built by you, from your experiences, your education and your imagination. Amenia tells me that when you went into your library you knew exactly where to go to find what you were seeking. This is because you organized it based on your own experience and needs. You may not remember doing it, but everything in this place should be completely logical to you once you discover everything it holds.

A warning, however; this place is vast beyond your imagining. Much like the Gateway Network, it leads to infinite possibilities. Most humans, even the gifted ones, never come close to mapping it all out in their mortal lifetimes. So, don't get over-anxious when you realize you don't know the half of it. You tend to be a bit of an over-achiever and you stress yourself way too much over what you can't do or don't know. So a lot of patience will be required. But you'll get there."

As soon as Liliath had pointed out the observatory, which appeared to be far away on the side of a tall hill, they were walking up the path that led there. Flowers bloomed in the edges of the path and the whole scene was framed in a brilliant blue morning sky. Jenny was fairly impressed with the detail. She found herself wondering, if you could enter into this part of a newborn's brain, would it be empty or would most of this be in place in some type of rudimentary format?

She noticed that Liliath had qualified the word "lifetime" with the word "mortal". She decided not to query Liliath about this, however. Even though she realized that time flowed much differently here in her mental fortress she didn't want to waste any of the time with philosophical debates.

The door to the observatory was human sized, but Liliath walked through it with no problem. Jenny realized, with a shock for not having noticed before, that Liliath wasn't much taller than Jenny in this place.

Inside the main entrance was a type of lobby with comfortable looking chairs spaced around it. Beyond the lobby were the laboratories, she knew without looking. Around the edge of the round lobby room was a wide staircase that ascended around the room to a balcony, similar to the main building in Miriha's village. The difference was that there was no closed door on the landing, just an archway that led to a high ceilinged room with a slit like opening in the roof that allowed for the extrusion of a humongous telescope.

"What will you see when you look through that, I wonder?" Liliath inquired in her soft voice.

"I had no idea it was here, so I'm not sure."

"Why don't you try it?"

Jenny only hesitated a moment before putting her eye to the eyepiece. "I don't see anything but a blur."

"Adjust the knob next to the eyepiece. You need to focus it to suit your vision."

Jenny complied, feeling a little foolish, since that step should have been obvious to her. As she turned the knob gently, she began to see something slowly come into view. The definition increased until she finally saw, very clearly, a human eye, looking back at her. She blinked and pulled away then looked again. When she blinked, the eye blinked back at her.

"Can you see what I'm seeing, Liliath?"

"If you allow me to, I can. Let me see through your eyes."

"How do I do that?"

"You actually know how to do it. Relax and allow it to happen."

Jenny let out a long relaxing sigh. Suddenly she felt Chidwi's small warm hands on her shoulders. She had nearly forgotten Chidwi was there. Chidwi had turned her reflection off before exiting the elevator, simply saying she didn't want to intrude. Now Jenny felt that amazing peace that Chidwi seemed to send out to Jenny exactly when she needed it.

"I can see it. What do you think it means?"

"Means? I don't understand."

"Remember, you built this land. You created everything in it, including any tech you see. Everything in your fortress has a specific purpose, to reveal different aspects of your gifts and talents and to help you become what you are intended to be. So why is that eye looking back at you right now?"

Jenny remembered Amenia had explained more than once that everything in this place was symbolic of something important to Jenny. So, what was with the eyeball? Of all the things she had expected to see in an observatory telescope, this wasn't a part of it. She decided to talk it through, as she often did when writing a difficult piece for a client.

"The eyeball must be huge. This is a telescope, after all. It was out of focus to begin with, so I had to focus to see it. The iris is blue like mine. The pupil is large, as if trying to take in more light, as if looking at something intensely. Large pupils also often represent excitement or seeing something that makes us happy..."

She paused, drawing another calming breath. "This is my eye looking back at me; me, looking at me, as if, instead of a telescope, this is a microscope with me under it. What do I need to see about myself? Why do I need to look so closely, so intensely?"

"Very good, Jenny; you are so very close. What do you see?"

"In the telescope? I just told you."

"No, put yourself on the other end and look. What do you see?"

"Um, I'm not sure I want to look."

"You get to choose. No one will attempt to force you, not that they could. As far as tricking you into it, that's not why I'm here."

"So why are you here? Is this a test? I don't see what this has to do with improving my ability."

Liliath only cocked her head, patiently, expectantly.

"But how do I get to the other end of the telescope?" Jenny said plaintively after a long moment of staring into the kind eyes of the dragon. Suddenly she was more than a little over-whelmed. How did this apply to her current mission? How was she ever going to learn enough in time to be truly useful to their cause? The words Burt spoke to her in his dream came back to her, "All you can do is all you can do. You can't be more than what you have the resources, intelligence and will to become. You've already exceeded all expectations. Give yourself a break."

She took a deep breath as Liliath pointed to a small circular staircase that led up into the slit that held the other end of the telescope. "All I can do is all I can do," she repeated to herself.

When she got to the top of the little staircase, she found a second eyepiece. Lowering her eye to it, she realized that she wasn't on the other end of the telescope, so what would she see? Adjusting the focus, what she saw was BaaGah, of all things. She knew the little creature was with Burt, so how was this possible? He looked like a little spaghetti squash with warts, a stubby tail, round eyes with no lashes and a wide grinning mouth with bovine-like teeth. The mouth stretched nearly the whole width of the body/face. No torso, no appendages, although Burt had told her that BaaGah had the ability to extend multiple arms and legs as needed. BaaGah was just a little round face with a tail.

So, what was he doing at the end of the telescope? She blinked and readjusted the focus and there he was, still blinking up at her. "BaaGah?" she sent, hopefully, but there was no response.

Climbing back down to Liliath she told her what she had seen. Liliath cocked her head and then shook it slowly.

"There was no one here but me. But your mind is trying to tell you something. There are two clues here. First, that this ability has to do, not with your mind, but your eyes. Second, BaaGah may have a clue for you as to what it is. Perhaps you may want to do another dream session with Burt when he is available. In the meantime, think on it. It is time to go to our next council session."

They came to in Liliath's Lair, as Jenny had decided to call it. Liliath didn't rise yet, however. She looked with interest at Jenny, making her squirm a little on her soft cushioned seat.

"That was very interesting," Liliath sent. *"Your mind appears to be very well ordered and yet, extremely creative. The observatory is well considered, as it appears to be about vision inward as well as outward. The fact that it exists in your mental fortress tells me that it is a placeholder for a specific talent or ability. For now, let your subconscious mind percolate on that idea. What is it about your vision or sight that might be out of the ordinary?"*

Suddenly Jenny recalled that at some point during her training with Amenia she had experienced some strange difference in her vision, nothing she could put her finger on, but that it was just different. And as she thought about it, she realized it was right after they had made the breakthrough that opened the mental fortress to her. She felt Chidwi's warm little hands on her face, turning her face to face the little creature.

"Jenny can see. Jenny can see more. Your eyes are new. You will see new things." Her serious little face, with the green moustaches trailing from the smiling little mouth and the matching green tufts over her eyes looked into Jenny's eyes. The warm gentle feeling that emanated from her was love in a way that Jenny had never considered. Jenny realized that she was feeling these feelings more and more strongly from all of those in her team. Was this another gift?

"Thank you, Chidwi and Liliath. I will focus on this thought in my process. You have both taught me so much and I cannot think of any way to adequately express my gratitude."

"Your actions and hard work are more than adequate, Jenny. Chidwi and I can feel the sense behind your words. Next session we will explore this more, but for now, let us get to our council session. You need to report your latest findings from Burt, and I understand the science team and strategy and tactics team have developed new tactics for their projects especially adapted to the dome environment. It sounds like it will be interesting. We are definitely making progress. That being said, typically regardless of how carefully you plan, there are always unknown factors, so more than one plan needs to be in place. There is still so much to be done and time grows short."

"I think Burt may be buying us some time at the moment. Emperor Peril seems to trust him, or at least that is what he would have Burt think. Of course, he is manipulating or he is trying to manipulate Burt. He has something devious up his little sleeve for sure and I think there is more than appears to the political structure here. In my writing career I covered a lot of political content for various companies and politics is so much of smoke and mirrors."

Liliath nodded in agreement as she led the way out of her lair. In moments they were walking into the private council chamber. Not everyone was there yet. Liliath took her accustomed seat. *"Let's keep the results of this session to ourselves for now, Jenny,"* she sent. *"Until we have something more conclusive, we need to be circumspect. I don't want the other teams distracted with speculation."*

"I agree. We don't even know what we've discovered yet."

"I have some suspicions, but, as Amenia has probably explained to you, these things work much better when you discover them on your own. Forcing things could ultimately damage your ability or even block it and we don't want that."

At last the others had taken their seats and Ingot stood. *"Welcome back from your break, or what we are calling a break. I doubt any of you really spent any of the time between sessions relaxing, other than some workouts here and there. This is why, although I admire your enthusiasm, we will do a workout up on the roof for one and all at the start of breaks from now on, with the exception of Jenny and Liliath, as I understand they are doing their own workouts between sessions."* He nodded at Liliath and Jenny with a wry twist to his mouth.

"Now let us get down to it. Jenny, I know you haven't really had a break yet, but I understand you have had further communication with Burt, and it is of importance to all of our efforts."

Jenny nodded and stood, looking into the eyes of the surrounding team members. She liked to do this before she spoke, because it gave her courage to see all of them, so attentive and open to what she was about to say. She remembered in the beginning she didn't always feel that way, but as the team had worked together and she got to know each of them better and now that she actually could communicate with each of them privately as she wished, she felt closer than ever to this disparate group of people tied together by such an important mission.

She told them of her time with Burt without going into describing their beautiful surroundings, which seemed somehow personal. She knew they were aware of her and Elizabeth's new trick and the slave, Elian, so Burt's surprise at their grand entrance sent a chuckle around the circle, including Myla whose hooting-like bird chuckle actually elevated the chuckle to a guffaw in many cases. When they had settled down, Jenny told them about Burt's report regarding his experience with the insensitivity of his guide to the subtle sub-text of Burt's interviews with the slaves of the domed plantation.

When she got to the part about BaaGah, she noticed many of the scientists twitched in their chairs, as if anxious to run off and discuss this with their fellow scientists. There were obviously nuances of the conversation that may have gone over Jenny's head.

Then she told of BaaGah's mysterious declaration about being one and many and the scientists seemed to swell and nearly explode.

"*Was he talking about reproduction?*" Megan burst in suddenly. Her zoological background was definitely showing in the excited tone of her voice. "*No sexes? Are we talking mitosis here? A being that can go 'between the spaces,' which sounds like the spaces of atoms to me. And with all of BaaGah's abilities? How can we get in touch with his people?*" Then with a start she looked around at the bemused faces of her team members. "*Oops,*" she said, blushing and hanging her head. "*Sorry. I got carried away. I'll try to restrain myself.*"

Jenny laughed. *"Not at all, Megan. This is why you are an important part of our science team. You are exactly right. Burt promised to 'have a talk' with BaaGah about this recent outburst. I am not entirely sure of the full ramifications of this newest development..."* She trailed off suddenly, realizing that an important connection had just occurred regarding her most recent session with Liliath.

At that same moment the building seemed to rock as a loud, violent blast nearly deafened all of them.

Jenny's guards sprang up at the same time that Tarafau covered Jenny with his body, attempting to shield her from falling objects. She knew that Miriha's death had ingrained a fear of something like that happening to her. She was grateful for his care of her, but it blocked her from the chaos amongst the group. Some were moaning in pain; others were trying to organize the group to check for injuries and to communicate with anyone outside the room as to what had just happened.

When Tarafau moved, she could see that Liliath and Myla were bent over Ingot. He had not been so fortunate. A long laceration on his head and blood streaming from his nostrils were evidence of what had happened to him. His face was gray, and his lashes fluttered.

Gariel was yelling into his version of a walkie talkie in his guttural language. There were few injuries, but some of the ceiling tiles had fallen and apparently Ingot had been hit by a large lighting fixture that had come loose.

"Healers are on the way, but it will be awhile, as the elevators haven't been certified to use. Tarafau, can you take Ingot to the infirmary's emergency section? He doesn't look good and isn't responding to mindspeech."

Tarafau nodded and simply took Ingot into his muscular arms and faded from view.

"The rest of you, please be seated. The moment we can use the elevators, we will get you to the gate to Sanglarka. You can disperse from there. Jenny will stay in touch with me and will relay information to you as soon as it is available. It looks like we have been attacked as there are never seismic events in this area of the planet. This is all I know for now."

Chapter 29: Putting Out Fires

Gariel looked around him. The only serious injury seemed to be Ingot, but that one was very serious. As a military man, he had seen some bad injuries, but had never become so hardened to become completely objective about it. Ingot looked really bad. The gray cast to his skin was a bad sign, especially when he had gone ashen so suddenly. Gariel knew that Tarafau would get him to the relative safety of the emergency section of the Infirmary almost instantaneously, but how much could be done for Ingot was questionable.

In the meantime, Liliath, Ingot's second was ordering everyone and checking for missed injuries due to shock. For the most part, the only thing that was bothering most of them was their hearing. The sound of the blast had been shattering. Myla was actually bleeding from his earholes and sat on his perch like chair, stunned. The bodyguards and strategy and logistic team members seemed to be organizing everyone for the descent down the tower. In the meantime, Gariel's team was doing reconnaissance to discover the source of the blast.

"I'll take Myla to the healers," Elizabeth offered.

"No, I want you to stay with Jenny, but perhaps Desminda and Elgyra can take Myla and Gissah to the infirmary and then report back. I'm kind of surprised Tarafau hasn't returned, so please be very careful. I suggest you take them to the reception area. I'm guessing ours aren't the only casualties."

The receptionist, Gissah, was unconscious, but didn't appear to have received any obvious wounds. Gariel suspected that her large, foxlike ears had been impacted by the high decibel blast and hopefully she would regain consciousness soon. Desminda and Elgyra soon faded away with the two injured in tow. He hoped he wasn't sending them into an even more dangerous situation.

Gariel had no idea whether this blast was just the Alliance Headquarters building or whether a larger scale attack was in process. If that was the case, he knew his troops had probably already engaged the enemy.

He hated having to stand still when, in all likelihood his troops were putting their lives on the line. His under commanders were competent. He knew he could trust them to keep a level head and, there were emergency evacuation plans for the building and even the city in case of an attack or natural disaster. That being said, the best plans only lasted intact until the first shot was fired, as his first battle commander had been fond of saying.

Jenny looked shaken but had not panicked at this emergency. She actually looked a bit distracted, not particularly surprising in a situation like this one. Survivors of disaster often remarked of unexpected thoughts and feelings when faced so abruptly with their own mortality. This wasn't the first time Jenny had found herself in a dangerous situation since coming on board as a Gate Guardian and now a Gatekeeper.

Tarafau returned to report

"I don't see any dangerous disconnections in the ceiling at this point," he sent to the group. *"However, please pay attention to where you choose to sit while we wait. I want to suggest that along the walls would be good, as this chamber is at the very center of this building. The outer walls of this room are reinforced with special materials to prevent eavesdropping, among other things. The fact that we could hear the boom of the blast so forcefully tells me that others were even more badly affected.*

In the meantime, please get any rest you can. I have no idea how long we will be here before we can leave the building. Once we do, however, if the situation allows it, we will get you directly to the gate to get you back to Sanglarka. Everything just changed radically, and we need to regroup.

So far, we believe that the Groga, the Insenium and the Fleistians have no access to Earth, so it is probably the best place to reasess our situation and mount an attack, if necessary. My assumptions may be premature. There is always the possibility that something exploded in the armory or the science lab..." and he waved down the objections of the science team. *"The point is, that we know next to nothing at this point and I would rather err on the side of caution, for now."*

Tarafau nodded, his amber eyes narrowed in thought. *"Do you have any ideas of who specifically might have done this, assuming it was an attack? Our information doesn't tell us if either the Inseni or the Fleistians have any potential access to this dimension. Up until now, the only enemy agents we are aware of are those we deliberately brought here, with the exception of Guaray."*

"No. I'm not even harboring any suspicions until we know if this was an attack or whether it was something less ominous. For all we know, at this time, it is simply some type of unexpected natural disaster."

"In that case," Tarafau said, nodding in agreement, *"Let's focus on re-establishing communications. I don't want to evacuate yet. As far as we know, it could be worse outside the building than where we are now. Everyone already has emergency food and water supplies in their MDPs, so no one will starve. If oxygen supplies get low, we all have rebreathers."*

Bob slapped his forehead. *"Jenny, get Lizziebot out and I will grab Fidget. They may have access to the in-building communications. Power seems to be functioning, but the network computer was probably destroyed or damaged with the same blow that took out Ingot. Our greatest need at this point is accurate information."*

Gariel watched as Lizziebot and Fidget materialized. *"How may I be of service?"* they said nearly in unison. He had forgotten about the bots and evidently both Jenny and Bob had been distracted enough by the blast as to have also forgotten about that particular resource.

"Fidget, I need you to see if you can connect with the local communications network. Lizziebot, I need you to do a scan of the council rooms and check for structural anomalies."

Gariel was astonished at how quickly the two bots went to work and came back with a report.

"*The communications network is partially down, but we have access to security and the main lobby. According to their reports, there is no outside damage, but the streets are in chaos. Security is analyzing security footage and is supervising an orderly evacuation of the building, with the exception of the badly injured,*" reported Fidget.

"*This section of the building is surprisingly stable, since seismic analysis tells us that the blast center was not far from here. Tell security to look at the floor above us. The blast appears to have been aimed at the private council chamber. Elevators are not functioning. Both secured stairwells are blocked,*" Lizziebot chimed in immediately following Fidget's report.

"*OK, thank you Bob, Fidget and Lizziebot. It appears we can evacuate using the Daringi on the team, if that works for you. Jenny, can you contact Sanglarka? I believe Arvid is on duty there.*"

Jenny agreed. She had been standing near Liliath's couch, Chidwi on her shoulder. She went gracefully into a seated position on the floor and her eyes took on an unfocused, faraway look. Gariel glanced at Liliath, who had taken on the attitude of a dragon watching over a hatching dragonet. They all felt that way about Jenny.

Gariel hadn't been much impressed by his first view of the new Gatekeeper. He had loved and respected Miriha as all of them had and wasn't ready for the change. But her fearless participation in the South American conflict with the encroaching Groga had won his respect and admiration. He knew her father was a military man and he found it sad that he didn't know what a heroic young woman he and his wife had raised.

Jenny's eyes refocused. "*Arvid reports all to be quiet at Sanglarka. However, he suggests that rather than all of us coming there; we sort ourselves back into our teams and retreat to our team headquarters, in case whoever did this decides to take another chance at wiping us all out at once.*"

"*Good advice. Tarafau, will you and Elizabeth transport Jenny and her bodyguards to Sanglarka to begin with and I will have everyone organized into teams for each of the next transports. Our enemy, if they are observing will think us all still trapped up here and I will arrange for security to set a little trap of our own, just in case they try to break in here. Desminda, if you will take the Tactical Team, except for me. Elgyra, if you will take Luz and Juan...*"

While he continued to give instructions Tarafau and Elizabeth nodded. Jenny had replaced Lizziebot into her MDP. Elizabeth grabbed Mynn and Myra and faded from view. Tarafau didn't' hesitate. He bent and grabbed Jenny's shoulder while she was still in her seated position with Chidwi on her shoulder, and then took Nona by a shoulder and vanished. They would be in Sanglarka in moments. Gariel and his team had already discussed the advantages of their new allies and had decided that as valiant and well trained as the Daringi were militarily, their transporting abilities would probably be the edge they needed strategically.

Gariel quickly arranged for Sardina and Desminda to take the Science and Logistics teams in shifts to Switzerland and Puerto Rico. By that time, Tarafau and Elizabeth had returned, but before he could give them their next assignments, Liliath got their attention. She had been surprisingly well controlled during the crisis, but telltale tendrils of smoke drifted from both nostrils. The spicy scent of dragon smoke lent a strange air of unreality to the whole scene.

"I would like to make an unusual request. As the ranking member of the Alliance Council, I would normally take Ingot's place while he is recuperating. He WILL recuperate," she said emphatically, a small trickle of additional smoke trailing up from one nostril. *"With Jenny's talent for communication and with the bots, I should be able to attend to my duties while Myla and Ingot are indisposed. I will assign a liaison with emergency powers to stay on top of the situation here.*

I have important unfinished business with The Gatekeeper. The talent she is developing could very well mean the difference between success and failure and prevent an interminable cycle of war across the dimensions. For the first three days I need to be in physical proximity to her. After that, I should be able to help her across dimensional space. So, I need to go to Sanglarka to complete the first stage of her training."

She turned to Elizabeth and Tarafau. *"Does size matter in your talent? Will it take more than one of you to transport me to Sanglarka?"*

Elizabeth grinned and turned to her father. *"Can I do it, please, father?"*

Tarafau nodded fondly and turned to answer Liliath's question. *"It doesn't take an ounce more of energy to transport a dragon than a dragonfly, Liliath. Any organic being can be transported by us as long as we can touch them."*

Elizabeth was practically dancing in anticipation. Liliath grinned her toothy dragon grin. For anyone who didn't know her it would have been intimidating, especially as the smoke continued to rise from her nostrils and her eyes were slits in her face with mirth. The whole effect was more than a little dramatic.

The funniest thing about it to Gariel was that in such a stressful situation, he could appreciate the excitement of Elizabeth and the kindness that Liliath's grin represented. It didn't change the urgency of the situation, but it did give him perspective.

Liliath turned to Gariel, looking into his eyes with draconic intensity. *"Get our people to safety. Jenny will be making contact with you soon after I arrive in Sanglarka. Establishing the contact with you will allow you to coordinate with all team members instantaneously. Just be aware that Jenny is not a machine. She still requires rest and time to do her other duties as well as ongoing training in her abilities.*

I will not be gone longer than 3 days. During that time, organize your resources here at headquarters. I am sending Arvid here to liaison with the other members of the general council. They all know him, and it will also allow him to be close to his nephew. I know that although he won't show it, he will be very concerned.

If, for whatever reason, you need me, I will only be as far away as it takes for Elizabeth to escort me back here. Do you have any questions?"

Gariel pondered this for a moment. *"What happens if Ingot doesn't make it? I know you are in line to take his place and traditionally Myla moves up to become your second and then you need a third. How is that choice made?"*

"*Our law states that the Chief Counselor can choose from a pool of candidates already approved by the Dimensional Alliance Council main body. We are careful to be sure that dimensions are equally represented and so no council presidency can be made up of all of one dimension. For instance, I can't choose another draconian. I have an idea of who I might choose, should that become necessary. For now, I want to move forward with the hope that soon Ingot can step back into his role. He only has one more year left to serve, and I would see him serve the full term.*"

Gariel nodded. "*Well, I suppose we'd best get on with it, then. Elizabeth, please escort the councilor to Sanglarka.*"

With a sparkle in her eye, Elizabeth laid one hand on Liliath's shoulder and they were gone.

Chapter 30: Spaces

Burt was grateful for his communications from Jenny. He admitted only to himself that when he had first gone through the gate to infiltrate the Inseni, he had felt cut adrift. He had been going on solo missions for the Alliance for years, and yet, this time it was different. He had bonded so tightly with the Earth team and he had gotten comfortable with their company and interaction. He had been a loner for so much of his life and it hadn't really bothered him at all. Or so he had thought.

Now, with his friends of the Earth team, he had experienced the bond of true friendship and the power of what people could accomplish working together.

Knowing that Jenny was often tagging along in his adventures with the Inseni added spice and more than a little comfort. His visit to two more domes the day before had been pretty much a repetition of the first one. He and Jenny agreed that the Inseni slaves were ripe for rebellion and they could help them with that, if they could work out the timing to coincide with their own efforts to take down the Inseni.

Today he would finally get to visit the "wizards", something he had been looking forward to with great anticipation. His analysis of the extent of their science and understanding would hopefully give them the clues they needed to determine whether or not they had multiples of the card their own science team was working so hard to hack into and whether they had any understanding of it at all. Burt suspected that this might have been some tech they had found in one of their raids and they still hadn't figured out any more than his own team had done.

He would be going off-planet for this visit. Evidently, they kept their wizards isolated from the general populace to eliminate distractions. Burt wondered if it was more than that.

There was a scratching at his door. Burt leapt up to answer. He was surprised to see Penchant instead of Mechi standing there. *"His Imperial Majesty will be accompanying you on this excursion,"* Penchant said by way of explanation. *"If you are ready, let us depart."*

There was a mental hiss from BaaGah. The little creature had become more antagonistic regarding the Inseni the longer they stayed here and interacted with the Inseni people and their slaves.

Burt was surprised to realize that BaaGah's indignation was as much for the treatment of the humanoid slaves and other beings the Inseni had enslaved as for the Mookookie. BaaGah's heart seemed to be bigger than he was. Another reason Burt was so glad he had fed the little guy in that dark cell that day.

As they had traveled between domes, BaaGah had pointed out the Mookookie peeking out from behind scrub and trees. Ordinarily they scampered about openly, but when an Inseni vehicle was spotted, all were immediately warned in the vicinity to hide. The only reason Burt had been able to see any of them was that they were curious because they sensed the presence of BaaGah in the vehicle. Otherwise they would have blended in with their surroundings, hiding in the "spaces".

Penchant led the way down the stairs into the common room of the inn. There, resplendent in crown and royal paraphernalia was Peril, His Most Royal and Supreme Emperor of the Insenium. His huge violet eyes solemnly acknowledged Burt and Penchant. Without a word he turned and led the three of them out of the inn.

They walked back toward the palace, encountering bowing and scraping citizens, slaves and Groga.

"Sire, when we have completed our visit to your wizards, I would respectfully request to visit your Groga training center. Your troops are so well trained and disciplined I would love the opportunity to witness their training in person."

If Peril's mouth was capable of it, Burt was sure it would have twisted in derision. *"The Groga are blunt instruments. We keep them only for intermittent raids. They train themselves under our watchful eye. We have no desire to arm them with more information or training than is necessary for our purposes. You can visit them if you wish. Their dome is nearby. Tomorrow.*

If you were able to stay longer, I would show you what real training is about. Our elite forces live and train off world and it is a bit of a journey from here. They aren't Inseni, strictly speaking. Our planet hosted two distinct races before we left it. They call themselves Inseni of the Warrior Way. Generally, our interests coincide, and they have agreed to operate under Inseni rule."

They entered the large plaza in front of the royal palace. The three of them were alone here. The private citizens did not seem to have a lot of business at the palace. At the end of the courtyard, Peril veered right to a small gate Burt hadn't noticed when he first came through there. Through the gate was a path that wound around the end of the main building where Burt got an opportunity to see just how massive the building was. For such small people, Burt thought, it was evident that the Emperor, at least, had really big aspirations.

Burt didn't push farther on the topic of the elite force Peril had mentioned. This wasn't the time, but he was sure he was going to pursue the topic when it was more appropriate.

The path led along the outside edge of the building for nearly 50 yards then turned left around to the backside of the palace. Looking up from this vantage point, Burt could see that this was the exact center of the dome. There, on a square cement slab rested a small aircraft, large enough to seat maybe a half dozen people, less, if they were all Burt's size.

On closer inspection he realized the platform wasn't cement at all, but some other substance, more plastic-like. From the corners extended cables that reached up to the top of the dome. The center top of the dome was the only part of the dome that Burt could see that was opaque.

As they entered the aircraft, and sat, Burt's knees uncomfortably close to his face, Burt heard the first sound he had ever heard from the vocal cords of Peril or any of his citizens and it wasn't pleasant. It was rather like the sound of a fax machine connecting, high pitched and screechy. At once, the doors to the cabin closed and the little ship began to rise on its platform toward the dome ceiling.

Just a few feet before they touched the ceiling, the opaque circle slid back. There was a sound of motors whirring and the craft took off vertically. Here was an opportunity for Burt to see a bird's eye view of the planet. From high above he could see that the area was spotted with domes, large and small. Most of the terrain seemed to be plains with very few hills. Beyond that a chain of mountains framed the flatlands, a wide stream winding between the domes.

"Home," came BaaGah's plaintive voice in his mind. *"My hooommmme."*

"I know, BaaGah. And we will do our best to get it back for the Mookookie."

BaaGah lapsed once again into silence.

"So where exactly are we going?" Burt inquired of Penchant. He thought it was probably politic to address the emperor through his lackey.

"We are about to launch. We just need a little more altitude."

"Launch? You mean in this little craft? Do you do this often?" Burt asked, trying to maintain his cool. He noticed there weren't even any safety belts.

"Certainly. How else would we be able to see what our wizards were up to? Wizards are powerful and not to be trusted. They come up with things that may not be in the best interest of the Insenium and they are easily distracted," Penchant replied tartly, as if it was too obvious to any reasonable person.

About that time the little craft paused and hovered for a moment below what might have been a cloud to a casual observer. They then rose into the little cloud. When they arose to the other side, Burt knew they weren't on the same planet instantly.

For one thing, it was dark, the stars clearly visible. For another there wasn't a dome in sight. The lights of a small city twinkled ahead of them.

"Wow! That was amazing! Did your wizards invent that?"

"Invent? No! It was a natural feature of the planet. We still aren't sure why it is there or how it works. We discovered it when a pilot accidentally flew through it."

Burt looked behind them, but there was no identical cloud to be seen.

"So how do we get back? I don't see a cloud."

"We have the coordinates of the entrance programmed into the aircraft. It requires no pilot and is powered by the sun. It uses nearly no energy because it never needs to fly but for a few minutes at a time."

Burt was impressed. A simple solution both technically and politically. Isolating their scientists this way and putting them under strict governmental controls was helpful to Peril's rule and was typical of the massive control policies that were evident everywhere they went. Arrogant, clever, diabolical and true to everything Burt had observed so far in the Insenium.

They landed just outside the main building of the small city complex. It was very similar in many ways to tech cities on Earth, self-contained communities devoted entirely to the scientists and technicians who created for them.

Exiting the craft, Burt noticed a small welcome committee waited for them. They weren't the tiny wide-eyed Inseni people at all, not one of them. These were humanoids similar in every way to Burt. These wizards were slaves. This made sense. At no time had Burt seen an Inseni who had any inclinations to technology. With the exception of the domes and the transportation devices and the basic necessities of power for lighting and the control of the dome climate, Burt hadn't seen a single Inseni, including Emperor Peril, use a single tech device.

There were three of them, around Burt's height, one with brown hair, one with red hair and one with blonde hair so white it was nearly transparent. All wore their hair long and wore a kind of uniform of dark blue, not so dissimilar to the "wizard robes" of Earth myth. Burt couldn't help but grin at the thought of how Merv would react when he referred to science as magic popped into his head. At closer inspection, the redhead was a woman. "Equal opportunity enslavement," Burt thought with a mental shake of the head.

She stepped forward and bowed. *"Greetings, Emperor Peril and guests. We are Lefa, Visker and Ghan."* Each bowed in turn to the Emperor. *"Please follow us."*

She turned along with her companions and held the door open for Emperor Peril, Penchant and Burt.

The interior of the building was well lit with unadorned white walls, a small, currently unoccupied reception area and a long hallway with doors on either side. Lefa led down the hallway nearly to the end and entered one of the doors on the right.

The lab felt so familiar. One of his favorite things at headquarters was to visit the labs and hang out with the scientists there. He found their conversations stimulating, not to mention that they often were willing to work on special projects to suit Burt's needs. They liked his ideas and the devices they developed from them often benefited all of the Alliance agents.

There were a few other "wizards" puttering around at their workstations. *"How can we aid the Emperor today?"* Lefa asked when they had seated themselves in an area that was obviously for the scientists to gather for brainstorming sessions and the like. Interestingly, there was, in the circle of chairs, one chair that was sized specifically for an Inseni. Evidently their overseers had a permanent place here. Burt found himself wondering why the person who usually sat in that chair was missing from today's events.

"Sir Burt is a delegate from The Dimensional Alliance, here to see what you do here. He has questions. You may answer him freely."

Burt couldn't help but feel that perhaps there was some code in those words. He had no illusions that these people had not been briefed earlier regarding his visit there.

"Welcome, Sir Burt. How may we assist you?"

"Tell me about your facility, Lefa, what do you do here?"

"We do great and terrible magics for our Lord, His Great and Imperial Majesty, Peril. He discovered our gifts when we were brought here from our planet and, in his wisdom, allowed us to pursue our arts in this community. We are sequestered here to allow us to focus on our wizardly arts without distraction. As you can see, the Emperor has provided us with everything we need as well as servants to assist us. Because of his generosity, we are free to create many great advances in warcraft and fighting to put down his enemies and secure the future of the multiverse in order and dominion."

Peril nodded with satisfaction. Burt could see clearly that this well-rehearsed speech met his approval. Funny that what Burt heard was not what Peril was hearing. The subtext in the careful emphasis on certain words sounded to Burt like a carefully crafted cry for help. He nodded at them, meeting each of their eyes in turn and receiving confirmation of what he heard. He was grateful that Emperor Peril and Penchant, like Mechi, seemed oblivious to the subtext of the conversation.

"What projects are you working on right now? It looks like there is a lot of, um, magic going on here. Could you show me around a little? Sitting here, drilling you with questions is not nearly as helpful, I think as seeing you in action...if that is permissible, of course," he concluded with a questioning look at Peril.

"Of course, of course! I want you to take a report back to your people that they may know that the Insenium is good and that the Insenium is strong and how important it will be to their future to join with us in setting the multiverse in order."

Burt smiled his best agreeable smile and they all stood. At this juncture, Visker took point. His nearly clear blond hair and lanky build would have made him stand out in any crowd. Even in the wizard robes you could see by his slender shoulders and thin arms that he was very skinny. You often found the extremes with sciency types, in Burt's experience and Visker was no exception. As he gestured with his right hand, Burt noticed, to his surprise that it wasn't a flesh hand, rather, a robotic hand.

Visker noticed him noticing. *"Blew my hand off in a lab experiment; the spell went wrong. Fortunately, we have excellent healers on staff. It's pretty necessary considering what we do. The hand was of Ghan's invention. His specialty is nonorganic magics, such as you see here. He is currently working on a prototype for a large cyber creature that can march for long distances, has multiple weapon attacks and is very hard to destroy. He keeps running up against roadblocks, but we think he is very close."*

Translation, Burt thought, they are stalling and really don't want to put such a weapon into Inseni hands.

He nodded and Visker continued. He finally paused at a worktable that held what looked like a computer chip.

"This will be the brain of the cyber creature. It can contain a very large amount of information and that information will be carefully bounded to the Emperor's specifications. The spells that guide this type of metal brain are complex and getting them right is absolutely vital to eventual success. Ghan is an expert spellcaster and he will eventually get the demons that reside in the brain to cooperate."

Burt nodded again, meeting Visker's deep brown eyes with a look of understanding. Visker blinked his acknowledgment that he knew he was getting his point across. Peril stood passively beside them, his stature a disadvantage when it came to seeing the implications of the looks that passed between Visker and Burt.

They moved on, entering a side room that was empty of tables but dominated by a construct the size of a Smart Car. It looked like an overly muscular cheetah, made of shining metal. This must be the creature of which they spoke.

"Wow! Impressive," Burt commented sincerely. *"I don't think I've ever seen anything like it."*

Peril swelled visibly with pride, as if he had been the one who had created this thing.

"As you can see, Sir Burt, my wizards have powerful magics. This golem will dominate all battlefields. We are constructing a production facility, even now on the other side of the compound that will be dedicated entirely to making thousands of these magical beasts who will work exclusively for the Insenium. Over time, they may replace the Groga. Then we can use them as slave masters for the massive number of slaves who will be captured by the ever victorious Insenium as we spread order and peace throughout the multiverse."

Burt wondered if he realized how ridiculous he sounded. They were building a massive war machine to inflict order and peace on a multiverse that was huge beyond his tiny little imaginings. He was a salesman trying to sell a motorhome to someone who wanted to buy a sports car. And he was proud of himself and sure he had made the sale.

"This is definitely impressive, Your Highness. I can see where something like this would be devastating to your enemies. Surely many will bow to you at just the sight of them. They will wish they had never heard the name of the Insenium."

Once again, the little emperor swelled with pride. *"I am sure you can see where the Insenium is much better as an ally than an enemy. My wizards are very good at producing great magics that will make us and our allies invincible."*

Ghan touched a panel on the back of the massive creature and it came to life, eyes glowing. It turned its head from side to side, scanning the group before it. Ghan reached into his pocket and pulled a small device similar to the device the Groga had used to activate their portal mechanism on Earth. The creature took a step forward and then back then raised up on its back legs, head nearly brushing the high ceiling. On its hind legs the creature was particularly impressive. The beast had been constructed with eyes facing forward and when it stood up, the head tilted down, so that the eyes continued to face forward.

Ghan pushed another control and the beast resumed its four-legged stance. He pushed another button and the creature's eyes dimmed.

"Ghan, this is amazing. You and your team have obviously worked some heavy magics here. Do you have other projects?"

"Indeed. Please follow me."

He led the way out of the robotics room into the main area again to a table with a small object in the center. A CARD! The little green card lying at the center of the table was being scanned by what was probably an assistant, since rather than wizard's robes he wore the standard slave clothing provided so "generously" by the Insenium.

"What's this?" Burt asked innocently. *"It doesn't look like much to me. After that magic beast you showed me, how can this be at all important?"*

"Important?" retorted Peril. *"You obviously don't realize that sometimes small things can be as important or more important than large ones. It is time the Alliance learned that vital lesson."*

The look in his even wider eyes was one of absolute incredulity. Burt had definitely hit a sore spot, he thought with satisfaction. Burt was really good at locating and pushing just the right buttons at the right time. In the Alliance he was practically famous for it. It was what made him a prized agent and had given him the lifestyle he most desired and the freedom to pursue it.

"And are you mass producing these as well? What does it do, anyway?"

"We weren't sure, in the beginning. There were a few of them and we destroyed the first two, trying to figure it out...spells went awry. The wizards who had created them had all been killed in the raid by the Groga and the lab had been burned after they had pulled out anything they thought might be of interest. If they hadn't been so ferocious in defending this particular, um, spell, we might have even thrown them away. They don't look like much, but our theory is that they represent a personal portal device. Emperor Peril is adamant we complete our research to the benefit of their invasion of the multiverse.

If we understand what we have learned so far, once a person has a specific coordinate and the proper interface, theoretically one could travel to anywhere, even places where no portal existed, natural or magical. It would be a formidable advantage to anyone who had access to them. Obviously, when we finally finish our study and decipher which spells would work on it, our Emperor would desire mass production of the devices which would only be given to trusted allies."

Peril nodded enthusiastically, his huge eyes now almost frighteningly wide and perhaps not quite sane. *"As you can see, Sir Burt, my magicians are powerful and wise. They work with great loyalty for the good of the Insenium Empire."*

"Yes...I can see that indeed. I can see that they are striving for the good of all beings of the multiverse. Their goals are very clear to me." Burt resisted the overwhelming urge to wink at the wizards. He could see they understood what he was really saying and felt their agreement, even though they could not, at risk to their lives, express it in any way the emperor would detect.

"Do you study the arts?" Lefa inserted. *"You seem quite knowledgeable."*

"I have some wizard friends and I have always been a curious person. Although I do not consider myself a wizard, I understand the basic concepts. My friends Bob and Merv are great wizards themselves. I am sure they would love to make your acquaintance."

"Alas," Peril broke in abruptly, *"I am afraid my wizards are far too busy for visiting or conferring with their fellow wizards. Perhaps in the future when our alliance has been approved by the Dimensional Alliance Council...*

This would be one of the great benefits of an alliance, the sharing of wizardly achievements and ideas. Please, Ghan, would you secure the card until you are ready to work on it again? I would hate for it to go missing at this crucial juncture."

Ghan nodded and pushed a button at one end of the table. Suddenly the card was just gone. Burt gasped, but the rest of the party didn't even blink.

"That's one of the best magic tricks I've ever seen," Burt said sincerely. *"And I've seen some doozies."*

"Indeed, it can be impressive when you don't know the secret," replied Lefa. *"Did you wish to study with us?"*

"What a generous offer! But, no, Lefa, I'm no wizard, but I love hanging out with them."

"Hanging out?"

"An old Earth term. It means to spend quality time with someone."

"Ah, I see. And what is Earth?"

"Oh, sorry. It means the planet I live on. Others call us Earthlings. You may use that term, if you wish."

His Imperial Majesty, Emperor Peril was shifting from foot to foot. It seems he didn't like being left out of the conversation.

"Your imperial Highness, I appreciate this tour of your wonders. Is there more I should see?"

"Indeed, there are many wonders to be seen, but we must return to our planet by evening time. I thought we might want to have a meal and then resume the tour. The cook in this facility makes a marvelous stew, almost as good as the stew at the inn."

What was it with these people and stew, Burt wondered? With those big shark-toothed mouths, he pictured them eating meat raw in great bloody bites. With a mental shudder, he composed his face and replied jauntily, *"Of course. That sounds wonderful. A great meal with interesting companions; what more could anyone wish for?"*

Peril flashed him a look, his big eyes reflective. Burt felt he was trying to decide whether Burt was being sarcastic or not. Burt decided to let him wonder.

The dining room of the lab facility was a bit of a surprise to Burt. Unlike the pastels that dominated the Inseni world, there were brightly colored tapestry scenes. One in particular caught Burt's eye. It featured women dancing in a forest glade in brightly colored costumes. The filtered light from the ancient-looking trees made the colors pop nearly off the page, giving it a nearly three dimensional look.

Burt expressed admiration for the paintings. Ghan, blushed to the roots of his hair.

"It is a representation of an annual festival of my country. I tried to get it right, but it doesn't fully express the joy of the occasion."

"You crafted this? Ghan it is breathtakingly beautiful. I've seen paintings in great art galleries that didn't even come close."

"It's one of his gifts," Lefa said, intervening for a very embarrassed Ghan. *"Not all wizards are about war machines. Ghan's sense of the aesthetic has many magical applications. He was the one who came up with the design for the beast. The desire was to make it as formidable as possible, both in appearance and function."*

Peril harrumphed and was seated at the dining table. His chair had a step up to the seat and a footrest. Evidently his Imperial Majesty visited often enough to have his own place at this table which answered one of Burt's questions, but he asked it anyway.

"*Your Majesty,*" Burt said with as much respect as he could muster in his mind voice, "*You visit here often. Why do you not just view the progress from your palace or communicate by voice with your wizards? Where I'm from we have devices that allow us to communicate visually and vocally from far distances.*"

"*I know not of such a thing. How is it done? Could your wizards teach mine how to do such magic?*"

"*I am sure, when we make alliance there are many things we can share to our mutual benefit.*"

Peril appeared to consider this and simply nodded.

Evidently the order for the meal had been placed in advance, because they had no sooner settled in when their food came, served by 2 slaves who set bowls and utensils before them and some kind of muffin for each on a small plate. The cook then rolled in a cart with a large tureen from which he carefully ladled a rich-smelling stew into each bowl, starting, of course with the Emperor. They then all bowed and retreated back to the kitchen.

All waited for the tiny Emperor to take the first spoonful and then proceeded to eat, watching their plates. It appeared that the wizards didn't enjoy watching Peril eat any more than Burt did. It was quiet for a bit. Burt made a show of accidentally dropping his muffin into his lap, and before retrieving it, broke off half for BaaGah, putting it into the MDP under the cover of his napkin.

They continued to eat in silence, so Burt was startled when BaaGah wailed plaintively into his head, "*Hungry! BaaGah eat more! BaaGah will BE more!*"

"*What are you talking about, BaaGah? I just fed you. What do you mean, be more? Of course, you can go into the MDP and have whatever you want.*"

Silence. Burt assumed BaaGah had retreated into the MDP and continued to eat the stew and muffin which were actually quite tasty.

Once again, he heard BaaGah's plaintive mind voice. *"BaaGah make MORE! BaaGah must leave spaces. Hurry, Burt! BaaGah leave spaces NOW!"*

"Um, could one of you point me to the necessary? Too much good stew, I'm afraid." Burt said to all.

Ghan pointed the way and Burt entered the bathroom and closed the door. *"OK, BaaGah. What's up?"*

BaaGah popped out of the MDP, quivering. *"On the floor, please."*

Burt put the little Mookookie on the floor, which was sparkling clean, as you would expect in a lab.

BaaGah began to quiver even harder. Was he having a seizure? He'd never seen BaaGah like this. Admittedly he hadn't known the little guy long, but still...

Suddenly the little mole-like orange dots that surrounded his ovoid frame began to swell like little balloons being inflated slowly. As they grew, they faded to the same golden color as the rest of BaaGah's skin and they began to develop new texture and details. Protruding eyes and a wide mouth.

"BaaGah, what's happening? Are you all right?"

"BaaGah try to tell Burt. Make MORE! Much good food. Much kindness. No threats to BaaGah. BaaGah make more!"

Suddenly there were two more in the little restroom. Elizabeth and Jenny stood next to him.

"Hi Burt. We wanted to be here to welcome the new Mookookie to the world. Congratulations, BaaGah!" said Jenny with a decidedly triumphant grin on her face. *"I had a suspicion about this from our last encounter with your little friend. We won't stay long, but I need to ask BaaGah something important."*

By this time the little BaaGah duplicates had separated themselves from BaaGah completely. There was a dozen of them, sitting calmly on their stomachs, little tails behind, balancing them and keeping them upright. They made no sound, but their little protruding eyes were looking around them and smiles wreathed each body-face. BaaGah had stopped trembling and seemed very pleased with himself.

"Yes, congratulations, BaaGah," echoed Elizabeth and Burt at the same time.

"BaaGah is very happy. Now has more family. Littluns. Lots. Lots and lots."

"Yes, BaaGah," agreed Jenny, *"lots and lots. Which is why I am here. May I have one of your...littluns? To care for and love? And may I talk with you and Burt in your mind in a few minutes? I have an idea how BaaGah can help Mookookie and Burt. Would you like that?"*

"Jenny is Burt's buddy, like BaaGah. Jenny is good and kind. Yes, please take Noony with you." They all looked alike to Burt, but it appeared they all already had names and BaaGah knew who they were. BaaGah had extended an arm and hand to the specified, Noony, patting the little Mookookie on top of its little body-head.

Jenny scooped up Noony gently and put him in the crook of Elizabeth's arm and they all disappeared.

Then Jenny's voice came into Burt's mind. *"Have them all go into the spaces and into the MDP so BaaGah can feed them in private. You can then return to the Emperor's presence with him none the wiser. Perhaps you should decide you need a nap after such a nice meal before continuing your tour?"*

Burt couldn't help but smile. Jenny wasn't ever what anyone could call bossy, but she had a very logical mind that seemed to grasp the implications of just about any situation quickly and was very good at coming up with workable plans on the spot.

He did as instructed, and BaaGah herded his new little family into the spaces of the flesh-like covering of the MDP and within moments he said, *"BaaGah feed littluns now?"*

"Yes, by all means, do feed them. Use the rations I showed you before, OK? I don't want them to eat something that might disagree with them."

"BaaGah very careful with littluns. BaaGah feed them carefully. BaaGah listen for Jenny's voice. Nice voice. Kind voice. Now Burt has lots of little buddies. BaaGah do good?"

"Very good, BaaGah. I am so happy for us."

Burt reentered the dining room, stretching and yawning. *"I may have eaten more stew and muffins than was proper. I feel very sleepy. Could I perchance lay down somewhere for a quick nap? I don't want to miss anything due to drowsiness."*

Penchant and Peril's eyebrows turned down. They obviously weren't impressed with Burt's lack of stamina, but Lefa quickly said, *"Of course, Sir Burt. We need to give Emperor Peril a detailed report of our most recent work anyway."* She waved a lab assistant over. *"Please escort Sir Burt to the rest area by the break room, will you?"*

The assistant nodded and gestured for Burt to follow her. Her dark hair was held back in a bun and she wore the nondescript clothing of a long term slave. She was neat and clean. None of the slaves he had met seemed to be dirty or scruffy. They went down a short hallway, through a very standard looking break room and through a door into a room that held a cot, a chair and a nightstand with a small lamp.

Burt thanked her and closed the door. He didn't lay down at first.

"Are you ready for this?" Jenny's mind voice was excited. *"Peril doesn't know it, but he has just let in the seeds of his destruction. Mookookie eat anything and everything. What you just witnessed was the Mookookie's unique form of multiplication. Noony is already developing little bumps on his outer skin and has demonstrated the ability to extend appendages at will by giving me my very first Mookookie hug. It was amazing.*

Before I go on, I need to tell you that there has been an attack on Alliance Headquarters. Either Peril is very good at dissembling that he is earnest for an alliance or there are other forces at work here. We are all safe at Sanglarka and the other team headquarters, but Ingot was seriously injured, and Myla is also hurt. Right now, everything is being run by Liliath and an assistant at Alliance Headquarters, but Liliath is here with me at Sanglarka for a few days. I'll tell you more about that later, but I thought you should know about the attack and that the rest of us were unhurt."

Burt took a moment to try to absorb all of this. An attack? He was sure Jenny would fill him in on the details later, but for now, that shook him. Was Peril that good an actor? He remembered how the little Emperor had tricked him into wearing the medallion and sighed. He would really have to watch his step, lest he fall into the trap of overconfidence.

"OK, Jenny. I'll be careful with Peril. What's your plan? Why did you abscond with Noony? It looks to me like you're raising your own little army. First Lizziebot, then Chidwi, followed right along with Elizabeth and now Noony? What's up?"

"Well, actually, Noony seems to have attached himself to Elizabeth. She was the first to feed him, so I'm assuming they imprint like baby birds do. If you feed them, you must be mom. At any rate, Noony has already found the spaces and likes to become a part of Elizabeth's sleeve. Of course, the little guy will eat pretty much anything, so we're going to have an interesting time of it, until we teach him what is ok and what is not. The rest of them, here at Sanglarka will be charmed by the little Mookookie. He wasn't even afraid of Liliath, so I think the attitude is inherited. Of course, we've only had him for a few minutes, so we will see.

For now, let's talk about how BaaGah and his little band can make a difference. BaaGah, can you hear me?"

"BaaGah is here, Jenny. Wants to help. Wants to help a lot. Littluns too."

"Wonderful BaaGah. Here's what I was thinking. Can you still talk to the littluns when you aren't on the planet? I got the feeling earlier that you could do more than we thought. Can you do this thing?"

"Littluns can hear BaaGah wherever I am."

"Good. How long before they can be on their own and, do they need to eat anything special while they are young?"

"Mookookie are ready to be alone as soon as they fall off. Mookookie eat stuff. All stuff. Especially chocolate. Chocolate good."

"So tell me about making more Mookookie," Jenny said; a chuckle in her mental voice.

"Every Mookookie has more Mookookie. Time and good food make more. Less food not make more."

"So the reason you made more Mookookie is because Burt fed you so well?"

"Especially chocolate," BaaGah agreed.

Burt was so amused by this exchange that he wanted to laugh, but he didn't. Jenny was kindly extracting useful information, and he was beginning to see where she was leading.

Jenny continued. *"BaaGah, can you speak to other Mookookie on your home world, even if you can't see them?"*

"All Mookookie can talk to all Mookookie. Talk goes through spaces easily. Doesn't it?"

Burt was sitting there in complete awe. In just a few minutes, Jenny had gotten more from this little guy than Burt had the whole time he had been with him.

"Through spaces...Sometime you and I will need to talk more about spaces. I only have a few more minutes. Burt, can you deposit the new Mookookie somewhere on the lab premises without anyone knowing?"

"BaaGah, can I do that?" Burt asked, remembering his resolution to not assume BaaGah was his slave or servant.

"This nice place, clean place, lots of food, lots of spaces. New Mookookie could live here. New Mookookie will do this?" This last question, Burt assumed was intended for the littluns.

"Littluns say yes. Littluns like it here."

"OK, will you tell them to stay in the spaces and only come out when the lights go out or when there are no big people doing things? Tell them they can eat whatever they want. BaaGah will tell them more later after he goes back to the home world. Is that OK with you?" Jenny asked BaaGah, her eyes crinkling.

"Yes. Thank you, Jenny. Now littluns have a home. Now littluns be safe."

Burt heaved a sigh. This was happening way too fast for him, but better than that then time dragging with no progress. He had an inkling of what Jenny might be up to, but that was a conversation for later.

"OK, all of you. I have to get back and report and then I have some studying to do. Can we meet later, Burt, during dream time?"

"Same place?"

"Of course. Maybe someday you and I can visit it together in the real world. I like it a lot. Bye then."

And she was gone.

Burt walked out into the break room to find the wizards, Peril and Penchant waiting for him. Evidently, they had retired there to give their reports. They all looked up. Burt yawned and stretched. He didn't have to tousle his hair, since it was always a mess.

"Nice little catnap. Now, where were we?"

Chapter 31: The Dilemma

Jenny opened her eyes to see Elizabeth with Noony sitting contentedly on her lap, Liliath reclining placidly and Chidwi at her side. She wasted no time in relating what had happened after Elizabeth and she had returned.

"*That's pretty amazing, that little trick of there and back again,*" Liliath commented acerbically. "*Is this new? I only thought your race could do that when they knew where they were going.*"

"*It's a new Jenny thing,*" Elizabeth replied. Liliath didn't intimidate her at all. "*I can extrapolate coordinates for us if she takes me along when she visits someone in a new place. It may change a lot of things with our people, although not many have this level of mental talent, but it bears exploring for sure.*"

"*I have never met anyone who could do that,*" Liliath admitted, "*which makes it even more important to explore the reaches of your talent. We need to make another visit to your observatory. I know there is a lot that has happened since your last session, but have you been considering the implications of your experience there?*"

"*Not as much as I would have liked, but BaaGah may have given me a clue. I'm going to try something when we get back. Elizabeth, are you able to mindspeak with Noony?*"

"*Yes. Noony is quite the chatterer, actually.*"

Jenny pulled a big bar of her favorite chocolate out of her MDP. "*Give her this. Or is it a him?*"

"*There is no her or him, but I think, since it is just us girls here most of the time, we can call Noony her. She seems to be ok with that.*"

"*Tell her to eat and then go into the spaces on your sleeve until we call her, OK?*"

"She's good with that," Elizabeth replied and began to unwrap the bar.

"According to Burt, she'll eat the wrapper too, so you don't have to do that. Are you ready? I want you and Chidwi to ride along this time."

"Ready."

They each assumed a relaxed position on the soft, plush carpeting of Jenny's mental workout room and soon Elizabeth and Liliath joined her on the drawbridge of her fortress. The guard at the portcullis waved them through, with a bow for Jenny.

In the observatory Jenny noticed that there was now an addition, a large, transparent plasma screen. Jenny at once had a remote in her hand.

"OK, you both remember that last time I had an encounter with the telescope that is also a microscope, the visualization was of an eye. There were so many possible interpretations of this that I admit to having been puzzled. However, I am beginning to understand more about how this all works. All of these visualizations are symbolic of different abilities, not necessarily indicative of some deep, dark psychological meaning hidden deep in my subconscious.

So, I realized that somehow this particular ability has to do with seeing. At first, I thought it might just be about the talent I already have to contact people I know and be able to see them at whatever they're doing, but then I realized that the telescope was the great big thing I had mentally skipped over.

This isn't just about seeing. It's about seeing in a particular way. Scientifically I know that lenses give us the ability to see both far away and also extremely close up. We also know that our body's neural system controls what we can see with what we call 'the naked eye.'"

At this point an eyeball showed up on the screen, looking back and forth and then looking straight at Jenny.

"BaaGah keeps talking about 'spaces'. He sees things differently than we do. I had to assume, since he is able to absorb his body into physical objects that he is able to see the spaces between molecules. He talks about the things between the spaces 'holding hands'. I think he means the molecular bond that holds all solid-seeming objects together. From a scientific viewpoint we think there is no such thing as something that is completely solid. If we could see from a molecular standpoint, depending on our relative size, the spaces between molecules might seem as far away as one planet from another."

The screen now changed to show a galaxy of molecules circling one another.

"I think this particular ability might involve being able to see between the spaces, as BaaGah puts it. Now whether it also involves the ability to blend into solid objects, I have no idea and I'm not sure I'm willing to try that yet, but so far, none of the abilities I have found that I can do have proven to be purely for entertainment, so I have to posit that there will be a use for it. Is this why you wanted me to explore this particular place, Liliath?"

Liliath nodded. "I was hopeful. I have seen only one person who could use this ability to her advantage, and she was dragonkind. Others have touched on it, but never were able to develop it in any useful way. But we have discovered that your mind is unusual, and you may be able to pull it off.

Jenny and Elizabeth exchanged looks of amazement. Chidwi was bouncing in place and hugging herself.

"Chidwi, what are you thinking?"

For the first time Jenny experienced Chidwi's natural voice and it was as soft and expressive as her mental voice had been. "It is like being able to turn your reflection off and on. You must be able to melt into the spaces of the air to do it. I didn't think manlings could do such a thing."

"Me neither, Chidwi, but I know a humanoid who can do something similar. Sneaky Sam pulled it off at Alliance headquarters once. If she could do it, then it is doable. If I learned anything from Amelia it was that proper visualization seems to be the key to me mastering these abilities. This is why I brought you all along. I need you to help me brainstorm the right visualization.

It needs to be something I can do when fully conscious and potentially when I am in grave danger. If I understand the process correctly, this means I need to create a key that will work in the fully conscious state. Liliath, what do you think?"

The screen showed a big red question mark. Evidently one of its functions was to show Jenny's thoughts, but to what purpose?

"I will give you a key," Liliath replied. "What do you envision when you see yourself accomplishing this thing?"

Jenny considered. She pictured herself standing in front of a wall of the room behind her. Obviously, she couldn't see behind herself, but what did BaaGah say about "the spaces"? Was he seeing those spaces with his physical eyes? Obviously not, as he often melded into something under him or behind him. He had also said, *Talk goes through spaces easily. Doesn't it?*" It was if he was saying that the spaces were easily permeable. As far as she knew it might be why she could speak across the dimensions, going between the spaces, so to speak.

She knew that there were stories about a "third eye", the ability to see something that wasn't physically there. Considering that so far, she had discovered that most of the stories she had thought of as myths had some basis in fact, perhaps there was something similar at play here.

The eyeballs she had seen in the telescope-turned-microscope was that they were looking at one another or seeing in multiple directions at once. She pictured in her mind this alleged third eye and how it might work. Perhaps it wasn't a single "eye" but an extension of all of her senses. So, instead of a single eye, she imagined every cell of her skin having an eye that saw in a 360 degree rotation.

The image kind of creeped her out, but she persisted to grow the concept. Liliath was right. She needed to know how it felt. She needed to be able to call on that feeling without having to think about it. As these thoughts passed through her mind, images representing them flashed one after another on the large screen in front of her. The screen was revealing her thought processes to Liliath and Elizabeth.

In her mind's eye she saw all of those little eyes turning into telescopes that could see the molecules of the wall behind her. Still facing away from the wall, she could see, nevertheless into the depths of the wall. The little eyes transformed into tiny magnets, each attuned to the spaces between the molecules. Jenny felt herself being pulled inexorably into the structure of the texture of the wall. She didn't feel constricted. There was plenty of room between the spaces of the wall. She turned her attention forward. From within the spaces of the wall she could see the room from which she had come.

Liliath and Elizabeth were standing in front of her, Elizabeth with her hands over her mouth and Liliath's dragon eyes narrowed to slits, a small trickle of smoke coming from her nostrils.

"Did I do it? Just now? Did I disappear?"

Elizabeth nodded. "It was like watching you melt. You kind of shimmered then were just sopped into the wall, like a sponge absorbing liquid. And you are still mentally communicating. Of course, this isn't the physical world, so it's still theoretical and you still need a key."

Jenny imagined herself melting into the wall. A sponge...maybe that was it.

"Liliath, what do you think about trying it in my room? I think I have the visualization now, a potential key. The worst that could happen would be I would stand there in front of the wall looking like an idiot, right?"

"Ah, but can you reverse the process? And how will it affect your key or how will your key affect the process?"

Once again Jenny was grateful for not being left to her own devices. Getting back out of it might not be quite as simple, if you could call this simple, as getting in might be.

"Maybe, before I try the process in real life I should have a chat with Noony. Elizabeth, do you think she is up to that?"

"She seems to be fine and she is pretty communicative. I think these littluns are born with a kind of race memory. She knows a lot of things and is already camouflaging really well, when she wants to. She melded into the quilt my mom sent along with my dad this morning. Mom was pretty worried when she heard about the attack on Alliance Headquarters. She thought the quilt would remind me that she is always thinking of me. Dad says he has something for you as well."

"Speaking of the attack, we'd better get back. Lova said she'd have a message from Gariel when we were finished this afternoon. I'll have to get back to this later."

They all nodded in agreement. Jenny simply stepped out of the virtual wall, it was her brain after all, and she could manipulate virtual matter easily here.

Chidwi was waiting happily next to her as she returned to reality. But as she thought of it, it occurred to her that what went on in her mental fortress seemed very real as well. And why not? She had been able to accomplish very real things in the real world as a direct result of her time in her mental fortress; real contact and interaction with real people. Real connections to the coordinates of the people she visited in her mental communications, so real that Elizabeth could use them to physically visit those people with her particular Daringi gift.

It was, she realized, absolutely necessary for her to understand that if she was going to successfully exploit this potential new ability. Fleetingly, she now wondered if Sam had gained her ability this way or whether it was intrinsic to her race. That might be an important question that needed some answers.

They headed out into her suite, where she was greeted by her bodyguards who had been engaged in their favorite pastime. Lizziebot was telling them stories of her past adventures. Mynn and Nona really got into it and had started haranguing Jenny to write the stories down. Jenny had tried explaining that they were mostly all already written in Lizzie's old journals. But they insisted that Jenny should publish Lizzie's adventures as a fiction book.

"No one would be the wiser. And they're really good stories. Just another fantastic fantasy; there could be movies..."

"I have no time to write at the moment, in case you haven't noticed," Jenny retorted good-naturedly. "I have enough on my plate to be going on with, but when we finally get a lock on this situation, I promise you I'll sit right down and start writing again, when my Gatekeeper duties will allow."

That was as much of a promise as she was willing to give them. If Peril had his way, there would be no more fiction books, or perhaps any books of any kind. After all, an educated populace was counter to his goals of an ordered multiverse. Educated people didn't much like being ordered around by the deliberately ignorant.

Burt's recent excursion into the Inseni lab was proof positive that Peril was an arrogant and ignorant fool with the power to back it up, a dangerous combination, for sure.

They trooped down to the lobby of the lodge. It was empty. Most of them were in the situation room. They were fending for themselves, food-wise; otherwise there would have been some mulled cider in the kitchen. Tarafau had taken Arvid to the Alliance Headquarters infirmary to visit Ingot. The last news of him had not been good. Healers had done their best, but they were pretty sure that the brain damage was permanent. They weren't yet sure if it would be fatal. Either way, Ingot would no longer be leading the Alliance. This meant Liliath was in charge. Myla's injuries were healing, but it would yet be several days before they would know if he would be capable of taking up the slack.

At Jenny's last update, the Great Council had been meeting to determine a replacement for Ingot and to sustain Liliath as the new Chief Councilor. They wouldn't have any further news on that front for at least another day. Gariel had told them he would have more information about the origins of the attack today.

When Jenny and her group entered the situation room where a special lounge had been placed for Liliath, she noticed that Lova looked a bit on the haggard side. Jenny was aware that Lova hadn't gotten a lot of sleep since the attack and she felt a little guilty that part of her talent required her to sleep. Yes, she knew it was necessary, but looking at the purple circles under Lova's beautiful blue eyes she couldn't help but feel like she got the easy end of the stick.

Nevertheless, Lova smiled at Jenny and stood, both hands held out to her as was her wont. Jenny took both hands and squeezed them and then reached out and hugged her fiercely. *"You need to get some sleep,"* she admonished her.

"Tonight, I promise. I have set up an on-call system for the lodge and a duty roster to be sure that our communications are monitored at all times. Gariel has set up troopers to guard the main gateway and there are troopers stations in the gateroom as well. We have stepped up security at Infinity Loop both for you and for Bob's home and laboratory, not that he left much behind..."

She and Jenny both chuckled at that. Once he had been assigned to work with the Alliance scientists, Bob had gone back and packed pretty much his entire lab into his MDP, so he could have access to all of his equipment, notes and the tools he was used to using. He told Jenny he was "all in" and didn't want to be "caught with my pants down".

When everyone had been transported away from Alliance Headquarters after the attack, Bob had requested that Tarafau transport him back to Cornelium's facility so he could continue to work on the card. Jenny would be contacting him later today to give him the information she had gleaned while at Peril's "wizard" lab.

"Thank you, Lova," Jenny replied to Lova's update. *"Are we all here?"*

"The other two teams will be listening in to the report from their respective gates on the Alliance communication network, which has been greatly improved, by the way, thanks to Mustapha. Everyone is on high alert and we nearly have a solid attack plan in place. Once Burt has safely completed his surveillance assignment, we should have all of the information we need to put a plan into motion."

"OK, how much longer?"

"Any minute now, if my calculations are correct. I hope they have more for us to go on. I'm feeling, um, itchy, like someone has sighted on my back and I can't see him, but I know he's there."

"I'd like to say I know what you mean, but having never been in combat, I can only imagine. I do feel like we're up against a 100 page deadline with only 5 pages written, though."

They both laughed at her comparison. Liliath had arranged herself on the chaise and the rest were standing, apparently not able to sit for anticipation. Jenny could feel the tension in the air as if there was a physical vibration. They were united in their concern for the implications of the attack, especially since, on the surface at least, Peril was trying to make some kind of alliance. So who really did attack headquarters at this crucial time?

Jenny had a fairly good notion that the attack wasn't due to internal strife. She was pretty sure she would have heard about it from Liliath, if nothing else, since few people had as high a security clearance as the Gatekeeper. Although they didn't clutter her office with all of the minute comings and goings of the various Alliance factions, she was certain that anything that might impact their current situation would have been included in her regular briefings by the Chief Council.

The air screen popped into being with Gariel's face, his beard squirming actively. He looked even more grim than the last she had seen him.

"We believe we have determined the cause of the attack and you aren't going to like it, Jenny or Tarafau. Your friend, Sam, aka Engoza was involved. Security cameras caught it on video..."

A video started playing on the screen. There was no sound, but one minute the hallway was empty and the next, Sam sat astride a humongous spider, of all things. Jenny recognized it as one of Glitha's community. What in the world could have possibly induced this creature to come to Sam's side?

Sam jumped down from its back, now sleek in one of her spandex body suits, the identical shade of black to the spider she had been riding. She bent and fiddled with something in her hands and stuck it to the door jam in the hallway, waved jauntily at the camera with an insolent grin, hopped back up on the spider's back and disappeared a fraction of a second before the camera went dark.

Jenny realized she was shaking with shock and anger. How was this possible? She looked over at Tarafau, who was shaking his head and rocking back and forth on his feet. His amber eyes met hers and he growled. It sounded so much like Tidbit's attack growl that it took Jenny aback. She didn't think she had ever seen him look so angry and absolutely formidable.

Gariel's face returned to the screen. *"We have no protection from this kind of attack, although every sensor in the building now has an alarm put together by Mervin's team that scans constantly for the DNA we pulled out of Sam the last time we had her in custody. For now, that's all we can do. The question is, was she acting on Peril's orders or is she taking matters into her own hands as vengeance?"*

"I'm guessing the latter," Jenny replied, barely constraining her urge to scream it at him. But she knew he wasn't the target of her anger and he had enough to deal with, without her going emotional on him. *"She has an ego the size of Gibraltar and she thinks she knows better than anyone else. But what about the spider person? How did that happen?"* She looked meaningfully at Tarafau and Elizabeth.

"Elizabeth is about to go home and find out. Elizabeth, go and see Glitha's people, but don't go alone. I can't afford to take the chance that Sam has coopted the entire clan. Take your brothers and their combat unit with you. Notify the Daringi council that there may be an issue. Report back as quick as you are able."

"Yes, father," Elizabeth said and without another word, she disappeared.

Jenny realized she was still shaking. She folded her hands in front of her and began her breathing exercises. This was no time to act like some kind of kid on her first outing. She straightened herself and looked straight into Gariel's eyes. It appeared that he too had gotten ahold of himself, as his beard was not squirming nearly so much.

"Peril doesn't seem to be heading in the kind of direction that makes me afraid of some kind of pre-emptive strike. This sounds like one of Sam's hair-brained schemes. But she knows exactly where the L.A. gate is. I would guess it might be a logical target. Both my home and Bob's are potential targets for her."

"Then it's a good thing we have added security and traps in both places, isn't it? She's never been anywhere near any of the other gates. She does know about the Brazil portal, however, not that she needs it with her current, um, conveyance. She's a loose cannon, which makes her dangerous, but as long as she isn't part of a coordinated attack, we have done everything we can at this point to see to it that she is limited in her mischief.

The damage to the building was surprisingly minimal and it looks like the only death may be Ingot. He expired about 20 minutes ago, Earth time. She has much to answer for, but the building is still usable and there were no civilian casualties. The city is pretty shaken up, however. Many of the dimensional ambassadors have gone home to report. The main Council is sitting today to make the final choice for 3rd councilor. Liliath is requested to attend as soon as she can get here. They will hold the start of the meeting until she gets here."

Liliath rose from her couch and hurried out of the room without a word. Jenny knew she would be in the council within minutes, ready to do her duty. In the meantime...

"Is there anything you suggest we do; other than the preparations we are already making?"

"Not at this time. Please make sure not to let your guard down. I have a feeling there is more to Engoza's plan than simply getting some kind of imagined revenge on the Council or the Earth Guardians or even the Gatekeeper. She strikes me as more sophisticated than that, albeit she is emotionally driven.

The dilemma is that we need to decide whether to wait until we have Burt's full report and pretend that he is still arranging for an alliance with the Insenium or do we begin to move forward with our current plans, which are, in some ways, still somewhat nebulous, even though we have much more information to go on than we did before Burt insinuated himself into Emperor Peril's confidence, shaky though it seems."

Jenny looked at Lova and Tarafau. Both nodded to her, conceding the decision to her, of all things! Jenny sighed.

"I think we need to give Burt a little more time. He and I are working on something that I don't choose to divulge at this time, due to the current situation. We think it has a chance to unsettle the Insenium and put them into considerable confusion before The Alliance confronts them. In the meantime, everyone should continue their preparations. Once Burt's plans are triggered, there will be a small window to deploy the rest of the Tactical Team. I believe, between the efforts of all of the teams and the progress we've made, we have the best chance of defeating them once and for all."

Gariel nodded respectfully to Jenny, then said, *"Thank you, Gatekeeper. I can see clearly why you were chosen. This seems wisdom to me. Lova, Tarafau, are both of you in agreement?"*

"We are," said Tarafau, determination firm in his voice. *"Jenny has the right of it. It would be precipitous to allow this isolated attack to determine our actions. It may be exactly what Engoza had in mind, to get us to betray our plans prematurely, so they can evaluate our strengths and weaknesses. I would like to mobilize the Daringi forces once Elizabeth comes back with her report, however. I think deploying them from Earth may give us an advantage that will allow us to move very quickly."*

"Then, I will leave you to it. Jenny, you have my mental coordinates?"

"I have your number, so to speak, Gariel. I can contact you regardless of where I am."

"Then let me know when Elizabeth returns, and I will stop in to Sanglar-ka to hold the official Council of War. Gariel, out."

And the screen went dark.

Chapter 32: Laying the Tinder

Jenny led her "girls" back to her suite. She needed to think. She went into her "workout" room, leaving them behind in the main suite to entertain themselves with Lizziebot, but she had the feeling there would be more serious interactions with Lizziebot at this point.

The three of them were good at their job, but although they didn't show it by any but the most subtle signs, a slight change in body language, a more vigilant look to their faces and the feeling about them of a cat prepared to spring, Jenny knew they were determined to see her safe.

She needed to see Burt. She needed to know he was safe. She needed to know what he knew and warn him about the newest threat. She wouldn't have believed this if Gariel hadn't shown it to them, which is probably why he did that instead of trying to explain it to them.

She also needed to clue Bob in on what she had discovered regarding the other key. If she understood correctly and assuming there was no subterfuge on the part of the "wizards" in Peril's lab, they might have a chance to eliminate at least that part of the threat from the Insenium. She knew they didn't yet have the full picture, but it was beginning to come into focus.

She realized Chidwi, seated on her shoulder, was crooning and running her soft, warm little hands rhythmically across the back of her neck. As she sat with a sigh onto her mat on the floor, she noticed that the knots in her muscles and her mind were relaxing considerably. She closed her eyes and mentally dialed Burt.

She found him in the little shuttle headed back to the Palace. They had just emerged from the little cloud which obscured the natural portal above the planet. None of them spoke, but Burt looked fairly pleased with himself and, surprisingly, so did Peril, as much as she could tell, at any rate. The lack of expression on the mouths of the Inseni made them a little hard to read, but the body language was open, and the huge eyes were fastened on Burt with wide open pupils and no tension around them. The brows were raised as if in amusement about something.

They landed on the little platform at the top of the dome and were lowered back onto the palace grounds.

"As you can see," said Peril, looking up at Burt as they exited the aircraft, *"Our wizards are without comparison. They will make us and our allies even more formidable."*

Jenny wondered if Peril had the slightest concept of how big the multiverse actually was. He might have the capacity to wage a long time war against great odds and even a strategy that would appear to allow him to do so on a galactic scale, but Jenny was beginning to think he was highly delusional. Unless, of course that was exactly what he wanted Burt to think and to pass on to his superiors at the Dimensional Alliance.

Burt only nodded. He was only a few years older than Jenny, but he had years more experience at this game. Jenny would have been highly tempted to speak her mind. However, she remembered that the last time she had done that, she and Tidbit had ended up bound to black marble slabs. Burt seemed to know what he was doing.

He ran his long fingers through his constantly ruffled hair. *"It's a great set up, Your Highness. Your wizards appear to be competent and committed. I am sure they will make a great asset for an alliance to unite the multiverse to order and dominion. I am sure the Insenium has every reason to be proud of their accomplishments."*

Peril appeared quite pleased with Burt's statement which had been stated in such a neutral voice that Jenny was sure Burt had been hard pressed to keep from sounding heavily ironic. He had not made a single dishonest statement. The difference was perception. Peril was sure he had won Burt over. He was sure he and his political machine were receiving high praise.

Actually, if Burt and her plans worked out, the "wizards" actually would be a great asset for the Dimensional Alliance, not any potential alliance with Peril or his minions.

She waited until Peril took his leave of Burt at the back palace steps. He proceeded around the perimeter of the palace and through the little gate to the side of the main courtyard.

"*That was well done, Burt.*" Jenny said. "*You never said a truer word. Those wizards will be a great asset to the Alliance. Are our little friends comfy and do they have their instructions?*"

"*They are to eat as they please whenever no one is looking. They are to hide from the scientists and staff. They will wait until BaaGah gives them further instructions.*

Learned a lot while we were there, especially that the Inseni don't have anything like video surveillance. That's a big deal and will give me lots of freedom to work with BaaGah and to have visitors at my little room at the inn. It also means I can use some of the tech I've been reluctant to use whenever I am out of sight of my 'guide.'"

"*So what's next on the tour agenda?*" Jenny asked. "*Did I hear something about visiting the Groga training dome?*"

"*Yep. I wonder how often BaaGah can do his little multiplication trick? It occurs to me that it would be great to have some mischief makers in the Groga camp.*"

"*I hear you, but how much danger will we be putting them in? What I would like is a meetup with the wild adults out there. I think it would be great to help the Mookookie get their planet back, don't you?*"

"*I like how you think. I wonder how we could do that? We've all got rebreathers, so if the atmosphere isn't breathable, we might be able to pull it off, with Elizabeth's help.*"

"*Speaking of Elizabeth, she is meeting as we speak with the Daringi council. The attack on the Alliance Council was bad enough, but...*" she hesitated to say it, to add one more burden on him, but Burt needed to know. "*Sam is loose, and she got loose using one of the huge spider creatures from Tarafau's planet.*"

"*Wait, but weren't they supposed to be guarding her? What in blue blazes could she possibly have done to get one of them to break her out? And she is the one who placed the bomb in headquarters? How insane is that?*"

He entered the little inn and ran up the stairs to his room two at a time. Once inside his room he flopped on his bed.

"*Look. Are you ok? You know she'll be after you next. Has Lova upped security? Of course, she has, what am I saying? Sorry, this has totally blown my mind. I thought we were rid of that witch. I thought you were safe from her.*"

He had bounced up off of his bed and was now pacing the tiny confines of his bedroom. His brows were furrowed, and he agitatedly ran his hands again through his hair. Jenny felt like she could actually see waves of heat emanating from the top of his head.

"*Jenny, you need to watch yourself. Remember, you have guards for a reason. You have Lizziebot for a reason. Even Chidwi is there for your protection. Please don't dishonor them by going off half-cocked after Sam.*"

"*Calm down, Burt. I have no such desire. There are too many other big issues for me to focus on her. As badly as she hurt me, I am more interested in her right now as a piece of the bigger puzzle. When we first found out about this threat, we thought of the Insenium as this looming, nearly undefeatable threat. The pure mystery of it gave it more ominous proportions than we could imagine. Now I am beginning to see that we may be missing the point here. And maybe the Insenium is just one more red herring, albeit a scary one.*

Now don't get me wrong. I don't think the Insenium isn't a threat or that it will be easy to defeat them, although, thanks to you we now know enough to be able to decide on tactics towards their defeat. What I'm really saying is the Insenium may be just one more step up to what might potentially be a bigger threat. I can't even put my finger on what that might be or why I feel this way."

Burt, who had calmed down enough to sit down, tapped one foot, releasing the residual energy he hadn't walked off. "*I agree, Jenny. The more I know about Peril and the Insenium the more I think he just doesn't have what it takes to put this all together. He's arrogant, despicable and just flat mean, but he isn't very bright. He honestly thinks he can wage war across the dimensions with his mechanized war cats and he is sure the personal portal card is the answer to getting them where he wants them, but he hasn't even started production yet on either thing.*

He really believes his scientists are wizards who are going to pull this all out of thin air any time now. We definitely need to pull him down and prevent his constant raiding for slaves, riches and tech, but I believe we can handle him.

What worries me is that we are missing something; something crucial. And, like you, I can't quite fathom what. It has been nagging at my gut all this time, ever since I first started touring this planet.

Peril tells me there are other Inseni planets, so I'm guessing that may give us more information. I do know the Alliance won't even pretend to ally themselves with this guy. They don't do business that way. I was worried about how long I could stall Peril, but the fact is we have a little more time than we thought, at least before some major onslaught, but Peril has not paused his raiding. Groga raids happen on a fairly regular basis, still. We can't allow that. So, the urgency is still there. I just don't want our forces to be blind-sided by an unknown factor."

Jenny nodded. *"I agree. Nevertheless, we need to proceed, if nothing else to discourage and hopefully prevent Peril from enslaving any more beings and plundering wherever he wishes. Let's make an appointment to get together on the Merced whenever you go to sleep."*

"I've already eaten. I'll give him this much, Peril feeds his guests well. I'll shower and head to bed in about 30 minutes. Will that work for you?"

"Sure. That'll give me the time to get in touch with Bob. I want to fill him in with what we learned about the card. I'm hoping it will be helpful to him."

"Sure. Tell him I said hi and if you see Mervin let him know he still owes me some money. I'll expect to collect on that when I get back."

Jenny couldn't help but grin. She knew Burt couldn't see her expression. She still hadn't figured out how to make an image for the other person when she contacted them in the waking world. And she was still working on how to include groups into her mental visits. One step at a time. But it was so hard when there was so much urgency to have every possible edge.

She dialed Bob. He was back in Cornelium's lab, Mervin and Anela and even Cornelium all gathered around Fidget, of all things, looking at him intently. *"Hey, Bob? Are you all alright? What's with Fidget?"*

Bob jumped slightly looking around and then grinning. *"Hi Jenny. Sorry, we were all pretty focused. What's up with Fidget is that he has incorporated one of the little MDP guys into his programming and he insists it isn't a virus. We've been running some tests on him to be sure this isn't a big mistake, but so far, he's passed all of the tests we could run past him. What's up with you? Any news about the attack?"*

"Yes, and I have some messages from Burt as well."

"Well, can you visit Fidget instead of me so he can broadcast you to the whole group? There needs to be a conference call mode on that gift of yours."

"Conference call? Whoa! That's it. Hold on a minute. I'll be right back."

Jenny dropped back into her fortress, going into the communications room and typed in Mervin, Cornelium and Anela into her computer, retrieved the phone numbers and programmed them into her mental cellphone. Then, she looked at the apps and right there, on the screen, was a nice little icon representing conference calls. She had no idea why she hadn't thought of this particular visualization before, but that's what learning was all about, she supposed, especially since even her teachers didn't know the extent of her abilities yet.

She quickly set up the call with Fidget and with all of the organic participants and pushed the button to establish the call.

The lab faded into view. *"Can you hear me now?"* she asked with her mental fingers crossed.

They all looked around and then, nodded. Once again, none of them knew where to look to see her, so their eyes were a bit unfocused while they listened to what she had to say.

"OK, so here's the scoop. The attack was perpetrated by Sam, aka Engoza, and a large spider creature from Tarafau's dimension. Since the spiders are supposed to be on our side, this came as quite a shock to many of us, as you can all imagine. Elizabeth has returned home to find out what has happened and to brief their leaders on the latest developments." She paused, waiting for that to sink in.

"You've got to be kidding me," Bob hissed, flushed with anger and shock. *"I thought we had eliminated at least that threat from the mix. What are they doing for security? What are the chances she will have other opportunities at the Earth gates?"*

Jenny told Bob about the precautions that they were taking. She noticed the look of satisfaction on Mervin's face when she told him about the security his team had put together at headquarters. *"Are they doing something similar at the gates on Earth? I'm pretty sure that's all she has access to, and that might prevent a serious breach,"* he said. *"But I'd sure like to get my hands on her. Ingot was my friend and Myla never did anyone any harm. That kind of terrorist gives no value to the lives of others and doesn't care how many are hurt or killed as long as they reach their target. A very old saying is that you can't negotiate with the insane. Now that she has, one way or another, found an ally with dimensional transport abilities, it could get dicey, but I don't have to tell any of you that."*

"You're right, Mervin, but it appears we have bigger fish to fry. I just hope this little fish doesn't bring a few great white sharks with her." Bob said, laying a hand on Mervin's shoulder.

"But wait...there's more." Jenny said, plowing on, hoping to give them something else to focus on. *"Burt's last outing was pretty fruitful. It appears the Inseni do have another card, but only one and they don't appear to know as much as we do about it. They know it allows for a personal portal, but they haven't gotten any farther than that. So, the card isn't in mass production although the prototype is pretty well secured. The thing is that their 'wizards', for that's what they call their scientists, are slaves. There are no Inseni scientists.*

Part two of that is that the 'wizards' are as ready to rebel as the other slaves on the planet. Burt and I think we have a way to make a coordinated rebellion to go along with any attack we make, 'to put a fox among the chickens', as my dad would say." Jenny didn't pause despite the looks on their faces that made her think more than one of them wanted to comment.

"Part three is that BaaGah can do the most remarkable thing! He reproduces by a type of mitosis. It's amazing. One minute there is one ugly but adorable Mookookie in the room with you and the next there are a dozen of them sprouting from his body and dropping to the floor! They are intelligent and are good at following instructions. When you add to that their ability to

camouflage themselves and massive omnivorous appetites on top of being intensely loyal to clan and those who feed them, we may have found an incredible ally. Burt and I will be meeting with BaaGah and other Mookookie later this evening to discuss an alliance to chase the Inseni off of their planet and perhaps make them a member of the Dimensional Alliance."

There was a stunned silence. The three scientists, Mervin, Cornelium and Bob appeared to be frozen, eyes bugging out, mouths hanging open and, in Cornelium's case, little tendrils of smoke drifting up to the lab ceiling.

"Wha? Um, huh?" Bob's mental voice came in a splutter.

"Are you kidding me? Are you sure you don't also want to tell us you've solved time travel too?" added in Mervin, with the beginning of an evil grin on his face.

"You are as amazing as Bob is always saying you are, Jenny," broke in Anela. *"You are worthy of your title, Gatekeeper. For one with so little advanced training in your duties, you certainly know how to make a valuable contribution. Well done."*

"Anela has said well, for all of us, Gatekeeper," agreed Cornelium. *"These are valuable keys you offer us. And if Bob has recovered himself, I think he will agree that you have given us much food for thought. Can you return tomorrow, perhaps? We need to absorb and discuss and see how all of this ties into our current projects."*

"I can't guarantee that, but I will try. Between training with Liliath and bouncing from relay to relay and my work with Burt, every day seems more than a little over-filled."

"Ah, Liliath. Jenny would you please give my cousin my regards and give her my sympathy at her losses. She takes on so much now, as she leads the Alliance. She has my utmost respect."

"I will do that. By the way, Mervin, Burt says to remind you that you owe him money. I hesitate to ask, what's that about?"

"It's a bet we had. I told him that BaaGah was going to be more trouble than he was worth, and he bet me that the little guy would prove to be more valuable than I imagined. He wins."

Jenny laughed. *"Well, I have to go, this was just supposed to be a quick in and out and back to work. Thank you for letting me try out the conference call thing. I learn new things every day, but it isn't in a vacuum. It seems everyone has a hand in my education. I'll be back when I can and when I know anything new."*

And with that, the room faded from view. She came to herself with Chidwi's little hands still warm on her shoulders.

She estimated that Burt would be asleep soon and that she only had a few minutes to grab a bite to eat. Her bodyguards stood immediately when she entered the room.

"Hey, Jenny, we need to go to the situation room. Elizabeth's back." Nona's rich alto voice was tinged with anticipation. *"We told them you would be out soon, and they are waiting for you."*

They all trooped down to the lodge lobby and crossed it to the door of the situation room. As before it was already crowded, especially with a fully grown dragon taking up her place on her special couch.

Tarafau stood with his arm around Elizabeth's shoulders. *"Did you bring Lizziebot? We should record this for the benefit of the folks at the Alliance and the other Guardians, so we can transmit it immediately after Elizabeth completes her report."*

Jenny realized she had left Lizziebot upstairs. Mynn offered to run and get her. While they waited, Jenny moved to Elizabeth's other side, putting her arm around her waist with a gentle hug. *"Glad you're back, sis. I know we're all anxious to hear your report. From the look on your face, it isn't good."*

Elizabeth shook her head sadly but waited patiently for Mynn to return with Lizziebot.

"Lizziebot, please record the following report and transmit it to the Earth gates and Alliance headquarters."

Jenny turned to Tarafau. *"Are we ready to begin?"*

Tarafau nodded. *"Elizabeth will be returning home after this report to organize and transport two battalions, one to Sanglarka and one to Alliance Headquarters, in preparation for an assault when we are ready. She will return in two days. In the meantime, she will make her report and say her goodbyes. Once she has everything organized and the troops are in place, she will return to assist Jenny and her guards. Elizabeth, please report."*

"*Thank you, father. I got to the arachnid community to find it in chaos. They were swarming all through their forest city searching for Sam and Ziggin. When I was finally able to talk to Glitha, she was beside herself. I had never seen one of her people so agitated before. Sam had disappeared with Ziggin when he was on watch with her. They can't imagine that she could have coerced him, so they are assuming he took her willingly. They had no way of knowing where they had disappeared to, but Glitha assumed they had gone to her home dimension.*

When I told her of the attack on Alliance Headquarters, she was devastated. But, as Lizzie was fond of saying, 'You can't put the genie back in the bottle.' Now that they are gone, Sam or Engoza or whatever she calls herself won't stay put and if she has gone home, she is out of our reach. I assured her that no one blamed them. Let's face it; Jenny doesn't call her 'Sneaky Sam' for nothing.

It didn't seem to comfort Glitha much, but she swore she would do whatever she could to make up for it. As a result, she is putting together an arachnid battalion to contribute to the attack on the Insenium. When I left her, she was already marshalling her troops. This is somewhat surprising as the arachnids on our planet are generally very pacific.

I left the arachnid city and went to the Daringi high council to report what had happened. They reiterated their commitment to aid the Alliance in any way necessary, with troops, supplies and whatever other resources we require. They are very concerned that someone like Ziggin is on the loose, since he has the ability to return to cause harm to the residents of our planet. They are stationing troops for defense in every city that will allow it, as there are some who are so pacific that they refuse any aid that includes a concession to violence, even if it means they lose their lives and they won't allow others to sacrifice their lives in their defense.

So, our entire planet's defenses are on standby awaiting your orders."

Elizabeth concluded her report with a little shiver. Jenny knew that, like herself, Elizabeth had led a fairly sheltered life, even though she had studied martial arts and trained as all Daringi do, in their defending army. Theory and practice was one thing. Putting it all into practice under a real threat was something else.

Jenny was glad Elizabeth had Noony with her. She had explained to Elizabeth about the Mookookie's protective powers and Noony had verified that she would shield Elizabeth if it ever became necessary. Burt had also told Jenny of BaaGah's skill at calming him when he was agitated. She had hoped Noony would be a soothing influence in a ticklish situation.

"I think I have some things to add to this report, while we're at it," added Jenny ruefully. *"First, thank you Elizabeth. You didn't find any more than we had feared, but it is good to confirm it. I have been to see Burt and Bob and the scientists at Cornelium's lab and so now I will get us all up to speed."*

Jenny proceeded to recount her two visits to an attentive room. They didn't interrupt, just listened, in some cases reacting with an occasional intake of breath or nodding, but they waited until Jenny was finished.

"Lizziebot, please send this transmission now," Tarafau said. *"I know Jenny has a rather urgent meeting with Burt, so we will let her go. You can ask your questions later. For now, Elizabeth will return home and the rest of us will adjourn for a meal."*

"Actually, I could do with a quick sandwich," Jenny said, hugging Elizabeth who hugged back and then faded from view. *"...nothing heavy as I have to get to that meeting with Burt and BaaGah."*

Jenny ran upstairs as soon as she had finished, Nona, Mynn and Myra right behind her. The girls had grabbed some snack trays and desserts to finish off their meals. Chidwi had nibbled daintily on part of Jenny's salad that Lova had insisted Jenny add to her sandwich. Now satiated, she left the girls and Lizziebot to their own devices and retired to her workout room.

Once again, seated on the floor, she melted into her mind and dialed Burt's dream. It was time to lay the tinder for the bonfire.

Chapter 33: Mookookie Mischief

Burt saw her face reflected in the deep glassy pool in front of him. The reflection of the two of them that way tightened his stomach against the fluttering creatures inside. How was it she could affect him this way? He knew that although he was dreaming that this was more than a dream. BaaGah was there beside him, able to be there because of "the spaces" somehow that he couldn't quite fathom. Jenny smiled at him and his heart was suddenly lighter. How did she do that?

"Hi, Burt. Hi, BaaGah. Glad to see you both. I don't have a lot of time, but we need to have this conversation, so I'll get right to it."

Burt heard the urgency in her voice and tried not to be disappointed that they couldn't talk about other things and to suppress the slight jealousy that she was really here more to talk to BaaGah than to him. Instead he contented himself to listening to her resonant voice and focusing on the animated expressions of her beautiful blue eyes.

"BaaGah, can you bring some of the Mookookie leaders to speak with us between the spaces?"

"BaaGah bring Mookookie old ones?"

"Yes, please. Are the old ones the ones who make decisions for the Mookookie?"

"Mookookie each decide, each choose, but we listen to the old ones, if we are wise."

"Perfect. How long will that..." She cut off as a hundred or more Mookookie popped in, encircling Bob and Jenny around the rocks surrounding the little pool. Some even perched up in the trees surrounding the rocks.

She and Burt looked at one another, grins of delight on both faces. Burt shook his head. "What have we gotten ourselves in for?" he sent privately to Jenny.

"The Mookookie are quick." Jenny sent to the group. "I am impressed. We have much to learn from you. Welcome and thank you for your interest."

"BaaGah tells older ones about Burt and Jenny many times. Mookookie want our world back. Will help Burt and Jenny. What can we do?"

"Burt and I have an idea of how we can chase the Inseni off of your planet. If we did this and if some of the slaves wanted to stay, would that be all right?" Jenny and Burt had discussed that some of the slaves might not have a place to go back to and they didn't want to displace them if they could live with the Mookookie in peace.

"Slaves not mean, not evil. Slaves could stay. Mookookie and slaves could make good things, do good things, together. BaaGah has learned about peoples. Not all peoples bad. Mookookie sad about slaves and mean Inseni peoples. Mookookie mad about bad peoples. Mookookie help. Help how?"

"We need Mookookie to help our people to free the slaves. We don't want a lot of Mookookie or slaves to be hurt. We have a plan to make the Inseni run away. We need Mookookie to eat things, important things, but at a special time. How many Mookookie are there?"

"More than lights in the sky," one Mookookie spoke up. He sprouted two legs and wobbled over to stand before Jenny. "Jenny is brightness. Jenny is heart beautiness. Jenny is wise. All Mookookie will be more, make more. That is a good thing?"

"That IS a good thing," Jenny agreed. "Will the Mookookie wait until we are ready? Will wait until we tell them?"

"Mookookie will do this. Will make more until then. Many and many and many more."

"Thank you. Do you know that some Mookookie may be hurt or even die if we do this?" Jenny asked, her beautiful blue eyes swimming with tears. "We do not wish this, but the Inseni may try to hurt the Mookookie who do this."

Burt's heart swelled within him and a lump appeared suddenly in his throat. How magnificent she was! He had always admired her, since they first met, but in such a short time she had become so much more, more than any of them had ever expected her to be. They had set a nearly impossible task before her and she had been through so much in that short time. And yet, she continued to amaze even the wisest and most experienced of the Alliance.

In this moment, he realized that what he felt for this young woman was so much more than simple admiration. She had stolen his heart irrevocably.

In a single, powerful mental voice, the Mookookie responded as one, *"Mookookie will do this thing. Mookookie will take back our world. Mookookie will follow Burt and Jenny and act when they tell us to."*

"Thank you, so much." Jenny said. Now I must go. Burt, I will be back to you in a bit while I get some things together with the Tactics Team. Please take care of yourself."

And then she was gone. The Mookookie, with the exception of BaaGah also disappeared until Burt was left staring into the crystal pool, feeling decidedly bereft. He knew his days of being the lone wolf were over forever. When all of this was done, he and Jenny would have to have a very long talk.

He awoke and realized his pillow was wet. He didn't have to wonder what the tears were about. It wasn't yet morning. He wiped his face on the pillow and turned it over to go back to sleep. He had a long day ahead of him tomorrow and regardless of his feelings, he was going to need his sleep.

But before he had settled himself enough to sleep, he heard Jenny's soft mind voice. *"Burt? One more thing, I will be riding along when you go to visit the Groga encampment later today. I think maybe we need to understand them more. When it comes down to it, they are also slaves. Do we know for a fact that they would continue to do what they do, if they were free to choose something different? Perhaps the same thing applies to them as to the other slaves. What do you think?"*

"I think you are amazing, Jenny. Why haven't any of us thought of this? I think we need to think more like you. Lizzie was this way, able to see so much more than the rest of us. It must be a family trait."

"*Wow, Burt, I don't know what to say. But do you think it is a good idea? We need to learn more about them. We need to know if perhaps they might decide to choose a better way if they were offered it. I don't think we would be any better than the Insenium, if we didn't offer them a choice.*"

"*I do agree, Jenny. How we can manage that, I have no idea.*"

"*I know, but I want us to be ready if the opportunity presents itself. Don't you agree?*"

"*I do. Agree, that is.*"

Jenny didn't appear to notice his Freudian slip and simply said. "*OK, so I'll see you later. I need to get back and get a little shut-eye of my own, if I am going to be any use to anyone. See you in a bit.*"

Before Burt could even reply, she was gone. How was he ever supposed to get any sleep now? He sighed, settled back again on his pillow and closed his eyes. He knew, even without Jenny actually visiting him in his dreams, what he would dream about when he finally fell back to sleep.

Chapter 34: Hidden Agendas and Outright Lies

Burt woke up with a start, realizing he must have been more tired than he had realized. He got up and got dressed, not bothering to see if BaaGah was awake. He wasn't even sure if BaaGah actually slept as he understood sleep. The little creature seemed to recharge by simply interacting with the "spaces".

As soon as he got to the bottom of the inn stairs, he saw Mechi, waiting in the common room. He smiled his most jaunty smile. *"Morning, Mechi! Have you arranged for our visit to the Groga training compound?"*

"Indeed, although why you would want to visit that slime pit, I have no idea. His Imperial Majesty has given me my orders and I will comply. I'm not sure what you will learn from those brutes that you haven't already learned. Didn't they put you into mortal combat and then arrested you and dragged you here against your will?"

Burt knew that it wasn't at all that way, but it wouldn't do for Peril or his minions to think so. *"I guess I'm confused. Aren't the Groga your loyal combat troops? Don't you depend on them to do your raiding and slaving and plundering?"*

"As I know His Imperial Majesty has explained to you, they are a blunt force instrument, suitable only for use in very straight forward and non-crucial missions where little supervision is required. Raiding and slaving and plundering is really all they are good for."

"But you have another force? An elite force, as the Emperor told me. How does that work? I understand they reside on a totally different planet in your galaxy. Why such a distance between you?"

"*That, erm, is probably something you should discuss with His Imperial Majesty, Sir Burt. I am not authorized to speak with anyone, including you about this and I have very little actual understanding of the workings of wars and things. I am a servant, albeit a trusted one.*"

Burt noticed the body language, the widening of the eyes in some kind of fearful expression he couldn't quite decipher. Was Mechi afraid of the "elite force" or the emperor or both? In any case, he wouldn't press the issue. For now, he needed Mechi as compliant as he was able to be. Today's expedition was crucial to their understanding of what they were up against.

"*I get it, Mechi. I won't inquire into it more. I want to spend some time with the Emperor after this, anyway. Let's see to that expedition. As base as the Groga may be, I need to understand enough to give a comprehensive report to my superiors. You understand.*" It was a statement, not a question. Creating a little empathy between the two of them might come in useful before he had to leave to make his "report" to the Alliance Council.

They went, once again to the transportation station and entered one of the little programmed vehicles. It was one of the few impressive pieces of tech he had seen. The little vehicles were quiet and probably not designed for long trips but worked fine as an enclosed environment for getting from dome to dome. These were the only vehicles besides slave pulled carts Burt had seen during his visit here.

Suddenly Burt heard a chuckling and realized it was BaaGah. "*What's so funny, buddy?*"

"*Buddy is happy. Mookookie are happy to see us. Mookookie peeking out from spaces and cheering for us. Burt and Jenny have Mookookie hearts. My peoples rejoice to know they will soon rid the land of the mean ones.*"

"*We haven't done it yet, BaaGah. There is still much to do, and we will need the help of all the Mookookie and the slaves besides just the troops of the Alliance.*"

But BaaGah continued his optimistic chatter along the road to the Groga dome, which seemed to be placed quite a bit beyond any of the other domes Burt could see. Mechi, as usual, remained silent, only speaking when spoken to. Burt was used to this by now. Burt had decided early on that Mechi just wasn't a talker. Fortunately, BaaGah kept him well entertained, so he was content to let Mechi sit quietly watching the countryside fly by outside the protective bubble of their little vehicle.

Finally, they approached a huge dome, larger by comparison than even the main dome which held the palace and the main city of the Inseni. It appeared to easily be 30 or more miles in diameter from his vantage point. As they got nearer, Burt realized it might even be larger than that. The Inseni guard who greeted them on the other side of the airlock was, as usual, efficient and humorless.

Mechi led the way to the entrance of the compound. Similar to the Fleistian Groga encampment, all of the buildings were what would have been considered on Earth as "cinderblock", squat, squared off buildings. The difference here was there were windows, albeit small, stingy, unadorned windows. With no weather to deal with in the climate controlled dome, there wasn't even any glass in them. Therefore, Burt could hear the guttural sounds of Groga speech intermingling with the noises of chanting troops, drilling on the various workout fields, the grunts of hand to hand combat and somewhere the repeat of some kind of energy weapon, presumably hitting targets like the practice dummies he had observed in the Fleistian compound.

They entered the grim squat headquarters building and Burt couldn't help but feel a chilly feeling of déjà vu, as he entered the main reception area. There were nearly identical Groga clerks bent over what appeared to be identical reports, only looking up with a sneer at the newcomers for a moment.

"We're here to see the Groga-ha. We have an appointment to review the troops and tour the facility," said Mechi somewhat imperiously to the room at large.

One of the clerks grunted irritatedly and left his work to stomp off down the hallway to what Burt assumed was an exact duplicate of the office of the Groga-ha at the other encampment.

The clerk came back and went straight back to his work without a word. The Groga-ha in full uniform regalia followed close behind. *"What would you like to see first,"* he growled without ceremony or introduction.

"Sir Burt would like to review the troops and perchance speak with some of them," replied Mechi acerbically. *"He is a liaison from potential allies and the Emperor commands he be given every honor and respect."* At this Mechi indicated the cursed medallion around Burt's neck. Burt had almost forgotten about the stupid thing. So far, try as he might, he hadn't been able to get the nuisance from off of his neck.

The Groga-ha simply nodded and then led the way out the door. They strode at a pressing pace past barracks and a workout and assembly area similar to the one where Burt had defeated Orgu what seemed like ages ago.

Finally, they went to the parade ground where there were several battalions of Groga assembled in long ranks. Burt was impressed despite himself. This was a force to be reckoned with, to be sure. The really scary thing was that he was fairly certain this was just a fraction of the forces Peril could call upon at a whim. And Peril did definitely have his whims.

The Groga-ha sent out a mental shout to the soldiers before them. *"Stand in ranks! Ordered march! Begin!"*

The Groga soldiers then performed a series of synchronized drills that were beyond impressive. Burt would not have suspected them capable of this based on his previous impressions of them both on Earth and on Fleist. This was a side of the Groga he had never seen. In his mind he had viewed them as undisciplined and brutish. This was a highly precise execution of a very complex drill pattern. When they came to a halt finally with their weapons raised and lowered with a resounding THUD, Burt nearly jumped and Mechi actually did. The fierce, unified shout of something Burt didn't understand only heightened the effect.

"Impressive," Burt sent at once. *"They appear to be very well trained in drill and precision, which requires discipline and a lot of practice. What are their primary weapons?"*

Of course, Burt thought he knew the answer to this question as they had faced the Groga in the past, but the Groga-ha didn't need to know this.

The Groga-ha answered without hesitation. *"Great hearts and willing hands."*

Burt didn't hide his surprise at this answer. *"An interesting reply; it sounds like you are very proud of your soldiers."*

"Their proper training and excellence is my life legacy. I know I can trust my troops to go wherever I point them and execute every command with exactness and diligence. I can give no greater compliment. You see before you, the result of my life's work."

Burt considered this. This was not at all what he had expected. How he would love to get this man alone to be able to speak frankly. He considered how he might do this, but for now he decided not to show his hand, especially in front of Mechi. He would have to be careful, but like the conversations he had pursued with the slaves, Burt was feeling a hidden subtext there. This person did not trust him or Mechi, but he had the feeling he would like this Groga-ha under different circumstances.

So, for now he replied, *"I can respect that, and I would like to have an opportunity to discuss the training of these troops with you before the day is out. I would like to see how these soldiers live when they aren't on the drill field and some more of your training. What can you show me of this?"*

"I will be glad to show you around the compound. We have many training operations going on at any given time. Our masters see to it that we have the equipment and resources to do this." Burt heard an "at least" implied by his tone and realized with a shiver that it was happening again. This man was desperately trying to communicate something to him other than what his words implied.

"Jenny are you there?" he asked, suddenly, thinking that perhaps he had just connected some unexpected dots.

"I'm here, Burt. I'm hearing every word and it is very, very interesting."

"It's you! That's what's happening here! I get it now. Jenny you have more than one mental ability. Some of them come as naturally to you as breathing and you don't even notice it when it's happening."

The Groga-ha had dismissed the troops and was leading them away from the training area. No one spoke, so he continued his conversation with Jenny.

"Do you understand what I'm saying?"

"Actually, I'm not sure what you're getting at."

"You are a magnet, a trust magnet. People naturally trust you. You radiate something and when you are riding along with me, others feel the effect of it as if you were standing in front of them. This is why these people are all open- ing up to me. This is why we're hearing all of these sub-communications from them. They trust me because of you."

"Are you sure you aren't reading much more into this than there is?"

"Actually, I don't think so. I believe I have hit the proverbial nail on its big fat proverbial head. You'll see. Ask Liliath about it later. I'll bet you anything she will tell you it isn't only possible, it's likely. In the meantime, we can lever- age this. Thank you for being you, Jenny."

Jenny was silent for a moment and for that small instant, Burt was con- cerned that he had offended her in some way. That was surprisingly painful for him. He had always decidedly been a "water off a duck's back" kind of a guy. This newfound sensitivity was foreign to him. Another evidence of Jenny's influence on the people around her.

They entered the village and Burt got another bit of a shock. It looked like any small town, shops, houses, apartment buildings and many Groga and some slaves milling about in the well-paved streets. The streets were clean, and it seemed very orderly but not somber like the camp. There were flowers in planters along the street. And children! Somehow, Burt had nev- er imagined Groga children.

And there were slave children playing with Groga children. Mechi, dwarfed by all except those children sniffed in contempt, wrinkling his lit- tle button nose as if something stank horribly. Actually, there were no of- fensive smells as was often the case in a bustling city. Burt, however, couldn't help but grin. Jenny had been right, as she often was. These were real people with real families and potentially they were as enslaved as any of the other slaves of the Insenium. This was something he could work with.

He felt a great surge of hope. It appeared that the Alliance may have had it all wrong. The Groga had never been the enemy. The Groga were tools like every other being enslaved by Peril and his people. It was now very clear to Burt that they would have to adjust their tactics and soon.

"Come," sent the Groga-ha. *"There is an event happening on the square that may be instructive."*

The Groga-ha sent him a look that Burt wasn't sure how to interpret. It wasn't a negative thing, although somewhat furtive, taking Mechi into account. Of course, as they were walking, Mechi would have had to look up to see it, something that he wasn't inclined to do. Instead, Mechi marched along beside the longer legged Groga-ha and Burt, nearly running to keep up with the Groga-ha's pace.

The Groga-ha seemed not to notice, but Burt had a sneaking suspicion that he was taking some perverse pleasure in making the little Inseni move at such a pace. That he wasn't terribly impressed with Mechi was patently clear to Burt, however, who suppressed a grin at the thought.

They marched along until they came to a great square; what might have been the center of the city. Fountains, trees (perhaps imported from the Groga world?) and flower boxes surrounded the cleared area. At one end was a raised platform about the size of a basketball court. On it were a number of Groga and slaves in brightly colored costumes. This was so unusual after the constant drab pastels of the Inseni. It was refreshing to his eyes and his heart.

Musicians with horns, percussion and string instruments waited off to one side of the platform. The Groga-ha indicated that they should seat themselves in some stadium style risers at the opposite side of the stage from the musicians. It appeared their seats had been reserved. So, Burt and Mechi sat down and waited as the Groga-ha climbed up to the front of the stage and addressed the waiting mass of people who immediately quieted and paid close attention to his words.

"My people, for you are all my people, Groga and not-Groga. Today we celebrate the days of delight and gratitude. We have much to be grateful for at this time. We are all well and well enough off. We have one another. We have all the necessary resources to sustain life and we have hope. Let us rejoice in what could be and find gratitude for what is. Let the festivities begin."

The crowd cheered and waved their hands in the air, then fell silent once again.

On the stage, those in their colorful costumes arranged themselves and the musicians struck up a lively tune. The women had colorful ribbon streamers on their sleeves and skirts which fluttered in arcs and patterns while their partners whirled them in a rhythmic and energetic pattern dance, much like the folk dances of his own Earth. The crowd began to clap along, and Burt found himself doing the same, much to the apparent disgust of Mechi, who sat there with his arms folded across his chest, his big eyes narrowed.

Burt admitted he was astounded at the complete joyfulness of this display. He had pictured this people as hardened, grim and violent based on his previous encounters. This community was ever so much different that he couldn't quite wrap his head around it. Perhaps this was the point the Groga-ha was trying to make. He wanted Burt to see his people as real, feeling beings with lives and culture and community.

He sighed as the performance came to an end and shouted his approval with the rest of the crowd. Mechi still sat, silent, his arms still folded firmly. Burt noticed he was looking at the ground, refusing to even acknowledge the performance. What was the matter with the Inseni, Burt wondered? How could this being not be touched by that display? But Burt decided to ignore it. Nothing he said or did would change the attitude of the little man.

Once again, the Groga-ha mounted the platform and addressed the people. *"All beings within the dome are hereby given holiday, with the exception of troops who have been slated for rotating duty, as is usual. Please, there are many food booths in the market square, and many things for your delight and entertainment. And don't forget to get something sweet for your children, with your festival bonuses and something pretty for your sweethearts. Let there be great rejoicing and gratitude and let us keep the hope we feel in our hearts."*

Burt rose as the Groga-ha descended from the platform and approached him and Mechi in the stands. *"I hope you can see the Groga in a new light, Sir Burt. Although we are destined to be the fighting arm of the Inseni, that is perhaps the least of what we are."*

Burt nodded. *"You have definitely given me much to think about, Groga-ha. I am again impressed. Is there a quiet place where we can talk?"*

"Indeed, Sir Burt. Mechi, will you join us?"

Mechi nodded sourly. Burt was getting better at reading the little In-seni, despite their lack of a mobile mouth. Mechi obviously was not enjoying this trip. He had little, if any, respect for the Groga and he made no attempt to hide it. Burt racked his mind to determine how he might be able to get a private conversation with the Groga-ha. This being was very much different than the Groga-ha at the Fleistian compound. The other had been cruel, rude and tyrannical. This person, on the other hand, seemed to genuinely care about his soldiers and his people.

And, when he thought about it, that made sense. He knew for a fact that not all soldiers or officers in any army were good, upstanding citizens. Many were drawn to military life for the opportunity to participate in legalized thuggery. He remembered listening to a man on a plane once, telling some pretty horrific stories of military types who bullied their soldiers and made the military a living hell. Why should he assume that every Groga had the same tendencies as the first Grogan officer he had ever met?

So he walked along until they came to a small eating establishment. It wasn't an inn. Burt assumed there wouldn't be much use for one, considering that they seldom had visiting travelers from dome to dome. He had gathered that much from the virtually deserted transport stations he had visited during his stay on the Insenium planet.

They were seated in a private area at the Groga-ha's request. They were no sooner seated then a Groga soldier came rushing in, out of breath. Evidently the message was directed privately to the Groga-ha, as Burt heard nothing. However, his jaw tightened. He turned to Mechi.

"We have been told it is the desire of the Imperial Majesty, Emperor Peril that any attacks by the little pests be reported directly to him. Since Sir Burt has very little time here with us, I would ask you, Sir Mechi, to please see to it that His Imperial Majesty is advised that there is a swarm of the creatures currently eating the barracks furniture and everything else they can get into their mouths. Every time our soldiers try to capture them, they simply absorb into the floor or a wall. Please notify the Emperor of this and have him advise us as how to proceed. We could probably use some wizardly help with this."

Burt listened with something akin to wicked glee. This couldn't be any kind of a coincidence. While Mechi was huffing and puffing and trying to argue with the Groga-ha that this was NOT his assignment, Burt sent out, *"Jenny?"*

"Yes, I did it. I admit it. Elizabeth and I helped a few Mookookie into the walls of the dome. Their instructions are to bother the Groga soldiers just long enough to get the attention of the Emperor and then to absorb into the spaces until Elizabeth and I return to take them back outside the dome. They could have done this by themselves, but this way we could clearly localize the damage without causing major mayhem on a day that is special to these people. Now is your chance to have some alone time with the Groga-ha. Elizabeth and I intend to keep Mechi busy for awhile. I'll warn you when he is headed back."

"Thanks, Jenny." And then, once again, she was gone.

Mechi had stomped off in disgust and the Groga-ha settled back in his chair with a sigh. *"The little pests don't generally bother us, but Emperor Peril was clear about our orders. He doesn't want the soldiers distracted from 'more important matters'. Sorry for the interruption. Let's have some celebration punch and be free with our conversation, shall we?"*

Burt decided that the best approach was to be blunt and honest with this man. He would have wanted the same. So he began, *"First, may I know your name instead of your title? It feels awkward to open up to you knowing only your title and you can just call me Burt."*

"I am Anwhal, Burt. You may speak freely without the withering ears of the Inseni to hear us."

"Thank you, Anwhal. Please, I think I owe you and your people an apology. I only knew of you through our encounters with some of your troops on my home planet, Earth. And I thought of your people in less than positive terms. Are you the supreme commander of the Groga under the Insenium or is there someone besides the emperor who you report to?"

"I am the final say when it comes to the Groga, under the emperor, of course. However, there is a group of Groga troops under direction of the Fleistians that I have little or no control over. While it is true that the Groga go where the emperor points, at this time, they have fallen into undisciplined chaos under the current Groga-ha in command there. If that was your first impression, I don't wonder that you think badly of us. Of course, regardless, on the battlefield is no place to gain any understanding."

"Good, there can be truth between us? I realize this well could be an Inseni trap, lulling me into a false security to speak my thoughts frankly."

"Something tells me that there can be trust between us. As well, this could be a trap for me and my people. So, let us drop all pretense. You have been lied to and I swear on an oath that I will not deceive you."

"Then it is mutual. I make a pact not to lie to you. You also have been deceived and I have a feeling you know this."

"Peril is good at thinking he is clever without realizing how easy he is to read."

Burt noted the lack of the honorific. *"However, he can slip one past you until you know what to look for."* He tugged uncomfortably at the medallion around his neck.

Anwhal smiled a rather wicked smile, even for a Groga. *"He caught us with a similar catchpole. It would do no good not to admit that. He thinks us subdued and at his beck and call. I think we may be about to give him a rather nasty surprise in the not so distant future, however. I have a feeling you might be the key to what we have been working toward for a long time. While it is true there are those of us who have bought into Peril's lies, there are many of us, the majority of us, who feel otherwise.*

He made a mistake by allowing his 'breeding in excellence' program to continue. We are a very fertile people and we have learned how to appear to comply without actually buying into the program. As a result, we have the numbers and now most of the resources we need to end this farce once and for all.

We don't have much time here and now to go into a great deal of detail, but I'm guessing you have your own lines of communication."

At that precise moment, Jenny and Elizabeth walked into the room, straight over to the table.

"Anwhal," Burt said, trying not to show his own shock at the sudden appearance in a possibly dangerous situation, *"Allow me to introduce, Jenny and Elizabeth, two of my compatriots and the very communications link you were just about to inquire after."*

Jenny smiled that amazing smile of hers and he watched the big Groga commander melt before his very eyes, from businesslike to enchanted. How did she do that?

"You know my name. I don't think we've ever met. I'm pretty sure I would remember that. And, Elizabeth is it? You don't look like any of the slaves I've ever met."

Jenny laughed, crinkling the corners of her eyes. *"No, Groga-ha, we have never met, but I know who you are and no, we aren't from around here. I do have a proposal for you, however. Would you be amenable to have me visit you less publicly to discuss how we can be of assistance in your quest to free the Groga? From what I just heard; you are ready to break the bonds of the Insenium. Am I wrong?"*

Anwhal's chin came up and he straightened in his seat. *"You are exactly correct, Jenny. How can we stay in communications without anyone knowing we are collaborating?"*

"I have a little trick. Now that you and I have met in person, we can have discussions in your mind without anyone knowing you are even communicating with anyone and..." she held up her hand to forestall Anwhal, *"I can't read your mind or see any thoughts you wish to keep hidden. It's only a conversation."*

Anwhal didn't say anything for a moment. *"I agree. Now, get out of here, both of you. I can't afford to be seen with you, nor can Sir Burt. I'm not sure how you got into the dome and I don't want to know. Good-bye."* He put on a stern face as if he had said something somewhat insulting to her and she took the hint and she and Elizabeth stalked out of the inn as if incensed.

Burt was mentally agape at what had just happened. *"Jenny?"*

"I'm here, Burt. Just thought it would help to show a little bit of our hand for the purpose of negotiations. I'd suggest you get the conversation back to something politically correct. We just saw Mechi stomping down the street towards the inn. We're on our way to gather our 'little pests' and get out of Dodge. I'll leave you to the rest of your tour while I get to Liliath. It's time for my lesson."

Burt relayed the communication to Anwhal who caught on immediately. *"As you can see, my people and our slaves are very well treated by the Insenium. I will be happy to take you to the training grounds to see what we're doing."*

Mechi tromped into the inn, a scowl evident in his huge eyes, the fine eyebrows tilted into a "v".

Burt and Anwhal stood. *"Hey, Mechi, we were beginning to think we were going to have to leave without you. Anwhal here is going to take me to watch the training exercises. Are you coming?"*

"Stupid pests; no idea how they got in here. Your sergeant seems to think they came in with the supply wagon, but I thought we scanned for them."

"Scanned for them? You can do that?" This sounded a little ominous to Burt, under the circumstances.

"Yes. That doesn't mean we can actually get them out of something once they're lodged there. We've tried burning the objects they're embedded in, but I'm not sure it works."

BaaGah's rumbling growl filled Burt's head. Mechi had definitely pushed the wrong buttons. *"Calm down, buddy. We're gonna fix 'em, remember?"*

"Fix 'em. Fix 'em good," BaaGah agreed. *"'Ems gonna get fried, like, 'em frying Mookookie. Surprise for them. Spaces safe. Mookookie just go from burning stuff into the ground or something. Burn 'em up. Burn 'em all up!"*

"OK, I hear you, BaaGah. We'll do it, but you need to calm down for now so I can get it done, OK?"

"OK it is, Burt. BaaGah calm, very, very calm."

He didn't really sound very calm to Burt. Only quieter, in a very deadly way. The Insenium had no idea what a mess they had made and how badly they were about to pay for it.

"*Shall we proceed?*" Burt said, without commenting on Mechi's grim statement. "*I'm sure the Groga-ha has much to do today besides just giving us the guided tour.*"

"*Indeed,*" agreed Anwhal, "*I'm sure there will be a report to file after we clear up the pest problem. Let us move forward.*"

Chapter 35: Lessons Learned

Liliath pondered the young humanoid female before her. Jenny was an anomaly as humans went. She was something more and she didn't even seem to realize it. She could tell that Jenny had only begun to scratch the surface of her potential. But, for some reason, Jenny seemed unaware of what an amazing being she was. Liliath could see her surpassing herself or even Miriha, who had been a formidable mental talent.

Liliath could see why Miriha had passed the key on at her death to Jenny. She knew that some thought it was merely a coincidence, but the fact of the matter was that Miriha had not needed to pass the key at all. Had she passed with no one present, the key would have simply dissolved, and the calling of Gatekeeper would have immediately passed to the Gatekeeper in waiting. But Miriha had already been paying attention to Jenny. When Lizzie had brought Jenny to her attention, she had confided to the Alliance Council that she felt Jenny should be the next Guardian for the L.A. gate when Lizzie passed.

Liliath could never quite understand the curious gift of Miriha. She was very good at seeing a trail of consequences to the point that her predictions (she hated it when anyone called them "prophecies") usually came to pass.

Now, here, before her, in her relaxed pose, prepared to enter the fortress of her mind, as she called it, sat this very amazing young woman who had no idea how delighted and impressed everyone was of her and, if she had known, it would have embarrassed her.

Little Chidwi stood behind her, tiny green hands resting gently on Jenny's shoulders. This was another interesting factor. Her understanding of the Linkling phenomena, according to Miriha and Lizzie, was that the kind of bond that existed between a Linkling and another being was a rare honor. Linklings had the ability to actually read minds, although they didn't gossip and Lizzie's Linkling had once confided to Liliath that most people's minds just weren't all that interesting and the ones that were, often weren't very pleasant.

For a Linkling to make this kind of bond was a serious commitment. Linklings bonded for life and beyond. This was why the Daringi had such immediate respect for anyone with a Linkling on their shoulder. It ultimately meant that the person was not only trustworthy, but worthy of admiration as well. Bonding with Chidwi was one more link in the chain of events that had shown Jenny to be more than just a pleasant or even talented individual.

Jenny's eyes closed and Liliath's did the same, following her onto the mental drawbridge that led to her fortress. They entered the observatory. Jenny stopped and held out her hand, a cellular device in it.

"Since our last lesson, I have learned how to make conference calls, to pull more than one mind into a call at the same time. I have also created a bond with Elizabeth that means she can find me wherever I am, across dimensions. We also discovered that she can pass those coordinates on to other Daringi, as necessary.

Interacting with BaaGah has taught me some new things about 'spaces'. On the one hand I am excited about these new abilities. On the other, I wonder if I am going too fast or if I am in danger of getting cocky about this. I see others with power doing terrible things and I find myself wondering if I even want all of these abilities. Will these gifts cause me to become arrogant and power-hungry? Am I in danger of becoming all of the things I despise in our enemies?"

Liliath paused before answering. Jenny often blind-sided her with questions she would have felt more comfortable referring to Miriha. And then she realized that was exactly what she needed to do.

"Do you have room for another teacher, Jenny? May I bring someone else into this conversation who might be more qualified than I am to answer your questions?"

"Of course," Jenny replied simply. "Anyone you trust would be someone I could trust as well."

Then Miriha was there, smiling her sweet smile, her Linkling on her shoulder. She looked as lovely as ever. Liliath missed her so. She had been one of the best and kindest Gatekeepers Liliath had ever met in the hundreds of years she had been a part of the Alliance.

Jenny's mouth flew open only for a moment and then, discarding all formality, threw herself into the welcoming embrace of the former Gatekeeper.

"Miriha! Oh, how I've missed you! How are you doing this?"

"As I told you once before, Jenny, there are more dimensions than you can imagine. I have only transferred to another in my progression towards further light and knowledge. Humans call it heaven or the spirit world. For me, it is just where I live now. But it is a fairly simple thing for me to pass through the spaces between dimensions now. I don't require a gate or a key."

"Whoa, what? I know you tried to tell me before, but that was in a dream. Wasn't it?"

"Actually, it was more like what you do with Burt and others now when you visit their dreams. Liliath, what is it that you need, my friend? I assume it is something about Jenny and her amazing progress..."

"Indeed. Jenny is concerned that these gifts will lead her down a bad path and she will become like many others who are addicted to power and misuse it for their own purposes."

"Ah, Jenny, that is so like you." Miriha smiled gently at Jenny, squeezing both her hands in her own and looking deep into Jenny's troubled eyes. "Your parents did a good job raising a truly decent being. Look into your heart, dear one. Ask yourself how you feel when you see the downtrodden and mistreated and ask yourself how you could ever do any of that? All of us make mistakes and you will too, but I have a lot of trouble seeing how you could ever go so far wrong as to take pleasure in the misery of others or to wish to force your will upon another person. These two things are the definition of evil and I don't see it in you.

That being said, there are precautions you can take to insure that this never changes in you. Start by always asking yourself if you are being kind, if you are being truthful and if you are honoring the rights and freedoms of others. If you can answer yes to all of these, you are on a good path that will lead you aright."

Jenny didn't reply right away. Liliath liked that about Jenny. She was thoughtful and seldom did anything on a whim.

"I think I can do that, Miriha. I hope I can. While I have you here, maybe you can answer one more question for me?"

"Of course, Jenny. What do you need to know? I have to be careful not to give you more answers than necessary, because the process of discovering your gifts on your own is important. Giving you too much information before you are ready for it would be much like freeing a butterfly from her cocoon to save her the effort of breaking free of it."

"I want to know about spaces. I think I have figured out how it works, the ability to see the spaces and perhaps even pass through them, but I don't want to find myself stuck in a brick wall or something. Is this something you know anything about?"

"Hmm, have you asked Chidwi about this? Linklings are clever about that, almost as clever as the Mookookie friends you have made. Yes, I have been watching, Jenny. Don't look so surprised. That wasn't a very kind thing I did to you back then, saddling you with such responsibility at such a young age, before you had even had a chance to figure out the whole Guardian thing. So, I do watch you, when I have time. I can't say how very proud I am at how quickly you have come into yourself.

So, have a conversation with Chidwi and use her as your guide. I am not sure yet, how far your talents will take you, but I believe you have much ahead of you that none of us have yet expected."

"Thank you, Miriha, I will. May I put your name into my contacts?" she asked wistfully, her eyes large and tears beginning to well up.

"I'm sorry, Jenny. That would not be wise. I don't think you need crutches such as any advice I might be inclined to give you beyond what has been said here today. Liliath is a great teacher and she will stand you in good stead. I will come and visit from time to time, but I have my own work to do."

"OK, thank you. I needed to ask. I miss you."

"And I you. But we aren't done yet and I will be there when I am needed, I promise you. I must go now but look for me from time to time in your dreams as in the past." And with that, she was gone.

Jenny blinked back her tears, but she looked Liliath in the eye, straightening herself and taking a deep breath. "Thank you Liliath, this has been a great session. I think I need some time to absorb all of this. Is this all right with you?"

"Of course, Jenny. I do think you have learned a very lot in a very short time today. I think it's about time you got some sleep and I don't mean, prowling Burt's dreams. Skip that tonight. You've put in a very long day. Do you get your work ethic from your mother or your father?"

"Both. My Uncle Joe often said that the two of them could pack more into any 24 hour day than anyone he'd ever met. My dad always said to do the work that was in front of you and not to stop until it was done, or the roof fell in."

Liliath couldn't help but chuckle at that. "Obviously they taught their daughter well. OK, so consider the roof fallen. Dismiss whichever of your guards isn't on watch this evening and get to bed. I'm sure Chidwi will agree."

Chapter 36: When a Plan Comes Together...

Gariel listened to Jenny's report with growing respect for the wisdom of so young a person. His animated beard lay quiescent at the moment, only the ends twitching languidly from time to time. Now that she and Burt had laid the groundwork for a coordinated attack, it was time to finish the strategic plan for the troops that had been recruited from around the dimension. This first attack would only serve to create chaos and slow down the plans of the enemy. Gariel had few illusions that this was a war that could be won in a decisive surgical attack.

However, Burt and Jenny had come up with a good strategy to reveal what they were truly up against. It was fortunate that the specter of a personal portal transport device was no longer hanging over their heads, but Gariel knew that, in war, commanders who assumed they knew what was going on with their enemy were often very sadly mistaken and if it looked too easy, that should be setting off loud alarms in his head.

They had begun without Jenny the day before and had been at it most of the day. Now as their planning session was coming to a close, he was beginning to feel that urgency that always started to build days before a battle. All of his senses were on alert, but he was yet calm. There was nothing you could do when you had already done your best.

"*OK, Jenny, you have the slaves queued up ready to rebel and the Mookookie are willing to join our ranks to rid themselves of the Inseni. But the Inseni are not the Insenium. Burt has already discovered that there is an elite force waiting out there ready to reinforce the Emperor and his Groga troops. Even if the Groga do fall in line and decide to join the revolution, that is just the opening gambit. While it does increase our available forces, as I understand it, not all of them are on board with this, am I right?*"

"*Absolutely. According to Anwhal, there are factions within the Groga. They aren't totally united, but the majority are ready to end the rule of the Insenium over them.*"

"*We can definitely use that. They are, of course aware that this could be a bloody business, correct? I don't want to mislead them that with the Alliance by their side, they would be invincible.*"

"*Of course not. Theirs is a military culture. The Groga-ha is convinced, however, that they have the numbers to make a difference and perhaps save their new home world from the ongoing tyranny of the Insenium by timing their revolt with our attack.*"

"*Then is there a best time to begin this, in your opinion? What does Burt have to say about it?*"

"*I wish he could be here to speak for himself but, based on what I have seen and heard and what Burt has told me, the sooner the better. Elizabeth has contacted her people and they have been in contact with all of the slave populations in the various domes at this point. We haven't had a single group of slaves say they'd rather stay a slave than take the risk. Most of them have lost relatives and loved ones to the Inseni on top of being enslaved and separated to different domes. For all of them, it will take generations to repair the damage to families and communities caused by the Inseni.*

I can see why this would be so very worth it to take the risk. What do they have to look forward to if they don't?"

"*Point taken,*" agreed Gariel. "*Then, do we have a signal for this revolution to begin? I believe we will have the most potential success if they all rise up at once. This should scatter the Inseni forces, such as they are and give the rebels the best possible chance for success. Since we know their communication technology is relatively primitive, we should be able to lock it down and have the Inseni capital in absolute chaos pretty quickly. Are we all in agreement?*"

The members of his team in addition to Jenny, Lova, Tarafau and Elizabeth nodded grimly. Every face was a picture of determination.

"*How do I and my space fleet fit into all of this?*" Brendan asked. "*It's fair dinkum that we aren't going to be bombarding them from space and I still don't see how these ships can travel from dimension to dimension. So far all of our drills have been in the galaxy around The Dimensional Alliance Headquarters planet.*"

"*There is a key part you will be playing, but not in this initial battle. Do not fool yourselves, people. This is not going to be a quick coordinated attack followed by a cleanup operation. When we initiate this first battle it will only accomplish one thing. It will buy us time and test the mettle of our adversary. If I am wrong, I will be happy to be so, but my experience tells me that we all need to be in this for the long haul. We are hopeful that making such a major strike will force the enemy to drop back and reassess their own strategy while we do the same for ours.*

As you will recall, according to Burt's report they are on multiple planets in that galaxy and potentially in some other dimensions as well. This will not be resolved by taking the Inseni capital.

As far as the space fleet is concerned, I think most of you realize that not all gates are planet bound. There are many identified gates. Burt has given us a potential opening at the 'wizard's' planet. We can create our own temporary gate near there and connect it to the Alliance Gate Network as we did on that planet to save the native populace from the Groga raid. It will be a bit of a ticklish operation, but the space drones our science team has created will allow us to do that.

The plan is to have one of Tarafau's people take one of our techs to the 'wizard's' planet and launch the drone with the gate creation equipment on it, which can be operated from the planet's surface. Assuming the scientists there are on our side, as Burt and Jenny's reports seem to indicate, this part should be simple. The rest of it, including temporarily hiding the space fleet from potential Inseni discovery, might not be so easy.

Jenny, can you see if the scientists working for the Insenium have any kind of star charts or observatories available?"

"*I'll put it on my list, Gariel.*"

"*Mustapha also has comm satellites ready to launch once we get into Inseni space. Juan has several MDPs to deliver to your logistics officer, Brendan. In them are the satellites, the space drones and supplies and new weaponry for your fleet. Be sure you have those installed in the next two days. We will put operation Freedom into play in three days, so you don't have a lot of time. The necessary techs have already been ferried up to your flagship.*

Adelle and her team have all of the bioweapons already transported to the Puerto Rico gate in an MDP as well. They have come up with several chemical options that include everything from a gas that will put the enemy to sleep to a chemical that will make the enemy horribly sick for a few days, enough to immobilize a particular force. They warn that these should be used sparingly as they aren't sure how fast they could reproduce more. Some of these will be issued to ground troops as well.

The Alliance Headquarters Science team also has come up with something they call buzzers. It consists of the little nano drones, but instead of being insects as they were in the Louisiana swamps, these send out a buzzing pulse that does two things. It makes it really hard to think and it jams communication. They caution not to launch them near your own troops, as they aren't partisan; they really don't care who they annoy."

They all smiled at this.

"*So, before everyone gets cocky and overconfident, let me say this. Yes, we have some amazing resources in this fight, but we still don't know for certain what the Inseni can bring to bear. This is why we plan; to give ourselves the best possible advantage, but quite likely the enemy has a few nasty surprises up their tiny sleeves as well. And if their size makes you feel superior, remember that your Napoleon was a tiny man with big ambitions and for a long while no one could beat him. Hitler was short compared to his generals, but he nearly conquered your entire planet before the allies stopped them.*

And yes," he added with a grin, *"we do study Earth wars. I'd cite many others, but that is not the point of this meeting. Mustapha has established an instant conference application that should work well once we have the gate and communication satellites deployed. Whenever possible, we need to meet as we proceed, so that every member of this conflict knows what is happening on all fronts that may affect their part in this assault. Communication and coordination is key, which is why each of you will be receiving a visit from Jenny also in the next few days, if you have not already. She will have all of you on mental 'speed-dial' as a backup of the tech communications network.*

Tarafau, do you have anything to add?"

Tarafau shook his head. *"We've been at this for two days. I'm sure things will yet come up, but we have covered the plan as thoroughly as we can until we know more."*

"Then I call this battle council adjourned. One final note, however. There will be a memorial for Ingot later today. It will be broadcast from the council room to prevent our enemy finding us all conveniently in one place again. Arvid will be home this evening and you may offer your condolences at that time."

Chapter 37: Before the Storm

Jenny walked through her little house on Infinity Loop, absentmindedly touching this or that and sorting through her mail. She had put most of it into the trash, except the two letters from her mom, decorated, as usual in cute stickers. These she put into her MDP to read later, perhaps before she went to sleep tonight. She had kept up random emails to her family, telling them of made up adventures with her new top secret job, explaining that there was so much she couldn't share, but she knew they would understand.

On a sudden whim she mentally dialed home. The living room with it's painting over the mantlepiece faded from her view. Her mom was in her sewing room, working on what was probably a gift for someone. She seldom made anything for herself. The silvery streaks in her mother's hair made her smile. Her mom called them "highlights", saying it was nice of Mother Nature to provide them without a trip to the hair stylist. She was focused on her sewing and Jenny didn't want to startle her by mentally calling out to her.

She heard her dad puttering in the kitchen. She could imagine yummy smells coming from there. Some men worked on cars or built things. Her dad cooked. Her parents were so...normal. It was the only word she could think of. They lived their lives quietly and happily. She had never seen either of them turn down someone who needed help or solace. These two strong people had given her their values; love, patriotism, kindness, curiosity and honesty.

She felt bad about deceiving them now, but she understood why it was necessary. There might come a time to tell them what she was doing, but now was not the time. She knew without a doubt that if she asked them to keep the information confidential, they would do so and keep that promise. She was even sure they would believe her without question because that was the kind of relationship she had always had with her parents, but she didn't want to put them in any possible danger.

She let the moment fade and sighed when she found herself again facing the portrait of herself and Tidbit over the mantle in her little house. So much had transpired since she first stepped through that doorway. So many doors since then...So many changes in her view of life and the world she thought she had understood.

Her bodyguards were on the patio, hanging out by the koi pond. Tidbit roamed the neighborhood and would return shortly. Bob had actually joined her in this visit, checking on his property. He had engaged Ted to take care of the grounds as Jenny had continued to do. On the one hand, all was normal and yet, none of this would ever be completely normal again.

This was the deep breath before the plunge. This was that moment when she girded herself for the battle to come. She couldn't say if she was saying good-bye or just taking a short break to take care of business, but the one thing she knew was that nothing would ever be the same again.

She had no regrets. What needed doing, needed doing and this went so far beyond simple patriotism. How could she bear the thought of so many people out there suffering when she had an opportunity to potentially stop it? How could she stand the idea of everyone on her planet under the thumb of the Insenium and their bizarre compulsion for "bringing order" to the multiverse? If it was in her power to stop it, how could she ever live with herself if she didn't do what she could?

And yet, a very whiny voice in her mind kept nagging at her that she could have taken the other option that Miriha had first offered her. She would have still had this lovely little house and a ton of cash and a cat and she would have had no idea that any of the terrible things were going on out there. She would not have had the scars on her arm that looked like a butterfly in flight. She would have never witnessed the torture and apparent death of Tidbit.

But she also would have never met all of the amazing beings she had become so fond of. She would never have met dragons and dwarves and bird people. She would never have seen a Linkling nor had her wonderful Chidwi as a companion for life and beyond. She would never have met BaaGah or traveled to fantastic worlds beyond her imagination. She would never have had all of the additional family that now graced her life and had helped her to grow and she would have likely never have discovered her mental abilities that now enriched her life so much.

So, she would go forward with her plans, the plans she had not confided in anyone, the plans that meant taking a big risk. But she knew it was the kind of risk her father would have willingly taken to defend his country, his family and his freedom. It was a risk her mother had lived with all of those years as an army wife. Both had been willing to make that sacrifice and they would have expected nothing less from their daughter, as much as they loved her, as much as they would never have wanted to see any harm come to her.

She took her courage in hand and turned around one last time. There was work to do.

She called Bob. "Are you ready? All squared away?"

"I had no idea how fast junk mail could pile up. I arranged for the post office to forward my mail to my son. He thinks I'm on safari and wants me to bring back an artifact, like I'm Indiana Jones or something." His rich baritone chuckle made Jenny laugh. "I have everything handled. My accountant has everything well in hand and my will is in order."

Jenny sobered at that. She too had created a will when she had first taken on her Gate Guardian duties, a requirement of her training. What it implied brought her back to her earlier contemplation.

"OK, well, I think I am good as well, so let's get back to Sanglarka. You are expected at the dragon keep and I have a ton to do before we give the go ahead for the assault."

She hung up and headed out to the patio to collect her guards. Chidwi sat next to Tidbit on the rocks at the edge of the koi pond, similarly fascinated by the undulating golden fish, sunlight glinting off of their bright scales. It was too late in the season for butterflies, Tidbit had noted grumpily. Lyra, Nona and Mynn straightened as Jenny walked out onto the patio, all attention. About the same time, Bob came through the garden gate and locked it behind him.

She knew the casual pose of her guards was deceptive. Those three were dangerous armed or unarmed and she had seen them arm themselves in less than a blink of an eye when necessary. One of the things they did for fun was to have contests to see who could come up with something out of their MDP the fastest. Jenny wouldn't have considered competing against them.

"Everything secured and ready to go?" he asked in his usually cheery fashion. Bob always seemed to have a smile and an attitude of optimism in pretty much every situation. He could be counted on not to panic or take the dark view of any given event. His almost childlike curiosity and sense of constant wonder made him a joy to be around.

His earlier offer to be a second dad to her still sat deep in her heart. She seemed to be gathering family as her time as a Guardian and Gatekeeper continued. Tarafau's family was also hers now. She felt very cherished and she knew if things went badly, she would cause pain to them all. But she also knew that she couldn't avoid doing what was necessary.

They left through the gate to Sanglarka, none of them looking back.

Walking through the gate at Sanglarka was breathtaking. The cool California fall was no match for the crispness of fall in Sanglarka where there would soon be snow waist deep along the path to the lodge. Not that Arvid wouldn't be right on top of it. He had returned from Alliance headquarters, a bit subdued, but ready to go to work. The first thing he did on returning was to make a batch of cookies and mulled cider so that all could raise a mug to salute the passing of Ingot and his respected memory.

Lova and Arvid were in the situation room with Gariel, Brendan, Aliki and Juan. Aliki and Juan had brought the requested MDPs filled with supplies and resources for the troops and the space fleet. It was good to see them. She knew that Luz would be back at the hacienda, supervising the others in their task and making sure that security remained tight. Jenny had been amazed to discover that Luz was even more versed in combat and defensive tactics than Juan. She had won marksmanship medals at a young age and was an avid tracker and hunter. So, Juan could leave her with perfect confidence that all would be well at home.

Lova stood as Jenny entered. *"So, all is well at home?"* she echoed, Jenny's thoughts, extending both hands as was her wont and taking Jenny's hands in hers. *"My, your hands are freezing! Arvid has some nice hot tea in the kitchen."*

She no sooner said this than Mynn piped up with, *"I'll go get some for all of us. Be right back."*

Jenny went to Arvid and surprised the dwarvish man with a gentle hug. *"We all miss Ingot so much, Arvid,"* was all she said. He nodded gruffly and she didn't embarrass him further by anything else. She knew they were planning a last group workout later that day and she would try to show her love and respect for him by sparring at the top of her game.

In no time Mynn returned with a tray of hot, steaming mugs of the spicy cider and a plate of Arvid's famous spicy sugar cookies. They all sipped and munched in silence for a moment, warming hands and hearts in preparation for what was to come.

Gariel looked around at the group assembled there. *"It looks like the base team is all here. Aliki and Juan will be leaving shortly for their station. In a few hours Jenny will give all the teams involved in the primary assault their cue. I won't belabor the plans we have made. Everyone knows their part. I just want to say how very proud I am to be one of you. You may have named me commander, but I think Tarafau, our chief, will agree with me when I say that I couldn't ask for better comrades in arms."*

"*Indeed, Gariel. I must agree. There could be no finer team than this. But we are more than a team, more than an alliance. Those assembled here and throughout the multiverse who now prepare to rid ourselves of the vile threat of the Insenium are worthy to be considered family. We are as prepared as we can be, given the time constraints and information we have. What happens next will be up to the courage and dedication we have in abundance and the kind and generous support of The Creator of All Things.*"

Every head bowed for a moment, contemplating and honoring Tarafau's words with a moment of respect.

That afternoon flew by. There was a group workout wherein Tarafau and Brendan ended up competing for the chance to confront Arvid. Even considering his obvious grief over Ingot, however, Tarafau didn't get in a single blow. They all showered and changed, and the evening culminated with a fine repast where Arvid completely outdid himself, which was truly saying something. One of his amazing stews with home baked rolls so fluffy that they were almost insubstantial, a huge salad with vegetables from their hydroponic greenhouse and cheesecake topped with fresh strawberries finished it off.

Then, it was time. Jenny's next step was to go to her personal "workout" room to get ready to give the signal to begin. She hugged all of her guards, once again feeling some guilt about what she was about to do. She knew they would be furious with her, mixed with worry and their own guilt for not figuring out her plans.

They wouldn't be the only ones. Only once she had put the ball into motion could she afford for anyone to find out, as she knew they would all want to stop her. She knew her plan was dangerous, and the risk was monumental, but she honestly believed that it was the one thing that would allow the ultimate success of what was likely to be much bigger and more formidable than they already suspected it would be.

She sighed. It couldn't be helped. Hopefully, assuming she was right, and this all worked out as she desired, they would eventually forgive her. She knew the pain she might be causing, but the time she had thought Tidbit to have been slain by Sam still lingered in her mind. A lesson well learned, she thought. Sometimes you had to endure some pain to get to the blessing.

Chapter 38: Smoke and Mirrors

Jenny closed her eyes, Chidwi in her usual place behind her. It comforted Jenny that Chidwi never judged her. She knew Chidwi understood perfectly well what she was about to do. Of course, Chidwi would be right in the middle of it with her, placing herself in equal danger of conflict, pain and death. She didn't allow herself to dwell on this but sent out her call.

"Elizabeth, are you and your troops prepared?"

"We are, Jenny. They are ready at your command, as am I."

"And you have made the required contacts?"

"I have. Here they are."

Elizabeth handed her the contact list like someone would download from one cellphone to another, only this was in her mental contact list.

"Does Noony understand what to do?"

"She does. She is ready to give the go ahead at our command. She tells me that the first day you told the Mookookie what to do they went into an eating frenzy and then proceeded to multiply. Each mature Mookookie is capable of reproducing up to a dozen new Mookookie and they are immediately ready to survive upon 'budding', as they call it. It turns out they are very similar to the bud-crawlers on my home world. They all come equipped with the race memory of all other Mookookie.

I think you will find you have a vast army of very determined and angry Mookookie ready to eat the Insenium literally out of house and home. It is of double benefit to them. They get the feast of their lives although it is at great risk and in the process, they help free their world from the 'hateful, evil and mean' Inseni, Noony's very words."

Jenny couldn't help but chuckle. She knew it was no laughing matter. The Mookookie would be risking everything in this attempt, and yet, their attitude and enthusiasm was delightful.

"OK, come and get me. No sound, please. I don't want the girls to know I'm gone until I tell them their part of the plan. They won't know I'm gone until I contact them after this part is done, as stage one will take almost no time."

Jenny opened her eyes and there was Elizabeth, dressed in a sand colored tunic and breeches and flexible boots fit for walking or tracking. Her long hair was bound back in a weaving that circled her head like a dark crown. Her dark eyes sparkled with excitement. Even though she was so much older than Jenny, her attitude was the same. They both realized the seriousness of what they were about to do, but it also suited their sense of adventure and curiosity. Both were scared, that was certain, but not so much that it blunted their natural desire to experience new things.

Chidwi sprang to Jenny's shoulder and automatically turned her reflection off.

Elizabeth said nothing, but with a wink, she laid her hand on the opposite shoulder and the workout room faded away.

They were on the speaking platform of the assembly room of the Apex. Crowded into the space which held upwards of twenty thousand people were the soldiers of the Daringi army. In moments they would be on their way to escort Gariel's troopers to the staging area for the assault. On Jenny's command, all of them would transport the entire force in a single moment to the Insenium capital which would already be in chaos.

After depositing those troops into each dome, the slaves would simultaneously rise up in revolt and the Groga who were in on the plan would turn on their masters.

The Mookookie were awaiting Jenny's command, as they would be the first part of the assault. Those assembled before her had already insinuated the massive numbers of Mookookie into the bounds of the domes. At her command they would begin eating everything in sight, especially weapons, vehicles and important structures, such as Peril's palace.

Jenny took a deep breath and dialed BaaGah. *"BaaGah, are the Mookookie ready?"*

BaaGah chuckled, his mind voice a humorous rumble, *"Some have already begun. We are ready. May I tell them to begin? Mookookie are very, very hungry. Mookookie are very, very angry. Mookookie are very, very ready."*

"Begin," said Jenny with a slight swoop in her stomach at the thought of what she had just started, *"and may The Creator of All Things keep you safe."*

"Hungry Mookookie! Begin! Eat for our freedom and our lives!" and Baa-Gah's image faded from her consciousness.

"The Mookookie have begun," she sent to the Daringi troops. *"You may proceed."*

At her words, the assembly hall emptied; the Daringi fading nearly instantaneously from sight. She turned to Elizabeth. *"Are you ready, my sister?"*

Elizabeth grinned. *"I am, sister of my heart. To the courtyard?"*

"Yes, the one behind the palace, in the little patch of trees just beyond the little gate. Our contact will meet us there."

Elizabeth nodded and the assembly hall faded from view to be replaced by the small thicket of scrubby trees at the side of the palace of Emperor Peril. Jenny hoped he was having a good day. It would be the last day he enjoyed that title if she or her comrades had anything to say about it.

It was yet quiet. Jenny knew that, at this point, the tiny emperor and his subjects wouldn't have a clue as to what was about to happen. There, in the shade of the little thicket was her contact, the Groga-ha, Anwhal.

"Are your troops in place?" he asked immediately as they appeared.

"They will be in moments. I have given the signal. At this point, however, the Inseni have no idea. I imagine it will be very apparent shortly. Did you bring the clothing?"

"I did." He handed her a small bundle and turned his back. *"Please be quick about it. Coincidental to your plans, evidently Emperor Peril also has something up his little sleeve today. We have been commanded to assemble before the palace. Something about some honor or other to one of his toadies, I imagine. I have arranged for you to watch from the crowd at the edge of the courtyard. When that is concluded, assuming it goes forward with the impending chaos, I will collect you and we can go to the Groga dome and through the gate to my planet, as you requested."*

"Good," Jenny huffed as she hurriedly pulled on the slave outfit and stored her clothing into her MDP. *"I'm done. How do I look?"*

"Your hair is too nice. Ruffle it a bit," was his terse reply. *"Good. Will your friend be coming as well? I didn't bring clothing for her."*

"No, Elizabeth has other tasks. She will know where to find me when the time comes."

Elizabeth nodded and winked out. Jenny squared her shoulders. *"Now what?"* she asked.

"You need to slouch a little more. You are a slave, remember? You are fairly newly captured and still a bit in shock. Can you do that?"

Jenny remembered the posture of the slaves she had observed in all but Anwhal's camp. Each had an air of unquiet resignation about them, as if they wanted to stand straight but couldn't see the point.

"Better," agreed Anwhal, looking her up and down. *"Don't look at faces. And don't speak to anyone unless someone asks you a direct question. Understood?"*

Jenny looked at his chest and replied, *"Yes, Groga-ha, as you say."*

"Well done. Follow me."

No one looking at her would have any idea she was The Gatekeeper, a key person in the government of the Dimensional Alliance. She shuffled along behind him, mostly watching his feet as they moved ahead of her. She could still feel the comforting light weight of Chidwi on her shoulder, but she knew that no one would have any idea she was carrying the Linkling as her camouflage was so complete as to not even leave a wrinkle or impression in the fabric of the baglike slave shirt she wore. The fabric wasn't itchy or uncomfortable, but it was still somewhat rough, like heavy muslin.

The color was nondescript, as if the cloth had never been bleached or dyed. The breeches or trousers were of the same sturdy, plain cloth. She had loosened her hair from its customary ponytail and had to keep brushing it from her eyes.

Anwhal stopped at the edge of the courtyard where slaves, Inseni and some Groga had gathered. He stopped before a Groga woman and what might have been her son. *"Jenny, this is my wife and son, Freia and Grephan. You may look into their faces to be able to recognize them."*

Jenny looked up. Freia was a tall, sturdy woman, but definitely female with hair the color of clover honey and dark eyes, so dark brown as to be nearly black. She wore the bright colors of her people, which definitely made her stand out. She nodded in acknowledgment of Jenny, her expression bland.

The young stripling Groga had black hair, like his father and the same dark eyes as his mother. He was built like every college linebacker she had ever seen. All the Groga she had seen had the same square build, sturdy, but not fat. There were no smiles of greeting, but neither were they hostile. Jenny assumed this was appropriate behavior for Groga interacting with a slave. Anwhal left her there and walked away to the front of the assembly of Groga soldiers, standing at their head facing them. His stolid face betrayed no emotion that Jenny could discern, although she knew that Anwhal's face could be animated with emotions at other times. This was the mask he was accustomed to wear in the presence of his men, especially when under the scrutiny of the Inseni.

Jenny looked around as the courtyard filled with not only the Groga soldiers standing at what Jenny assumed was a kind of "parade rest" stance, but also Inseni who were privileged to stand in the courtyard, rather than the perimeter as the rest of the populace seemed constrained to do. There were no guards preventing the lesser people from coming forward, but evidently, they knew their place and weren't inclined to take the consequences of moving out of it.

On the raised entrance to the palace there were but two guards in uniform standing on either side of the large doors that filled the entrance of the palace. The series of broad steps that led down onto the courtyard were also bare of anyone. The silence, due to the prevalence of mind speech was somewhat eerie, although Jenny could sense that there were multiple silent conversations going on all around her.

Over the silence however, far behind the crowd that extended down the main street behind Jenny came the faint sounds of something unusual in the Inseni city. Someone was shouting. Many someones. There were also other loud noises that seemed to come nearer as they waited. The sounds were still faint, perhaps miles away yet, but Jenny found herself having to restrain the grin that kept wanting to creep onto her face.

Feet shuffled and she noted that a number of the Inseni and the others standing near her were occasionally looking worriedly over their shoulders. They were having trouble keeping their eyes on the palace steps. Jenny kept her head down noticing all of this under somewhat lowered eyelashes. The wave of sound behind her was far enough away that she was sure it would take yet awhile to make it to the courtyard, but she knew it would come and strove to keep her expression disinterested.

All at once the men at arms snapped to attention audibly, raising their weapons in salute as custom required. The doors to the palace had opened and out stepped Emperor Peril, his servant Penchant, Mechi and Burt. Jenny couldn't help but think how small and insignificant the little emperor looked standing next to Burt, even in his crown and royal robes. Burt was dressed neatly and simply in the same pastel colors that all Inseni and their minions tended to wear. The sun flashed briefly on the cursed medallion around his neck.

She saw him scan the crowd. Could he see her? As far as she knew, he didn't have any idea of this part of her plan. She doubted he could, but she was sure he assumed she was riding along in his mind. She hoped that gave him some kind of comfort at this crucial point, but she didn't try to contact him or soothe him. She did feel a surge of pride however at his courage and at how well he compared to the supposed royalty standing next to him.

Emperor Peril surveyed the crowd. His wide eyes narrowed nearly imperceptibly at the faraway noise of the ruckus in the street behind Jenny. She wondered if he had any idea what was causing it. She suspected he really had no clue. The one thing they had discovered about Peril and his people was that they used nearly no communications devices. That had puzzled Jenny when she thought about all he had done so far, but she had begun to realize that he was a bully. Bullies never picked on anyone more powerful or advanced than they considered themselves.

Without exception, every place he had raided had been peaceful people with no clue they were bait for him and no idea that their tech would fall into the hands of a would-be despot.

So, there he stood, scanning the crowd with a look of disdain on his face for everyone who was not Inseni. Finally, his eyes lit upon his people and they softened.

"My people," he began in a booming mind voice that was out of place with his face and stature. *"As many of you know, we have recently been graced with the presence of a representative of the Dimensional Alliance, those who guard the dimensional gateway system of renown with diligence and cunning. Sir Burt has spoken to representatives from every part of our realm here upon this planet, both Inseni and representatives of other lands who serve in our kingdom."*

He paused. Was that sound coming closer? Was it getting louder?

"Indeed, the sole purpose of his visit was to learn of our people, to understand the high purpose of our empire and to seek to return to his people with a good report, that we might ally ourselves in the quest to finally bring order to the multiverse and take away the burdens of the common people. Never more will they be plagued by the necessity to discover truth for themselves. Never will they be forced to ferret out the secrets of how to get the things they need. No need to worry about food or shelter or employment. This is our quest."

A crash of something large echoed in the distance. The trample of feet afar off rumbled like an angry swarm of hornets.

"It is our extreme pleasure therefore to bid Sir Burt farewell that he may return to his superiors and bring our offers of friendship, peace and power and to relieve them of the tiresome burden of government and keeping the peace. We will be the peace of the multiverse. We will alleviate the necessity to choose anything but the right path. They will see this, and our power will increase. Join with me in rejoicing!"

There were no cheers, but the Inseni all raised their hands above their heads, fluttering them and waving, looking like a sea of ripened grain in the courtyard. In the meantime, the sounds behind them increased in volume.

The emperor pointed at Burt, who bowed and straightened, a grin on his face.

Then, for a moment the sound in the background receded from their consciousness as another voice, a mental one roared into existence.

"FOOL! You pitiful, tiny, big-eyed, bloody fool! Have you lost your Imperial mind? Are you blind as well as STUPID? We give you a little bit of power and this is what you do with it? You got to wear that ridiculous crown and your pathetic little jewels, and you think yourself a ruler? IDIOT! Baby-faced little MORON!"

Peril stood with eyes wider than Jenny ever thought possible, looking around himself in panic. Gone was the regal bearing. Gone was the snide superiority. This was the very epitome of a man terrified.

"Where are you?" the emperor's mental voice beseeched. *"What are you talking about? Why are you here?"*

"You don't really think we let you alone all this time, do you? Such a child? Such an idiot? Alone with no supervision?"

Instantly there stood before the ranks of the Groga, back to the courtyard, facing the little Emperor, a huge humanoid with even whiter skin than the Inseni. Jenny's mind went back to her days in Sunday school learning about David and Goliath. This being was a good foot and a half taller than any of the Groga. He wore forest green robes that were nearly black.

Peril took a step back, eyes appealing to the Groga-ha, who stood motionless.

The man took not a single step closer.

"You, Sir Burt are a snake, a conniver. You are no emissary. But you are a very clever spy. It is good that you will never return to those fools in the Dimensional Alliance to deliver the information you have gathered. It is only a shame that they will never know what happened to you. They will assume you have betrayed them. They will assume you have joined us and we will make it appear that you have indeed done so. Behold!"

Beside the huge man appeared what could have been Burt's twin from his tousled hair and lanky frame to his cocky grin.

"Our tailors did much more than measure you for a suit of clothing, did they not?"

Burt's eyes widened only slightly in surprise then his brows furrowed.

"I should have known there was no way Peril could have been running the show. I hadn't been here a single day before I started to wonder. Tell me; was the medallion your idea? Your technology? Obviously, you have much more than your tricked out big-eye despot here. Have you been behind this all along?"

On top of this thought sent to the being before him, Burt sent another directly and only to Jenny. *"Are you taking notes, kiddo? I think we may have left a few things out of our calculations."*

"I'm here, Burt," Jenny replied. She didn't mention she was actually, physically there. He didn't need that distraction right now.

"A little clever and a little too late for you, Sir Burt; yes, the medallion is my personal creation. I give Peril a toy or two to play with from time to time, so he will feel like he is in on the joke. But I'm afraid the joke's on you. As long as you wear it, you can never leave this planet or go through any portal on it. Unless you don't care to keep your head, that is. You see the chain is unbreakable, as you have no doubt discovered and if you attempt to go through any portal while wearing it, not that you have a choice, then it will tighten until your head comes loose from your shoulders."

Burt straightened and stood even taller. On the raised veranda on which he, Peril and his minions stood when Burt straightened to his full height, he could look his nemesis directly in the eyes. Jenny's heart swelled within her. He was magnificent. There was no breeze, but his hair always looked as if it was windblown. His dark eyes, usually so mischievous and kind, were now deadly serious and earnest.

"You are right, whoever or whatever you are. The Alliance has no desire to champion your cause, such as it is. We value the freedom and worth of every living being. We believe in the right of every being to choose their own path as long as that path doesn't obliterate the path of another. What you are attempting is wrong and will result in eons of war, terror and conflagration. It cannot be allowed. Too bad my compatriots do not know you for what you are, the true villain; the true evil that leads this travesty of a quest. We will never give in."

The huge man turned his back on Burt and the little emperor and faced the waiting crowd. Behind Jenny she could hear that the sounds were indeed coming closer, but to what end? Had she and Burt, who had thought themselves so clever to defeat the Inseni only wasted precious life and resources to no purpose?

This humanoid's face had but one large electric-green eye in the center of his forehead, a long hooked nose and a wide red mouth full of fangs like a picture she had once seen of a vampire bat on a movie poster. His long green cloak had swirled as he had turned dramatically and now, he raised his hand imperiously as he sent to the crowd.

"I am Gall. I am the puppeteer who pulls the strings on the little man who thinks himself Emperor. He has served his purpose and you see what little he has accomplished. Therefore, we will leave him to face the consequences of his stupidity, but not before we correct one thing. The Dimensional Alliance will fall and the dimensions with it. It will be ours and so will all living things, in all places seen and unseen.

Look a last time on life and on the beings you thought to have deceived, Sir Burt."

A keening, like the sound of a thousand fax machines all sending a signal at once pierced the air, coming from the throats of all of the little Inseni gathered there.

Gall turned again to the front of the palace. As he raised his hands, to Jenny's shock, Burt's mental voice sent directly to her, sweetly, calmly and unafraid. *"I love you Jenny. I always will."*

From Gall's long clawed fingers shot a pulse, a huge fireball directly at Burt. Burt stood there without flinching. In a shower of sparks, Burt exploded into a fountain of brilliant lights.

At the same time, the sound behind Jenny finally washed over her like the crashing wave of a tsunami. Something hit the back of her head and everything went black.

Epilogue:

Elizabeth saw it all, traveling as she had been instructed, from dome to dome. The Inseni, completely caught off guard had been simply over run. Between the slaves, the Mookookie and those Groga who had also turned on their masters, it had nearly been no contest.

Soon after the uprising had begun, Gall's soldiers had found their way into most of the domes. This was a vulnerable point, as most of the revolutionaries had been transported by her people to the main dome, where the highest concentration of Inseni lived.

As they had expected there had been a high cost. She would have estimated the number of dead and wounded to have been in the thousands on both sides. Foodstuffs and equipment, weapons and even buildings had been devoured by ravenous and deliberately destructive Mookookie. To her surprise, she even saw Mookookie place themselves between slaves and their attackers, saving more than one life.

Slaves had turned on the Inseni and any Groga who were still loyal to the Insenium. They had nearly no weapons of their own, but gladly used those supplied via MDP by the Alliance.

She didn't remain long at any one dome, only long enough to assure that the fighting was well and truly in process and moved on. The fighting was fierce on both sides, but it was obvious that the Inseni had met their match in the righteous anger of the slaves and Groga.

She was interested to see that the slaves only fought as needed, willingly taking capture as many as would put down their arms. This aligned with the teachings of the Daringi and she felt that these would make great allies as the fight continued as she knew it must, beyond creating chaos on this one planet under Insenium rule.

By the time she returned to the main dome, she was pleased to see that the fight was well under way. She transported into the crowd around the courtyard, interested to see how Burt was going to give his parting address before returning to the Alliance to make his final report. She knew Jenny would be all ears for his clever remarks. She had noticed how Jenny looked at him and the change in her face when she had spoken of him, which was oftener than Jenny would have admitted.

The plan was that Burt would continue his subterfuge of arranging an agreement with the Alliance and would return to report all he had learned.

As she edged towards the front of the crowd, she thought of the next part of Jenny's plan. The part no one knew but Jenny herself. Jenny had not even confided to Burt the urgent need she had been consumed by for the last few weeks. It was something that had come to her during one of her mental exercises with Liliath. Jenny had sworn Elizabeth to secrecy, and she hadn't even told her the whole of it.

She got to the front of the crowd moments before a huge being appeared suddenly between the veranda at the top of the steps to the palace and the crowd.

She gaped with the crowd as the being roared his insults at the little emperor and then at Burt. It dawned on her a moment too late what was about to happen after Burt gave his unexpected and courageous reply.

She could only gasp in shock as Burt disappeared in that flash of light and sparks.

She looked around for Jenny but at that exact moment, the rebellion she had set in motion was upon them. It rolled over her, ignoring all but the Inseni masters who had earned their wrath. Desperately she called out Jenny's name over the clamor. But her words, both verbal and mental were lost in the chaos and the keening of the Inseni. She could not take Jenny out of this if she could not sense her. She was determined to take Jenny out despite her careful and audacious plans. She knew Jenny would be angry with her, but she did not care. However, try as she might it was of no use. The horrible being who had slain Burt was nowhere to be seen. The emperor, no longer protected by his troops, pounded desperately on the door of the palace begging, she surmised, to be let in, but to no avail. He disappeared beneath flying fists and heavy boots and was no more.

With the revolution apparently successful and the emperor permanently deposed, Burt dead and Jenny disappeared; there was nothing further for Elizabeth to do but to return and report. Wiser heads than hers would have to take it from here.

MIRIHA TURNED FROM her pool with a sigh. She knew she had watched the breaking of a heart and it grieved her that Jenny should feel such pain. The Dimensional Alliance had been thrust into another violent conflict, as she had suspected it would be. And this one would not be resolved by the force of arms alone.

Jenny was still the key to victory. Miriha was sure of this. But choices still had to be made and trials overcome. In all things, choice was the pivotal factor. Miriha knew what she hoped for. But no one could choose for Jenny. The outcome depended on it. So, she gazed into her clear crystal pool in her garden and sent up prayers for wisdom, for Jenny, for the Dimensional Alliance and for herself.

If you loved Infinity on Fire and The House on Infinity Loop, please take a moment and do a review:

Or any social media groups or book clubs you may participate in. This helps me know how best to continue to provide good reading for you, my audience, and it will be greatly appreciated.

If you can't get enough of The Dimensional Alliance and want to know more about the characters, not to mention giveaways, events, release dates of new books in the series and much more, you can get a free monthly story by joining the free Dimensional Alliance Stories Club at:

http://storiesclub.dimensionalallianceheadquarters.com/ .

For news about upcoming books, audio books, contests, giveaways and fan gear, visit my fan page on Facebook: The Dimensional Alliance – Fan Gate

About the author:

Bonnie K.T. Dillabough

At 16 years old I started having a recurring dream that pestered me most of my life. Time and time again I would discuss the dream with people I thought were wiser than me and time and time again the repeated answer came, "No idea. I've never heard of such a thing."

At age 63 after having the dream once again I decided that maybe if I wrote it down it might leave me alone. I did so and filed it on my desktop, but didn't think of it again until I started hanging out with published authors.

Mercedes S. Lackey told me at one point, when I confessed I had often considered writing a book, "Put your butt in the chair and write!" It was some of the best advice I had ever gotten.

In search of material to write about I stumbled upon that dusty text file about my dream and the rest is history. From it came the science fiction - fantasy series "The Dimensional Alliance" beginning with "The House on Infinity Loop". Now, at the launch of "The Infinite Publishing Alliance, I find myself grateful for the events leading up to setting myself upon this path.

To my readers: Never give up on your dream. The first book in this series was published two weeks before my 64th birthday. It is never too late. There are many more to come.

Don't miss out!

Visit the website below and you can sign up to receive emails whenever Bonnie K.T. Dillabough publishes a new book. There's no charge and no obligation.

https://books2read.com/r/B-A-ZNYK-OHJLB

BOOKS 2 READ

Connecting independent readers to independent writers.

Also by Bonnie K.T. Dillabough

The Dimensional Alliance 2nd edition
The House on Infinity Loop
Infinity on Fire
Mirrors of Infinity

Watch for more at https://dimensionalallianceheadquarters.com.

www.ingramcontent.com/pod-product-compliance
Lightning Source LLC
Chambersburg PA
CBHW051555100726
47898CB00001B/104